A/F
AUGUST
2010

DATE DUE

1581	AUG 16 2010
	AUG 31 2010
2384	SEP 30 2010
3103	1-24-13

F
JOH

Shadow zone.

SHADOW
ZONE

SHADOW ZONE

IRIS JOHANSEN

AND

ROY JOHANSEN

ST. MARTIN'S PRESS ≈ NEW YORK

This is a work of fiction. All of the characters, organizations, and events portrayed in this novel are either products of the author's imagination or are used fictitiously.

www.stmartins.com

ISBN 978-0-312-61160-6

First Edition: July 2010

10 9 8 7 6 5 4 3 2 1

For Jerry

A faithful friend
who brought much love and laughter into the world

SHADOW ZONE

PROLOGUE

Venice, Italy

10:35 P.M.

MARINTH.

Samuel Debney piloted his motorboat up Venice's Grand Canal, wishing he had never heard that word.

Marinth.

He had been only vaguely aware of it before, but in the past two weeks the name had come to mean many things to him. Awe. Wonder. Wealth. Fear. Ugliness. Death.

Marinth.

Had it only been two weeks since it had totally consumed him, wrenching him from his old life? It had been a good life, a comfortable life, but one that was now lost to him forever.

He shook his head. Can't look back. He would soon have plenty of time to wrestle with his regrets.

He hoped.

The lights of Sestiere di Castello shimmered on the water as he eased off the throttle and turned down Fondamenta San Lorenzo. Three turns later, he was facing the white-plaster back side of an art gallery. He heard music in the distance, but other than that there was only the sound of water lapping against the building foundation. It was deserted and only partially visible from the adjacent waterway.

He cut the engine. Why in the hell had he agreed to this?

He knew why. Because he was tired. Because he wanted it to be over. Because he just wanted—

"Thank you for coming, Mr. Debney."

He turned. Two men appeared from around the corner of the building. Debney tensed. He recognized them both. Gadaire's men, whom he'd seen when he'd made the attempt to contact Gadaire. The red-haired man with the narrow face who had spoken was Tad Bekins. The smaller man with gray hair and muscles like a weight lifter was Ralph Johnson. Nasty bastards like all of Gadaire's goons. This was not good.

Debney tried to smile, and only then did he realize that his lower lip was trembling. "Hello, Bekins, I didn't expect you."

"Why not?" Bekins and Johnson jumped off the concrete walkway and landed on his boat. Bekins stepped closer to him. "Mr. Gadaire was intrigued by the information you claim to have."

"I do have it." His lips tightened. "And if he was so intrigued, why didn't he come himself?"

"Mr. Gadaire is a very busy man."

"So am I. I don't have time to waste with—"

Johnson slipped around and grabbed him from behind. As Debney struggled to break free, Bekins grabbed his arm and sliced his left wrist. Blood spurted onto the boat deck.

Debney reached for the revolver tucked into his waistband, but Johnson got there first. The man hefted it and struck him on the back of the head. In the next instant, he felt an icy cold shiver of pain on his right wrist. He looked down and saw that Bekins had cut him there, too, and his blood was now pooling at his feet.

"What in the hell are you doing?" Debney screamed.

Johnson pushed him down onto the weather-beaten seat. "You're losing blood fast. You'll be unconscious in seven minutes, and dead in twelve. *Unless* you tell us exactly what we need to know."

"You're out of your minds! I had a deal with Gadaire!"

"Deal canceled. This is the new deal," Bekins said. "Talk. Tell us where we can find the sample."

He was going to die. Debney rocked back and forth. "Mother of God . . ."

"The sample," Bekins repeated. "Tell us where—" Bekins suddenly arched, his face drooping. He stumbled backwards toward the side of boat.

Debney stared in bewilderment as Bekins tried to speak. Blood. Blood pouring from his chest. Another step back, and Bekins tumbled into the canal.

"What the—" Johnson spun around to face the walkway.

A man was standing there, a tall, powerful shadow in the dimness. He took aim with the automatic handgun and fired two muffled shots. Johnson collapsed onto the cushion next to Debney, almost as if dropping down to rest.

The man with the gun stepped down onto the boat.

Debney looked up. A fog was creeping up from the back of his head. Must fight it. Must stay awake. Fall unconscious, and he was a dead man. "You . . . killed them . . ."

"Yes. I'm sure neither of us is going to miss them." The man was powerfully built, a gleam of silver burnished the hair of his temples, and he spoke with a slight accent. Russian? "I'll offer you the same deal those gentlemen did. Tell me what I need to know, and I'll save your life. The difference is, I will keep my word, which those two had no intention of doing."

"Who . . . are you?"

"Kirov." He checked his watch. "Your time's running out. I suggest you begin talking now. If you talk fast enough, I'll have time to stop that blood before those wounds kill you. But I won't start until I have what I want." He added with lethal softness, "Believe me. I don't bluff, Debney. Marinth. Let's start there, shall we? Before this is over, I'm going to know everything that you know about Marinth."

CHAPTER 1

"HEY, I DIDN'T SEE YOU IN the galley for breakfast, Hannah," Josh Carnaby said as he strolled down the deck toward her. "You okay?"

"Fine." Hannah Bryson made a face as she gestured to the satellite phone in her hand. "I'm just trying to get through to my sister-in-law before we go down in the minisub. I want to talk to my nephew, and the time difference between here and Boston usually screws everything up." Her lips tightened determinedly. "But I will get through, dammit."

"An emergency?"

She shook her head. "It's my nephew Ronnie's twelfth birthday." Her expression became shadowed. "It's the first one since my brother's death. I want to touch base with him. It's going to be tough on Ronnie. It's going to be tough on all of them."

Josh nodded soberly. "It's only been a couple months since

Conner died. The wound has to be still raw." He was silent a moment. "Damn, I miss him. The entire crew misses him. Every time I see you, I expect Conner to be right beside you."

As he'd been beside her all through the years, she thought. They'd not only been brother and sister, they'd worked together on hundreds of undersea projects, traveled the world together, and been best friends. She missed his sweetness, his humor, his gentle way of opening her eyes to the good things around her when all she could see was darkness. Dear God, how she missed him. "Yeah, I know." She swallowed hard and quickly gazed out at the sun-dappled sea. Get control. She mustn't be all teary when she talked to Ronnie. "Conner would have loved this job. He was always telling me that I spent too much time involved with machines and not enough enjoying the wonders the machines could uncover." She smiled with an effort. "Here I don't have a choice. The wonders are all around me whenever I go down to that lost city that all the historians are trying to link with Atlantis."

"That city would be damn hard to uncover if you hadn't been so brilliant and designed those minisubs." He was silent a moment. "I just want you to know that I appreciate you letting me go down with you and having a part in this show. It's the chance of a lifetime, and you've always been the best boss a guy could have. I'll never be as good as Conner, and I know it probably hurts you to work with anyone else. But it's been an experience I'll never forget."

"Bullshit," she said unevenly. "If you weren't terrific at your job, I wouldn't have chosen you. We make a good team." She drew a deep breath. "Now get out of here and let me make my telephone call. We're supposed to dive in thirty minutes, and I won't go down until I've talked to Ronnie."

He grinned. "I'm on my way." He moved down the deck. "I'll

even keep Ebersole away from you. He was asking for you at breakfast."

Hannah groaned. "Then I'm glad I skipped it. For the last three days, he's been cornering me and squeezing every bit of progress information out of me."

"Imagine that. But since he's chief operating officer of AquaCorp, and AquaCorp is funding our little expedition, you can understand how he'd have a *slight* interest in the operation."

"Moneymen," Hannah said. "The bane of my life." She made a shooing motion. "Go. Keep him off my back until I finish my call, and I'll be eternally grateful."

"Consider it done."

She smiled as she watched him stroll away from her. Yes, Josh would find a way to give her these few moments' respite. He'd been a member of her team for years, but she'd learned new respect and affection for him since she'd lost Conner.

She dialed Cathy's number again. It rang six times, but Cathy finally picked up.

"Hi, I've been trying to get through to you. Everything okay?"

"Sure, we're about to cut the cake. Ronnie's been on the phone with my mom." Cathy chuckled. "And Donna had to have her turn. She doesn't totally understand the concept of special treatment on birthdays."

"She's only five."

"And Ronnie doesn't mind. He's a very protective big brother with her." She was silent a moment. "Particularly since Conner died. He thinks I need help with her."

"He's a great kid."

"You bet he is. The best."

"How are you doing, Cathy?"

"I'm surviving. Some days are better than others. This one is not so great." She changed the subject. "We saw you on the Discovery Channel this week. Donna was very excited."

"And Ronnie?"

"Thoughtful. I was worried that he might be thinking about Conner. I tried to talk to him, but he closed me out," she said. "We're okay, Hannah. Stop worrying about us."

"You're my family. It goes with the territory."

"We worry about you too. We're not the one who's careening around in the depths of the ocean in that weird contraption." She paused. "You named that exploration minisub you use after Conner. It came as a shock when that announcer started talking about *Conner One*."

"Conner would have liked this sub. I can hear him laughing because it's so crazy-looking."

"Yeah, he always teased you about your mechanical 'creatures,'" she said. "It's kind of . . . comforting to have his name on one. Thank you for doing it, Hannah."

"I'm selfish. I did it for me."

"You did it for us, too. Now I'll let you talk to the birthday boy. He's right at my elbow."

Ronnie came on the phone. "Hi, Aunt Hannah."

"Happy twelfth birthday. I wish I was there."

"Me, too. Thanks for all the new soccer equipment. It's cool."

"No, *you're* cool. I'm expecting stellar things from you next season."

"I'll try." He was silent a moment. "I was thinking about skipping soccer next year. Mom may need me."

"She needs you to be a normal kid." But he wasn't a kid any longer, she thought sadly. He'd always reminded her of Conner, and since her brother's death, she could see all Conner's caring and serious responsibility mirrored in the boy. "She's trying to hold everything together. Don't make her feel like a failure."

"Mom's great." He was silent a moment. "I saw the TV show about you and Marinth. It looked . . . cool."

"It is."

"They said there are hundreds of dolphins who live down there."

"Yes, the people of ancient Marinth had a special relationship with dolphins. That's why my friend Melis Nemid became involved in searching for the lost city. She's a marine biologist, and she loves dolphins. She has two, Pete and Susie, who are her special friends. They're absolutely amazing."

"I'd like to see them," he said haltingly. "I think I should come there, Aunt Hannah."

She had been afraid this was coming. "To see the dolphins?"

"No, to take care of you. My dad told me that you were alone, and we had to take care of you. Now that he's gone, it's my job."

So solemn, so endearing. It was breaking her heart.

She would *not* tell him that she didn't need him. "We all have to take care of each other. But right now you need to take care of Donna and your mom." She paused. "Maybe I could arrange for you to have a working holiday with me next summer. Sort of an apprenticeship."

"Working together?" His voice was eager. "Doing stuff like Dad did for you?"

"Exactly. I'll look forward to it, Ronnie."

"So will I." He paused. "But that's months away. Is that okay? I don't want you to be lonely, Aunt Hannah."

"It's okay. I'll keep busy, and you'll be here before I know it. Now go back and have your cake. I love you, Ronnie."

"I love you too. I'll study all the books in Dad's library that have to do with mapping and scientific—"

"You do that. I'm sure it will help. Enjoy your birthday. Goodbye, love." She hung up.

What had she gotten herself into?

Dealing with a twelve-year-old. Responsibility. Duty.

Love.

As long as there was love, she could handle the rest. In fact, she was beginning to feel excited about the prospect of having Ronnie with her on the job.

She gazed out at the sea. She hoped that Ronnie would be able to come here and see the wonders she'd viewed in the last weeks. If AquaCorp had its way, her team would be sent on their way long before next summer.

I don't want you to be lonely.

She didn't want to be lonely either, but she'd made her choice. She'd tried marriage, and it hadn't worked out. She was too driven and obsessed by her work to be able to make that kind of commitment. It would have to be an extraordinary relationship to ever tempt her to try again.

Kirov.

She veered away from the name that had suddenly slid into her mind like a seductive whisper. That was a promise that had never come into being. Just as well. Kirov might be extraordinary, but he was also deadly. She was better off alone than walking that path.

Stop moping, she thought impatiently. She worked with great people, and she had Cathy and the kids to love and nurture. That was a hell of a lot more than most women had going for them.

She turned and headed for the minisub at the docking station on the vessel.

And she had work that was headily exciting and filled her life. When she was in that minisub exploring those wonders she had wanted to show Ronnie, there were exhilaration and curiosity and endless possibilities.

And there was no loneliness.

DAMMIT, HE'D MISSED HER again, Ebersole thought with annoyance as he watched Hannah climb into the minisub. He had an impulse to go down, pull her out of that sub, and throttle her. He knew she'd probably been avoiding him again, and Josh Carnaby had been a party to it.

Yeah, sure. If he laid a hand on her, she'd very likely deck him. There was nothing fragile about Hannah Bryson. She was tall and slim but with shapely broad shoulders and beautiful long legs. Her wild curly dark hair reached her shoulders and framed a face whose deep-set brown eyes, high cheekbones, and wide lips made you want to keep on looking. The cameras loved her, and that face had been a bonus to the corporation when the Discovery Channel had been doing the interviews. Science was great, but charisma made it go down a hell of a lot smoother.

But now she was proving to be a complete pain in the ass. She didn't understand the common dollar-and-cents rules that governed expeditions like this. She wanted things her way and fought any limits they tried to put on her. She was stubborn and hardheaded and thought that the ships she built were almost human.

And some of them seemed to come very close, he had to admit. She had been a valuable asset. Past tense. He was feeling regret as well as irritation, he realized.

Because in these months aboard the research vessel, he had become caught up in the camaraderie and excitement that Hannah and her team had felt exploring the underwater city. At times he had actually thought of himself as one of them. It had been . . . different.

Hannah turned, smiled, and waved at him.

Be professional. Smother the annoyance. He lifted his hand and waved.

Enjoy the trip.

I'll be waiting.

HANNAH GLANCED AWAY FROM staring out into the murky water at the minisub's forward port. "Once more around the spire, Josh."

Josh smiled as he pulled back on the control stick. "We've already photographed it from every conceivable angle."

"I don't care. Let's get it again."

"Aye, aye. And for the record, I don't blame you, Hannah. I'm going to miss this place."

Hannah took in the magnificent vista before her. Even after all these weeks, the sight still took her breath away.

Marinth.

In the decade since its discovery, the fabled four-thousand-year-old city had sparked a cottage industry of books, television shows, a hit IMAX documentary, and even a new-age religious movement. It could be even older than scholars estimated because mention of Marinth was made on the wall of Hepsut's tomb in Egypt. No matter how ancient the city, the glory was in the architecture and sweeping symmetry, streets laid out in perfect order. Huge white columns built to last forever, a people so advanced that universities were vying for every word of their lives and studies. There was even speculation that it might be the Lost Atlantis.

But none of the media frenzy could match seeing it with her own eyes, Hannah thought. She had designed *Conner One* and its almost-identical twin, *Conner Two,* as state-of-the-art undersea-research vessels, and she couldn't think of a better way to break them in. She had browbeaten the sub's manufacturer, AquaCorp, into financing this trip not only to evaluate their new minisubs' effectiveness, but also to demonstrate their abilities to potential customers.

Hannah aimed the digital cameras at one of the tall golden spires as they moved around it. "The lighting is better today. This looks fantastic."

"Amazing what a couple million watts of candlepower can do, isn't it?"

Hannah nodded. Dozens of movable billboard-size light towers had enabled them to map and photograph every square foot of the site with incredible clarity and detail. Finally, the world would see Marinth for the magnificent city that it was, with long boulevards, breathtaking statues, and grand buildings that were as beautiful as they were functional. Tall golden spires marked north, south, east, and west on what was once a four-hundred-square-mile island, and miraculously, three of the four spires still stood, almost a quarter mile beneath the ocean.

They circled downward around the South Spire until they found themselves cruising over what was once one of Marinth's main thoroughfares.

Josh smiled. "Get Matthew on the horn. Tell him to bring *Conner Two* down for a drag race."

"Not in my subs."

"Funny how AquaCorp thinks the subs belong to them."

"Not bloody likely." Like all her other creations, the subs would always be hers, no matter what company or branch of the military financed their construction. A nautical magazine had recently run a series of articles on "Hannah's Fleet," which, to her surprise, now numbered over two hundred vessels—thirty-six individual designs—not including her early sketches dating back to a drawing on the place mat at her senior prom. She stood on the deck of her first launched sub on her twenty-fourth birthday, and in the thirteen years since, she prided herself on her versatility, from large nuclear attack subs to tiny one-man exploratory vessels.

To the general public, however, she was best known as the woman who mapped and photographed the *Titanic* wreck like no one before, enabling armchair explorers to explore large sections of the doomed luxury liner through an interactive Web site and a 3-D software program. Although others played key roles in the expeditions, it was Hannah and her revolutionary subs that captured the lion's share of attention from the world's media outlets.

Those subs were positively conventional compared to this new design, Hannah thought. It was a round pod with winglike structures on each side. Each wing featured a retractable mechanical arm and hand that had become a trademark of her research-sub designs, manipulated by a pair of controller gloves in the pod.

She was still amazed that she had ever been able to get such a ridiculous-looking little sub built. Its wings, exotic curves, and retro lighting panels looked more like something out of Jules Verne than a product from one of the world's largest defense contractors. The design was adventurous even by her usual standards, and it had been the source of much controversy ever since she had submitted her preliminary sketches over three years before. Many within the Aqua-Corp company had ridiculed her concepts as impractical, but the craft's speed and maneuverability had silenced most of the critics in the past few weeks.

Josh stared in awe at a statue garden even though he had seen it a dozen times before. "This was all under a hundred feet of silt?"

"Most of it. And it would still be there if—"

"Shit!" Josh pulled back the stick, and the minisub veered hard to the right.

Hannah's gaze flew up to see that the dark superstructure of an inactive light tower, fallen on its side, now filled the entire front window. "Pull up," she yelled. "Pull up!"

"I'm trying!"

Before she could brace herself, *Conner One* spun to the right, struck the remnants of a building, and brought down a pile of debris. A dull roar sounded in her ears, and the hull of the submersible shook as it was carried along by the debris.

Piercing alarms sounded, and Hannah heard her own voice—a temporary audio track—repeating "Collision imminent!" over and over again.

"Any thrust?" Hannah called over the rumbling and alarms.

Josh struggled with the control stick. "I got nothing!"

She felt as if her teeth were vibrating out of her mouth. After over a minute of the sliding, rumbling, and the sounds of groaning, twisting metal, they finally slowed to a stop.

She looked out the window ports. Total darkness. They had been carried away from the light towers, and the silt further cloaked them.

She turned toward Josh, whose face was covered by a glaze of perspiration, despite the fact that the minisub's interior was now quite cold. Condensation from his rapid breathing frosted on the instrument panels in front of him. "What's the power situation?" she asked.

He pulled back on the stick, and *Conner One*'s thrusters whined weakly. "I guess that's your answer." He tapped the button on his headset. "I'll call for help."

"Save your breath." She was staring at her diagnostic screen. "The antenna system is damaged. No A/V communication, no GPS beacon, no lifeline to the surface."

Josh shook his head. "This keeps getting better."

"You don't know the half of it. The aft oxygen tank has also ruptured. We have maybe forty minutes left."

"Tell me you're making some kind of sick joke."

"No joke."

"Dammit, we shouldn't even be here. This expedition should have been finished a week ago."

"You volunteered to stay on. You believed in what we were doing here. We all believed."

He managed a rueful smile. "Sorry, Hannah. I guess I'm believing a whole lot less right now."

She glanced around the small compartment, which was illuminated only by the glow of the panels in front of them. Beyond the instrument panels were two forward-facing window ports.

And beyond that, Marinth.

Josh shook his head. "This is my fault. I hit that wall like a bulldozer. I tried to spin away before it came down on us, but I wasn't fast enough."

"It wasn't your fault. There isn't a soul on earth who's better at piloting this thing than you are."

"Except you."

"I designed it, but that doesn't mean my reflexes are better than yours." Hannah flipped a switch that toggled between the minisub's observation cameras. Three of the six cameras were operational, offering murky views of the right, front, and rear of the sub.

Josh squinted at the carved features that surrounded them. "How far away did the collision carry us?"

"Half a mile, maybe more."

"The rescue team may have a tough time finding us. If our GPS pulse cut out when the wall first came down . . ."

"I know, Josh. I guess we need to stay positive." It was all very well to say that, she thought ruefully.

She studied the monitors. The rockslide had kicked up so much silt that visibility was still at only a few yards. She didn't want to say the words, but she knew that their oxygen would run out long before full visibility was restored.

She had to think of something. Fast.

The diagnostic screen blinked red wherever there was damage on the sub. It scared her to see that warning lights were flashing all over the vessel's superstructure. Damn.

She pointed to the power indicator. "We're losing juice."

"Great. Fuel-cell rupture?"

She nodded and bit her lip. "Those cells are made up of a liquid hydrogen-carbon compound . . . Heavier than water."

"Yeah? So?"

She leaned forward and pulled a lever that would activate the left retractable arm. The servo motors whined, and the arm lurched from its place beneath the wing.

She slipped her left hand into the controller glove and flexed her fingers. Outside, the mechanical hand vaguely mimicked her motions, as if crippled by arthritis.

"You're not going to do much with *that*," Josh said.

"It's okay. This isn't exactly a delicate operation."

"What kind of operation is it?"

Hannah drew back her arm. "I'm sure they sent *Conner Two* down here as soon as they lost touch with us. It can't be that far away."

He shook his head. "It could still be a mile. And in this muck, it might as well be a hundred."

"We need to send up a flare."

"How are we going to do that?"

Hannah raised her arm, and the mechanical appendage outside struck a stone wall. She made a clawlike motion and dragged the mechanical hand back toward the rear of the pod, where the ruptured fuel cells rested.

"See any sparks?" Hannah said.

"Sparks? Down here? Why would there be—?"

He was interrupted by the blinding, white-hot flash of light, accompanied by a low rumble.

Josh threw himself back in his seat. "Holy shit! What did you do?"

"I ignited the fuel-cell compound."

"Are you trying to blow us up?"

"Yeah, kind of."

Sparks flew from the mechanical arm, and yet another flash lit up the ocean floor.

Josh was almost hyperventilating.

Hannah scraped the mechanical hand against the rock wall a few more times. Although sparks flew, there were no more ignitions. "I guess that's it." She pulled her hand from the controller glove.

"Dammit, you could have killed us!" Josh said.

"It was a distinct possibility."

"Then why the hell did you do it?"

"I had a pretty good idea that the compound was diluted enough not to blow apart the entire sub." She looked out the forward port. "We don't have time to wait and hope they stumble upon us."

"Even so, it would be a miracle if they—" He stopped. "Sorry. I know it's no good being negative. Is there anything else we can do?"

Hannah shook her head. "We wait. We conserve air, we keep movements to a minimum." She added quietly, "And we try not to stare too hard at the oxygen gauge."

"IT'S BEEN A LONG TIME," Josh said. "They should have been here by now, shouldn't they?"

"It's only been fifteen minutes." It had seemed longer to Hannah too. She had hoped that the rescue ship would have come long before this. "I think we're both a little on edge. They may be having trouble finding us in all this silt and—"

"Look!"

Another shaft of light shined through the port windows, but this was no explosion.

Hannah leaned forward. "It's *Conner Two*!"

The minisub descended from above and came to rest less than ten feet in front of them. Matthew Jefferson's dark, chiseled face appeared in the craft's forward-right port. He smiled when he saw Hannah. He looked down for a moment, then raised a small whiteboard on which he had scribbled "R U OK?"

Hannah grabbed the whiteboard from underneath the console in front of her. She wrote her response and showed it to him: "BOTH FINE. O2 < 20 MINS!"

Matthew nodded and backed away from the viewing port. After a few moments, *Conner Two*'s two mechanical arms extended before it. The hands gripped the wall pinning them, then slowly raised it and pushed it away. The mechanical hands, with a dexterity that could only be Matthew's work, then attached a steel tether cable to *Conner One*. *Conner Two* slowly rose, once again kicking up the silt and totally obliterating Hannah and Josh's view. Their craft lurched, and they felt themselves being pulled from the ocean floor.

"Thank God," Josh said fervently.

After a few minutes, they completely cleared the silt and could once again see the intense blue and green lights that accented the underside of *Conner Two*'s pod and wings.

"How's the oxygen?" Hannah asked.

"Good. Still over ten minutes left." Josh shook his head. "I still don't know how in the hell they found us. Even if they were right on top of us when you triggered those fuel-cell blasts, it must have taken them a while to get here. Do you know how lucky we are?"

"I know, Josh. I know."

After a few minutes, Hannah peered through her port. "You know, I don't think it was just luck that they knew where to find us."

Josh smiled. "Are we talking about destiny, Hannah? That's not at all like you."

"That's not what I mean." Hannah pointed outside. "Look."

Josh leaned forward to look out his port. "What are—"

Then he saw them. Two sleek dolphins circled the two minisubs, playfully tapping the windows with their snouts.

Hannah smiled and tapped the window with her fingers. "Hello, Pete," she whispered. "Hello, Susie. Nice to see you . . ."

THIRTY MINUTES LATER, HANNAH and Josh stood with several members of her team on the top deck of the research vessel *Copernicus,* gazing at a twin-masted schooner floating fifty yards away. "When did *Fair Winds* get here?" Hannah asked.

Captain Danbury, a red-haired bear of a man, shrugged. "A couple of hours ago, right after you went down. Melis radioed and said she'd join us for dinner."

Hannah nodded. "Good thing she brought Pete and Susie with her. I have a feeling we'd still be down there if she hadn't."

"You got that right," Matthew said in his thick Australian accent. "But give credit where it's due. I was the one who zoomed to save you from the murky deep. Not a bad bit of rescuing, eh, doll?"

She smiled. Matthew was a tall, good-looking black man whose easy charm made many forget that he was one of the best minisub pilots in the business. "I'll let you get away with calling me 'doll' only because you just saved my neck."

"I know how to pick my moments." He smiled at the dolphins chirping and turning back flips in the waves between the two boats. "As soon as we hit the water, Pete and Susie bullied and cajoled us until we headed in the direction they wanted us to go. I thought they were way off base, but they wouldn't take no for an answer."

Kyle Daley, her hydraulics specialist, pulled off his SEE ROCK CITY baseball cap and scratched his curly brown hair. "Okay, am I the only one here who doesn't believe that dolphins are the sea world's Einsteins? They're *fish*, people."

"Mammals," she corrected.

"Whatever." He made a face. "I'm happy you're okay, Hannah, but it's just as likely that they were leading Matthew to a school of yummy salmon they had their eyes on."

Hannah shook her head. "You can be a skeptic about a lot of things, but not about Pete and Susie. Not after the things we've seen them do in the past few weeks."

"Right. And next you'll have them doing your taxes." Kyle motioned toward the banged-up hull of *Conner One*. "It's amazing you guys were able to walk away from that thing. Looks like a scene from one of those old driver's-education films. You know, the ones where you see a mangled car all covered with the blood of a couple of careless teenagers?"

Hannah crouched beneath the left wing. "Thanks for the mental image, Kyle. But I see what you mean. It doesn't look like something a person could survive."

Hannah tuned out Kyle as he prattled on in the clichéd deep baritone of a driver's-ed instructional-film narrator. She usually welcomed the tension-breaking humor he brought to their long weeks at sea. Now, however, she couldn't focus on anything but the wounded *Conner One*. Josh knelt beside her, examining the twisted plates on the wing's underside. "Nothing a month back in the machine shop can't fix."

"Six weeks. Everything was going so well, too."

"It's still going well. If we had been in any other minisub ever built, we'd be dead now. This only proves what an incredible design you've given them."

"I have a feeling Ebersole isn't going to look at it that way."

"You're damn right I'm not," Sean Ebersole's raspy voice said from behind them. He gave Kyle a cold glance that stopped his narrative in the middle of the sentence. "You think this is a joke?"

Hannah and Josh stood and turned to face Ebersole, the chief operating officer of AquaCorp. His short, stocky frame was practically bristling. Even in the open air he smelled vaguely of McClelland Dark Star pipe tobacco. He always carried the scent with him even though she almost never saw him puffing on his pipe.

Hannah patted the minisub's damaged plates. "Yeah, it's a howler of a joke, Ebersole. You should have seen us laughing down there on the ocean floor. We're both fine, by the way."

Ebersole nodded toward *Conner One*. "More than I can say for your vessel."

Josh stepped forward. "It was my fault. I thought I'd left enough clearance, but I misjudged the distance. I still think this is the best craft I've ever piloted."

"Do you? Hannah, let's talk inside."

"Now? I need to run diagnostics and—"

"Your people can take care of it. Let's go."

Josh and Matthew moved to follow him, but Ebersole turned and raised his hand. "Just Hannah."

She turned toward them. "It's okay, guys. Finish up here." She followed Ebersole, who was already halfway across the deck. The crew was looking at her as if she had been sent to the principal's office, and she knew it was taking every ounce of Kyle's self-control to hold back a taunting "Uh-oh . . ."

They walked downstairs and made their way through the long, narrow corridor to the conference room, which was papered over with schematics for the submersibles. *Conner One* and *Conner Two* were virtually identical, but Hannah had designed subtle variations so as to evaluate the best total design for the final product. Three-foot models of the two vessels were suspended over the long table by almost-invisible strands of wire.

Ebersole closed the door behind him. "I'm shutting the mission down, Hannah."

She tensed. "Don't do this."

"I'm the only reason you're still here. Corporate wanted it over weeks ago."

"I know that. But you need to buy us some more time."

"Every day we're out here is costing the company a fortune. The rental of this boat, payroll for the crew . . ."

"AquaCorp is all over the Discovery Channel TV special, not to mention a logo placement in every newspaper ad and bus-stop poster. Plus the *National Geographic* spread. The exposure will be huge."

"It will be. But the Discovery Channel television people are gone, and the National Geographic team has finished. And you've completed your trials on the XP38 vessels."

"*Conner One* and *Conner Two*," she corrected.

"If you prefer. The point is, AquaCorp has gotten everything out of this mission that it's going to get. Your creations have performed magnificently, and everyone in the industry knows it. Even more people will know it when the magazine pieces and television profiles hit. We already have a three-year wait list on orders."

"So doesn't that entitle me to two more weeks?"

"The company has nothing to gain by keeping us out here and everything to lose. Everyone will know that one of the best underwater pilots in the business cracked up in your sub. That won't give our potential customers a comforting feeling."

"It's still a story without an ending."

"You mean Marinth."

"Yes." Hannah crossed to the far wall, where dozens of eight-and-a-half-by-eleven-inch color printouts had been pieced together to give a complete mosaic of what remained of the ancient city. "We've learned so much about the people who lived here. How they ate, worshipped, married, raised their children, governed themselves . . ."

"Your minisubs made that knowledge possible."

Hannah turned away from the mosaic. "But we didn't solve the biggest mystery of all . . . We don't know how they died. It was a brilliant, beautiful civilization that just seemed to . . . vanish. Almost no trace of their language or customs has ever existed anywhere else. What happened to them?"

"That's a question for another expedition, Hannah."

"But with just a few more dives, we might be able to answer it with *this* expedition."

"I'll give you one more day. Tomorrow. Then we're heading home."

"When all the TV specials and companion books come out, I'll promote the hell out of them. I'll give AquaCorp all kinds of credit."

"You've already promised to do that. That's why we're out here." Ebersole shook his head. "When I report your accident, it will be out of my hands anyway. We're done here, Hannah."

He strode out of the conference room.

Dammit. She had been half expecting it after the crack-up, but she had hoped that she could persuade Ebersole to stall for more time with the corporation.

Okay, he had pulled the plug. That didn't mean she had to give up without a fight. She just had to think of some way to make that fight as effective as possible.

CHAPTER 2

MELIS NEMID POURED TWO GLASSES of sangria from a pitcher and handed one to Hannah. "You gave it your best shot. I can't ask for more than that."

"I can." Hannah took the glass and leaned back in her chair on the deck of Melis's ninety-foot twin-masted schooner. Although it looked for all the world like a nineteenth-century sailing vessel, the belowdecks area contained one of the most sophisticated research labs on the sea, manned by a half dozen of the smartest and hardest-working marine scientists Hannah had ever met.

But none was more impressive than the young woman sitting across from her. Melis Nemid was blond and gorgeous, with an intelligence that was truly remarkable. She was the marine biologist who had discovered Marinth and unlocked many of its secrets years before, and the previously lost city and its people had become her life's passion. Hannah had met Melis at various scientific conferences back when the impossibly young marine biologist was still trying to convince skeptical colleagues of Marinth's significance. Hannah and

Melis had formed a close bond, allies against an establishment that was increasingly closed to new ideas. They were kindred spirits, then and now.

Hannah looked at the *Copernicus,* parked just a hundred yards from *Fair Wind*'s starboard side. Her team was still on deck evaluating the damage to the minisub. She knew she should be there with them, but she had to get away from that boat, away from Ebersole, away from all things AquaCorp.

"My best wasn't good enough, Melis." Her hand tightened on her glass. "Dammit, I know we're close to an answer."

"I feel it, too. But I'm grateful for what we've been able to do. Only you could have convinced that company to turn your routine sea trials into a massive archaeological expedition. I've been trying for years to mount a project of this scope. Without you, I would have waited years longer. My husband, Jed, has poured millions into this project, but I won't let him sink any more into it. He shares my dream, but I have to take over now. This is *my* responsibility." She made a face. "And money is tight in the academic world."

"I take it that you weren't successful yesterday."

"It was a complete waste of time. I can't tell you how many times I've had to take some foundation chairman on a personal tour of the Marinth Museum in Athens, endure a long, excruciating lunch, then hear them tell me that they *might* have a few dollars to spare in the next fiscal year . . ."

"I've done the fund-raising circuit. It's no fun."

"The executive I met with yesterday told me that I'd better my chances if I would go to dinner with him wearing the silver gown I wore at the Save the Oceans fund-raiser last year."

"You're kidding."

"I wish I was."

"You didn't do it, did you?"

"What kind of woman do you think I am?" Melis smiled and sipped her drink. "Besides, the gown was a loaner from Halston. It's against my principles to buy designer gowns when I could put the money toward something more worthwhile."

"Ah."

"So I pulled up anchor and got back here as soon as I could."

"It's a good thing you did. I guess you heard that Pete and Susie just saved our bacon?"

"Captain Danbury said something to me about it. It doesn't surprise me. Those two have helped me out of a hell of a lot of tight spots over the years." She gazed affectionately at the dolphins as they raced each other around the *Copernicus*. She turned back to Hannah. "As much as I hate to say it, it may be a good thing you're ending the expedition now. We've already been out here a couple weeks longer than we expected, and your people are getting tired. We both know how dangerous that can be. Accidents do happen. You could have been killed."

"But I wasn't. And the answer is still here somewhere. It's probably right in front of our eyes."

"If it is, we'll find it. You've given us enough data for years of study. Thanks to you, we'll be able to explore every inch of this city from the comfort of our computer keyboards. We'll be able to look up, down, left, and right from any vantage point. It'll be even more amazing than the mapping work you did on the *Titanic*."

"I hope it amounts to something."

"It will. In time, schoolchildren will be able to log in to the Marinth Web site and explore the entire city, just like you've helped them do with the *Titanic*. Maybe one of them will make the discovery we're looking for."

"I guess I'm just more impatient than you are."

Melis smiled. "I've been living with Marinth for most of my adult life, and delving into its mysteries has never been an easy battle.

When I first found it, we were able to swim down to it wearing scuba gear. But after the underwater earthquakes along El Hierro Ridge, the island sank more in the next five years than it had in the four thousand years previous. It seemed so unfair . . . like some deliberate slap of fate. But vessels like yours have brought it back to us. And new underwater currents have cleared away hundreds of feet of silt and exposed far more of the city than we ever realized was there. So maybe those earthquakes weren't such a disaster. Marinth seems to give up its secrets only when I'm best able to understand their meaning."

"That's why I grabbed a skiff and came over here. I needed some of your Zen-like perspective on things."

"You should take some time off. That will give you loads of perspective."

"I'm not giving up, Melis."

"Neither am I. My Zen only goes so far. Marinth may be over four thousand years old, but I want to find out all her secrets in my lifetime. But it doesn't hurt to stop and take a breath . . . or a vacation."

"I've never been good at vacations."

"Take one. Go someplace frivolous. It's been a difficult time for you, Hannah. Your brother's only been gone two months, and you haven't properly grieved for him."

"I've grieved for him. I grieve for him every day of my life." Hannah looked down. "Because I can't bury myself in my work to forget when he was my right hand on these kinds of jobs." She smiled faintly. "He was looking forward to coming with me on this one."

"I was looking forward to seeing him. Conner was a good man."

"Yes, he was."

"You don't blame yourself, do you?"

Hannah was surprised at the bluntness of the question, but then again, Melis had never been one to hold back. "No. Even though it happened on one of my jobs."

"You were supervising the retrofit of an old Russian nuclear submarine for a U.S. museum exhibit, right?"

Hannah nodded. "I'm sure you heard all about it. There was a lot of history connected to the sub that we didn't know about. It seems that there were men who were willing to kill to find what was aboard that sub. If I had been inside *Silent Thunder* that night, I wouldn't be here now either."

"All the men responsible are now dead?"

"Yes. It didn't bring Conner back, but it's a relief to know they won't hurt anyone ever again."

Pete and Susie broke the water's surface near them, playfully clicking and chattering.

Hannah looked at the dolphins and smiled. "They always know when someone needs cheering up, don't they?"

"As much as I'd like to give them credit for that, this time your Mr. Daley would be right if he said they probably just wanted a snack." She picked up a plastic bucket of salmon and held it up toward Hannah. "Would you like to do the honors?"

"Sure." Hannah took two of the fish and tossed them out to Pete and Susie, who immediately devoured their treats.

Melis put down the bucket. "While I'm probing you on subjects you would rather not discuss, what about Kirov?"

"You're right. I'd rather not discuss it."

"Tough. I've been holding back my curiosity on all this for the past two months. Now I want some answers."

Hannah sighed resignedly. Of course Melis wasn't going to let her off the hook. "Okay, what answers?"

"Well, I know that someone named Kirov who had a connection to you signed on for this project as a security chief, but he never showed up."

She shrugged. "Then you know as much as I do. Kirov has

intelligence-agency contacts, and they used their influence with Aqua-Corp to get him the gig."

"Then why didn't he show up?"

"I have no idea. He hasn't been in touch with me."

"Wonderful. I see that your taste in men hasn't improved since your divorce." Melis glanced at the deck of the *Copernicus,* where Hannah's team was still working with the minisub. "Okay. We'll forget about him. What about Matthew? He absolutely adores you, you know."

"Matthew? Are you serious? He has women falling for him in every port city in the world."

"But he doesn't fall for any of *them.* At least, not the way he does for you. He acts like a schoolboy whenever you're around him. A schoolboy who speaks with an incredibly charming Australian accent. And one who happens to be ripped. I've been sitting here hoping he'll take his shirt off, but I don't think it's happening."

"Maybe you're the one who needs to hook up with him."

"Not an option. I already have the perfect man. At least, the perfect man for me. Jed is everything I want or need. Matthew is all yours."

Hannah smiled as she shook her head. It was amusing to see Melis in matchmaking mode. Melis was usually as intense and obsessed with work as Hannah. "You know he's not my style."

"A gorgeous man who worships you?" Melis thought for a moment. "You're right. Not nearly complex enough. Not your style. But maybe you should consider changing your style."

A loud, insistent beep sounded from the walkie-talkie clipped to Hannah's belt. She unfastened it and held it up. "This is Hannah."

Josh's voice blared from the tinny speaker. "Hannah, I'm inside *Conner One.* You and Melis need to get over here now. Right now."

Hannah exchanged a glance with Melis. Josh's urgency surprised her. She raised the walkie-talkie. "What's going on, Josh?"

"You're not going to believe this. Hell, I can't believe it." Now she could hear the excitement and jubilation that vibrated in his voice. "Screw Ebersole. I think we've found it."

"Found what?"

"What we've been looking for. The end of the story."

HANNAH AND MELIS STARED AT the murky eight-foot projected image in the *Copernicus* conference room. There were over two dozen crew members crowded behind them, all trying to make sense of what they were seeing.

"What are we looking at?" Hannah asked.

Josh adjusted the focus. "This is the captured video from *Conner One*'s aft camera right before we struck the wall. I was reviewing the footage from the moment of impact, to see what happened."

Matthew smiled. "You're a screwup, that's what happened. You shouldn't need instant replay to figure that out."

"Thanks for the support, Matthew. I wanted to see *how* I screwed up." Josh advanced the image a few more frames. "When the wall came down, it hit the edge of a mosaic of colored glass that had been covered by silt. The stained glass tilted up for a second, and our lights shone through it. We don't have a clear shot of the glass itself, but you can see the image that it cast on another wall. Look."

Josh froze the image, and they could see the multicolored images projected with astonishing clarity.

"It's incredible," Hannah murmured. "So sharp and vivid."

Melis walked toward the screen. "This may have been the top surface of a trellis, probably designed for the sun to shine through and project these images on a white patio. We've seen these in a few other places, mostly schools and libraries. They were often used to recount histories of various buildings and institutions."

"Exactly what I thought," Josh said. "I've seen enough of these in the past few weeks to get an idea what I was looking at. If it's anything like the others, the top line tells us what story we're being told." He turned to Melis. "You're the expert. What does that say to you?"

Melis studied the image. "It's sunrise/sunset signs, meaning birth and death. We're being told a life story."

"Whose life?" Ebersole asked from the back of the room.

Melis's eyes narrowed on the sign to the right. "It looks like the birth and death of . . ." She gasped. "Oh, my God."

Josh nodded. "So I'm not crazy?"

Melis studied it for a moment longer. "This last picture is in the shape of what was once the island. Marinth itself." She looked up at Hannah. "This is the story of Marinth, from the beginning to the end."

"You always said this was here someplace," Hannah said.

"It had to be here. The people of Marinth had too much regard for their history for them *not* to have had some kind of record. And since their civilization was dying long before the tsunami, they would have had time to tell it." Melis walked toward the projected image and ran her finger across the lines, which looked as much like cave paintings as a written language. "But only the first part is visible here. Look, here are the early settlers in their fishing boats, and this is the great war they had with the invaders. We already know about this from statues and monuments we've found. Immediately afterward, there was a long period of peace in which art and music blossomed . . ."

"What else?" Josh said.

Melis turned around. "Nothing else. That's all we can see here. We need to see the rest of this pane." She looked at Hannah. "Is it possible to bring it up in one piece?"

Hannah thought for a moment. "It would have been easier with both submersibles, but we might be able to pull it off." She looked at Matthew and Josh, and they each nodded in response.

Kyle chuckled. "Somebody better tell the Discovery Channel to get their asses back here!"

Laughter exploded from the other members of team. But Hannah noticed that Melis didn't smile. She was still transfixed by the colorful images projected in front of them.

Hannah stepped closer to her. "Are you okay?"

"Yes. I want to know *more*. Hannah, I heard somewhere that you have a photographic memory. Is that true?"

"Yes, for what it's worth."

"It would be worth a good deal to me right now. Did you see anything down there that isn't here in front of me?"

"Maybe. I don't know. It's not that easy. It takes a hell of a lot of concentration."

"You don't want to do it."

She shook her head. "I'd rather not rely on mental hijinks. Let me bring up the trellis and let you see for yourself. Okay?"

Melis nodded. "I'm just impatient." She finally looked away from the screen. "And I think I'm a little frightened. That's what happens when a dream comes true. It's been so many years. This could be it, Hannah. The last piece of the puzzle . . ."

Zabyd Province

Afghanistan

VINCENT GADAIRE CLIMBED OUT of the armored Hummer and ignored the sand blowing across his face and hair. His half dozen guards and associates wore thick scarves, but he could not let his newest client see anything but strength and supreme confidence. He was also aware that the boldness of his strikingly handsome face was one of his chief assets, and he knew better than to hide his strengths.

"Welcome, Mr. Gadaire!" General Fetssel stood on a hillside that served to block some of the cutting winds. Fetssel was a tall man with salt-and-pepper hair and a mustache to match. Although his dozen or so uniformed men wore scarves, Fetssel did not.

Gadaire smiled. The general, of course, knew a thing or two about leadership. "Thank you for meeting me, General. I'm sorry it was on such short notice, but I've found that the longer in advance I set up a meeting, the greater chance there is of security leaks."

Fetssel nodded. "I understand. But I'm disappointed your lady friend isn't with you. Her beauty is almost legendary."

"Anna chose to sit out this meeting. I wouldn't want her to distract you from the demonstration I have planned."

"Ah, very wise. You're aware of my situation?"

"I'm aware." Gadaire had been put in touch with Fetssel by a satisfied former customer who had outlined the general's needs. The general had allied himself with local insurgents, with whom he hoped to overthrow the fragile government and instate himself as leader. There were obstacles in his path, of course.

"We're prepared to pay well if you can give us what we need."

"General, I understand that remote-controlled aircraft have been a problem for your friends. These drones have most of the countryside under constant surveillance, and without warning, they fire missiles on your allies."

"That is correct."

"Then I have the solution to your problem. It wouldn't have been wise to bring you within close proximity of the merchandise because of those drones we were just discussing. My equipment tells me there are two overhead right now, and they may be watching our meeting."

"So where are your toys?"

"About two miles from here." Gadaire pushed a button on his cell phone, and after a moment, a high-pitched whistling sound echoed from the west. He pointed to a pair of objects rocketing upward. "There. They can be remote-controlled, but you're better off using them in autopilot mode. They will seek and destroy any drones in—"

Gadaire's phone buzzed in his pocket, and he pulled it out and glanced at the screen. "Forgive me, but I have to take this."

Fetssel scowled. "We're in the midst of a business demonstration, Gadaire."

"And I promise you'll be very impressed, and I wouldn't take this call unless it was a matter of life or death. I'll be back with you in just a moment." He turned and stepped away as he pushed the TALK button. "This had better be important, Devlin," he said through set teeth. "You know where I am and what I'm negotiating. I told Fetssel this call had to be life or death, and it will be if you've embarrassed me for nothing."

"You'll want to hear this," Devlin said. "I just heard from our contact on the *Copernicus*. He thinks they found it."

"He *thinks*?"

"He couldn't talk long. He was afraid of being discovered. But they're going to follow up with another dive tomorrow morning, and he's pretty sure it will give you exactly what you've been wanting."

Yes. Gadaire's hand tightened on the phone as excitement surged through him. "I'm flying to Dublin tonight. I need our team to meet me there."

"Which team? The scientists? Or our own men?"

"Both. We'll need everyone on this." Gadaire looked back at the general, who was staring coldly at him. He wanted to tell him to go screw himself. The cash he was going to pry out of Fetssel was small change compared to what was beckoning on the horizon at Marinth. This could be bigger and more powerful than anything he'd ever been involved in before. "And make damn sure you choose men who won't be squeamish no matter who they come up against." He added grimly, "When I tell them to pull the trigger, they'd better not hesitate."

Marinth Underwater

Archaeological Site

Atlantic Ocean

HANNAH FLEXED HER FINGERS inside the controller glove and looked at the robotic arms outside *Conner Two*'s triangular side portholes. The metallic fingers flexed in time with her own, without any apparent lag. The gloves sensed subtle physiological cues that enabled the controller to anticipate the wearer's movements, and it was not uncommon for Hannah to see the robotic hands performing movements before she had even fully executed them herself. Although she would have loved to take credit for the controller, it was actually the brainchild of a brilliant young kinesiologist from Cornell who still e-mailed her weekly software updates as he refined his creation.

Matthew and Josh were at *Conner Two*'s controls, piloting the minisub down to the ocean floor. Matthew squinted at the color monitor trained at the artifacts below them. "The GPS stamp says it happened around thirty feet from here. Any of this look familiar, Josh?" He glanced slyly at him. "Why am I asking you? You're so blind that you bumped into the damn thing."

Josh scowled. "Lay off. It could have happened to you."

Matthew had spent most of the journey torturing Josh about the accident the day before, and although Josh had responded in good humor, Hannah could tell he'd had enough. Time to step in and stop it.

"Josh's right. It was an accident and it should be—What's that?"

A jarring, a subtle whump, on the submersible's port side.

Her gaze flew to the controls. "What's happening?"

Another jarring. Stronger this time, from the rear.

"It's not mechanical." Matthew was looking out the front and side viewing ports. "I think something's hitting us."

Hannah pulled her hands from the controller gloves. She reached up to the instrument panel and flipped on all of the exterior lights. She powered up the six HD video cameras, offering views in every direction.

Whump.

"What the—" Hannah squinted at the monitor. "Good God, it's a dolphin. I think it's hitting us with his tail."

"Several dolphins, maybe half a dozen," Matthew said. "I've got 'em on sonar."

Hannah looked at the sonar screen. Several blips circled them, moving over and under as they moved through the water. "This is bizarre. They've always given us a wide berth down here. They've never hit us before."

Whump.

Josh looked out the starboard port. "And it's not just one. They're all doing it. Do you think they're playing with us?"

It was a possibility, she supposed. It was true Pete and Susie could be playful. But there was something . . . determined about the assault by these dolphins. "I don't know." She nibbled at her lower lip. "Let me get Melis on the horn. She needs to see this."

While Hannah established contact with the surface, the dolphins struck their submersible three more times. Melis's voice finally came over their headsets.

She sounded surprised. "Are you on the ocean floor already?"

"Not yet. I wanted you to see this. Do you have feeds from all of our cameras?"

Hannah knew that Melis at her bank of HD monitor screens would have an even better view than they had down in *Conner Two.* "All feeds accounted for," Melis said. "What are you seeing?"

Whump.

"Did you get that?" Hannah asked.

"Yes." Melis sounded stunned. "A dolphin just slammed into you."

"It's happened several times in the past few minutes. There are six or seven dolphins following us down. They're all deliberately striking *Conner Two.* Sometimes with their tails, sometimes with their entire bodies. I've never seen anything like it. Have you?"

"No, not with a submersible. But look how their mouths are opening and closing, almost like they're popping their jaws. That's a sign of aggression. Whatever is going on, it's not a game to them." Melis's tone was serious. "Look, you've been lucky with your past dealings with the dolphins, but it may be time to back away. Forget about all that media image of sweet, cute Flipper. They're not like us, and we have to learn to coexist with them on their terms. Dolphins are fascinating creatures, but they can be dangerous."

Hannah flinched as a tail slapped angrily at the port closest to her. Violence. "It didn't start until we got close to the site. It's almost as if they don't want us to get near it."

"Too bad for them, because we're heading right toward it," Josh said. "I'm going to power up the Marinth light towers." He hit a switch that remotely activated the large towers of illumination on the ocean floor. He stiffened in shock. "Oh, my God!"

There were thousands of dolphins swarming, gliding over the ruins of Marinth.

"What's happening here, Hannah?" Matthew whispered.

She shook her head in disbelief. "I wish I knew." The sight took her breath away. She had never seen so many dolphins in one place before. The dolphins moved erratically, and their jaws opened and closed in the same disturbing manner as the ones that had assaulted the submersible.

Hannah spoke into her headset. "Melis, are you seeing this?"

"Yes, but I'm not believing it. Tell me you're recording all these feeds."

"Every single one in the magic of high definition. And two angles in 3-D."

"Good. I wish I were down there."

"You could have had my seat," Matthew said. "Something about all this creeps me out."

"I know what you mean," Hannah said. "Let's get what we came for. Head for the GPS coordinates of where we cracked up yesterday."

Whump.

Josh gripped the stick harder. "That was another dolphin. And there are more heading toward us."

Whump.

Another jarring hit.

Whump.

Again.

Whump!

The last blow rocked the minisub as three dolphins struck it in tandem.

"Get out of there," Melis said. "Get to the surface now."

Whump.

Matthew shot an inquiring glance at Hannah.

Hannah shook her head. "No. Keep going. We only have one shot at this."

Whump.

Hannah pulled on a pair of 3-D goggles. Her view, generated by the video cameras mounted outside, changed with the degree by which she turned her head. She slipped her hands back into the controller gloves and flexed her fingers to activate the mechanical arms.

"What are you doing?" Josh asked.

"I'm going to try to swat them away."

"Good luck," Matthew said. "Those dolphins weigh over a thousand pounds."

"Just keep going." Through the goggles, Hannah could see four dolphins heading toward her from the right. She extended the right mechanical arm and waved it back and forth, effectively blocking the vessel's side from another tandem blow.

The dolphins swerved away at the last second.

She blocked another blow from the left. And another after that. "Almost there, guys?"

"Another hundred feet."

"Hurry. I think I spooked them with the mechanical arms, but it may not last."

After a few moments, Matthew's eyes narrowed at the color monitor trained on the structures below them. "The GPS stamp says it happened around thirty feet from here. Does this look familiar, Hannah?"

"You're asking the wrong person." Hannah spoke into her headset. "Melis?"

"I think these were the gardens of a school," Melis said. "An institute of higher learning."

Matthew chuckled, but there was still perspiration beading his brow. "University of Marinth."

"I see it," Josh said. "It's at ten o'clock. I'll take us over."

Josh piloted the minisub over to the fallen wall that had almost crushed them the day before, then used a touchpad to aim a spotlight over the area. "There. There's our trellis and colored glass. Are you getting this, Melis?"

"Yes, that's it. I can't tell how much more there is under the silt. Got your leaf blower handy?"

"I'm already on it." Hannah extended the left mechanical arm and activated a compressed-air nozzle mounted on one of the steel fingers. Silt scattered across the trellis, exposing the intricately carved stone framework containing hundreds of interlocking pieces of colored crystal.

For the first time, they were able to take a good look at the entire artifact. It measured approximately twelve feet by eight feet, cut from a dark brown slab of granite less than an inch thick. The bridges between the colored translucent pieces were approximately an eighth of an inch thick, and a few of them had broken, leaving gaping holes in the elaborate jigsaw puzzle.

"Some restoration work needs to be done, but it's fairly intact," Hannah said.

Whump.

Another dolphin hit, this time from the rear.

"Shit!" Josh yelled. "More coming!"

Hannah whirled around. Ten to twelve dolphins were fast approaching from the left. Hannah raised the mechanical arm and repelled them with a blast of compressed air.

"Look fast. I don't mean to rush you, Melis, but things are getting intense down here."

"Just another few seconds, Hannah."

"No more than that."

Melis was silent for a moment. Hannah imagined she was leaning forward at her console, lips slightly moving as she read the ancient writings.

"I'll be damned," Melis murmured.

"Melis?"

"It's a gravesite. There was someone buried here."

Matthew exchanged a look with Hannah. "I thought you said this was a school."

"It was," Melis said. "But the historian, the one who is telling the story of Marinth here, was a high-ranking official. He may have even been the top man. The dean, if you will. It was a sign of great respect, a tribute, for people to be buried at institutions they had founded. You guys photographed markers at the central marketplace and the courthouse, remember?"

"I remember," Hannah said. "What else does this mosaic tell us?"

"I'll need you to bring it up. There are just enough broken crystals to obscure the key parts of the story. But there's a specific reference to a massive shadow descending over these waters, laying waste the people of Marinth."

Josh shook his head. "A massive shadow . . . Great. Is this a ghost story?"

"I don't think so," Melis said. "The Marinthians weren't particularly superstitious. There's something here we aren't getting. Look around for his funeral marker. Educators were often denoted with a circle motif, maybe a ring of circles. See anything like that?"

"Not yet." Hannah pushed *Conner Two*'s exterior lights on high, then swung the spots to illuminate the surrounding area.

Dolphins.

Everywhere she looked, there were sleek gray creatures darting about, taking positions around the submersible. Great dark eyes and that menacing snapping of the jaws. Her heart was starting to pound. "Help us, Melis. You're better at spotting this stuff than we are, and those dolphins aren't making it easy."

"I'm looking, but so far I don't—Wait. Move your starboard spotlight back a few feet, where it was a second ago."

Hannah slowly swung the spotlight back. There was now a wall of dolphins blocking all visibility. She called out to Matthew and Josh. "Move through the dolphins, guys. Slowly. We don't want to hurt them."

They backed up slightly and pushed through the mass while Hannah hit the dolphins with low-pressure blasts from the compressed-air jets. This time, however, they were much slower to move out of the way.

"Uh-oh," she said. "The air nozzles aren't working so well any longer. They must have figured out that the air won't hurt them."

"Any sign of a marker?" Melis asked.

"Not yet. So far, just a lot of—That might be it!" She directed a camera toward a circular outline on the ocean floor. "See that, Melis?"

"Yes. How big is it?"

"About eight feet in diameter."

"Dust it off, will you?"

Matthew piloted the minisub toward the circle and hovered in place while Hannah blasted away the silt. The wheel-shaped stone was carved with hundreds of detailed figures, different than the writings she had seen elsewhere in the city.

"Is this what you're looking for, Melis?"

"Yes, it's definitely a grave marker. I can't read everything there, but that isn't unusual. All the grave markers we found have been written in a different style than their normal written language. It may be an older dialect, or maybe even their version of poetry." Melis paused. "I guess there's no way you can bring that up."

"Sorry, doll," Matthew said. "Not now. We probably couldn't swing it even if we had both Conners in service. We'll do well just to get that trellis up."

"I knew the answer," Melis said. "Sorry I asked."

Josh positioned the exterior cameras over and around the marker. "But we'll have some spectacular 3-D video for you. Next best thing to being there."

Whump.

Jarring force.

Whump.

The submersible skittered to the side.

Whump.

Three more dolphin hits, each more forcible than the one before. Another hit!

Hannah tried the compressed air again, but this time the dolphins did not even hesitate to body-slam *Conner Two*.

"We're out of time," Hannah said. "Let's put that trellis into the sled and get the hell out of here."

Josh and Matthew piloted the vessel back to the trellis, struggling to keep it steady against the crush of pounding, circling dolphins.

Hannah pushed a button, and the sled's protective cover slid open.

First hurdle overcome. Kyle had struggled to coax the larger cover to open and close properly using a hydraulic system that had been designed for a much lighter sled.

Using every bit of the mechanical arms' articulation and sensitivity, Hannah gently picked up the trellis and swung it toward the sled. Before she could lower it, she saw a dark cloud racing toward the artifact.

Dolphins. Dozens of them.

"No!" she said through clenched teeth. "Don't you dare. It's *mine!*"

The dolphins pounded the trellis, the sled, and the mechanical arms.

The trellis flipped out of her grasp, and chunks of colored glass floated downward. Before the trellis could hit the ocean floor Hannah managed to swing the arms underneath and guide it down gently.

"Great catch!" Matthew said. "But you gotta work fast. Our friends are coming back for another blitz."

Hannah looked up. There was an even larger shadow advancing on them this time, building speed with each passing second.

No time to spare.

She spun the trellis around and quickly attempted to gauge how best to lower it into the sled. Normally she would have spent several minutes making adjustments to the position, but today she didn't have that luxury.

She held her breath and let go of the trellis.

As the gray cloud loomed ever larger, the trellis, riding the current, eased into the sled.

Matthew and Josh whooped, but she wasn't ready to celebrate yet. She hit the switch and watched as the cover slid shut in jerky fits and starts.

Just a little bit more . . .

Success!

"Move!" she yelled. "Get us out of here!"

Conner Two raced from the site as hundreds of dolphins pounded the submersible and sled from every direction.

It was crazy, Hannah thought desperately. This couldn't be happening.

"They're following us up," Josh said in disbelief.

And how much more pummeling could the sub take? Hannah

held tight as the submersible pitched from side to side. "Don't go up yet. Follow the ridge along the ocean floor."

"Why?"

"Just do it."

Conner Two changed direction. The onslaught of the dolphins lessened almost immediately.

"It's working!" Matthew said.

Hannah glanced back at the sled. "Keep moving. We're not out of this yet."

As they left Marinth behind, the dolphins thinned considerably. After another few minutes, there were none to be seen.

Matthew turned to her. "How did you know?"

"I didn't. It was a crapshoot. But they were so concentrated in Marinth, I thought they might not want to venture away." Hannah pulled the bandanna from around her neck and wiped away a layer of perspiration that had collected on her brow. "Okay, guys. Let's get topside."

CHAPTER
3

"ARE YOU OKAY?" MELIS ASKED Hannah as she exited the minisub. "That was completely weird. For a little while I didn't think you'd make it."

"For a little while, I didn't either. When we went down before, we had no trouble with the dolphins. It was as if that accident we had that uncovered the trellis triggered something. Crazy." She nodded at the sled, now resting on the deck. "But I know you can't wait to get a close look at the trellis. Go for it."

Melis hesitated.

"Go ahead." Hannah grinned. "You've been properly concerned and caring, now go see what your Marinthians have to say."

Melis made a face. "I do care." She started to unfasten the sled containing the trellis. "But I've waited a long time for this. And it may be only the beginning. I wish you could have spent more time down there."

"Blame your beloved dolphins. They weren't willing to have us down there." Hannah fell to her knees beside her. "Let me do it. Your hands are shaking."

"You're damn right they are." Melis's face was glowing. "I have a right. This could be the bonanza, Hannah. You saw it down there. Now I want to see it, touch it."

Hannah nodded, smiling. "I can see that you do. Just give me a minute." She carefully opened the sled and sat back on her heels, watching Melis's expression. It wasn't often that she'd been privileged to be present at the realization of a dream. It was a rare and special moment. "It's dirty. There's a lot of silt floating around down there."

"That doesn't matter." Melis stared at the intricate pattern on the glass. "It's beautiful."

"Yes, it is."

Melis glanced at her. "You're not impressed?"

"I guess I'm more excited about how things work than the actual physical beauty of an object. Conner used to shake his head and tell me I had no soul."

"You have a soul. Your focus is just different." She looked back at the trellis. "When I first started exploring Marinth, I couldn't understand why my husband, Jed, could be so excited about the artifacts that the crew brought up from the depths. I was only interested in the huge dolphin population that lived down there in the ruins."

"You were a marine biologist."

She nodded. "But that changed one day. I reached out and touched one of the goblets they had brought up on deck. It might have been warmed by the sun, but it felt oddly . . . alive. As if it had just been set down by some young Marinthian before he strolled away. I began to think of those men, women, and children who had lived and studied and loved all those thousands of years ago. I felt a connection and then I felt . . ." She reached out and touched the panes of glass with gossamer gentleness. "Wonder."

Hannah's throat tightened. She knew about wonder. Wonder was when she had stood with Conner by the bedside of his sleeping children. Children were wonder. Connecting with someone you loved was wonder. As she had told Melis, her life had been more involved with machines than human interaction but she knew that truth. "I guess I don't have your sensitivity."

Melis laughed. "Heaven save me from the gentle souls who tell you how sensitive they are. We're all different. We all have our own priorities. I'll take you anytime over them. Particularly when you risked your pod to keep from hurting my dolphins."

"It came close," Hannah said ruefully. "It was pretty scary down there. Dolphins can be intimidating, and there were so many. I can handle Pete and Susie, but those dolphins reminded me of those Foo dogs that guard Chinese temples. Very fierce." She looked down at the trellis. "Were they protecting this artifact, Melis?"

"I don't know. You can't make the mistake of thinking all dolphins are like Pete and Susie. They're not; they can be as lethal as sharks in some situations. Something triggered that ferocity. We'll have to think about it." Melis began to set up her camera. "But right now I want to study and photograph and not worry about the dolphins."

"Can I help?"

She shook her head. "Just keep Ebersole out of my hair until I finish." She nodded at the AquaCorp executive on the bridge. "He's been salivating to examine the trellis, and I've told the crew they're not to let him near it."

Hannah could see that he'd pose a problem. He was frowning, and he looked as if he were pulling at an invisible leash. "No problem."

Hannah made a face. "Well, actually I'd rather take arsenic than have him cross-examine me about the retrieval. How long?"

"Three hours. Then I'll have the crew stand guard while I arrange transport for it. I need to ship it to the museum. My lab isn't equipped for this kind of restoration. You can bring him to view it then . . . at a distance."

Hannah nodded and turned away. "I'll go do my duty right after I change."

"Hannah."

She looked over her shoulder.

Melis smiled. "Thank you."

"I just did my job."

She shook her head. "You took that extra step. You retrieved my trellis, and you protected my dolphins. That qualifies as damn terrific."

Hannah grinned. "I guess it does. But the hardest task is yet to come. Just get that trellis off the ship and out of Ebersole's view." She strolled down the deck toward the steps that led to her quarters.

"Hannah," Ebersole roared. "I need to talk to you."

She sighed, then forced a smile. "Right away. Just let me change first." She started down the steps, then heard the familiar chirping off starboard. She glanced out to sea and saw Pete arc high out of the water. Susie followed only seconds later.

Beautiful. Splendid creatures.

Mysterious creatures.

And what had happened today down in the ruins of Marinth had been full of mystery.

And wonder?

Perhaps. If she had been able to stay here longer, then she might also have been able to reach out and touch the wonder . . .

* * *

"A *HELICOPTER?*" JED KELBY SAID it as if he hadn't heard Melis correctly.

Melis walked toward the stern of *Fair Winds,* holding the satellite phone tight against her ear. "Yes. It's necessary, Jed. I wouldn't ask if it wasn't. You know I don't like asking you for help with Marinth."

"No, dammit, I wish you would. I'm your husband, and that place is as special to me as it is to you."

"That's not entirely true."

"Well, *finding* it was special for me."

Melis smiled. Marinth had been the passion—no, *obsession*—of Jed long before she had even heard of it. As she had told Hannah, her interest in Marinth had originally centered on the ancient civilization's unusual interaction with dolphins, and how, thousands of years later, the local dolphin population still exhibited unique social behaviors with each other and human visitors. In addition, the Marinth dolphins' highly evolved skeletal and respiratory systems allowed them to dive deeper and longer than any other dolphins on earth. But Marinth had held her once she'd been caught up in its unfolding story. Jed, however, had quickly moved on to other challenges, other adventures that took him to the far reaches of the world. He was currently in Micronesia, on the trail of a sunken Japanese destroyer that might have gone down with a fortune in diamonds in its hold.

"Marinth was only special to you when it was still so blasted elusive," Melis said.

"That's not true. It will always be special to me. It brought us together, didn't it?"

"Don't get all sentimental on me. I'm still not through teasing you about your attention deficit disorder."

"Let's get back to the helicopter. Why do you need it?"

"Hannah brought up the trellis. It's reasonably intact, but there are dozens of missing glass pieces that need to be reconstructed before we can interpret the message on it. This could be it, Jed." Lord, she hoped that was true. It had gone on so long, she was almost afraid to hope. "This could tell us what happened to the people of Marinth."

"I hope so, Melis. It would be everything you've been working for."

"It would." She added lightly, "Don't you wish you were here instead of chasing diamonds?"

He chuckled. "At this very moment, yes. No, not this minute. Every minute of every day. I miss you. Screw the diamonds. They don't compare."

She felt her throat tighten. No, they didn't compare. Treasures were dazzling and the search exciting, but what she had with Jed was truly remarkable. Yet their relationship was based on freedom as well as love, and she would no more interfere with his life and purpose than he would with hers. He was an adventurer who traveled the world, but when they came together, it was fantastic. "I miss you too. If you get a chance, fly in and see what we're doing here."

"I might do that. The Japanese are giving me a king-size headache about that sunken sub. Things aren't going so well here."

"Which means that there's no way you'll change your focus until you get what you want. So I'm not going to see you anytime soon."

"Unless you tell me to come." His voice was suddenly grave. "Then I'll be there for you. Anytime. You know that."

"I know that." For an instant she was tempted. No, she'd probably be so busy that she'd end up ignoring him for sixteen hours of the day. But oh would those other eight hours be fantastic.

Stop being selfish.

"No, go persuade the Japanese that they should let you have your diamonds. I'll call you when you can come for a celebration."

"I'll be there. I'm happy for you, Melis."

"Don't be. Not yet. My lab here isn't up to the job. I need to get that trellis to the museum right away."

"Hence the helicopter."

"Can you help?"

"I'll get Wilson on it. If one of the corporate copters isn't in the area, we'll hire one with the juice to go out there and airlift your relic out. We'll get it to you within a few hours. Happy?"

"Extremely. But I thought you had finally talked Wilson into taking a vacation."

"I thought so, too, but an hour before we left Guam, he turned up at the dock. He said he was bored."

"Well, working for you could never be boring."

"That's exactly what Wilson said. He'll find you a copter, don't worry."

FOUR HOURS LATER, HANNAH stood with Melis on the deck of the *Copernicus,* watching as the rented helicopter lifted off and headed east with its precious cargo. All around them, champagne corks popped, and crew members brought up bottles of whatever alcoholic beverages they could get their hands on. The first corks had popped the moment that *Conner Two* broke the surface, and Hannah had lived through enough end-of-expedition celebrations to know that the corks would still be flying at dawn.

Hannah turned toward Melis, who gazed wistfully at the helicopter as it disappeared into the distance. "I'm surprised you didn't make them take you, too."

Melis smiled. "It occurred to me, but I didn't want to leave Pete and Susie. Not here."

"They're comfortable with the other people on your team, aren't they? The crew of the *Fair Winds*?"

"Of course. They're like family. And if it was anyplace else, I wouldn't hesitate to leave. But here . . . Every time I come back to Marinth, I know I could lose Pete and Susie. They might decide to leave me."

"That could never happen."

"It could. They have a special connection to the other descendents of the Marinth dolphins. I don't know what it is. Their brains may just be wired a certain way, but they communicate differently with them than they do with any others. Dolphins communicate with each other, you know. Every time I come here, Pete and Susie disappear for a few days. I think the Marinth dolphins call them."

"But they always come back."

"Their time away has been getting longer and longer. And when our last expedition ended, they didn't leave with us. That was a first. They finally caught up with us almost a week later, but they were . . . different. A bit listless, maybe even depressed. It took almost a month for them to get back to normal. I'm afraid it may have been a turning point for them. They were young when I found them, but I may be losing them as they grow to maturity."

Hannah watched Pete and Susie as they sped back and forth across the stern of the *Copernicus,* putting on a show for the crew. "You could stop bringing them here."

"No, I couldn't do that, especially if this is where they would rather be. I'd miss them, but they know what they want."

"I can't imagine you without Pete and Susie."

"I can't imagine it, either." Melis managed a smile. "Anyway, I didn't want to just copter out of here in case this is the last day I'll ever have with them."

"I think you underestimate how they feel about you."

Melis's gaze never left the dolphins. "That may not be enough,

Hannah. The relationship of the dolphins with the citizens of Marinth was a strange and powerful bond. Very powerful. The Marinthians protected the dolphins, and the dolphins protected them. I know it sounds weird, but I think it seems to be still in existence. It's as if they believe the Marinthians are still here." She shook her head. "I know. Those ancient Marinthians perished thousands of years ago. But who knows if there's not still a lingering memory in the dolphins' DNA. I've heard of genetic memory, and dolphins are strange and wonderful creatures."

Hannah had to agree with her as she remembered how Pete and Susie had saved her life in the pod only a short time ago. She had run across many odd phenomena in her career on the sea, and she could accept that there was too much she still didn't know to discount anything.

And Melis knew worlds more than Hannah did about dolphins and was troubled. Dammit, she didn't know what to do to help. Okay, skip the deep stuff and just rely on distraction.

She took Melis's arm. "Come on. Stop frowning. You may have found the mother lode. It's a great way to end the expedition, and the guys deserve their celebration. So do we. Let's go see if we can out-party them."

Customs Warehouse
Tenerife Airport

MADRE DE DIOS, HE WAS CURIOUS about that box.

Carlos Nelazar stared at the large box he'd ordered stored conveniently close to the ramp doors for pickup. What was in it that could be worth the bribe he'd been offered to ignore the theft of some scummy artifact from the depths of the sea?

And was he a fool not to have demanded more? He had only a few more years before he retired from the Customs Department and got his pension. What if they found out he was involved in the theft?

Maybe it wasn't an artifact, maybe it was jewels or coins, and he could grab a few handfuls. Yes, it would be smarter to open the box and find out if he should ask for more money or grab a percentage on his own. Screw those bastards who'd told him not to examine it. He had a right to know. He checked his watch. Nine thirty. They weren't supposed to pick up the box before ten.

He lifted the crowbar. If he was quick, he'd be able to open, examine, and then nail the crate shut before anyone came to pick it up.

He had the box open within five minutes. Excitement gripped him as he first glimpsed the gleam of the colored stones. Jewels, it must be jewels.

Disappointment came over him. Only cheap crystals. No reason for anyone to be willing to pay such a high—

Or was there? There was something there, something that was holding him, drawing him closer . . .

"Pretty, aren't they? Like drops of sunlight."

He went rigid and slowly looked over his shoulder.

Relief surged through him. Only a woman, a pretty woman in a dark pantsuit, her hair in a tight chignon.

"You should not be here," he said sternly. "This is a restricted zone. Please leave."

Her gaze was still on the colored glass in the trellis. "I must have taken a wrong turn. Those corridors are so confusing. I'll leave soon."

"Now."

She smiled sweetly and took a step nearer to him. "What were you looking at? You seemed to be so interested." She stared eagerly down at the crystals. "Oh, yes, there seems to be a strange depth in those stones, isn't there?" She stepped still closer. "Personally, I prefer emeralds or rubies, but I admit there's a sort of mystique to—"

Pain.

Carlos doubled in agony as her needle-thin stiletto entered his heart.

BY NIGHTFALL, THE TOPSIDE deck of the *Copernicus* was packed with crew members from both it and *Fair Winds,* drinking, dancing, and watching the four-member amateur rock band led by Josh, Matthew, Kyle, and a bikini-clad blond research specialist whose only function was, as far as Hannah could tell, to look good while she shook a tambourine.

Hannah turned away. The expedition was over, and she had gotten through it. Her first job without Conner. It was as difficult as she thought it would be, but working with Melis in addition to her usual team had been a good way to ease back into the groove. If only she had been able to finish what she had started.

She heard footsteps behind her and caught a whiff of that familiar pipe tobacco.

Ebersole.

"You know . . . I'm not the bad guy here," he said.

She turned to see that he was holding a drink and wearing a tropical-print short-sleeved shirt. Very out of character for the buttoned-down executive with whom she had been working. "I know that, Ebersole. There were times when you went to bat for us, and I appreciate it."

"I wish you would tell that to the crew. They're looking at me as if I'm a monster."

"They know what you've done for us. But you need to understand that these people are sailors, no matter how many advanced degrees they may have. And they'll always think of you as a corporate bean counter." She wrinkled her nose as she looked him up and down. "No matter how obnoxious you get with your wardrobe choices."

He smiled and gripped the lapel of his brightly colored shirt. "Too much?"

"A tad. But I appreciate the effort. Next time wear it on the first day of the expedition instead of the last."

"Good tip. I'll keep it in mind." He leaned against the railing. "AquaCorp didn't just do all this out of the goodness of its icy corporate heart, you know."

"Of course not. This was a great public-relations opportunity."

"It goes beyond that. We did this for you."

She laughed. "Now I know you're lying."

"No lie. You're the only top-level designer who won't tie yourself to one manufacturer. We know about the offer you received from Deepstar last year. Very generous. It would have given you a sizable stake in the company."

"It wouldn't have given me the biggest power of all."

"What's that?"

"The power to say no. That's more important to me than stock options."

"Evidently. Still, when bidding on lucrative government contracts, any company would love to guarantee that Hannah Bryson will be on board."

"You have my phone number and e-mail address. I'm happy to discuss your contracts on a project-by-project basis."

Ebersole leaned closer and spoke quietly. "You'll be hearing from us sooner than you might think."

Hannah studied him. "Good heavens, Ebersole. You're talking like you want me to join your mob in a jewelry heist."

"Nothing that glamorous, I'm afraid. But AquaCorp wants your help on a very delicate project. A project, we're afraid, you may not be too keen on. We had hoped not to involve you, but we knew it was always a possibility that your assistance would be needed. That's the real reason you had such an easy time talking us into this multimillion-dollar expedition."

"What the hell is it?"

"I've said too much already."

"Don't give me that bullshit. You didn't just accidentally say too much." Her gaze narrowed. "There's no one more calculating than you are, Ebersole. You dress up in your Hawaiian shirt and come here to smooth the way for the bomb AquaCorp is planning to drop on me. Then you take one step forward and two steps back. Talk to me."

He shrugged. "Can't do it. I have my orders. I told them I should be up front with you, but they preferred I try to be subtle. Anyway, don't be surprised when you get our call. And please keep in mind what AquaCorp has done for you." He turned away. "We've been good partners. We could kick it over the top with this project."

She watched him walk away.

He was the quintessential company man, and the company had sent him to feel her out on working with them on this "project." She was uneasy. Secrecy was not uncommon in her business; aside from the national-security issues of military contracts, corporate espionage was always a concern. But Ebersole seemed to be talking about something else entirely. Of course, his odd demeanor could have been the result of nothing more than the tall, colorful drink in his hand. Maybe she was reading too much into it. At any rate, she wasn't going to let it bother her tonight. She was going to go back to Melis and the guys and what might be their final party at Marinth.

CHAPTER
4

IT WAS PAST ONE A.M. WHEN Hannah heard the sound of a powerboat engine in the darkness. At first she thought it might have been one of the small crafts shuttling between *Copernicus* and *Fair Winds,* but she soon realized it was coming from the opposite direction. She glanced around the deck. The other revelers had heard it, too, and they gathered along the portside railing. Captain Danbury fired up a spotlight and shined it into the darkness.

Hannah walked toward him. "What is it?"

"I can't see it yet." Danbury nodded toward the lights of a larger boat several miles away. "Whoever it is, they might have come from there. That boat's been anchored for the past couple of hours."

As they watched, a beacon flashed from about fifty yards away. Danbury flashed his spotlight in return, then angled the spot toward the small craft, which Hannah saw was about ten feet in length. She could see three men on board. Two were seated, but the third, a distinguished-looking man in a dark suit, stood looking up at them.

He smiled. "Permission to come aboard, Captain Danbury."

Danbury stepped from behind the spotlight and looked at the three men. "State your purpose."

"I'm Agent Elijah Baker with the U.S. Defense Intelligence Agency. I need to speak with Hannah Bryson. And Melis Nemid, if she's here." The man gestured toward *Fair Winds*. "That's her boat, isn't it?"

Hannah glanced at Melis and Ebersole, who had joined her at the railing. They looked just as bewildered as she was feeling.

The man smiled as he held up a wallet displaying a badge and an ID card. "I'm the real deal, I promise. Would you mind throwing down a ladder?"

Danbury nodded to a couple of his crew members. They threw open the lid of the strongbox, pulled out a rope ladder, then hooked it over the railing. The three men from the smaller boat climbed aboard the *Copernicus*. By now the music had stopped, and all eyes were on them.

The man who had identified himself as Elijah Baker extended his hand to Danbury. "Sorry to crash your party." He glanced at Hannah. "You're Hannah Bryson. I recognize you from your documentaries." He turned to Melis and again showed his ID. "Ms. Nemid?"

"Yes, what are you doing here?"

"I'll try to take as little of your time as possible. Is there somewhere we can go to talk? An office?"

Ebersole stepped forward. "I'm the COO of AquaCorp. We're funding this expedition. Is there something you wish to discuss with me?"

"Absolutely nothing. My business is with Ms. Bryson and Ms. Nemid. They can bring you up to speed after we've spoken. I'm very busy. I really don't want to waste any more time. Ladies?"

Hannah nodded toward the stairwell. "Follow me."

Hannah had intended to lead Baker and Melis to the conference room, but at the last minute she decided to detour to the dining area. For some reason, Baker's crisp air of command annoyed her. She had dealt with Feds before, both on expeditions and after Conner's death, and she wasn't about to let him dictate to her and Melis. She threw open the door of the galley, where covered platters of food were prepped and ready to be carted up to the party. Hannah pulled back a corner of one of the plastic wraps. "Want a salami-and-cheese finger sandwich?"

Baker shook his head. "No, thank you. This won't do. Is there someplace more private we can go?"

"No one will bother us here. What's on your mind?"

Baker glanced at Melis for support, but she only smiled. "You really should try the salami. It's quite good."

Baker shook his head. "I heard you had a problem with authority, Ms. Bryson."

Hannah nibbled at a bit of cheese. "First of all, we would have to recognize you as *having* some kind of authority. We're on an archaeological expedition in international waters. I don't like orders. We're happy to help you out in whatever it is you're doing, but don't pretend we're in any way obligated to jump when you snap your fingers."

He folded his arms across his chest. "I'm not pretending anything. I just want your cooperation. I did come a long way to talk to you."

"I've been wondering about that. We do have satellite phones and e-mail."

"I thought this warranted a personal visit. You recently dispatched an artifact recovered from this site. Is that correct?"

Hannah and Melis exchanged a glance.

"Yes," Melis said. "It went out by helicopter this afternoon."

"Would you care to tell me what the object was?"

"An artifact we recovered from the Marinth site. From a school."

"Describe it. In detail."

Melis frowned at Baker's curt order but she continued. "It was part of a trellis, with inlaid colored jewels and crystals."

"Valuable?"

"From a historical perspective, yes. It's priceless. It fills in a major missing piece about the decline of this civilization. But the gems themselves are nothing spectacular. It's not as if they're diamonds and rubies. Most of them are colored quartz."

"That's what brought you out here?" Hannah asked.

Baker nodded. "Do you know where that artifact is now?"

"The helicopter took it to Santa Cruz de Tenerife. From there, a cargo jet is flying it to a lab in Athens." Melis checked her watch. "It's on the plane now."

"Wrong," Baker said. "Your artifact never made it onto the cargo plane."

Melis stiffened. "What the hell are you talking about?"

"The helicopter brought it to the airport, right on schedule. But sometime in the next ninety minutes, while the crate was waiting to clear Customs, it vanished."

"No!" Melis said.

"Vanished?" Hannah said. "Nothing vanishes into thin air. Was it stolen?"

"Probably. A Customs official's body was found in the warehouse. But we suspect he may have actually helped with the hijacking."

"It can't be gone. I *need* that piece." Melis's hands were clenched into fists at her sides. "It's the culmination of everything I've been working toward for years."

"We'll get it back," Hannah said. She turned toward Baker. "And this still doesn't explain why you're here. Or even why you're in this part of the world. What business does the intelligence community have with Melis's artifact? What were you doing nosing around that cargo plane anyway?"

"Are either of you familiar with Vincent Gadaire?" Baker asked.

"Never heard of him," Hannah said. "Should we have?"

"He's an arms merchant. He's been getting rich selling high-tech weaponry to every side of every conflict in the past fifteen years. Governments have even used him in situations in which they don't want to get their hands dirty." Baker unzipped a tablet computer and filled the screen with a photo of a strikingly attractive couple entering what appeared to be a red-carpet gala. "This is Gadaire and his mistress, Anna Devareau. He sometimes refers to her as his wife, depending on the social situation."

Hannah studied the screen. "They look like supermodels at a movie premiere."

"This was at last year's Cannes Film Festival. He occasionally finances films, which means that he often has every actor and filmmaker with a pet project cozying up to him."

Hannah studied the image of Gadaire and his girlfriend. Baker had chosen the picture wisely, she thought. It told her a lot about this couple, from their grace, easy confidence, and sheer power they had over the people around them. It was immediately apparent that they had a magnetism shared by many successful people she had known.

"What does he have to do with us?" she asked.

"That's what I came out here to find out. We monitor his activities for a variety of reasons, and recently we got word that he's taken an interest in your expedition."

"Marinth?" Melis asked. "As an investment?"

"I doubt it. We've learned that at least three people have been murdered because of your lost city."

Hannah stared at him. "*Murdered?* You think people have been killed because of what we're doing out here? This is a historical expedition. As Melis told you, the artifacts she's brought up are valuable but not priceless."

"Something about your work here attracted Gadaire. He's definitely involved."

"That's insane," Melis said. "We're not doing anything that you can't watch on the Discovery Channel."

"I guarantee Gadaire isn't interested in the Discovery Channel. What else are you doing that could be important to him?"

Melis shook her head. "Nothing." She frowned. "A weapons dealer? Around the time we discovered Marinth, there was some thought that their ancient technology could be harnessed as a weapon. It was impressive, but in the end it was too inefficient to be used that way. I really don't think the Marinthians possessed anything that Gadaire could use."

"What you think doesn't matter," Baker said tersely. "It's what Gadaire might think, even if he's wrong. You said this stained-glass piece was important to you. Could it have been just as important to him?"

She shook her head. "It's important only from a historical perspective. We've put together almost all the pieces regarding their civilization except the last one. Thousands of people have been studying Marinth ever since we found it, but no one knows how the civilization died out."

"The island sunk, right?"

Melis made a face. "You probably saw that awful TV miniseries, with waves crashing over the island while the residents tried to escape. We do believe the actual submersion was caused by a tsunami that happened in the Canaries. But that was the last tragedy that took place. Marinth was already dying before that catastrophe. It was almost a ghost town at the time of the tsunami. We don't know what happened to them, or if it was disease, invading armies, or some other natural catastrophe that cleared out this place. Whatever it was, the tsunami was only the final deathblow. The Marinthians documented everything, but until yesterday, we didn't think anyone had recorded what ended their civilization. Once we restore the trellis, it might tell us exactly what we've been looking for."

"Or maybe what Gadaire is looking for." Baker glanced at Hannah. "I wonder if I may speak to Ms. Bryson alone for a moment."

Melis started to leave, but Hannah put a hand on her arm. "No, anything you want to say to me, you can say in front of her. This is her city, dammit. It's her artifact that was stolen. Melis and I have been friends for years. If you want to talk to me, she stays."

His lips tightened. "This is a national security matter. The choice isn't yours to make, Ms. Bryson."

"Then we're done here, Baker. Good luck with your case."

Baker cursed under his breath. He pulled up a pair of pictures on the computer and displayed them side by side on his tablet. He swung them around toward Hannah and Melis. "Go ahead, look. Not the prettiest pictures, are they?"

Hannah instinctively recoiled. The photos were of two male corpses, one in a small boat, the other floating in a canal. Blood covered the seat of the boat and drenched the corpse.

Blood. She had a sudden memory of her brother's blood-soaked body the night he died.

Push it away. These bodies had nothing to do with that horrible night when Conner had been shot. Focus on the here and now.

She looked up at Baker. "Gadaire killed them?"

"No. They're victims of a friend of yours." He paused. "Nicholas Kirov."

Kirov.

She felt as if she'd been punched in the stomach. Baker's gaze was on her face. The arrogant bastard had obviously hoped to get a reaction from her. Don't let him see he'd scored. She was determined to deny him that pleasure.

She stifled the shock and tried to keep her face without expression. "What do you want me to say? I don't know anything about this." She paused. "But in my experience of him, Kirov never killed anyone who didn't deserve it."

"That gives him the right to act as judge, jury, and executioner?"

"I didn't say that." She moistened her lips. "How do you know he did it?"

"There was an eyewitness. Have you been in touch with Kirov?"

"No, not since I've been here."

He lifted a brow. "I understand you were very close. Should I believe you?"

"That's entirely up to you," Hannah said. "But I'm sure you've gone back and combed every satellite transmission to and from these boats."

"Of course we have, but we know that Kirov is very adept at telephone relays. If he wanted to contact you without anybody knowing about it, he could have done it."

Yes, the Kirov she had known might well have been able to do it. "Yes, and who taught him? He worked for the CIA, didn't he?"

"They had an arrangement, but actually I'm sure you know Kirov works for no one but himself."

"But they were willing to use him. For all I know, they might still be using him. What does he have to do with any of this?"

"That's what we're asking you. These two men worked for Gadaire." He held up his hand as she started to speak. "And he wasn't playing good guy disposing of the scum. Kirov isn't clean, believe me. He has a lot in common with Gadaire, especially where his interest in Marinth is concerned."

Hannah wrinkled her brow. "What are you talking about?"

"He was after the same information these two men were. Information about Marinth."

"If Kirov wanted information about Marinth, he could have asked me himself."

"My feelings exactly. That's why I thought he might have been in touch." Baker tilted his head to one side. "Are you sure there's nothing you want to tell me?"

Hannah closed her eyes. More violence, more killing . . . Naturally Kirov was involved.

"Ms. Bryson?"

Her eyes flicked opened. "No. I have nothing more to tell you. What about this eyewitness? Maybe you should spend more time with him."

"I'd like nothing more. His name is Sam Debney. Do you know him?"

"No."

"He was in a Venice hospital for a couple of days last week, terrified for his life. He wanted protection, and apparently he was quite talkative."

"Protection from Kirov?"

"No, from Gadaire. Two of Gadaire's men worked Debney over pretty good. He almost died, and he probably would have if your friend Kirov hadn't stepped in and eliminated them. Those are the men in the photos I just showed you."

"As I told you, Kirov tends to kill people who deserve it."

"And as I told you, he's no white knight. He wanted information from Debney, and he was willing to let him bleed to death if he didn't get it."

"Information about Marinth again. What exactly did he want to know?"

"Debney didn't say. He was holding back that little tidbit in exchange for protection from us. In the end, he gave us the slip. He walked right out of the hospital in scrubs."

"Funny that he was able to pull that off under your noses. Maybe he was right in thinking that you didn't have much to offer in the way of protective services."

Baker raised his hands in surrender. "I think I've had my chops busted enough for one night. I'm becoming irritated. If Kirov gets in touch with you for any reason, we ask that you let us know." Baker handed her his card, then another one to Melis.

Hannah shrugged. "Fine, but I really don't expect to hear from him."

"We think you will. Aside from his personal relationship with you, Ms. Bryson, he's apparently very interested in Marinth. You and Ms. Nemid here have more knowledge of it than just about anyone. I suspect you'll hear from Kirov sooner than later." He turned and headed for the door. "And you'd be wise to share anything he tells you with us. I'd hate to have to consider you an accomplice in this dirty business. I could make things very difficult for you."

The threat lingered in the air after the door shut behind him.

"Ugly." Hannah turned to Melis, who was very pale, her expression shocked. "It's going to be okay, Melis. I feel the same way. I was over the moon when I thought that trellis could tell the end of the story. No, maybe not the same. Your emotional investment was a hell of a lot bigger than mine. But I wanted it to happen. Dammit, the answer was in our hands. No one is going to cheat us out of it."

"Well, it's not in our hands now." Melis raised shaking fingers to her temple. "It seems impossible. What the hell is going on?"

"We'll find out."

"Yes, we will." She stared Hannah in the eye. "And one of the things I have to find out is about your friend, Nicholas Kirov. I'm going to know a good deal more about him before we go any farther. For one thing, you didn't mention that he leaves dead bodies in his wake."

"It's not quite—"

"Hannah, you're not being fair. I was respecting your privacy, but this is about Marinth. I have to *know*. And you're going to tell me."

Hannah hesitated. Why was she still trying to protect Kirov? It had been instinctive with Baker, but Melis had a perfect right to know about someone who might be an accomplice in stealing that trellis. Lord, she hoped Kirov was clean. "You're right, I'm not being fair. Okay, let's go on deck, and I'll tell you what I know about Kirov." She grabbed two glasses of wine from a tray on the counter. "I don't know about you, but I need a drink."

"I need something to put the starch back in me." Melis took the glass and opened the door. "Though I'm not sure this will do the trick."

Hannah wasn't sure either. But to talk about Kirov she would have to talk about Conner, and she could use all the insulation alcohol or anything else would offer her.

The moonlight was bright on the water and, as she reached the railing, she could see the lights of Baker's boat as it picked up speed and left the *Copernicus*.

"Talk to me." Melis leaned her arms on the rail. "Kirov."

"You know that Conner was murdered aboard a Russian nuclear sub, *Silent Thunder*, that I'd been hired to go over with a fine-tooth comb and make sure it would be safe as a museum exhibit."

"Yes."

"Conner and I were pawns. The CIA knew there was a map on the sub that was going to draw Pavski, a Russian bureaucrat who had been climbing the political ladder in Russia during the last days of the Cold War. He had been responsible for the release of a bacterial agent that caused the deaths of *Silent Thunder*'s entire crew during a training exercise. The CIA knew *Silent Thunder* was going to be targeted, and they let us take the job anyway." She gazed out at the sea. "Conner was alone on the sub when Pavski's men came. They blew his head off."

"Dear God, Hannah."

She took a drink of wine. "And the CIA wouldn't tell me anything. It was classified. I wanted to kill them."

"I can see why."

"So I went after Pavski myself." She looked at Melis. "And I ran across Nicholas Kirov, who had been after Pavski and the men on his committee for years. He taught himself to be an assassin. He'd teamed up with the CIA so that he'd be under their protection when he took out those politicians who had made *Silent Thunder* a death ship. He'd found and disposed of them all by the time I met him. Except for Pavski. He was the last and the one most responsible for all those horrible deaths. Kirov was after him."

"And so were you."

"It seemed intelligent to team up with him. He knew everything about Pavski. Everything about *Silent Thunder*. He was a man who would never stop until he'd killed Pavski." She took another drink. "I don't blame him. Pavski was responsible for the death of his wife, he'd made him go on the run. He was to blame for the death of Kirov's entire crew."

"Kirov's crew?"

"Kirov was captain of the *Silent Thunder*." She finished her wine. "He loved that sub, loved his crew, loved his wife. When I met him, it had all been taken away from him. His crew had suffered a horrible death from a bacterial agent set loose in his sub; his wife had been murdered by Russian agents trying to find him. But he was still the most remarkable man I've ever met."

"Even though you said he'd trained himself to be an assassin?"

"I didn't care. He could help me find Conner's killer." She looked back at the ocean. "And he did. We found him together. I owe him more than I can say. And I trusted him, Melis." She grimaced. "Well, sometimes I had problems with that, but when it counted, he was there for me."

"You were under great strain."

"And my judgment was impaired?" She shrugged. "It's possible. But it didn't matter to me at the time." She paused. "I've worked shoulder to shoulder with men all my life because of my profession. I've never met a man who I'd rather have with me in a tight corner. He saved my life, Melis. Twice."

"It seems the partnership is over," Melis said dryly. "And you may trust him, but I don't. I can't. He's clearly in this mess up to his neck."

Hannah couldn't deny that when the sight of the bodies in those photographs were still fresh in her memory. "Then I have to find out why and if he knows anything we can use to get that trellis back."

"We have to find out," Melis corrected. "It's my battle."

"The hell it is." She started to turn away. "I fought those crazy dolphins down there for that trellis, and I'm not letting any two-legged jackasses take it away."

"Even if the jackass's name is Kirov?"

She glanced back over her shoulder. "I didn't deserve that. Particularly if it's Kirov."

"Sorry, I'm upset. I know you wouldn't be anything but straightforward with me." She paused. "But there's one other thing I have to know so that I can put suspicion behind me. Were you lovers, Hannah?"

"Did we go to bed together? No. Would it have happened if I hadn't still been in mourning for Conner and not able to think of anything else? Possibly. Kirov is sexy as hell. Very male. Very confident. Charisma galore. Sort of Sean Connery meets Harrison Ford." She met Melis's gaze. "But our relationship was founded on revenge, and I guarantee that Kirov won't be able to persuade me to hurt you or Marinth by luring me into the sack."

"I know that wouldn't happen," Melis said quietly. "But I had to have all the facts."

"You have a right to a little suspicion." Although that question had hurt. It probably shouldn't have stung her. In Melis's position, she would have wanted to make sure that she knew everything that was going on. She moved down the deck. "It's my job to clear this up so that you don't have to worry about Kirov any longer."

"Where are you going?"

"To call for transport." She started down the steps to the cabins. "And I have to pack."

Cobh, Ireland

1:10 A.M.

NICHOLAS KIROV LEANED FORWARD and listened to the footsteps in the hallway. Driscoll?

He listened for a moment longer, then heard a woman's voice chattering into her cell phone. Her footsteps grew louder, then softer as they receded into the distance.

Not yet, he thought. Soon.

Kirov leaned back into the large leather easy chair and glanced around the small living room of the modest two-bedroom flat. The lights were off, but a streetlight outside the window cast enough illumination for him to see fairly well. The flat was located in Cobh's working-class Holy Ground neighborhood, a community immortalized in an old sea shanty that had somehow found its way to crew members with whom he'd served in the Soviet Navy.

Kirov looked at the frayed carpet and water stains on the ceiling. He had expected to find better living quarters for the great Martin Driscoll.

Of course, anyone would probably expect that, which may have been the point. If Driscoll wanted to keep himself hidden, this would be an excellent choice for him. Kirov remembered some of the shabby places *he* had lived when he didn't want to be found. Places that made this flat look like a mansion. Places that—

More footsteps in the hallway. Heavier this time. A man's footsteps.

Keys jingling outside. The lock turned, and the door opened wide.

A man with silver hair was silhouetted in the hallway, wearing a denim coat with a large fleece collar. Driscoll.

The man closed the door. He froze. "Who's there? Charlie?"

He paused, waiting for an answer. Driscoll cursed and flipped the light switch and dove to the side.

"No lights. I removed the bulbs," Kirov said.

Driscoll was on the floor, crawling behind the couch. "Who are you? What do you want?"

"Relax, Driscoll."

"Who in the hell is Driscoll?"

"Do you really want to play it that way? We both know who you are, and I really don't want to waste any more of our time than I have to."

"I don't know who sent you, but I can make it worth your while to forget you ever found me."

Kirov chuckled. "You think I'm here to kill you?"

"It had occurred to me."

"I know about your difficulties with the Brogan crime family. Trust me, I couldn't be less interested in their problems."

"Then who are you?" Driscoll was inching toward a small oak cabinet.

"If you're going for the derringer in the drawer, it's not there anymore. You should really have had it on you." Kirov held up the gun, silhouetting it against the window. "But then violence isn't really your area of expertise, is it?"

"Dammit, if you're not here to blow a hole in me, what are you doing here?"

"I know this is a rather disturbing way to approach you. I'll give the gun back after I'm finished."

"Finished with what?"

"I have a business proposal for you."

Even in the dim apartment, Kirov could see the annoyance on Driscoll's face. "Cripes. You're one of those."

"One of what?"

Driscoll shook his head. "You're here to lure the master thief out of retirement for one last job, right? One last score that will let me get out of the game once and for all. That's it, isn't it?"

"Not quite." Kirov laid the gun down on an end table. "But close enough, I suppose."

"You're wasting your time. I don't do that anymore. And if I did, I wouldn't be hiring myself out to a lowlife who breaks into my flat and scares me half to death."

He was beginning to like Driscoll. He was honest and had no false bravado. "It seemed to be the thing to do at the time. I didn't want to waste time, and catching you off guard was a way to cut to the chase. I apologize."

"I'm not believing this. This was all so that you could ask me to pull a job . . ."

"It's not just any job. I knew you couldn't be tempted unless the stakes were high enough. I guarantee that the stakes are going to interest you. This could be of huge benefit to you."

"Huge, eh?" Driscoll's voice was bitter. "It's always huge, isn't it? The last time I heard that, I ended up on the run from the most dangerous organized crime family in Europe. So get the hell out of here with your huge score."

"I can't do that. I'm afraid I've left the situation in a bit of a mess. I detest disorder. I have to straighten it out."

"Screw your mess. Just get out of here."

"You don't understand." Kirov stood, switched on a lamp on the table beside him, and walked toward the closet. He opened the door to reveal a young, dark-haired man who was bound and gagged, his hands strapped over his head and hooked on the support beam of a high shelf.

Driscoll's eyes widened. "Charlie!"

"He got here half an hour before you did," Kirov said. "I invited him to sit down and join me, but it seems he was only interested in killing me."

"Because he's a smart kid."

Driscoll pulled the tape from the young man's mouth, and a string of Irish-accented obscenities tumbled out. He glared at Kirov. "I'll still kill 'im, just say the word!"

"Calm yourself, son."

"Son?" Kirov produced a knife and stepped closer to Charlie.

Driscoll blocked his path. "Don't touch him. You'll have to go through me first."

"That isn't necessary." Kirov reached over Driscoll's head and cut the tape from Charlie's wrists.

The young man pushed Driscoll out of the way and hurled himself at Kirov. "You son of a bitch!"

Kirov smoothly grabbed Charlie's wrist, twisted it behind his back, and pushed him facedown on the sofa. "I thought you would have had enough of this by now." Still holding Charlie down, Kirov pocketed his knife and looked over at Driscoll. "I didn't know you had a son. He doesn't look much like you. He's a good-looking kid, but lacks your sense of style."

"He's young. He has time to develop. But he's mine all right. I was surprised, too, when *I* found out two years ago." Driscoll looked down at Charlie. "Ease up, boy. This man means us no harm . . . I hope."

Kirov let him go, and Charlie jumped to his feet and started toward him.

Driscoll shook his head. "I said enough, Charlie."

The young man's eyes never left Kirov as he spoke. "You don't actually trust him, do you?"

"Believe me, if he was one of Brogan's men, I'd be dead now. And so would you." Driscoll walked over to his son and pulled the remaining tape from his feet and wrists. "Relax, Charlie. It's just another ass trying to recruit me for a job."

Charlie snorted. "Another one of those."

Kirov's brows lifted. "Do you really get that many offers?"

Driscoll looked up with a faint smile. "Of course I do. I was the best."

Kirov could see the pride in that smile. It didn't surprise him. Driscoll had developed his thievery into an art form. "I know. But evidently no one is perfect. You went to prison."

"I served my time. Four and a half years in prison for the only job they could pin on me. It was awful, but in a way it has given me more freedom than I ever would have imagined. I don't have to hide that entire part of my life anymore."

"That *entire* part . . ."

Driscoll shrugged. "Every man has his secrets. I imagine you have one or two, Mr. . . ."

"Kirov."

"Kirov. Ah, I'll wager that's not even your real name."

"It's real to me, even if it's not the name I was born with. It's the name I've been using for the past few years. It's the name my friends use."

Driscoll nodded. "That's real enough. You obviously know who I am, and this young man is Charlie Diehl."

Kirov nodded to each of the men. Charlie was still glowering at him as if he'd like to cut his throat. He might prove difficult. It would be too bad if he had to eliminate him from the equation. "New start? Just hear me out, then I'll walk away from you if you're not interested."

"You're wasting your time."

"It's my time to waste. I need your help, Mr. Driscoll, and I guarantee it's not like any proposal you've ever been offered."

"I sincerely doubt that." Driscoll smiled. "What is it? A payroll job? Jewels from a family estate?"

"Nothing like that. I wouldn't insult you. I know I'd have to hand you a challenge."

Driscoll studied him thoughtfully. "Talk."

"What if I told you that this involves at least two governments, one of the world's richest men, and quite possibly millions of lives? You hide out in cheap flats because you're afraid to surface and let anyone know where you are. You know as well as I do that Brogan's killers will find you eventually. You're a dead man walking." He paused. "What if I told you that I could settle your problems with the Brogan crime family? Then what if I give you enough money for a world cruise before you settle down in a lucrative consultant's job with one of the world's biggest security companies?"

Driscoll stared at Kirov for a long moment, then slowly settled down into the easy chair. "I would say . . . I'm listening."

CHAPTER
5

"YOU'RE INSANE, HANNAH. YOU know that, don't you?" Melis followed Hannah through the narrow passageways of the *Copernicus,* which was eerily deserted due to the party still under way on the top deck. The music thumped from above as the party had once again kicked into high gear after the government agent's departure just ten minutes earlier. "All right, I was a little suspicious, but I never wanted you to go trekking after Kirov."

"I have to do it. We found what could have been the most important discovery in the history of this site. You said it was exactly what you've been looking for after all these years. You want that piece back, don't you?"

"Of course I do. But that doesn't mean you need to—"

Hannah stopped and turned toward her. "You heard what that government agent said. There's something going on with Marinth that we don't know about. People are getting killed. And whatever it is, Kirov is in the middle of it. He's the key. When I find him, I'll make him tell me what's happening and get that piece back."

"You're making it sound far too easy. The government is already looking for him. What makes you think you can do any better?"

"I know Kirov."

"How can you say that? Evidently you didn't know him all that well. You had no idea he was even involved in this."

Melis was right, Hannah thought angrily, she didn't really know Kirov. He was his own man and had more secrets than the sphinx. He had only allowed her into a tiny part of his life. What right did she have to think that she understood anything about him?

And why did it hurt so much to have that realization hit home? "No, I didn't know. He must have found out something that spurred him into exploding like this before I left for Marinth. That's why he took off." Her lips tightened. "Whatever it is. I want to throttle him for not telling me."

Melis grimaced. "Maybe he knew you would interfere with his plans."

"And I may have. You can be sure when I find him, I'll make sure he tells me exactly what those plans are." Hannah turned and continued walking toward her cabin. "Dammit, I feel as if he used me. He wouldn't have even been interested in your Marinth if I hadn't told him that I was taking a job here. I thought—" She broke off. "He always has to go his own way. If he found out something about Marinth, why couldn't he share it?" And why was she even wondering about Kirov's motives? Hadn't she learned he was an enigma? "He's a loner and would never willingly open to anyone. I led him here into your world. If he's responsible for hurting you or your project in any way, I'm going to know about it. I'll stop it, Melis. There aren't many worthwhile dreams in this world. No one is going to destroy yours."

Melis stood in the doorway of Hannah's cabin and watched her as she threw a suitcase on the bed. "You don't need to do this. My husband, Jed, has resources. He has private investigators on his company payroll. Let me call him."

"Don't do it." Hannah said quickly. "If those investigators managed to find Kirov, and he felt threatened, they might end up like those two men in Venice."

"Why didn't you tell me about Kirov's nasty habit of killing people?" Melis asked quietly.

"Do you think those Intelligence men who were here tonight were squeaky clean? They all live in a dark world. It's not our world, but I don't think Kirov would kill unless he was threatened or if he—" She stopped before she said wearily, "But I'm not sure about anything about him. All I know is that Kirov helped me track down the man responsible for Conner's death. I never would have been able to do it without him."

"I can see how that would make you want to believe in him," Melis said gently. "But this is something else entirely. You don't know what's going on here. *You* could end up like those men in Venice."

"I won't."

"Where would you even start?"

"I'd use the same method as your husband's private investigators. I'll start with his friends and associates."

"I thought you said he was a loner. Do you know any of his friends?"

Hannah thought for a moment. "Just one."

New York City

HANNAH LEANED BACK IN THE taxi, gazing at the buildings on Lexington Avenue as the driver argued with someone into his

Bluetooth headset. Only at that very moment did Hannah wonder what she would do if she wasn't successful here.

Typical, she thought. No safety net, no backup plan. She'd left herself no option but to succeed, which was just the way she liked it. That's why she had flown to New York instead of just picking up the phone. If the response wasn't immediately favorable, a phone call could be too easily terminated with the mere press of a button.

Terminated. Funny word, Hannah thought, considering who she was there to visit.

Eugenia Voltar was in her late teens when she had served as an agent in the waning days of the KGB, where she cultivated a reputation for eliminating her enemies with lethal efficiency. But she had also rebelled against the increasingly corrupt higher-ups in her agency, and by the time the Soviet Union had dissolved, she was finished in the intelligence community. More recently, she had found great success as a facilitator for American corporations wishing to make inroads into the Russian economy. Eugenia and her network of contacts routinely overcame obstacles that stymied armies of lawyers and corporate negotiators. Eugenia was the only friend of Kirov's that Hannah knew, and if she wasn't willing to help, the trail could go cold mighty fast, Hannah thought.

The taxi turned onto East 51st Street and stopped in front of the converted brownstone that served as Eugenia's office. Hannah paid the driver and walked up the few steps to the front stoop. She rang the doorbell, and after a minute the door swung open and a pair of long, slender arms suddenly wrapped around her.

"Hannah, what a wonderful surprise!" Eugenia squeezed her for a long moment before letting go. Her smile was luminous, and along with her soft brown hair and youthful skin, Eugenia looked more like a popular sorority girl than a successful international

businesswoman. Hannah could not even begin to reconcile Eugenia's warmth and youthful looks with what she knew about the
woman's former life as an intelligence agent.

Before Hannah could utter a single word, Eugenia grabbed her
wrist and whispered in her charmingly half-Russian, half-British accent. "I need your help, Hannah."

"*My* help?"

"Yes. There's no time to explain, but I need you to wait in the foyer
for sixty seconds, then walk up the stairs to my office and scream at
me."

Hannah stared her. "Scream at you? Scream what?"

"Listen carefully. I need you to say, 'Okay, you bitch. We have a
deal. And we'll waive the Apraxin clause!'"

"Are you serious?"

"Yes. And I need you to sound angry at me. Then walk down the
stairs, slam this door closed, and wait in that coffeehouse down
the street. When you see my visitors leave, you can come back."

Hannah repeated under her breath, making sure she had heard
Eugenia's instructions correctly. "Okay, you bitch . . . We have a
deal, and we'll waive the Apraxin clause."

"Perfect. Remember, sixty seconds."

Eugenia ran upstairs.

Hannah stepped into the foyer, trying to comprehend what had
just happened. Everything connected to Eugenia was always unex-
pected but not this strange. Oh, well, go with the flow.

After a minute, she marched up the stairs, swung open the oak
office door, and yelled her line to Eugenia and three startled men in
dark suits. She slammed the door and hurried back down the stairs.

She left the building, walked down to the coffeehouse, and was
deciding whether to order something when she saw a limo pull up in

front of Eugenia's office. The three men she'd seen earlier hurried down the steps and climbed into the car, which then sped down the street.

By the time Hannah made it back to the brownstone, Eugenia was waiting on her front stoop. "*Magnifique!* A wonderful performance, Hannah!"

"I'm happy you're so pleased. What did I just do?"

"You just helped me close a two-billion-dollar deal, that's what. A Russian automotive company is looking for a transportation partner, and those gentlemen were trying their best to give them the short end of the stick." Eugenia shrugged. "I may have hinted that there was another suitor, and I suppose they jumped to the conclusion that you were negotiating on their competitor's behalf. In any case, they were in a much greater hurry to close the deal after your appearance."

"That's how billion-dollar business deals are done?"

"*Two* billion. The numbers may get bigger, but that doesn't mean the players are any smarter." Eugenia waved her inside. "Come in. You made me a lot of money today. That's worth at least a cup of tea and some pastry."

Hannah followed Eugenia up two flights of stairs to what the woman called her "real" office, which was the polar opposite of the second-floor office's dark woods, granite countertops, and heavy furniture. Although she used that imposing room for meeting clients, her upstairs "real" office, with its shag carpeting, beanbag furniture, hammock, punk-rock posters, and ever-blaring stereo, was where Eugenia actually did most of her work.

Eugenia turned down the stereo and slid out of her tailored jacket. Her white blouse, which had appeared as buttoned-down conservative as her pin-striped suit, was now revealed to have sleeves covered with psychedelic designs. Noticing Hannah's surprise, Eugenia held up her sleeves. "Like this? An artist in Greenwich Village did it for me. He's quite talented, yes?"

Hannah nodded. "Yes. And quite possibly under the influence of some strong hallucinogenics."

"Ha! You might be right. Or not. Artists can also live in their own world which has nothing to do with drugs. At any rate, he was very charming." Eugenia poured two cups of tea and nodded to a pair of canvas folding chairs in the corner. "Have a seat and tell me what brings you here."

Hannah took the cup and sat down. She sipped the tea and took a deep breath. Time to lay it all out. "Kirov."

Eugenia's face tensed. "Is he all right?"

All the humor was gone from her expression. Eugenia and Kirov had been friends for years, and it was a friendship based on hardship and danger. Hannah knew that Kirov had saved Eugenia's life at one time, and it was probable that she had returned the favor. At first, Hannah had thought they were lovers but, as Eugenia said, sex would have gotten in the way. In their world, friendship could be much more precious. "What's happened to him?"

"I don't know," Hannah said. "I haven't seen or heard from him in over two months. But he killed two men in Venice last week, so he can't be doing too badly."

"Oh, that's a relief," Eugenia said dryly. "But I thought those days were behind him."

"Old habits die hard, I guess." Hannah held her cup with both hands and took another sip. "I'd like to say it has nothing to do with me, but it does."

"Ah, but Kirov has everything to do with you." Eugenia smiled. "I was very interested in watching the interaction between you. You were fighting it all the way, but you found Kirov very sexy. Yes?"

She should have known that Eugenia would jump straight to

the personal aspect. Hell, yes, she found Kirov sexy, but she wasn't about to discuss it. "That's not what I meant. What disturbs me is that I know it had something to do with my project at Marinth."

"Oh, yes, Marinth. I watched that special on the Discovery Channel. Fascinating."

"I've been at the site for the past several weeks. Kirov was supposed to be there with me, but he took off with no explanation just before we left."

"That sounds like him." She made a face. "Kirov has a way of dropping in and out of his friends' lives without notice."

Hannah nodded. "So I've found."

"With you, though . . . It's different." Eugenia bit her lip. "You're special to him. I didn't know him when he was married, but I've never seen him behave with anyone the way he does you. He's very careful about giving too much of himself."

"I noticed," Hannah said.

"But then you're a very private person, too, Hannah. I imagine the two of you coming together would be like trying to break into a Swiss bank." She threw back her head and laughed. "I admit I would like to see it. I'm not usually a voyeur, but there is always an exception."

She had to deflect Eugenia and head her in the direction she wanted her to travel. "I admit Kirov and I formed a certain attachment. How could I help it? He helped me at a time when I was at my lowest point after my brother died. But this isn't about any personal relations. It's about Marinth. Kirov may be over his head this time, and if it involves Marinth, it also involves me."

Eugenia smiled. "I sincerely doubt that Kirov is over his head. He's quite good at taking control of situations."

"For God's sake, he's not Superman."

"Do you know, I never found Superman interesting. Too pure."

"Eugenia, listen to me. I understand there's someone else in the mix. A man named Gadaire."

Eugenia's eyes narrowed. "*Vincent* Gadaire?"

"You know him?"

"Not personally, but I see why you might be worried. Where does he fit into this?"

At last, she had Eugenia focused, Hannah thought with relief. She quickly told her about the recent Marinth discovery, its theft, and the previous evening's visit by the U.S. agent.

After she finished, Eugenia was quiet for a long moment, lost in thought. She finally looked up. "Before he left, did Kirov have access to any special information about Marinth?"

"He had access to the same materials I did. Which is to say nothing that hasn't already appeared in thousands of books, articles, and documentaries."

"There must have been something else that set him off." Eugenia shook her head. "Why are you here? Why did you come to me?"

Hannah moved to the edge of her seat. "I need you to help me find Kirov. I need to know what's going on, and I need to get that artifact back. And despite what you think about his control of the situation, he needs help. Between Gadaire, the Feds, and whoever else he's crossed, Kirov is in deep trouble. He's wanted for murder."

"If what you say is true, he killed those men to save another man's life. He may not be charged."

"And then again he may. The Defense Intelligence Agency wants him, and that would be an excellent tool for manipulation. At any rate, he's still being hunted for it. You know him much better than I do. The people he knows, the way he operates . . . Will you help me find him?"

Eugenia was silent again. "But what if Kirov doesn't want to be found?"

"Even by me?"

"Especially by you. I'd guess that's why he hasn't been in touch. He doesn't want to put you in danger. He also probably knew that the authorities would come to you looking for him, and this way you didn't have to lie to them."

"Or give him up?"

"You and I both know you wouldn't have done that. I'm sure Kirov knows it, too."

No, she owed Kirov too much. But that didn't mean she was feeling anything but extreme annoyance toward him at the moment. "You're right, I'd want to deal with Kirov myself. But, dammit, I can't do it if I can't find him. I need your help, Eugenia. Please."

Eugenia looked away. "You're putting me in an awkward position. I owe Kirov my life, and my loyalties have to be with him. And if I were to guess what he wants, it's that you stay as far away from him right now as you possibly can."

It was the answer she expected, but she couldn't accept it. "Eugenia, I'm involved in this whether he wants me to be or not. My communications have been monitored, I've had government agents boarding my boat, a priceless artifact has been hijacked . . . I don't understand any of it, but I believe Kirov does. Don't you think I deserve an explanation?"

Eugenia did not reply.

She threw in the one argument to which she knew Eugenia would respond. "And Kirov may need help. *Our* help. And I need to know whatever you can tell me about Gadaire. I take it he's someone we should be worried about?"

Eugenia nodded. "Oh, yes, he most definitely is."

"Then don't do this for me. Do it for Kirov. And if we find him, and he tells me to go to hell, I'll go home."

Eugenia's brows arched skeptically. "Just like that."

"Well, maybe after I get some answers." Hannah put her hand on Eugenia's. "Will you do it, Eugenia?"

Eugenia let out a long breath. "Kirov will be furious with us, you know that?"

Hope soared within her. "I don't doubt it. Are you saying you'll help me?"

"Yes." A brilliant smile lit her face. "I've been bored. I need a challenge. Let's find that stubborn, secretive son of a bitch."

Paris, France
Rue de Rivoli

AH, ANNA . . .

Beautiful as ever, Gadaire thought as he caught sight of Anna Devareau standing waiting for him on the sidewalk near the Café Marly. She was wearing a short black skirt that showed off her long, tanned legs. In the thirty seconds it took him to reach her, he counted at least a half dozen passersby—both male and female—who felt compelled to turn and catch another glimpse of this woman with long dark hair, full lips, and sparkling green eyes. He felt the familiar surge of lust. He was never more turned on than when he saw others admiring his Anna.

He stopped at the curb, and she climbed into the passenger seat of his Mercedes.

She smiled. "You're late. No driver today?"

He kissed her and continued driving. "No. I had a few sensitive phone calls to make on the way, and I didn't need anyone listening. How did your meeting go?"

"Good. Dr. Hollis has agreed to do everything we need him to do. It didn't take much prodding after I offered him the money.

He's a fanatic about anything relating to Marinth, and you're right, he feels very competitive toward Melis Nemid. He's excited to know that he can look at that trellis before she has a chance at it."

"But you made it clear he can't discuss it with anyone?"

"Of course. And I made sure no other employees were present at his office at the Louvre." She tilted her head. "But once he's examined the trellis, you don't really think he'll keep his mouth shut, do you?"

Gadaire shot her a sideways glance.

She smiled. "Ah, it's going to be one of *those* jobs? You didn't tell me. Am I going to get a bonus?"

"Why should I bother? You like it. Who was it who insisted on going into that Customs warehouse in Tenerife? You should pay me." He turned left at the corner. "Once we're finished with him, it shouldn't be too difficult to get him to take you someplace out of the way."

She laughed. "Someplace secret, someplace remote, someplace he won't be telling anyone about . . . He is a married man, after all."

"You don't anticipate a problem with him?"

"I rarely have problems in that area."

"I know."

"It wouldn't have taken much encouragement for him to jump me right there in his office in the Louvre. When he's given you what you need, let me know. I'll take him into the countryside and dispose of him." She leaned forward, brushed her lips across his cheek, and whispered, "Unless you want to come along and watch. I don't mind screwing him before I kill him. I know you like that sometimes. Remember Mordalen?"

"Yes." He could feel himself getting hard as he recalled that night when he'd ordered her to kill Lew Mordalen, one of his competitors in an arms deal. He had been filled with power as he had stood over them and ordered her to perform every variety of the sexual act on Mordalen. Then as a climax he had ordered her to cut the bastard's throat. She had not hesitated and when she had come to him only minutes later, her body had been covered with blood. She had been wild that night, and the term bloodlust had taken on a new meaning.

"You're thinking about it." She reached out and slowly rubbed him. "Anything you want. You know that, Vincent. I only want to please you."

Yes, he knew she was willing to do anything he wanted because it was what she also wanted. He had never met a woman who was more sexual or more lethal. Anna had no sense of right or wrong, but only what gave her pleasure. She could be totally reckless, and there had been moments when he had even felt a hint of trepidation at some of her suggestions. But excitement always overcame any reluctance. As it was doing now.

"We'll see." He put his hand on her knee. "It might be amusing."

"I'll make sure it is." She leaned back in her seat. "So, have you thought about where you're taking me to dinner, darling?"

Brooklyn, New York

HANNAH WALKED WITH EUGENIA down Meserole Street in Brooklyn's Greenpoint neighborhood. The street was lined with small family-owned shops, which were now mostly closed, though the few restaurants were packed. Sharp odors wafted from the dining establishments and hung in the humid evening air.

"You think your contact down here can help us?" Hannah said.

"One thing I know about Kirov is that he always carries a firearm. He feels naked without it. But he almost never travels across borders with one since that would make it too easy for governments to detain him at airports and railway stations."

"I can see that any number of governments would be eager for an excuse to close their borders to him."

"They are. That means he has to buy a gun wherever he goes. Fortunately, I know some of his sources. If Kirov has recently contacted one of them, I might be able to find out where he is."

"Then why are we here? Shouldn't you be calling someone overseas?"

"I will be. Kirov's favorite contact is based in Rome, and this man can arrange transactions pretty much anywhere in Europe. But the only way we can call him is through a computer in the back room of his brother's store. That's it up ahead."

"Couldn't he just buy a disposable cell phone?"

Eugenia smiled. "You *are* an amateur, aren't you? If he tried that, the Italian authorities would zero in on him in no time. He uses custom software to scramble Internet telephone calls from several stations around the world. If his system doesn't recognize the IP address of his brother's broadband connection or one of the others, the call doesn't come even close to going through."

Hannah grimaced. "I'm still getting up to speed on this business."

"Trust me, there are some things you're better off not knowing."

They approached a small store with red-painted lettering in the front window that read GORECKI'S BICYCLE SALES AND REPAIR. Although a CLOSED sign was displayed on the front door, they could see a bald middle-aged man at a workbench in the middle of the store. A cigarette protruded from his lips as he balanced a bicycle's rear wheel.

Eugenia rapped on the front window, and the man's annoyed look quickly gave way to an expression of eagerness. He ran to the door, unlocked it, and pulled it open. "Eugenia, my dear! You have made my day, my week, my month . . . Why do you never come to see me?"

Eugenia hugged him. "The Brooklyn Bridge goes both ways, Ed. Good to see you."

He stepped back and looked at Hannah. "And who is your lovely friend?"

"Hannah Bryson, this is Edmund Gorecki."

"Ed, please," he said.

Hannah smiled. Ed still hadn't taken the cigarette from his lips, making his voice sound like a bad ventriloquist struggling to keep his lips still. Yet somehow, the man's warmth and excitement managed to come through. "Nice to meet you, Ed."

Eugenia lowered her voice. "Are you alone here?"

Ed nodded.

"I need to call your brother."

"Of course. But you realize that it's very late there."

"This can't wait. It's important I talk to him right away."

"For you, Eugenia, I'm sure he won't mind. Come this way."

They followed Ed to the back room, which was a miniwarehouse of bicycle parts packaged in plastic bags and hung from pegboard hooks. Ed walked over to a desktop computer, where he picked up a headset and handed it to Eugenia. She adjusted the earpiece and microphone while he opened a software application and keyed in a series of numbers.

After a moment, Hannah was startled to hear Eugenia speaking rapid-fire Polish into the headset. Ed chuckled as he saw her reaction, and said quietly, "You're surprised."

Hannah nodded as they stepped away from the computer. "Yes, but of course Eugenia surprises me quite a bit."

Ed finally removed the cigarette from his mouth. "She speaks like a native. If I didn't know better, I'd say she grew up in my neighborhood in Warsaw. She picks up languages as easily as most people pick up bad habits." He tapped his ears. "Language lessons on her iPod."

After a couple of minutes, Eugenia finally took off the headset and turned back to Hannah and Ed. "I may have gotten a lead."

Ed raised a hand. "Save it, please. I don't wish to hear. For your protection and mine."

Eugenia nodded. "I understand. I am in your debt, Ed. If there's ever anything I can do for you . . ."

He shrugged. "My wife's mother wants to become an American citizen, but she's having some difficulty. Anything you can do?"

"I might." Eugenia thought for a moment. "There are people in the State Department who owe me favors. I'm about to leave the country for a few days, but when I get back, I'll call you and get the details."

"Thank you, my dear." He walked with them to the door. "I'll tell my wife. She'll be delighted."

Hannah turned to Eugenia as they left the store. "When you said you'll be out of the country, do you mean we'll *both* be out of the country?"

"Yes. Gorecki's brother wasn't exactly forthcoming at first, but he and I go back a long time. He still made me swear I would never tell Kirov where I got my information."

"He's been in contact with Kirov?"

"He didn't supply Kirov with a gun himself, but he recently put him in touch with someone else who did."

"Where?"

"Dublin. This was just in the past couple of days, so there's a good chance he's still somewhere in Ireland." A troubled expression crossed her face. "But I'm uneasy. I don't like this at all . . ."

"What's wrong?" Hannah asked. "It's a lot more than we knew just a few minutes ago."

"Gorecki told me something else," Eugenia said grimly. "Kirov didn't want only one weapon. Apparently he was looking for enough weaponry to equip a small army."

AFTER A QUICK STOP AT EUGENIA'S Union Square apartment, they made their way to JFK Airport to catch a 10:50 P.M. flight to Dublin. At midnight, Hannah found herself in the alcove of the 787 Dreamliner wide-body aircraft, sipping her sparkling water. She had been peppered with questions by a nearby couple who recognized her from the Discovery Channel specials, and she hoped they would be asleep by the time she returned to her seat. She checked her watch. Three and a half hours before they reached Dublin.

Eugenia approached her and leaned against the bulkhead. "You're more famous than I thought. Your two fans are wondering where you went."

"I usually like talking to people, but I have a lot on my mind right now. I hope I wasn't rude."

"No, you were quite gracious. After you left, the woman made her husband get a camera out of her carry-on bag. I think they want a picture with you before we land."

Hannah smiled. "I'd better freshen up, then. I'm sure I look like hell."

"Only a little bit like hell. It won't matter to them anyway."

Hannah finished her sparkling water. "Thank you, Eugenia. I don't know where I'd be if you didn't help me."

"You would have found a way. Your whole life is about finding solutions to problems. I'm quite sure you would have found a solution to this one."

"Well, I'm happy the solution turned out to be you."

"I'm happy to help you, Hannah. I'm very loyal to my friends, and I count you as a true friend. But like I said, I owe Kirov my life. I would never do anything that I thought might hurt him."

"I was afraid you would feel like you were betraying Kirov."

She shook her head. "No. I wouldn't be here if I thought that's what I was doing. As much as I want to help you, my real mission here is to help Kirov. And not the way you were talking about. He's quite capable of taking care of himself. But when you told me that he was involved in the deaths of those two men in Venice, that worried me more than anything else."

"Why?" Hannah asked.

She was silent a moment. "After his wife was murdered, Kirov was totally consumed. You know how that feels. You went through it after your brother's death. But for you, it was only a matter of a couple weeks. Think about what it would have been like to have that rage inside you for fifteen years. That's how long it took Kirov to eliminate the people responsible for his wife's killing."

"But he succeeded. It's over."

"That's what I thought. All those years he traveled the world and lived outside the law, all for the sake of vengeance. I thought he might finally find peace. But from what you've told me, I don't believe he's found it."

"How can you be sure? We don't know what he's doing."

"I'm not sure. I'm just trying to work my way through this." Eugenia shook her head. "He may be like a man who's spent most of his life in prison, unable to function in the real world. Kirov spent almost fifteen years in the prison he made for himself, and he may not know how to live any other way."

"Lord, that sounds terrible. I hope that's not true." But that might explain why Kirov left so abruptly, she thought. Oh, what the hell, she just didn't know, and she refused to speculate until she was face-to-face with Kirov.

"I may be wrong. But if I'm not, he needs to know he has connections in this world, people who love and care about him." Eugenia gave her a cool smile. "And I'm very fond of you, but in my mind, that's what all this is about. And it's especially important that you be there, Hannah, because I know how he feels about you."

"You don't know any such thing. It's all guesswork on your part."

"I'm very good at guessing. If you're important to him, then I'm going to do what's necessary to bring you to him."

"Why do I feel as if I'm being served up to Kirov on a silver platter?"

"Nonsense. I'm too much of a feminist to ever do that. But I owe him my life, and he comes first. I had to give you warning that I want Kirov to have whatever he needs or wants."

"Including weapons to supply an army?"

"If he can convince me it's good for him. That's the bottom line." She turned and started down the aisle. "Now you'd better get back to your seat and have that picture taken with your fans. I don't want to waste any time when we reach Dublin."

AFTER THE PLANE LANDED AND they cleared Customs, Hannah stepped outside to make a phone call to Melis while Eugenia went to the business center to print out and sign some e-mailed documents. Melis answered on the first ring. She was still on the *Fair Winds,* heading home.

"Ireland?" Melis asked after getting a full update. "I didn't think we'd find any answers there."

"We still may not, but it's the only lead we have. I'll let you know what we turn up. By the way, how are Pete and Susie?"

"They left even before we moved away from the site. Their usual communion with the local dolphin population."

"Don't worry. They'll find you."

"We'll see. By the way, Ebersole wants to find *you*. He was annoyed that you helicoptered away from the *Copernicus* without talking to him. He says you two have some unfinished AquaCorp business to discuss."

"They have another job for me, but he wouldn't discuss it at the time. I didn't push him. I got the impression I wouldn't be happy about it. Frankly, I don't need the aggravation right now."

"Well, I gather Ebersole's bosses are putting a lot of pressure on him. I'm sure you'll be getting some frantic phone calls."

"I saw them in my voice-mail box. I'll be sure to screen my calls while I'm here."

"Good idea."

Hannah could hear a somber note in Melis's voice. She wasn't accustomed to hearing her sounding so depressed, but between the theft of her prized artifact and the possible loss of Pete and Susie, who could blame her? "Melis, get back to your lab and work. It's the only way you're going to get your mind off all this. I'll bring back that trellis, I promise."

"Thanks, Hannah." She paused. "But I can't leave it entirely up to you. This is my job, my Marinth. I'll give you another few days to locate Kirov and get some answers. After that, I'm going to let Jed hire those investigators, and I'm going hunting myself."

Dear heaven, that was the last thing she wanted to happen. "Don't do it, Melis."

"My Marinth," Melis repeated quietly. "I'll be waiting for your call."

Hannah cut the connection. Damn. As frustrated as she was, it was only a fraction of what Melis must have been feeling and no wonder she—

"Hannah?"

She whirled and saw Eugenia behind her. "I've just finished talking to Melis and—" She stopped as she saw the expression on Eugenia's face. "What's wrong?"

Eugenia glanced at the man who had come to stand next to her. He was a middle-aged man with a pencil-thin mustache, and his suit and overcoat made him indistinguishable from the scores of other business travelers waiting in the busy airport pickup area.

"Tell her," he said.

Eugenia leaned closer to Hannah. "Trouble. According to this man, a sniper has you in his sights, and he'll fire if we don't do exactly what he says."

Hannah turned to look at the man in astonishment. "That's crazy. Do you believe him?"

"Look at the sign next to you," he said quietly. "Pay particular attention to the final 'o.'"

Hannah turned. The sign read PASSENGER LOADING AND UN-LOADING ONLY. While she looked, a neat, round hole appeared in the middle of the "o" from "only."

Hannah spun toward a building facing them, knowing that the bullet must have come from there. If there was any noise from the shot, it had been masked by the sounds of the traffic and nearby jets. No one else had even noticed it.

"George is a very good shot, an expert sniper," the mustached man said. "It could just as well have been any part of your anatomy. Or that of this other lady."

A black Mercedes-Benz limousine pulled to a stop in front of them. The man opened the rear door for them. "Please get in. I don't want to signal George to give you another demonstration."

Hannah glanced at Eugenia. She hesitated, then nodded. They climbed into the car, and he stepped back and slammed the door. The car sped away from the airport.

"How do you do? Thank you for joining me, ladies."

The man who had spoken was sitting facing them from a rear-facing seat. He was a fiftyish, obese man who seemed to be all gray-white hair, spectacles, and pouty pink lips.

"Your sniper didn't leave us much choice," Hannah said dryly.

He chuckled. "Well, since your only alternative was for you to fall dead onto the sidewalk, I do see your point. So just let me commend you for your excellent decision." The man's Irish brogue somehow made even the threatening statement sound less intimidating.

But there couldn't be anything more threatening than the bullet that had been fired so close to her, Hannah thought.

"Who are you and what do you want?" Eugenia asked crisply.

"Ah, the direct approach. Refreshing. I don't get a lot of straight talk from the people in my world. Alas, you are not in a position to demand information from me. You will tell me what I need to know, and if you are still alive at the end of our car ride, I will decide what to share with you. Do you understand?"

"Ask your questions," Hannah said.

"Excellent. What brings you two ladies to Dublin?"

Hannah glanced at Eugenia before responding. "We're looking for a friend. We heard he was here."

"Perhaps I can help. Your friend's name?"

Hannah hesitated. "Nicholas Kirov." She studied the man's face for any flash of recognition, but there was none.

"And what is your business with this man?"

"He's just a friend," Eugenia interjected suddenly. "We didn't come all this way for you, if that's what you're thinking, Mr. Walsh. You are Anthony Walsh, aren't you?"

The gray-haired man chuckled. "Very good, Eugenia."

"Look, Walsh. I spoke to Gorecki in Rome last night," Eugenia said. "He told me that he sent Kirov your way. I suppose he told you that we would be coming to Dublin."

"Yes, he told me as a professional courtesy. I would have done the same for him. Men in our profession can't be too careful. In America, I know they give away guns in boxes of cereal, but here an untraceable firearm is a precious commodity."

"I thought Gorecki would vouch for me," Eugenia said. "He and his brother are old friends of mine."

"Oh, he spoke very highly of you, and he promised that I could trust you. Pardon me for being cynical, but the only reason I'm still alive and in business is that I've learned to trust no one. And even if you mean me no harm—something of which I'm still not entirely convinced, by the way—I couldn't risk the two of you compromising my operation by blundering into the country and asking questions about me and my whereabouts. I assume that would have been your first step in order to track down your friend."

"Our only interest is in finding Kirov," Hannah said. "We didn't come here to hurt you."

"Perhaps not intentionally, but it easily could have happened. And assuming that you're telling me the truth, why do you think I would willingly expose a customer?"

Eugenia smiled. "I negotiate for a living. I thought we could come to a meeting of minds."

"My clients need to stay anonymous. If it got around that I was less than discreet, I wouldn't stay in business—or alive—for very long."

"It won't get around," Hannah said. "And we only want to help your client."

"I never said that he's my client. Just because someone referred him to me doesn't mean we've actually done business together."

"If that was the case, why bother with the bizarre airport pickup?" Eugenia said.

"I told you. I need to protect myself. While I'm beginning to believe that you're using me to get to Kirov, I knew it was possible that you were using Kirov to get to me."

Eugenia nodded. "I understand."

They were both so cool and businesslike, and it suddenly made Hannah furious. She had been frightened and threatened, and they were acting as if it was commonplace.

"I don't understand any of this bullshit," Hannah said. "What I do understand is that because of your paranoia, a sniper just had me lined up in his sights."

Eugenia patted Hannah's arm comfortingly. "The first time's always the hardest." She glanced back at Walsh. "Now, Mr. Walsh, how do we fix this and both get what we want?"

Walsh gave her a cold glance. "I don't have to fix it. I have you, and that's all I need."

Eugenia appeared taken aback. Her stance changed from confident to wary. "May we at least talk?"

He was silent, gazing at her without expression. "I don't believe I have anything more to say to you."

CHAPTER
6

Aviva Stadium
Dublin, Ireland

KIROV AND DRISCOLL WALKED along the top level of the four-tiered soccer stadium, looking down at the match under way on the field. Almost fifty thousand fans were packed into the modernistic venue, which boasted a sweeping, curved design and translucent roof that covered the spectators.

Driscoll made a face. "What a pity. I suppose this place is all right, but there used to be a better one here. Much more charm, you know. Progress is one thing, but you can't buy the feeling that the old Landsdowne Field gave you."

Kirov spoke quietly. "I assure you that you're going to look back at this place with a good deal of fondness. Do the job right, and you'll be free to go anywhere, do anything you want with no threat hanging over you. Maybe that will give you warmer feelings for it."

"The Landsdowne Field would have been an easier job."

Kirov glanced at the security cameras trained on the concourse. "I won't dispute that. If this was going to be easy, I wouldn't have brought you in."

Driscoll looked across the arena at the third-level concourse, which housed most of the corporate boxes. "Gadaire's suite is over there?"

"Yes. Straight down that corridor."

"Why isn't it on any of the blueprints I looked at?"

"Gadaire acquired a forty-percent stake in this facility just last spring. Part of the deal was that he got a two-thousand-square-foot hospitality suite that he can use for entertaining clients. He also has an office there. They shifted some of their corporate sponsors out of their boxes and created a megasuite for Gadaire."

"Amazing. I wasn't aware that he lived here."

"He doesn't. He occasionally jets in with friends or clients for games. Gadaire was born in France, but he was educated here at Trinity College. He became quite a fan of the Ireland National Football team while he was here, and it stayed with him."

"And you're positive he keeps that packet in his owner's suite?"

Kirov nodded. "Yes. Where exactly, I can't tell you. I assume there's a safe in the office. I don't know where it is. But that doesn't mean he'd keep the packet there. Though it would be reasonable."

"Reason sometimes has nothing to do with where people hide valuables," Driscoll said. "But give me thirty minutes in that office, and I'll be able to tell if he's the type who has to lock it away or has the nerve to put that packet out in plain sight."

"Thirty minutes is a long time. Fifteen maybe. When we start to move, it's going to have to be at the speed of light. You should be able to get an idea of the complete layout tonight. That should help."

At that moment, Charlie swaggered by with a serving cart. Dressed in a green jacket and black slacks, he didn't break stride as he spoke to his father and Kirov. "Follow me, gents."

Kirov smiled as he strolled after Charlie. "Looks like your son located the uniforms."

Driscoll nodded, beaming as if his son had made the honor roll. "Warms my heart. He has great initiative. Makes me wish I hadn't missed his first twenty-five years. His mother never let me know he was alive until she had to go into the hospital with tuberculosis. She wanted to make sure I'd take care of him."

"He's a bit old for a father's tender loving care."

"You're never too old. I owe him. We get along just fine. He listens to me. He got into a lot of trouble with the law when he was a teenager, and if I'd been around before, I could have kept him out of trouble."

Kirov arched a brow. "You're going to tell him how to keep out of trouble with the local magistrates? Don't you think that's a little strange?"

Driscoll laughed. "Well, I would have shown him how to be so good that they would have never caught him."

"No wonder his mother kept him away from you."

"Yeah." His smile faded. "She did the best she could. I didn't have any business around a kid. I was too busy being Mister Big Shot. I'm older, and I've learned a few things now." He glanced at Kirov. "Charlie's beginning to like you. I can tell."

"Because he hasn't tried to strangle me lately?"

"Well, Charlie tends to be a little violent. But he respects you now, and that goes a long way with him."

They turned right down a corridor that led into a stairwell. Kirov closed the stairwell door behind him while Charlie pulled the tablecloth off the serving cart to reveal two more uniforms.

"I found these uniforms in a closet near the first-floor kitchen. The servers in Gadaire's suite are all wearing them," Charlie said. "There's probably a hundred people there, and at least ten servers. We should be able to get in and out without attracting too much attention."

"Well done, Charlie." He had been pleasantly surprised at the eagerness and efficiency of Charlie Diehl. He was smart and enthusiastic, if a little on the rough side. But once he had gotten over his first resentment toward Kirov, he had obeyed instructions without question and with alacrity. Kirov handed tiny button video cameras to the other two men. "Thread these over the collar and attach them to your top button. There's only twelve minutes of recording time, but if we split up, that will be more than enough time for us to capture the entire layout in there."

Driscoll pulled off his flannel shirt and slid into one of the green serving jackets. He smiled as Kirov helped him position the camera. "When I started out in the business, I had to remember everything and draw it out on paper later. I like your way better."

Kirov smiled. "It just proves how talented you were to be able to do that. But it's good to be appreciated. You'll be interested to see what I can do with these videos after we get back."

Kirov and Driscoll finished changing, and once they were sure their button cameras were placed for maximum coverage, the three men lifted the cart and carried it down to the third level. They emerged from the stairwell and pushed it toward the owner's box, where they glided past the gray-suited security man standing watch at the entrance.

Kirov spoke quietly to the other two men. "Okay, I'll meet you back at the stairwell in ten minutes. Go."

Each of the men grabbed an empty serving tray from the cart, moved through the crowd, and began taking empty plates and glasses from the guests.

Kirov angled his body in every direction, making sure his camera captured as much of the area as possible. The suite was fronted by floor-to-ceiling windows overlooking the playing field, with two tiers of seating just behind them. Beyond that, where most of the

guests were spending their time, was a luxuriously appointed entertainment center with two full bars, several flat-screen monitors, and
areas of sectional sofas. As with most corporate boxes he visited, very
little attention was focused on the game. It amused him to notice
that the participants in almost every conversation were constantly
stealing glances at the entrance, looking to make sure they shouldn't
be talking to someone more important. He didn't know most of the
guests, but he recognized four well-known actors, a somewhat-past-
his-prime rock star, and a professional athlete milling around.

A young male server passing canapés caught his eye and gave
him a curious look. Kirov gave him a friendly nod that was quickly
returned. The server went about his business.

Kirov glanced toward the back of the suite, where a door was
slightly ajar. Gadaire's office? He moved toward it, balancing his
tray as he negotiated his way through a bottleneck of guests.

He paused at the door and glimpsed Gadaire leaning against his
desk. He was talking to two seated men.

"May I help you?"

The soft, husky, voice came from behind him. He turned and
found himself facing Anna Devareau. In her bronze velvet cocktail
dress, she was even more beautiful than the photographs he'd seen,
though obviously annoyed.

"I was going to see if Mr. Gadaire would like anything."

"He'll ask if he wants anything. You should know better than to
bother him otherwise. Didn't Arthur tell you?"

"Yes, ma'am. I'm sorry." Don't be too subservient. He knew his
years of commanding a sub had given him an assurance that couldn't
be suppressed. If he tried, it came off phony as hell. He could only
be dignified and polite. "I forgot. I'm just a fill-in."

"And not very experienced." Anna studied him. "You were a
sailor, weren't you?"

"Ma'am?"

"I was watching you. There's a roll to your walk. It's slight, but it's there. You've spent a lot of time at sea."

Kirov smiled. "I was on a commercial fishing vessel for nine years. You're amazing."

"And you've never worked as a server before, have you?"

"There's no work on the docks right now. What gave me away?"

She sipped her champagne. "The way you're holding that tray. You're resting it entirely on your palm. Look around. All the other servers also use their forearms. It's better for balance."

Kirov eased the tray back onto his forearm. "That's a good tip. Thank you."

She gazed at him thoughtfully, then flashed him a smile that he could only describe as dazzling. "My pleasure." She glided into the office and closed the door behind her.

Kirov stared at the door for an instant. Anna Devareau was going to be a force with which to be reckoned. Observant, intelligent, and probably unpredictable. He wasn't at all sure if she had been satisfied by his explanation. Anything out of place or unusual would probably trigger an uneasiness in her. It wouldn't surprise him if she checked on him with Gadaire's majordomo, Arthur. Time to beat a fast and discreet exit.

He made one last sweep of the room before leaving the suite.

LESS THAN AN HOUR LATER, THEY were back at Driscoll's flat, and Charlie was still talking about Anna.

"I've never even seen a film star who was that gorgeous. She's positively electric."

Kirov smiled as he connected Charlie's button camera to his

laptop computer. "If I look at your surveillance footage and all I see is pictures of Anna Devareau, I'm going to be extremely annoyed."

"Don't you worry. I got the place covered. But tell me more about her. Where is she from?"

"She claims to be from a farm outside of Limoges, France."

"What do you mean 'she claims'?"

"Gadaire was involved in a sensitive financial transaction a few years ago, and one of the companies' boards of directors did a background check on him and Anna. His past has always been fairly well documented, but hers didn't check out at all. None of the villagers there remembered her or her family. She still sticks to her story, but I guess the answer to your question is, no one knows where she's really from."

Charlie shook his head and grinned. "Do you know what I think? I think Gadaire created her in a secret laboratory. He set out to create the perfect woman, and she's the result."

"It depends on what you term perfect. She's brilliant, beautiful, and she hides her ruthlessness well. But I don't think even Gadaire would think she was without flaws. She's been a big help to Gadaire and his business, but it wouldn't surprise me if she was already planning how to take it over herself."

Charlie's eyes widened. "Could she do that?"

"Probably not if Gadaire was alive. I doubt if that would be an obstacle for her."

Charlie thought about that. "You really think she's capable of committing murder?"

"Yes." Kirov looked up from his laptop. "No proof. Just instinct. There's a definite cold streak there. She helped build his organization into what it is today. She may have already decided that she doesn't really need him."

"Gives a whole new meaning to 'high maintenance,'" Charlie said.

"Of course, Gadaire is a smart man. I'm sure he's already on his guard."

Driscoll shook his head. "Or maybe not. I've used pretty women to distract attention from my sleight of hand. Women that beautiful have a way of altering men's perceptions."

Charlie grinned. "She sure altered mine. I'd be willing to put her to the test."

Had he ever been that reckless and sure that anything he wanted was worth the risk? Kirov wondered. From the time he was a boy, he had trained for the sea, and discipline was a way of life to him. He'd had his wild moments, but they were few and far between and always jettisoned when his duty called. He almost envied Charlie's blind sense of his own immortality. "You'd be wise to keep in mind what I've told you," Kirov said. "She may be even more dangerous than Gadaire."

A tone signaled that the footage from Charlie's button camera had finished downloading. The men turned toward Kirov's laptop.

"Okay, what now?" Driscoll asked.

Kirov sat and opened a software application. "Now that I have all of our footage of Gadaire's suite, I'm going to tag elements that the pictures have in common." Kirov pointed to three windows on his screen. "Here are the three videos we shot with our hidden cameras. Each of us got a shot of the back wall, so I'm going to click to mark the room's top left corner in each of our videos and label them each A1. That way the computer will know it's the same spot. The thermostat also appears in each, so I'll label that A2. I'll continue through the videos, looking for common points of reference between any two or all three of the videos. This will only take a few minutes."

While Driscoll and Charlie watched, Kirov marked several

common reference points, including windows, a spot on the wall, and even a half-empty glass of champagne on a coffee table.

"Okay, I think that's enough," Kirov said. "Now the program will take the videos along with information I've supplied and give us a complete representation of Gadaire's suite. It will take hours to do a complete render, but we can get a rough idea sooner than that."

After a few minutes, a 3-D representation of the suite appeared on the computer screen. Kirov pressed the arrow keys to move through the various areas almost as if playing a first-person computer game.

"I love it!" Charlie murmured. "Where did you learn to do that?"

"I bought the software and practiced on my own. I was inspired by a friend of mine." He had a sudden vision of Hannah, her expression intense as she described the process. She had always been intense, vital, earthy. Even the most difficult problems were only a challenge to her. Hell, every moment with her had been a challenge. Don't think about Hannah. Concentrate on the problem at hand. "She used a similar technique to create a digital 3-D model of the *Titanic*."

Driscoll grabbed a dining-room chair and dragged it in front of the computer. "It's fantastic. This way we can roam around the suite to get an idea where to find what we're looking for."

"That's the idea."

Driscoll watched the screen for another few seconds, then burst out laughing. "My oh my . . . It's a whole new world. It's almost enough to make me want to come out of retirement for good."

Kirov could see the excitement and intensity that was beginning to stir in Driscoll. Good. It was what he'd wanted to happen. Driscoll would be more productive if he saw a challenge and the answer to the challenge on the horizon. "You won't need any more scores. Not if you focus on this one. Now sit down and start gathering info so that we can put together a plan."

Driscoll gave him a shrewd glance. "I'd bet you already have a plan. You're not what I'd call a team player. You like to pull the strings, Kirov." He looked back at the computer screen. "I don't have a problem with that as long as you don't do something that will get me killed."

Kirov didn't answer.

"No comforting assurances?" Driscoll said.

"I'll try to keep you both alive. That's all I can promise. If it's not good enough, walk away."

"No way," Charlie said. "I'm going to get that packet, and we're going to thumb our noses at Brogan. Then I'm going to make a lot of money and get me a fine house and a woman like Anna Deva-reau. Hell, maybe I'll get her."

Driscoll shook his head. "Charlie, I think maybe we'll take Kirov up on that cruise and make it a long one. I'm sure you'll find a woman on board who can satisfy you and who's not a black widow. Now, get a pad and take down the notes I'm going to give you . . ."

Kirov's mobile phone vibrated in his pocket. It was a new phone, and he'd made sure only two people had the number.

He pulled it out of his pocket. "Yes."

"Kirov, my boy . . ."

He recognized the voice and Irish intonations immediately. No great feat when the field was narrowed considerably down to two. "Hello, Walsh, I've been waiting for your call."

"I'm still working on the merchandise you requested. Don't worry, it's coming."

"I wasn't worried, I have every confidence in you and your orga-nization. You were highly recommended."

"You flatter me. But I'm calling you because I've recently come into possession of another item that might interest you. I'm prepared to give you an excellent price."

"You have my order. I'm really not interested in any other merchandise you may be trying to—"

A female voice cut in. "Kirov, don't bargain with him. Don't pay
the bastard a cent."

An icy chill ran down Kirov's spine. "Hannah?"

Walsh came back on the line. "I see you're familiar with the
product."

Kirov's hand tightened on the phone. "What the hell are you doing?"

Driscoll and Charlie glanced up at the harshness in his voice.

"I'm just doing what I always do, Kirov. I obtain things that
people want and sell them for a fair price. Check your phone. I just
sent you a page from my most recent catalog. Go ahead. I'll wait."

Kirov pulled the phone from his ear and saw that he had an instant message waiting. He tapped the phone and a photograph of
Hannah appeared. She was wearing wrist restraints and holding that
morning's edition of the *Irish Times* newspaper.

"I'll cut your heart out if you hurt her, Walsh."

"That's entirely up to you."

"What do you want?"

"Five hundred thousand euros cash. Tonight."

"You're insane. I can't pull that much cash together on such
short notice."

"I'm a reasonable man. Perhaps I can take it out in trade. I have
a rather sensitive assignment you can do for me instead."

"I won't kill for you, Walsh. Despite my reputation in some quarters, I'm not an assassin."

"Who said anything about killing? Though I find it odd that
that's the first thing that came to your mind."

"Maybe it's the company I keep."

"Meet with me tonight. We'll discuss it like reasonable business-men."

"Only if I speak to Hannah first. Put her on again."

"I don't honor requests. Nor orders, Kirov."

"How do I know that wasn't a recording I heard? You might have already killed her."

"Do what I say, and you'll be able to see her this evening."

"She's here in Dublin?"

"You saw the photograph with the newspaper."

"You could have gotten a copy of the *Irish Times* in any city in the world."

"She's here, Kirov. Actually, she made it quite easy for me."

"Put her back on the phone. I'm not going to do anything you say until I talk to her again."

Another long pause. For a moment Kirov thought Walsh had hung up. Then Walsh finally replied, "Very well."

Hannah's voice returned to the line. "Don't do it. Whatever he wants, don't do it."

"Shhh. Are you all right?"

"Yes."

"I'm sorry, Hannah. I'll get you out of there no matter what it takes." He paused. "No matter what I have to do for Walsh."

"I don't want you to do anything for him. I don't understand. Why is this happening?"

"I don't understand either. But we won't be in the dark much longer. You'll be free soon. I promise you."

"I'm so touched." Walsh's voice startled Kirov as it returned on the line. "Make good on your promise. Meet me tonight on the Sean O'Casey Bridge."

"The Sean O'Casey Bridge. And how am I to be sure it's not a trap?"

"You don't. But if I wanted to set you up, I could have just waited until it was time to deliver your weapons. All this wouldn't have been necessary."

Good point, Kirov thought. "Then what do you want from me? Tell me now."

"We'll discuss it when I see you. Ten tonight. Come alone, or the deal is off."

"But how am I supposed to—"

Walsh cut the connection.

Kirov stood there, thinking, for a long moment. It was only when he was pocketing his phone that he realized his hands were shaking. What the hell? He'd dealt with a lot of scumbags like Walsh, and he was probably low on the lethal scale in comparison to some of the others he'd put down.

But this time Hannah was caught in the middle, and it was scaring the hell out of him. He didn't know Walsh well enough to be sure of his volatility quotient. He didn't know which way he would jump if cornered. He didn't know if he would strike out at the nearest person if he felt threatened.

And Hannah was that nearest person.

"That sounded like rather an intense call, Kirov," Driscoll said quietly.

Kirov nodded jerkily and grabbed his jacket. "I have to go."

"Just like that?" Charlie asked. "But what about our—"

"It will have to wait. A friend of mine needs me."

"So we heard," Driscoll said. "It sounds as if you could use a little help. I can't speak for Charlie, but I've got nothing better to do tonight."

Kirov shook his head. "Thank you, but I have to play this low-key. If I don't show up alone, he might panic and decide to kill her."

"He might kill you both," Charlie said. "You need a backup."

"I already have a backup." He pulled out his automatic and checked his ammo cartridge. "One that Walsh understands."

"Don't be a fool," Charlie said harshly. "You go off alone, and you'll get yourself killed."

Kirov smiled. "Why, Charlie, I didn't think you cared."

Charlie's face flushed, and his words came awkwardly. "Well, you know . . . We're counting on this job. You'll be no good to us floating in the river with a couple slugs in your back."

"And here I'd thought we'd made a turning point in our relationship."

"Screw off. We're partners, aren't we? I just thought partners were supposed to back each other up."

Kirov secured the gun in his shoulder holster. "I believe that's the usual procedure. I wouldn't really know since I usually work alone, but I applaud the concept. However, not in this case."

"I understand." Driscoll stood and offered Kirov his hand. "Call if you change your mind."

Kirov shook his hand and turned away. "I'll do that."

Charlie jammed his hands in his pockets. "You're a fool, Kirov."

"I've been called far worse. I'll see you both here later tonight. "

He walked out of the flat and ran down the steps.

CHAPTER 7

KIROV STRODE QUICKLY PAST THE life-size statues that, from a distance, appeared to be people loitering on this walkway that ran along the Liffey River's north bank. Instead, it was one of the city's many monuments to victims of the potato famine, with its haunting sculptures of men, women, and even a dog, all on the verge of death.

Not what he needed to see right now.

Detach. It was the only way he'd been able to stay alive all this time. The moment he let emotions dictate his actions, he was finished.

It wasn't working. Not when it was Hannah. He had stopped being able to separate his emotions toward Hannah a long time ago. He had fought them, tried to reason them away, and now could only accept that they were here to stay and he had to deal with them.

He glanced around. It was almost deserted here, in stark contrast to the hordes of people at the O'Connell Street intersection a few blocks behind him.

If Walsh had wanted a quiet meeting place, he had chosen well.

Up ahead he could see the angular gray spans of the Sean

O'Casey Bridge, a narrow steel pedestrian structure capable of separating and swinging open to allow larger boats to pass.

He stopped. Someone was standing in the shadows on the bridge. Walsh?

No, too thin.

Maybe the goon with the mustache he'd seen with Walsh during his one and only encounter. It would figure that the big man might bail when things got a little risky.

Kirov warily glanced around, then moved onto the bridge, moving between the large round automobile barriers. There was mist on the river, and spheres of condensation swirled around the streetlights. The bridge's steel railings glistened.

The figure on the bridge hadn't moved; his back was to him. Maybe it wasn't Walsh's man at all. Maybe Walsh was hiding in the shadows of a nearby building.

Kirov's hand tightened on the handle of his automatic. It was pure irony that it was Walsh who had sold him the weapon. Well, he'd make good use of it.

"You won't need your gun."

That voice . . .

The figure turned and moved out of the shadows.

Hannah.

She walked toward him. "Hello, Kirov."

Same wild curly hair, strong beautiful shoulders, and a face that he'd known from the moment he'd seen it that he'd never be able to forget.

He jerked his glance away and his gaze flew around the surrounding area. "Where's Walsh?"

"Having a pint down the street. I told him I wanted to see you alone."

"You told *him?*"

"The situation is a little different from what you were led to believe."

Kirov dropped his hands to his sides. "How different?"

"Almost completely different. Sorry about that."

"He didn't kidnap you?"

"Oh, he did, most definitely. But after I showed him a few Web sites with my pictures on them, I convinced him I'd be stupid to forsake my career as a marine architect just to come here to cause trouble for him . . . and you."

"You set me up."

"Yeah, I guess I did. With Walsh's help. Once you get to know him, he's really a romantic at heart."

"Bullshit."

"No, it's true. He knew I needed to see you, and he thought he was doing it in the name of true love."

"You set *him* up."

She nodded. "But he was well compensated. Eugenia gave him a few thousands for his trouble. I think she expects you to reimburse her."

"Eugenia . . ." He nodded slowly. "Of course. That's how you hunted me down."

Her lips tightened. "I could have called you. If you'd had the courtesy not to have left me without so much as a phone number."

"I'm sorry. I don't keep phones for more than a few days. It's too easy to track me through them." He smiled ruefully. "Although you don't seem to have had a problem."

"Dammit, the real issue wasn't about your lack of a phone. Forty-eight hours before we were to leave for Marinth, I had to hear from a hotel clerk that you had checked out and called a cab to take you to the airport." Her eyes were glittering with anger. "You couldn't have told me that you were leaving?"

"No, I decided that it was best you didn't know. I never meant to hurt you."

"You didn't hurt me. Annoyed, maybe. Confused. Pissed off. Not hurt."

"Then I'm sorry to have . . . pissed you off. Is that why you've gone to such lengths to find me?"

"Don't flatter yourself. I wrote you off."

"Then why are you here?"

"For one reason." She jammed her hands into the pockets of her coat. "An important artifact of ours was stolen. We brought it up from Marinth just yesterday. The Feds think someone named Gadaire took it. What do you know about it?"

Kirov tensed. "What kind of artifact?"

"Why should I tell you? I don't even know if I can trust you."

"That's not true. You know you can trust me. What kind of artifact?"

She ignored the question and asked in turn, "Why do the Feds think you might have had something to do with stealing it?"

"They probably don't. More than likely they were fishing. Tell me about the artifact."

She shook her head. "Not unless you tell me what's been going on. You left me out in the cold before. It's not going to happen again. I'm going to get that artifact back for Melis. You're going to be honest with me."

"Always."

"Don't tell me that, you Machiavellian Russian."

"I think that's a little confusing terminology. Machiavelli was an Italian, and he was—"

"Did you kill two men in Venice?"

"Yes," he said with no hesitation.

She waited. "That's it? No explanation?"

"What do you want to know? Those two men were working for Gadaire and were in the process of trying to murder a man."

"So you were just being a Good Samaritan?" she asked sarcastically.

"Not at all. You know me better than that. This man, Debney, possessed some information I needed. Gadaire's men were hunting for the same info, but they would have killed him before they got it." He shrugged. "I did what I had to do. I don't think anyone would dispute that the greater good was served by eliminating them."

"The Venice police might dispute it."

"Possibly. That's why I didn't stay around to discuss it."

"What information?" she asked. "I want to know everything, Kirov. Don't just give me bits and—"

"Ah, I see you've found each other." Walsh was strolling toward them from the south-bank quay.

Kirov called out to Walsh, "I expect a discount on my order now. You've caused me a good deal of trouble."

"You'll get nothing of the kind." Walsh waddled toward them, huffing and puffing from the exertion. "I expect a bonus for reuniting you with such a lovely lady."

"A lovely lady you abducted."

"At gunpoint," Hannah added.

"A misunderstanding." Walsh beamed. "I was merely looking after your interests and mine, Kirov. We're having such a happy ending, let's let bygones be bygones." He turned. "Come along, I'll walk with you to the pub on the quay, then I'll disappear and let you have your reunion. This pub is one of my favorites, full of light and music." He grimaced. "I really don't like it here. All those starving statues on the quay . . . The thought of famine deeply depresses me . . ."

*   *   *

CHARLIE STOOD IN THE SHADOWY entrance of a closed photography shop on the south bank, watching Kirov on the bridge with the woman and the fat man. Kirov had called the man Walsh, he remembered. Although Kirov claimed he didn't need help, Charlie knew better. Too much could go wrong. He had grown up on the streets of Dublin, and he knew that a human life—or two—meant nothing to thugs like Walsh over there.

Charlie braced himself against a brick wall and raised his handgun. He aimed at Walsh's shock of white hair.

Make your move, fat boy. I'm ready for you.

He frowned, puzzled. Although he couldn't hear them, the body language and mood between Kirov, Walsh, and the woman seemed almost . . . civilized.

Uh-oh. Walsh was going for something beneath his jacket. Why couldn't Kirov see it?

Dammit, that's why he needed to be here. Charlie took aim with his revolver, applied pressure on the trigger, and slowly . . .

A cold metal barrel was pressed to his temple.

He heard the chilling click above his ear.

His gaze flew to his right, and he saw a small, attractive woman holding a gun that seemed too large for her. Then he saw her eyes, and he knew that no weapon would be too big for her to handle.

"Friend of Kirov?" She smiled. "So am I. My name is Eugenia. They're having such a delightful time. Let's not spoil it for them."

KIROV SMILED AT THE WAITRESS as he ordered two pints of Guinness. The waitress smiled back and patted his arm as she walked away.

"I'd almost forgotten," Hannah said.

"Forgotten what?"

"How perfectly at home you are in almost any environment. We've been here two minutes, and two men have already nodded hello to you, and a group of women asked you to play darts. You said you've never been here before."

"I haven't."

"And naturally you've never seen these people before."

"No. The Irish are famous for being gregarious. And I guess I just have one of those approachable faces."

Approachable when it suited him, she thought. He was wearing a casual cream-colored wool sweater and a gray-tweed jacket, and he looked completely at home in this pub. Kirov wasn't a handsome man in the traditional sense, but his strong cheekbones, pronounced chin, and piercing blue eyes were arresting. It was the sheer force of his personality that increased his attractiveness to megawattage, an effect that took only a few moments to work on most people. She should know. She was angry and wary, and yet she was once more being enveloped in that force. She wanted to keep on looking at him, bask in that lazy confidence that was almost sensual in nature. Ignore it. Pull away.

Kirov tilted his head. "But I'm sure you didn't come all the way to Ireland to discuss my irrepressible charm."

"Damned straight. Did you think that I'd be less likely to tear into you if we were in a public place?"

"I know you better than that, Hannah. You would be perfectly willing to tear into me anytime, anyplace." He glanced at the glowing fireplace across the pub. "But Walsh is right, this just seemed like a warmer place for two friends to share a drink."

"Dial down the charisma, please. I'm not in the mood right now. I have some questions I need answered."

"Ask away. What would you like to know?"

"What would I like to know?" She stared at him in disbelief. "I don't even know where to begin."

"Why don't we start with why I didn't join you at Marinth?"

"That's your own business." And it hurt too much. "You changed your mind about wanting to go with me. That's okay. I never asked you to go. There are more important things to talk about."

"Actually, it's all related. I assume you've made the acquaintance of Elijah Baker, the agent of the U.S. Defense Intelligence Agency?"

Hannah nodded. "That's why I'm here. He told me you were roaming the European continent, killing people and making inquiries about Marinth."

Kirov smiled at the waitress, who was approaching with a tray. He waited until she set down their mugs and left before answering. "I suppose that's technically true. Did Baker tell you that he wanted to hire me?"

"For what?"

"Marinth."

"No, he left that part out."

"Of course he did. It wouldn't suit his purpose to tell you that. As you know, I spent a few years working with the CIA on projects in which we shared a common purpose. They wanted to continue the relationship, and I declined. But when Baker heard I was going to Marinth, he wanted my help in a case he was working on. He knew Gadaire was interested in Marinth, and for someone in Gadaire's business, that usually means the possibility of a weapon."

"Baker told us that."

"But to truly understand, you have to go a little further back. To a man named Samuel Debney."

"Debney. Baker said that you saved him when you killed those men in Venice."

"Well, sort of."

"He also said that you didn't do it out of the kindness of your heart."

"True. Did he tell you who Debney was or where he came from?"

"No."

"I didn't think he'd want to share to that extent. Debney is a botanist who was working with a major pharmaceutical company in France. They were studying some of the marine life brought up from previous Marinth expeditions. They knew about your upcoming expedition, and the lab was preparing to request more samples to be brought up. Organic material that might be worthy of further study."

"There's nothing unusual about that. I'm sure Melis was in touch with several labs to find out if they needed more samples for their work."

"Of course. But those other labs didn't make the discovery that Debney and his boss, Raoul Lastree, made. They were studying a new subspecies of alga that had been designated as TK44 by the marine biologists with the Marinth expedition that apparently doesn't exist anywhere else but in the waters near Marinth. While they were experimenting, they discovered that this alga is capable of leaching all oxygen from the surrounding seawater. It's been harmless on the seafloor for centuries, but if properly activated, it could spread and lay waste to all sea life along large areas of coastline." He lifted his pint to his lips. "Imagine if someone could control such a destructive force."

She shivered at the thought. The seas were constantly under attack from the advance of civilization with all its carelessness and greed. She had witnessed the results on many of her expeditions, and it had sickened her. But a deliberate threat of devastation was a greater horror. "I'm sure Gadaire has imagined it."

"Yes. And before that, Debney and Lastree did, too. They had cracked the riddle that had plagued historians and scientists for years—the secret of what had ended the Marinthian civilization. Unfortunately, that wasn't enough for Debney. He saw the discovery's potential as a weapon that might be worth tens of millions of dollars. It was a lot of temptation for a weak man. Debney cut the brakes on his partner's Mercedes and Lastree ran off a mountain road into a valley two hundred feet below. Debney took the activated sample of TK44 alga and he was in business."

Hannah shook her head. She had seen enough ugliness and horror that she shouldn't have been surprised. "No one else knew about it?"

"Apparently not. It was such a momentous discovery that they were trying to keep it quiet until they were ready to publish. Debney tried peddling his sample along with the know-how necessary to unleash its destructive properties."

"Enter Gadaire."

"And a few other players as well. Debney was out of his element. He wasn't ready for the hell that rained down on him. I knew that if I didn't find him fast, he wouldn't be alive for very long. Fortunately, I caught up with him in Venice, just as Gadaire's men were about to finish him off."

"So you got him to talk?"

"Not enough. I was most interested in the location of the sample packet of TK44, but he lost consciousness before I could get that bit of information from him. He was trying to use it as a bargaining chip with the authorities, but he eventually managed to slip out of the hospital. Ironically, he contacted Gadaire again and eventually managed to strike a deal with him for the packet. You'd think he'd have avoided him like the plague. I guess he realized that Gadaire really wanted that packet if he was willing to kill for it."

"So why the hell did Gadaire still go after that artifact?"

"I think something happened before Debney could impart the information needed to activate the alga's special properties."

"You don't know what happened to him?"

He shook his head. "He disappeared. I can't find a trace of him. He may be dead. Even if he was cautious in dealing with Gadaire a second time, there's no guarantee he survived. Or he may have taken his first payment and left the country. Or maybe it was his partner who had the activation process, and Debney decided to bluff his way into the big bucks. In any case, Gadaire is desperate to discover how to make it work. He's looking for any clue that can help him make that happen."

"A clue like our stolen artifact?"

He nodded. "That would fit the description of the type of thing he was looking for. Anything that would document the end of Marinth." He gazed at her inquiringly. "Which I assume is what you found?"

"We don't know if it goes into that kind of detail. If this alga devastated their food supply and killed them off, they may not have even known the cause."

Kirov shrugged. "They may not have. But as your friend Melis has shown the world, the Marinthians were very clever and techno-logically advanced. And when Gadaire sets his mind on something, he exhausts every possibility."

"So I'm beginning to understand. But what brought you here to Ireland?"

"Did you know that Ireland has the best lamb stew in the world?"

"Kirov."

"Oh, aside from the lamb stew?"

She had to clench her hands to keep from hitting him. "Yeah, aside from that."

"Gadaire has been spending quite a bit of time here recently. I've been keeping watch on him, and I'm certain he has Debney's sample here with him."

"What makes you so sure?"

"He's been spending a lot of time with a botanist, Dr. Simon Lampman, from Trinity College, which happens to be his alma mater. I believe Gadaire has hired Lampman to find out what activates the destructive properties of the Marinth alga. I've seen Lampman come and go several times from Gadaire's office in Aviva Stadium, each time carrying a small cooler. I think Gadaire is keeping Debney's original sample in his office and doling out portions as Lampman needs them."

"If that's true, Gadaire really is leaving no stone unturned."

He nodded. "And think about the scenarios if he manages to get what he wants."

"I haven't been doing anything else." It could be a nightmare, she thought, chilled. "There are hundreds of nations that rely on their waters for their food, their very livelihoods. If this is what destroyed Marinth, then whoever controlled it could hold entire countries, maybe even continents, hostage."

"And anyone who paid Gadaire's price would have that same power over their enemies." His lips twisted. "I don't think I want to live in that world."

"Do you think I do? You have to report this to someone."

Kirov's brows rose. "Really? To Baker?"

"I know you're suspicious of government types. Hell, so am I. But you can't screw around here. You can't let Gadaire get what he wants."

He took another swallow of his beer. "I don't intend to."

"Your intentions might not be good enough."

"Intentions seldom are unless followed by effective action."

"What action?"

He didn't answer.

Her hand tightened on her mug. "Dammit, tell me you have something in mind."

"Oh, I do." He met her gaze. "I'm just not sure you want to hear it."

"Try me. I came a long way to hunt you down. I'm not leaving without answers."

"Answers can be dangerous. If we end our time together right now, you'll have no idea of any action that could possibly cause you megatrouble later. It falls under the category of prior knowledge."

"Prior knowledge of what?"

"You're not going to give up, are you?" He stared at her for a long moment, weighing his options. He finally smiled. "I'm going to steal the sample from Gadaire."

She had been afraid he was heading in that direction. "According to both you and Baker, Gadaire is a criminal heavyweight with all the manpower that implies. Are you insane?"

"No, insane would be to just hand this over to a government man. Even if he claimed to have your country's best interests at heart."

"What do you intend to do with it? Hide it under a rock?"

"It's tempting. That alga stayed down at the bottom of the sea for centuries without disturbing the balance of power." He held up his hand as she opened her lips to protest. "No, I know it's too late. But wouldn't you like to know what we're dealing with? If it turns out to have the weapon potential Gadaire believes, I'm not entirely opposed to eventually turning it over to someone for safekeeping, but I'd never give it to just one person or even one government. That's entirely too much power. Marinth, of course, is Melis Nemid's passion, and I think she should have a say in the matter."

"Of course she should."

"How much input do you think the Defense Intelligence Agency would give her? How much input would it give any of us? I'm not inclined to bring in the police or any government authority. That would be the quickest way to lose control of the situation."

"And you can't stand not to be in control, can you? You were sole authority on that submarine for too long."

"Practically all my adult life. It was a necessity that I learned to trust my own judgment."

"And you never made a mistake?"

"I made mistakes, but I never tried to cover them up, and I never made the same mistake twice. As captain of a nuclear submarine, I was too visible to get away with that shit. But government agencies are different. They can hide their corruption or inefficiencies in a thousand tiny cubbyholes. I'd rather depend on myself." He leaned back in his chair, and added softly, "Like you, Hannah. I'm not the only one who is a control freak. You're getting over the first shock and feeling the same dread I am of letting Baker come in and run the show."

Hannah stared down at the tabletop. "What makes you think you can just waltz into Gadaire's office and walk out with the sample?"

Kirov smiled.

Hannah knew that smile. She was starting to waver, and he knew it. Damn him.

"I got a little outside help. Martin Driscoll, a man who has made a career of waltzing in and out of supposedly secure places. I'll introduce you to him tonight."

Hannah stared at him. Was she actually considering this?

Kirov pointed to her mug. "Drink up. Contrary to what most Americans believe, the beer here is served cold. You don't want it to get warm."

"You're pretty damn sure I'll go along with this. Otherwise, you never would have told me about your plans."

He shrugged. "You and I look at things very much the same way. I could be wrong, of course. In any case, I'm now at your mercy. It's whatever you say, whatever you want."

"You'd never allow yourself to be at anyone's mercy, Kirov."

"Oh, but I would," he said quietly. "It just has to be under very special circumstances. It would be my pleasure to be at your mercy in any number of situations, Hannah."

Look away from him. She mustn't feel like this. She could feel the heat rise to her cheeks but finally managed to pull her gaze away. "I don't believe you're capable of giving up power to anyone. I may call your bluff someday."

He smiled. "I look forward to it. But now I think you have a decision to make."

Yes, she did. She thought about it for another moment. Then she sat up straight in her chair. "If we're going to do this, we need to do it right."

His lip curled in the faintest smile. "We?"

"We. And we can't just hit Gadaire's office." Hannah picked up her mug and took a long drink before setting it down with a firm click on the tabletop. She was thinking hard, weighing options. "We need to break into the Trinity College lab at the same time."

CHAPTER
8

GADAIRE STROLLED ACROSS THE grassy main square of Trinity College and made his way toward the vine-covered herbarium, a building that housed hundreds of thousands of botanical samples.

Lights were illuminating the building. Good, Lampman was burning the midnight oil on the project. That was what he liked to see.

As he entered, Dr. Simon Lampman lowered his clipboard, obviously surprised. And, perhaps, even a bit frightened.

Excellent.

"Mr. Gadaire . . . I didn't realize we had a meeting scheduled."

"We don't. I'm just here for a bit of reassurance."

"About what?"

"Convince me that I'm not wasting my time with you."

Lampman scratched his face in the place once occupied by a bushy white beard he'd had when Gadaire had first met him. The facial hair was gone, Gadaire noted, but the nervous habits remained. "I told you there were no guarantees. You may think this is a colossal waste of time, but in science most of our time and effort is spent eliminating possibilities."

"And how many possibilities have you eliminated?"

"Thousands. But you have to realize that this is a most unusual assignment you've given me. You want me to tell you what can cause these TK44 alga samples to acquire very dramatic properties, which is all well and good. I've tackled projects like this before, but it helps to have a sample that reflects the final state."

"As much as I'd like to provide you with the 'after' sample, it probably hasn't existed for thousands of years. You knew this going in, Dr. Lampman. If this is too much for you, perhaps Taylor McDaniel or Chad Foushee at Oxford would like my money. I understand they're doing some impressive things in the botany program there."

He stiffened. "They're good. Not as good as I am, but good enough. But if you're still concerned about confidentiality, you'd be making a mistake. Your secret might be safe with them until the first scientific conference, when they'd be in the hotel bar bragging to all of us about the money they were making off you. A drink or two after that, they'd be telling us exactly what the project is about." Lampman shrugged. "But if you don't care about that . . ."

Gadaire hadn't expected such a well-thought-out defense. Lampman might be intimidated, but he wasn't going to cave. "Don't play me. We need to move this along. What more do you need?"

"It's not a matter of resources. We're dealing with living cultures that need time to grow. We must be patient."

"I don't have time to be patient. Is there anything else I can supply you with?"

Lampman thought for a moment. "Information. A clue, a hint, anything you can give me from the historical record."

"We're working on that." Gadaire felt his sinuses closing as they always did when he came into the herbarium. Damned plants. He was probably allergic to a dozen of them. He should have waited and had Lampman come to him, but he'd wanted him to know that he might drop in on him at any time. A little pressure never hurt. Lampman worked here in his ivory tower and forgot who was in control. He was sensing that the professor might have ambitions, and that could be dangerous. Lampman didn't seem to realize his only task was to produce and produce fast. Gadaire might have to reinforce that part of their agreement. But right now he had to get out of here. He backed away from Lampman and turned toward the door. "As soon as I know anything, *you'll* know. But in the meantime, I expect results from you. Instead of relying on historical data, creative thinking seems to be in order." He headed for the door. "I want something on my desk by next week."

HANNAH WALKED WITH KIROV DOWN a back alley in Dublin's Liberties district. The cobblestone paths were wet, and the night air was thick with the spicy odor of hops from the nearby Guinness brewery. She smiled. "I see that you've wasted no time making yourself comfortable in another city's seedy underbelly."

"I'm comfortable wherever I am. It's only a mind-set. This is just temporary. As a matter of fact, my partners and I are relocating tonight."

"Relocating where?"

"I've rented a place closer to the target. I already have a surveillance camera there trained on the arena's private entrance to chart the comings and goings of Gadaire and his team. I figure it's time we move our base of operations there."

They rounded a corner, and Hannah spotted a white-paneled

van with three people standing next to it. As Kirov led her toward it, she turned to him. "Friends of yours?"

He nodded. "And of yours."

As they came closer Hannah tried to make out the figures gathered beneath a building-mounted streetlight. A man in his sixties, a less-polished man in his midtwenties, and . . .

"It's really not nice to keep people waiting," Eugenia said as she started toward them.

Hannah sighed and shook her head. "I thought you were going to wait at the hotel."

"I thought so, too. Not my style. Too boring. I decided to shadow you to the bridge and make sure nothing went wrong. Good thing I did, because Charlie here was going to put a bullet into our friend Walsh."

Kirov said curtly, "I told you to stay here, Charlie."

"Sorry, Kirov," Charlie said. "I thought you needed backup."

"I would have asked for help if I'd needed it," Kirov said. "What's wrong with your hand?" Charlie's right hand was tucked between his left biceps and torso. "What did you do to it?"

"Actually, I did it," Eugenia said. "On our way back here, he tried to overpower me. He thought he could pin me down."

Charlie showed Kirov his swollen hand. "She tried to break my hand."

"If she had really tried to do that, she could have done it and much worse," Kirov said. "You're lucky you're not in a hospital emergency room trying to get your hand reattached to your wrist."

Eugenia smiled as she hugged Kirov. "You always know just the right thing to say to flatter me." She turned back to Charlie. "Put it on ice, and it will be fine in the morning."

Kirov stepped back from Eugenia and shook his head at her. "I *suppose* it's nice to see you again, my indiscreet little busybody."

She clicked her tongue in response. "I didn't like the way you had treated my friend Hannah. The aloof-asshole routine worked for you when you were younger, Kirov, but now it's just rude. Don't do it again."

"I'll try, but the aloof-asshole persona fits me too well, Eugenia." Kirov turned back toward the group. "Hannah Bryson, meet Martin Driscoll. He's the man I told you about."

Driscoll took her hand with an elegant panache. For an amused moment she thought he was going to kiss it, but he only gave a quick squeeze. "My privilege, dear lady. I've gotten into many tougher places before, so don't you worry. Nothing's going to stand between me and a few paltry dishes of your alga."

Hannah smiled. "Nicely put. It's not exactly diamonds on the French Riviera, is it?"

"No, ma'am. But a job is a job. And I already have some ideas about how we're going to pull it off."

"Good," Kirov said. "Because I've just been informed that we're also going to be raiding the labs of Trinity College."

Driscoll looked as if he had just heard a joke he didn't understand. "Right. So will this be before or after we break into the headquarters of an international arms merchant?"

"We'll figure that one out later," Kirov said. "But Hannah made a believer out of me. We should do it."

"And I suppose you do everything that a pretty woman tells you to do. Not that I blame you. Hormones can do crazy things to a man's judgment." He nodded to Eugenia. "And here's another lovely lady. My boy goes out for a pack of smokes, comes back with this pretty little woman, a mangled hand, and a story about how you were duped into meeting another woman from your past. And now you tell me that this woman wants us to break into Trinity College?"

"It's not like we're after the *Book of Kells*," Kirov said. "But I have a feeling you'll charge me as if we were."

"A fair day's wage for a job well-done." Driscoll winked at Hannah. "I'm sure the lady agrees."

"The lady agrees," Hannah said.

Kirov rolled his eyes. "Before the lady drives me to the poorhouse, I propose we discuss this later. Right now, we're packed up and ready to move to our new base of operations. I propose we pile into the van and continue our conversation there."

HALF AN HOUR LATER, THEY entered the sparsely decorated eighth-story apartment that Kirov had rented. The ancient building elevator had groaned and whined all the way up, but the apartment itself was in new condition, featuring a window that offered a spectacular view of Aviva Stadium.

"It looks like a spaceship," Hannah said, gazing at the illuminated structure in front of her. "I like it."

"I knew you would," Kirov said. "It was my first thought when I saw it. Those modernistic curves are your aesthetic all the way."

Eugenia stepped around a tripod-mounted video camera set up in front of the window. "Your camera, Kirov? I thought your Peeping Tom days were behind you."

Kirov peered at the camera's LCD viewfinder. "You know what they say . . . Once a voyeur, always a voyeur." Satisfied with what he saw in the viewfinder, Kirov moved back. "I actually set this up to keep tabs on one of the arena's private entrances, the one that Gadaire, his driver, and his private security team use. The video is stored on a hard drive down there on the floor. Charlie, it will be your job to scan through the recordings and write down the make and license-plate number of every vehicle going in, plus the day and time."

Charlie made a face. "Aw, you're giving me the shit work."

"There's no such thing," Driscoll said. "Each piece of the mechanism is a necessary one, and that's a fact."

"It's a fact that some pieces are less necessary than others," Charlie said.

"Well, if that piece is you right now, it's only because you're still paying your dues. And it has to beat digging trenches for fiber-optic cable, which is what you were doing when I found you."

"*I* found *you*," Charlie corrected.

"Whatever. As long as Mr. Kirov is true to his word, I'll be in a position to hire you for a good job in that fancy security company."

Kirov handed Charlie a clipboard. "I am true to my word. Consider this your internship."

Hannah turned toward Driscoll. "So what's your plan? Are you breaking in during the dead of night?"

"Afraid not. I might have tried that thirty years ago, but modern technology has made that kind of caper very difficult. We'll need a bit more daylight finesse." Driscoll flipped open the lid of Kirov's laptop and placed it on a small folding card table. "While you were gone, I studied the video we stitched together."

Hannah looked at the screen and was surprised to see the representation of Gadaire's suite. "You've actually been inside there?"

Driscoll nodded. "Today. And I noticed that there's an extra video feed in the folder." He clicked on it and revealed a multicolored video that bore only the slightest resemblance to the feeds from their other cameras. "Am I correct in assuming that these are infrared pictures?"

Kirov nodded. "Yes, I was going to tell you about that. It came from my tie clip. I thought it might prove useful."

Driscoll leaned toward the screen. "It has. We know that our items must be kept refrigerated, so it would follow that there's a thermal footprint somewhere in here."

"Something cold?" Charlie asked.

"Probably not. More than likely, we'll be looking for a heat source."

"A cooling unit and compressor," Hannah said.

"Exactly." Driscoll fast-forwarded the infrared feed to the point that offered a glimpse of Gadaire's office. "Here we see a strong heat source at the bar, which we can assume to be from a minifridge. I sincerely doubt he's keeping it there, though it would make our jobs much easier."

Hannah pointed to a patch of orange-red high on the ceiling. "What's this?"

"Heating vent. But look at this panel." Driscoll wiped his finger across the bottom of a wooden shelving unit next to Gadaire's desk. "There's a heat source here."

"A printer?" Kirov said.

Driscoll shook his head. "Too hot for a printer. I'm willing to bet that this is from a refrigeration unit. But if these samples are as important to Gadaire as you think, this wouldn't be a standard-issue refrigerator. It's probably something much more secure with backup capabilities. I have the dimensions, so now I just need to do a bit of research."

"See, what did I tell you?" Kirov said to Hannah. "He's the best."

Hannah nodded. "He's remarkable. But if he was really the best, you wouldn't need all those guns you requested from Walsh."

"Guns?" Driscoll said.

Kirov shrugged. "A precaution. Before I enlisted your services, Driscoll, I thought that I might have to resort to a more direct approach."

Driscoll smiled. "An old-fashioned commando raid? Is that what you had in mind?"

"Something like that."

"Sounds good to me," Charlie said. "Much better than all this planning and homework. I could have stayed in school if I'd wanted this rubbish."

"You should have stayed in school anyway," Driscoll said.

Charlie snorted. "You should talk. Mum told me you didn't see a day of school after age eleven."

"Your mum told you almost nothing about me your entire life, yet she told you that. Lovely woman." Driscoll turned back to Kirov. "No gunplay required, my friend. It's a point of pride with me."

"That's why I wanted you to be a part of this." Kirov glanced at Hannah and Eugenia. "If you're interested, we can use your help."

Hannah smiled. As worried as Eugenia had been about Kirov, she could see that he had never been more in his element. This is what he needed to be doing, totally in command, leading others as he had when he was captain of his nuclear sub. Although this endeavor was clearly outside the law, he reminded Hannah of a medieval warrior attacking a castle, battling against huge odds. Bold, clever, and yet somehow noble.

Noble? Where the hell had that come from? Kirov would laugh in her face if he heard her say it, but that adjective wouldn't leave her. Even as he was plotting a heist.

Eugenia nodded. "Why not? It might be interesting. You obviously need my help since you're teaming up with boys like Charlie, who shoot before they think. What can I do for you, Kirov?"

"It might be necessary for us to leave the country rather quickly once we have the samples. That also means no entanglements with Customs."

"That's it? You insult me, Kirov. I thought you'd have me doing back flips over laser sensors, and all you need is for me to push some papers around?"

"You have a way of negotiating the impossible, Eugenia. I need that skill right now."

Hannah shrugged. "Does that leave me for backflip laser-sensor duty? Guess I'd better start limbering up."

"Not quite. But since you were insistent that we retrieve the specimens from Trinity College, you're going there with me tomorrow. I doubt that a college research laboratory will have quite the same level of security as that athletic stadium, so I thought we might take a look around and see what's involved with securing the samples there."

"Good idea." She frowned. "Before we leave Ireland, I'd like to remove every bit of them from Gadaire's control."

Kirov nodded. "It's the only thing to do." He paused. "But you realize that Gadaire won't hesitate to kill anyone who stands between him and a lucrative payday."

Hannah tilted her head. "My, my, how ominous. Are you trying to scare me?"

"No. To warn you." He glanced at the others. "To warn you all. I pulled you into this, but you have to know what you're facing. If we take Gadaire's prize away from him, he'll take it personally. Gadaire is a vicious egotist on the highest level, and he's not going to like having egg on his face. He won't quit until he gets his revenge on each and every one of us."

Silence.

Driscoll spoke. "Then we'll just have to make sure he doesn't know what hit him, won't we?"

"Enough of this," Eugenia said. "We're all adults. Stop trying to take responsibility for everyone around you, Kirov. It was always a fault of yours. Being a commander on that submarine twisted your thinking."

"My apologies." His lips quirked. "Though only you would find a responsible attitude toward a nuclear sub unacceptable."

"I'm only saying it was bad training for real life." She turned to Charlie. "I need a ride to the Temple Bar. I called a few friends while I was waiting for Kirov to come to Hannah's rescue, and I'm meeting them for drinks. Will you drive me?" She added slyly, "You may get your chance to get your own back for that sprained thumb. I'm always ready to play tutor."

"I don't need any lessons from you," Charlie said. "You caught me off guard."

"Did I?"

He grimaced. "No. You were good."

"Yes." She smiled. "And you weren't terrible. Will you drive me?"

He hesitated. "If we can drop off my dad first."

"Ah, such devotion," Driscoll said. "It touches me that you're not willing to leave me in the lurch, son."

"You're actually going partying?" Hannah asked. "What stamina. Don't you ever wind down?"

"When I do, I wind myself up again. Life's too short. And it sometimes turns out to be shorter than you think." She turned away. "I'll see you later back at the hotel. Come on, Charlie, show me your wheels."

Hannah watched the three walk away from them down the block. "She's amazing. Has she always been that energetic?"

"Ever since I've known her." He opened the door of the van and helped her into the passenger seat. "And she just gave you her philosophy in a nutshell. She's lost too many friends not to keep in touch and cling to everyone that she has left." He climbed into the driver's seat. "Where is your hotel?"

"The Reardon. It's a quaint little inn on the Liffey. Do you know where it is?"

"I know the general area." He started the van. "I'll find it."

"I don't doubt it. You seem very familiar with the city."

He shrugged. "I like it. I appreciate the spirit of the country. Hard, a little reckless, but enduring."

"Not romantic and mystical?"

"That's not how I see it. But, then, I'm neither romantic nor mystical in nature. I have problems keeping in touch with my softer side."

"That's no surprise."

Kirov gave her a wary glance and fell silent. He did not speak again for the fifteen-minute ride. Kirov parked on the street and cut the engine.

Hannah turned toward him. "Tomorrow then?"

"Hannah . . ."

"Ten A.M.? Eleven?"

"I'm sorry, Hannah."

"Sorry for what?"

He made a face. "You're not going to make this easy for me, are you?"

"Why would I ever want to do that?"

"I should have told you. You have every right to be angry with me."

"Angry? I'm just surprised. Especially after all we've been through together. I thought I deserved better from you."

"I was trying to protect you," Kirov said quietly.

"Okay, now you've hit a nerve. Since when have I needed protecting? I've been taking care of myself for a long time, Kirov."

"I'm not saying you needed it. It's a flaw I share with a good many of the male population. It's just something I do instinctively."

"Do me a favor and smother those instincts from now on, will you?"

"I'll do my best, but I have an admission to make—I *like* feeling protective of you."

She felt a rush of heat surge through her. Ignore it. "Too bad."

"I've missed you, Hannah."

"You don't get to say that. Not after the way you left."

"I'm telling the truth." He paused. "Leaving you was one of the most difficult things I've ever done. You know the life I've lived. I don't permit myself to make attachments. But you came close to me and wouldn't go away. And after we were together a while I didn't want you to go away. We were heading somewhere that was . . . exciting me. Then I had to break away and leave. I knew it was only temporary, but it still hurt me to do it."

"Well, I *didn't* know it was temporary. Imagine how I felt."

"I know. I thought it necessary. I'm sorry."

She couldn't look away from him. She was being wrapped in that charisma that was such an integral quality of Kirov, she realized. Dear God, not again. Hannah let out a long breath. "Look, we have a job to do here. I suggest we just focus our energies on that. I'm a big girl, and in the end, none of this other stuff really matters." She opened the car door and climbed out. "Meet me here at ten tomorrow morning."

"Hannah . . ."

She slammed the van door closed.

Hannah could feel Kirov watching her as she walked to the hotel's front door, through the lobby, and straight back to the elevator. She watched the van's reflection in the elevator's mirrored paneling until the doors closed behind her.

I was trying to protect you.

Her reunion with Kirov had been every bit as exasperating and painful as she thought it would be.

I like feeling protective of you.

She couldn't let him get to her. Not again. It had hurt too much. Those tentative steps she had made toward a relationship with Kirov had been a mistake. She could never really be sure of him or what he would do down the road. Stick to the plan, get what she needed, then wave good-bye when he once again decided to take off.

If she didn't take off first.

HANNAH'S CELL PHONE WAS ringing as she unlocked the door of her room.

Melis?

She hurriedly slammed the door behind her and accessed the call.

"Aunt Hannah?"

Ronnie.

"Hi, honey, how are you doing? Why are you calling? Is everything okay? How is your mom?"

"Mom is fine." He hesitated. "Is it all right that I called you? I didn't want to bother you. I didn't wake you or anything?"

"No, I just got back to the hotel." She dropped down in an easy chair. "I'm glad you called. It's good to hear your voice." She said gently, "Don't ever worry about bothering me. If you need to talk, I'm here for you. Just as you would be for me, Ronnie."

"I would be there, if you'd let me." He was silent. "I had a dream last night, Aunt Hannah."

"Did you?"

"It was about Dad."

Hannah's hand tightened on the phone. "That's natural. You want him to be with you, and he's always in your thoughts. I've had a few dreams myself since he died. Was this the first one for you?"

"No, I dream about him almost every night. I don't tell Mom because I don't want her to be sad."

"She'd understand, Ronnie. She wouldn't want you to be sad either."

"I know. But most of the dreams aren't sad. They're just . . . Dad. I'm only sad after I wake up."

"Maybe you and your mom could talk your way through it so that the sadness would go away."

"Maybe. But right now she's . . . I don't want her to worry about me. She's having enough trouble with Donna and just getting through this."

They were all having trouble getting through Conner's death. He'd been such an important part of their lives that there were memories around every corner. Hell, she was tearing up again, just thinking about him. "How can I help, Ronnie?"

"I didn't really call because of the dream. Or maybe I did, but it was because it made me start thinking and—"

"Tell me about the dream, Ronnie."

He was silent a moment. "It was a little different. It was just Dad standing leaning against the doorjamb and smiling at me. He was wearing that gray sweater Mom knitted for him . . ."

"The gray sweater?"

"Yeah, he always wore it because of Mom."

She knew that. She also knew that Conner had worn that sweater on the night he was killed and that it had been cremated with him. But she hoped Ronnie didn't know that. No, he couldn't, they had carefully kept all those details from Donna and him. And he certainly wouldn't have spoken so casually about the sweater if he'd known. "Yes, he told me once that he remembered Cathy knitting it when she was expecting Donna."

"He teased her all the time because she kept making mistakes with it. But she didn't mind." He paused. "I remembered that last night."

"And you just saw him and the dream was over?"

"No, he talked to me like he used to do. He talked about you.

He said that I had to remember to take care of you. He said it was important now. He said you were sad and hurting. He said I should protect you."

"Ronnie, you were just remembering what he told you when he was alive. And we're all sad and hurting," she said unevenly. "You love me and want the best for me."

"Yes, but I promised him."

Cripes, I have to keep control. "You are going to help me. Next summer you're going to come and work with me. We'll be together for at least a couple months."

"That's a long time away," Ronnie said. "I thought . . . maybe I should come to you now."

"Don't be silly. You're in school. I'll be fine, Ronnie."

"I could make it up. I think I should be with you. He said now. He said I should protect you."

"It was a dream."

"I know . . . I think. But he never told me to protect you before. Just to keep you from being lonely."

"But you're a very loving and protective boy. Look how you take care of Donna and your mother." She swallowed to ease the tightness of her throat. "The jump between keeping me from being lonely and protecting me isn't such a big leap. Look, nothing's wrong. I'm doing my job and just waiting for the summer so that we can be together." She tried to laugh. "Have you forgotten what a tough cookie I am? I'm sure your dad has told you stories."

"Yes, most of them were funny."

"That doesn't surprise me. He always loved it when the joke was on me. He said that it was good for my ego." She took a breath. "I'm not saying I don't want you or think you could help me, but we have to be patient. I'm fine. Why don't we set up a time to talk to each other every week? That way we'll know what's happening in each other's lives and can jump in if needed. Is that a plan?"

He was silent. "I think I should come."

"No, Ronnie. How about calling every Friday evening about this time?"

"I guess so."

"It's for the best. If you want to talk, don't wait until Friday. That's only a guideline."

"Okay. You're sure everything is all right with you?"

"I'm sure."

"How are Pete and Susie?"

Thank Heaven. She was glad his thoughts had turned away from his father to the dolphins. "Well, mischievous and independent. More independent than Melis would like. We're going to head for the Marinth Museum in Athens, and she's afraid they won't go with her."

"I'd like to see them."

"You will. I promise. It's time I got to bed, Ronnie. I've got a full day tomorrow. I imagine you do too."

"Yes." He paused. "I love you, Aunt Hannah."

"I love you, too. Take care of the family."

"I will. It's my job now." He hung up.

She hung up and leaned back in the chair.

Damn. Damn. Damn.

What kind of world was it that men like Conner were butchered and boys like Ronnie had their childhoods taken away by responsibilities. He should be thinking of his next soccer game and whether he liked that cute girl in his math class. Not about shouldering the responsibilities of the family. She knew it didn't matter how much she talked to him. He'd do it anyway. It was his nature.

Responsibilities. Eugenia had been teasing Kirov tonight about his penchant for shouldering responsibilities. It was strange that she had come face-to-face with another male who had that same characteristic. Had Kirov been an intelligent, grave little boy like Ronnie? They certainly had the same instincts, she thought ruefully.

I was trying to protect you.

And Ronnie had said the same thing.

Or rather he had said that Conner had wanted her to be protected. He wouldn't admit it, but he'd wanted to believe that experience last night had been more than a dream. It had been her duty to discourage him. She was a hardheaded realist, and a dream was a dream.

But somewhere deep in her heart she wanted to believe that Conner was still with them. If not with them, somewhere safe and happy and surrounded by love.

Oh, shit.

The tears were running down her cheeks. She got to her feet and headed for the bathroom to wash her face.

Dream, Ronnie, keep him close to you. Let him help you heal.

Let us all help you.

Fair Winds **Research Vessel**

Atlantic Ocean

I CAN'T GIVE IN TO THE SADNESS, Melis thought.

She felt it every time she left Marinth, with each mile that separated her from the place that had become such an important part of her life. Her husband, Jed, teased her about her obsession, but he understood more than anyone how hard it was for her to leave the ancient city and its secrets.

Stop being ridiculous. She shouldn't be mooning around about how things weren't absolutely perfect. Life wasn't perfect. This trip

to the lab at the museum in Athens was essential. Hannah was trying desperately to retrieve the trellis, and Melis had to do her part.

She sat cross-legged on the upper deck, her sweater pulled tightly
around her as she looked between the bars of the stern railing. It
wouldn't be light for another few hours, but this was when the sea
was at its most alluring, beckoning her from the dark void beyond
her vessel's running lights.

It was only that it was harder this time, she realized. The rush of
emotion that had accompanied their new discovery, followed by the
crushing disappointment of abruptly losing it, had exhausted her.
Then, too, there was the uncertainty about Pete and Susie. The local
dolphin population's recent odd behavior unsettled her, driving home
just how little she knew about them. She was already afraid of losing
Pete and Susie, but that fear had only intensified in the past two days.
They, like Marinth, still had secrets to share, but at the moment that
seemed trivial next to her love for them.

"Melis?"

She looked behind her to see Aziz Natali, a biochemist she had
recruited only days before the expedition's departure. It didn't surprise her that he would still be awake at three thirty. She was accustomed to seeing him in the lab at all hours of the day or night.

"Get some sleep, Aziz."

He smiled. "I already have. Between 1:20 and 1:55. It was most
refreshing."

"Oh, good. That should do you for another day or so."

"It just might." He crouched on the deck beside her. "I've been
running simulations against the TK44 alga sample you told me
about. So far I haven't found anything unusual."

"Run it against all plant and animal life unique to Marinth.
Whatever it is, the combination has to be extremely rare not to have
occurred anywhere in the world in the thousands of years since."

"I've been doing that. I've been using the bioscanner I brought on board to analyze and break down all of your Marinth samples to the molecular level. Once that's done, I can run computer simulations of the various combinations to examine interactions."

"The bioscanner is why you're here, Azis. That YouTube video of your university demonstration made a real impression on all of us."

"So you use YouTube to staff your expeditions. I'm lucky I'm not sharing my cabin with a sneezing cat or a teenage blogger."

Melis laughed. "Maybe next trip. Right now I don't want anything to distract you from the work you're doing."

"It would help if I had access to more samples of the marine life you've collected in Marinth. You have thousands in your lab here on board, but I know there are more."

"Many more. They're in the museum laboratories in Athens. I've already alerted the staff to start preparing them for you."

"Ah, I can see I won't be getting much more sleep even after we dock."

"Sorry about that, but this is important."

He stood. "No big deal. I have a tough time sleeping when I'm immersed in a problem anyway. You may have noticed."

"I've noticed."

"You've given me a challenge. I'll do my best to test everything on board before we get to the museum."

"Thanks, Aziz." She suddenly grinned. "I'm so glad I picked you over the sneezing cat."

CHAPTER
9

Reardon Hotel
Dublin, Ireland

TO HER SURPRISE, HANNAH managed to sleep until seven thirty. Throughout the night, she had still felt the familiar rocking motion as if she was on a boat. It was a feeling she knew would persist for a week or so. The sensation had never bothered her as it did some of her colleagues; to the contrary, she found comfort in the sensation. The sea was as much home to her as the shore.

She checked her voice mail. Ebersole and another AquaCorp executive had left a total of sixteen messages for her. What in the hell did they want? If indeed the company had bankrolled a multimillion-dollar expedition just to curry favor with her, they must have had some humongous favor in mind. And probably one she wanted no part of.

She was tempted to call back out of sheer curiosity, but after a few seconds she turned off the phone. She didn't need the aggravation.

She slipped on sweatpants, tennis shoes, and T-shirt and went downstairs for a run along the quay. Before she even stepped out the hotel's front door, however, she spotted a familiar face outside.

U.S. Intelligence Agent Elijah Baker sat on a bench facing the hotel. "Good morning, Ms. Bryson."

She stared at him warily as office workers passed between them on the sidewalk. "What in the hell are you doing here?"

He smiled. "My great-great-grandparents were from Ireland. I figured it would be as good a time as any to visit the Old Country."

"You had me followed."

"You flatter yourself. We wouldn't waste the manpower to shadow you to the ends of the earth."

"Yet here you are."

"Well, it's much less labor-intensive to follow a data trail. Your friend Kirov is much better at covering his tracks."

"I'm not a criminal. I have no reason to cover my tracks."

"Lucky for us, I suppose. But when we saw you had gone to Ireland, that piqued my interest. Because as it happens, Vincent Gadaire has been spending a lot of time in Ireland lately."

"Did his great-great-grandparents come from the Old Country, too?"

"I just find it interesting you would suddenly find yourself in the same city with this person you claimed you'd never heard of."

She shrugged. "Small world."

"Kirov is here, isn't he?"

"You didn't tell me that you tried to hire him."

Baker's eyes narrowed. "So you've spoken to him."

She ignored the question. "You tried to hire Kirov to spy on our expedition."

"Gadaire had someone on the inside. I thought I should have someone in there, too."

"Who was Gadaire's inside man?"

"Who says it was a man?"

"*Who was it?*"

"I don't know."

"You don't know? I don't believe you. It's just another secret you've chosen to keep from me."

"I honestly don't know. But this person's intel is most likely responsible for the theft of that relic."

As usual, Baker was dropping little hints, then skipping away. Whether he had knowledge or not, it was clear he wasn't going to reveal anything. "What do you want from me, Baker?"

"Just Kirov. We need to talk to him."

"Because you think he has information that can help you nail Gadaire? Do your own intelligence work."

"That's what I'm doing, Hannah. Tell us where to find him and go back to your life. You don't need to be involved with this. I believed you when you said you didn't know who Gadaire was. I still don't think you know what he's capable of." Baker stood up and stepped closer to her. "I once found the body of a business partner who had tried to cut him out of a transaction. The man's teeth had been crushed all the way to the nerve, one by one, by a pair of pliers. I found the guy's tongue in his shirt pocket. Gadaire is an animal. Don't get mixed up with him."

Baker was obviously trying to shock and frighten her. It was a form of intimidation that always made her angry. "As far as I'm concerned, your job is to get our artifact back," she said curtly. "Talk to me again when you've done that."

Baker studied her. "And what will that get me?"

"I'll make you a deal. Find the artifact and return it to Melis, and I'll help you with Kirov, Gadaire, and whoever else is on your agenda. You'll have my full cooperation."

"Time may be running out, Hannah. Help me, and I promise to make a good-faith effort to find the artifact and—"

"Not good enough."

"Be reasonable."

"That's my offer. Don't talk to me again until you've put that trellis in Melis Nemid's hands." She stretched her calf muscles. "Now if you'll excuse me, you're cutting into my morning run."

AS HANNAH JOGGED THROUGH the City Centre, she found herself imagining that she saw Baker's surveillance men several times along the route, tracking her every move.

The bastard had made her paranoid.

Perhaps with good reason.

If her scanned passport had been enough to bring him to Ireland, it wasn't unreasonable to think that he might have her watched. She would have to take precautions.

She ran alongside the river, thinking about the words she'd hurled at Baker.

Find the artifact and return it to Melis, and I'll help you with Kirov, Gadaire, and whoever else . . .

She had offered it up so easily without coercion. What the hell was she thinking?

You'll have my full cooperation.

She needed to get that artifact back to Melis, that was what she was thinking. Wasn't that worth any bargain, any price? Kirov could take care of himself. Surely Melis would agree. All those years, searching for the final pieces of the puzzle . . .

But even Melis knew where to draw the line. Come to think of it, she probably would have told Baker to go to hell.

Perhaps it wasn't so much about Melis but about Kirov himself. She was still experiencing the hurt and anger that wouldn't leave her. He was coming too close, and she had to find a way of pushing him away.

Even if it meant betrayal?

No way. Everything inside her rejected that thought.

Dammit, she would just have to find a way of dealing with Kirov in her own fashion.

Sorry, Baker, there's not going to be any bargain with the devil.

Trinity College

Dublin, Ireland

EVEN FROM THE OTHER SIDE of the campus rugby field, Hannah recognized Kirov's strong, confident gait. He exuded power with each step, with a bearing that suggested total ease with himself and the world around him.

He smiled as he drew closer. "That was a rather cryptic message you left on my voice mail—'Meet me in front of the place.'"

Hannah pointed toward the botany building behind her. "The place. You didn't seem to have any problem finding it."

"No, but I had thought we were meeting at your hotel."

"If you had gone there, you might be spending the next few days being interrogated by U.S. intelligence agents. Baker's here, and he really wants to see you."

Kirov nodded. "I see. He must have tracked you. Are you sure you weren't followed here to the campus?"

"Positive."

"You're forgetting something. Your mobile phone. They can use it to track you within a few yards." Kirov glanced around. "I suspect we're about to have company."

Hannah gave him a disgusted look. "Who do you think I am?" She held up a plastic disposable phone. "Fifty euros from a shop on

Nassau Street. I paid in cash, and it came with a hundred minutes of talk time."

Kirov smiled. "Well done. And that smartphone of yours?"

"I took out the SIM card, erased everything, removed the battery, and threw it into the trash."

"Hmm. The river would have been better."

"I agree. But it would have been hypocritical for a Save the Oceans spokeswoman to discard her old electronics into the Liffey River." She shrugged. "In any case, no one is tracking me right now."

Kirov smiled slightly. "Is it my influence that has made you so good at evading the long arm of the law?"

"Stop looking so pleased with yourself. It's really nothing to be proud of."

"Oh, but it is."

"Whatever. I can't go back to my hotel or use my credit cards until we're finished. This has become quite inconvenient for me."

"Then go back home to Boston. I'll take care of things here."

"That's not going to happen."

"Somehow I didn't think it was."

"We're wasting time." She jerked her head back toward the botany building. "Let's check out the lab."

"No, not yet. Because we're not wasting time. We're waiting for you to get a glimpse of Dr. Simon Lampman. He's the one who's studying the samples for Gadaire."

"Naturally you have his entire routine committed to memory."

Kirov shrugged. "I do my homework. It's actually a fairly simple schedule. One doesn't need a freakish memory like yours to master it." He pointed to a nearby building. "There. That's Luce Hall. He'll cross in front of it any minute now on his way to Pearse Street. He always goes there for lunch."

"What does he look like?"

Kirov pointed to a man carrying a brown satchel and several plastic mailing tubes. "Like that. Introducing Dr. Simon Lampman."

Hannah stared at Lampman as he walked past the building to the busy street beyond. He was slightly overweight, with unkempt hair and clothes that were a size too small for him. He moved awkwardly, struggling to keep the tubes under his arms.

Hannah shook her head. "Does he have any idea how dangerous Gadaire's project is?"

"With the money he's getting, he probably doesn't care."

"Maybe he'll care after we take the project away from him," Hannah said. "What's to stop us from going into the lab and taking it right now? How much security can there be?"

Kirov smiled, amused. "How eager you are to commit grand larceny. Probably not much, but we can't risk tipping off Gadaire. We'll have to hit his office and this lab at the exact same time. Otherwise, he'll be hypervigilant."

Hannah nodded. "You're right."

"Plus, however we do this, we have to make sure we get all the materials that Lampman has in his possession. It would defeat our purpose if we leave behind even one sample."

"How do we do that?"

"I'm not sure. That requires some thought. That's why this trip is purely to reconnoiter and find out what we're going to have to deal with." Kirov was still staring at the sidewalk where Lampman had just passed. "Okay, look over there. See that young man in the striped shirt?"

Hannah glanced over to see a boy with longish brown hair, jeans, T-shirt, and a denim jacket. He carried a book bag over his right shoulder. "Yes. What about him?"

"That's one of Gadaire's men."

"That kid? Are you sure?"

Kirov nodded. "Look at the bulge under his jacket. It's a shoulder holster. He's one of three men Gadaire has assigned to shadow Dr. Lampman. They work in shifts, and they each blend in with the student population fairly well."

"I would have believed he was a student. Does Lampman know he has a shadow?"

"I don't think so. I'm sure their purpose is as much to spy on him as it is to protect him."

"Spy on him? But he's working for them."

"Gadaire probably wants to make sure Lampman isn't cooperating with the authorities or perhaps selling out to a competitor. Gadaire is extremely suspicious of his own people. I'm sure he's also monitoring Lampman's telephone and e-mails. Whatever we do, we'll have to take that into account. Wherever Dr. Lampman is, one of Gadaire's men won't be far away."

"Good to know."

Kirov motioned toward the botany building. "Now that both of them are off campus for the next hour or so, this would be an excellent time to have a look at that lab. I need to get some photos of the setup."

He led her to the side of the botany building, and they walked down the short flight of stairs that took them to the basement, where signs pointed them in the direction of LABS 1–8. Hannah looked at the students in the corridors and felt positively ancient. It wasn't unusual. She often felt the same when working with interns on her own projects. They seemed much too young to be college students. Who let all the ninth-graders in there?

Kirov pointed to a closed door. "Lampman teaches all his advanced laboratory classes in here, and it's also where most of the advanced equipment can be found . . . Stereoscopic imaging scanners, plotters, everything he might need for his own research."

Hannah peered through a narrow window on the door. The lab was empty. She tried the knob. Locked. "So are we going in or what?"

Kirov glanced at a group of students clustered around another lab entrance down the hall. "Cover me."

Hannah casually stepped between him and the students. Kirov produced a small pick gun, inserted it into the knob, and unlocked it within seconds. They stepped into the lab and closed the door behind them.

Kirov was scanning the room as if trying to memorize every detail. The lab was lined with sinks on all four walls and packed tight with two-person lab stations. At the front of the room, a large lab desk sat atop an elevated teaching platform. Kirov crouched to study the room from a lower level.

"What are you looking for?" Hannah said.

"Opportunities." He looked at the room for a moment longer. "Hmm. No real places to hide. One door. No windows. There are locked storage cabinets here, but there's also a refrigerated archive center at the end of the hall."

Hannah thought for a moment. "We need Lampman to show us where all the samples are."

"I thought you were opposed to the brute-force approach."

"I am, if there's a subtler option."

"And you have one?"

She studied the elevated teaching platform. "Well, if I was Lampman, and I was working on a project that was paying extremely well . . ."

"For a boss who might punish failure with a bullet to the head," Kirov interjected.

Hannah nodded. "I would do anything to protect it, especially if it was endangered somehow. Maybe that's the key. We could—"

"May I help you?"

Hannah was startled by a cold voice from the door.

She and Kirov whirled to see Dr. Simon Lampman standing in the doorway.

Kirov seemed unfazed. "Good morning. We were just admiring your facilities. Much nicer than others we've seen. It's refreshing to see an academic institution that keeps up with the times."

Hannah glanced down to see that Lampman was holding a take-out bag from a sandwich chain. So much for his leisurely lunch. The professor was clearly annoyed. And definitely a bit suspicious. "How did you get in here?"

"The door was open," Kirov said. "I hope you don't mind. We're looking at schools for our daughter, and we don't want to send her anyplace that doesn't have the very best tools."

Lampman pressed the lock button and tried to turn the door-knob. "Strange . . ." He looked up with a frown. "There's something wrong. The lock's okay. You can't be in here."

"Obviously we can." Hannah smiled. "Even if it's by accident. Do you mind if we ask you a few questions about your department's offerings?"

"I'm very busy," Lampman said curtly. "You really should arrange a tour through the admissions department."

Kirov crossed his arms. "Surely you wouldn't mind answering just a few—"

"I'm sorry," Lampman said. "I must ask you to leave."

Hannah slowly nodded. "Very well. You've just made our decision much easier. My daughter is a fine student. She deserves the coopera-tion and respect of her professors."

She and Kirov left the room. They had scarcely entered the corridor when Lampman closed and locked the door behind them. Hannah leaned closer to talk to Kirov when he abruptly placed a hand on her arm. She followed his glance down the corridor.

The young man with the backpack was only five feet away from them, punching a number on his mobile phone.

Kirov bumped into him, knocking the phone out of his hands. "I'm so sorry," Kirov said. "Here, let me—" Kirov stepped back, and the phone cracked under the heel of his shoe. "Oh, no . . ."

The young man bent over and picked it up. "You prick!"

"I'm sorry," Kirov said. "Let me pay you for it."

The kid glared at him, squeezed the shattered phone in his hands, and kept walking.

Kirov was smiling as he and Hannah left the building.

"What was that about?" she asked.

"He wasn't making a call. He was taking our picture with his phone. I didn't want him to have it. He probably overheard some of our conversation with Lampman and was doing it as a precaution. Hopefully, he just thinks we're a couple of parents blundering our way through the campus. Or maybe not." Kirov checked his watch. "Let's head back to the apartment and see what kind of progress Driscoll has made on the stadium. I hope he's done better than we have."

"THIS IS IT." DRISCOLL POINTED to the large flat-screen monitor connected to his laptop. "This is the unit in Gadaire's office."

Kirov, Hannah, and Charlie were gazing at the screen from their canvas folding chairs. The studio apartment now had a much more lived-in look than it had the evening before, with chairs and folding tables set up around the room. The forty-two-inch television monitor was mounted on the wall, next to several large sheets of blueprints for Aviva Stadium.

Driscoll pointed to a chrome refrigeration unit in a Web site photo. "This is the Fenwick 9500." He pushed a button on his laptop keyboard and pulled up a frame from their surveillance of Gadaire's office. "And there, behind his desk, is the same unit."

Kirov stood and approached the screen for a closer look. "Are you sure?"

"Positive. Gadaire's designers added cherrywood panels so it would match the rest of his built-in cabinetry, but that's definitely it. Look at the three-door layout, plus the rows of vents on top and bottom." Driscoll punched the keyboard, alternating the shot from Gadaire's office with the Web site photo.

Kirov nodded. "You're right. That's the same unit. What did you find out about it?"

"It's essentially a refrigerated safe, marketed to clinics and physicians' offices to store narcotics and other controlled substances. If there's an intrusion, it notifies either an on-site alert panel or an alarm-monitoring service of the client's choosing. If someone breaks into Gadaire's unit, I'd wager that it's programmed to notify stadium security, Gadaire himself, and the private security force he has in his employ."

"Not promising," Kirov said. "Especially since the stadium has twenty-four-hour security on patrol just steps away from Gadaire's suite. Do you have a way to bypass the unit's alarm system?"

Driscoll sighed. "Not quite. One slipup and we'll have all hell raining down on us."

Hannah's brows rose. "So that's the report from the world-renowned master thief? It's too hard?"

"I didn't say that, dear lady. I merely mention it to explain why I'm discounting a rather obvious possibility." Driscoll pointed back to the Web site photo. "There's another interesting feature with this unit. If the primary refrigeration unit fails for any reason, a battery backup kicks in. An alert and a diagnostic report is transmitted to the company's local service representative, who is dispatched immediately to repair it."

"Interesting," Kirov said.

Charlie grinned. "Even more interesting if Dad and I are the repairmen."

"I understand." Kirov thought for a moment. "But you know you'll be watched every second you're in there."

"Of course," Driscoll said. "But it won't matter. I'll get you what you want. It's what I do."

"I appreciate your confidence, but I'm a little concerned," Kirov said. "If you're caught by Gadaire or his men, you won't be arrested. You'll be killed in the most unpleasant manner imaginable. He'll torture you both until you tell him everything about why you're there and who you're working for."

"Then if we're caught, you'd better hit the road." Driscoll chuckled. "Because I'm telling him every damned thing he wants to know."

"It won't matter," Kirov said. "He'll still kill you."

"Do you want me to pull this job or not? I have to tell you, my enthusiasm is waning."

"Of course I do. But you need to be aware of the risks."

"You're doing that responsibility thing again that Eugenia was talking about. It's beginning to get boring. I'm always aware and so is my son. Right, Charlie?"

"Bet your arse," Charlie said.

Kirov nodded. "Well, I'll try to restrain myself from now on. I wouldn't want to bore you. How do you propose to make the unit malfunction?"

Driscoll stepped over to one of the large blueprint pages tacked to the wall. He jabbed his finger in the lower left-hand corner. "The stadium power plant is here, down two levels on the north side.

We'll insert a virus into the system that will cause an extreme power surge on the circuit that powers Gadaire's refrigerated locker. I got a computer guy working on it now. We need to damage the refrigeration system without shorting out the entire unit. It's a delicate balance, but we'll figure it out." He turned from the blueprints. "I think we'll try it first at a holistic pharmacy in Donnybrook. They have one of these units, and it's visible behind the front counter. We'll get a telescope, stake out an empty building across the street, and watch the repairman arrive and key in his service code. That should tell us what we need to know."

Kirov nodded. "I'm impressed. I see why everyone says you're one of the best."

"*One* of the best?" Driscoll said, insulted.

"A slip of the tongue. I'm sure you're so talented you'll be able to get me those samples without even a chance of getting yourself killed."

"Not a problem. How did things go at the college?"

"Not so good."

Driscoll chuckled. "You blew it?"

"We didn't get what we needed. We had a few problems," Hannah said. "We'll have to go at it from another direction."

"Need my help?"

Kirov and Hannah exchanged a look. "Actually, I think we can handle it. We'll need to coordinate our efforts. It would be best if we found a time when Gadaire is out of town, and Dr. Lampman is actually at the college."

Driscoll gave him a curious look. "You say you want Lampman there while you raid his lab?"

Kirov nodded. "He has to be. Our plan won't work otherwise."

"And you're worried about *us* getting caught?"

"Gadaire is out of the country at the moment, but he's hosting another reception in his owner's suite this weekend. We need to strike before then."

"Then you'd better get out of here and see if you can come up with something a hell of a lot more productive than your last effort," Driscoll said slyly. "After all, I can't carry the entire show alone."

Citronelle Restaurant
Washington, D.C.

GADAIRE TOOK ANOTHER SIP of wine and cursed under his breath. Nibal Doka was playing head games again, making him wait. The arrogant asshole.

Doka was nothing more than a middleman, and an unnecessary one at that. He was Pakistan's ambassador to the U.S., a position bought and paid for by Doka's well-heeled friends who could count on him to do whatever the hell they wanted.

They were the ones he should be meeting, Gadaire thought. Not this ineffectual idiot. But this is the way they wanted it. If things went south, they would let Doka take the fall.

Even Doka had to realize that was his primary purpose. The idiot probably thought that his benefactors would ride to the rescue, but Gadaire knew their only thought would be to save their own necks. They could always get themselves another puppet.

"Sorry." It was Doka's nasal voice behind him. "I was delayed by an important meeting. Have you been waiting long?"

Only since our agreed-upon time, Gadaire wanted to say. Instead, he turned, and replied, "No. Good to see you."

Doka sat down across from him. "They have an excellent wine list here."

"I'm sure they do. But don't get comfortable."

"Why not?"

"We're not having our conversation here."

Doka tilted his head questioningly.

"This discussion requires the utmost secrecy. Too many people could have known we were meeting here, and I always have to be vigilant for electronic surveillance."

Doka half smiled. "You're being paranoid."

"I assure you that I'm not."

"I'm surprised you don't think I'm wearing a wire."

"If you were, my mobile phone would be vibrating like mad right now." Gadaire smiled. "There's an app for that."

Doka lost a little of his arrogance. "Where do you propose we go?"

Gadaire stood and tossed a twenty onto the table. "Let's take a walk."

Gadaire led Doka out the door and onto the redbrick sidewalks of Georgetown. They walked along M Street, passing the mostly closed boutiques and restaurants.

Doka was clearly annoyed. "You're carrying this too far. I'm a busy man, Mr. Gadaire. Is there a point to this?"

"Your bosses will appreciate it, even if you don't."

"They're not my bosses," he snapped.

Gadaire intended to irritate him, and he was happy that he had succeeded. "Pardon me. Your associates. Your extremely rich and powerful business associates who have been extremely frustrated with your government's current unwillingness to engage India in open conflict. It's very bad for business."

Doka nodded. "Many people share their frustration."

"The attack in Mumbai was evidence enough of that. But your associates wish to do something more. They want to make a statement that will resonate for years. They approached me for my help a couple of years ago, and I finally have something for them."

"A nuclear device?" Doka's pace faltered, and his voice lowered. "Interesting."

"Better."

Doka chuckled, but all humor ebbed from his face when he saw that Gadaire was dead serious. "What exactly are we talking about?"

"Their life blood. India has the world's third largest fishing industry. If that was suddenly taken away from them, their economy would crumble."

"That's what this is about? Fishing?"

"If you dropped an atomic bomb, they would just rebuild. But take away their livelihood, and they would never recover. They can't feed all their people as it is."

Doka stopped in his tracks. "I see. And how would you accomplish this?"

"I've discovered a way of destroying all marine life in hundreds, perhaps even thousands, of square miles of coastal waters. With coordinated attacks, it would be possible to wipe out inland fishing areas as well. And this condition would last years to come, perhaps even decades. It would ruin them. And if your associates made it appear as if the Pakistani government was behind the attack, war would be a certainty."

Doka stared at Gadaire as if he were trying to decipher a foreign language. "This is . . . amazing. You're not one to go in for hyperbole, so I can only assume you're telling me the truth about your ability to execute this?"

"I am. There are just a few last details to sort out."

"And the price tag?"

"Two hundred and fifty million."

"Dollars?"

"Yes."

"They'll never pay it."

"I think they will. Together, the six gentlemen you represent are worth almost two hundred billion dollars. They probably have two hundred and fifty million that has fallen between their couch cushions."

"That's an insane amount of money. How can I possibly go back to them with that?"

"Tell them that's less than what a blockbuster Hollywood movie costs. I'm giving them a bargain. When they consider the alternatives, they'll be smart enough to realize that."

"I'll speak to them tonight." Doka's expression was suddenly eager. "They were most excited to hear what you have for them, and I suspect they'll be even more excited now."

He'd finally broken through the prick's puffed-up vanity to a level where he could trust him to be an enthusiastic messenger of good tidings. Or bad tidings, depending on the point of view. "Good. Tell them I need an answer in forty-eight hours. I'll be waiting for your call." He turned on his heel and strode away.

CHAPTER 10

Dublin, Ireland

KIROV WALKED OUT OF THE small house he had rented for Hannah near St. Steven's Green and lingered on the sidewalk for a moment. He had brought Hannah back here after a day of strategizing with Driscoll, and he felt uneasy leaving her. He'd had no choice. Hannah had practically pushed him out the door. He knew better than to invade her space when she wanted to be alone. Their relationship was too fragile for him to take any chances with it.

"Stop worrying. She'll be fine, Kirov." He looked up to see Eugenia strolling toward him on the narrow sidewalk.

She smiled. "Believe it or not, there are many of us who manage to survive without your personal protection. Hannah knows how to take care of herself."

Kirov nodded. "I can't argue with that."

"Good. It's about time you realized you can never win an argument with me." She took Kirov's arm and pulled him down with her to sit on the house's front steps. "Besides, I'll be here with her. And I've taken every precaution to make sure that no one followed me here when I brought our things from the hotel." Eugenia smiled. "I was most thorough. I did a sweep before I left, and I found GPS tracking pellets injected in the heels of each of her shoes. I dug them out."

"Really?" His eyes narrowed. "What was the make?"

"U.S. government issue all the way. They must have entered her room and planted them while she was out running this morning." Eugenia shook her head. "It's amazing how small those things have gotten. In my days with the KGB, they were the size of a box of matches."

"Efficient as usual." He shot her a cool look. "But I'm still not at all pleased with you."

"For helping Hannah find you?"

He nodded.

She smiled sweetly. "I make people angry almost every day of my life, but they can never stay mad at me. One of the virtues of my winning personality."

"And of your immense modesty."

"Modest? No. Modesty is highly overrated. One should celebrate his or her strengths. And, of course, be honest with oneself about any weaknesses."

"Thanks for the life lesson."

She grinned companionably. "Just one of many that you could benefit from."

"It was dangerous for you to bring her here. Dangerous for her and dangerous for me." He added, "And for you, Eugenia."

"I made my choice. I decided it was worth it to me. She has every right to be here. She has more at stake in this than you do. And when I heard about the way you left without even a word to her, I really didn't give a damn about your safety."

"I had my reasons."

"Stupid reasons. You may have told yourself you were protecting Hannah, but you were really protecting yourself."

"More life lessons, Eugenia?"

"Shut up. All those years you spent avenging your wife's murder . . . You forgot what it was like to have real attachments, real relationships. Maybe because it was safer for you not to."

Kirov looked away. "It was safer for the people in my life. My wife was killed by my enemies to get back at me. I couldn't risk exposing anyone else to that." Not Hannah. Never Hannah. The mere thought sent panic racing through him.

"That's in the past now. And you can pretend to be angry with me, but I noticed the way your eyes lit up when you saw Hannah on the bridge last night."

"I really don't think you could see that from a hundred feet away," he said dryly.

"I could see that from a *thousand* feet away. I'm exceptionally good at reading you, Kirov. I've made a study of it over the years." Eugenia smiled. "Whenever you walk into an unfamiliar area, you're usually scanning the area for possible threats to your person. I did it myself for years even after I left the agency. But when you're with Hannah, she's the one you're watching out for, not yourself. You're always aware of where she is and what's going on around her." Eugenia shrugged. "It's subtle, but I notice it."

"You have a great imagination. Did it ever occur to you that I might feel responsible for her?"

"That boring word again. Yes, it did, but I dismissed it. I prefer my own interpretation. It's much more interesting. Trust me, no one's responsible for Hannah Bryson except Hannah Bryson."

Kirov smiled. "You're right about that."

"She doesn't need your protection, but she deserves your respect. You didn't show her a lot of respect when you left the way you did."

"No. I screwed up."

Eugenia beamed. "See, my life lessons are already working. Be honest with oneself about any weaknesses. Okay, I'm finished with my lecture." Eugenia stood. "Now go. Shoo. Stop loitering in front of my house. Don't you have a couple of heists to pull off?"

"THOSE BASTARDS!"

Eugenia had come into the house and had just begun to unpack when she heard Hannah's exclamation. She came back into the living room. "If you're talking about bastards, you must be referring to Kirov. He's the highest on your list."

"Not at the moment. Unfortunately, there are other bastards out there."

"Who?"

Hannah turned her laptop around to show her. "This is actually classified, but right now I'm so mad I don't give a damn."

Eugenia studied the screen, which was filled by a photograph of a submersible similar to the Conner vessels.

"Why is this classified?" Eugenia said. "Half of America has already seen it on the Discovery Channel."

"No one has seen this. Including me."

Eugenia wrinkled her brow. "Isn't this one of your new Marinth subs?"

"Close, but not quite. It looks like AquaCorp modified my design and built this version for military use." Hannah ran her finger over the top viewport. "These are missile launchers. These holes along the side are gun ports. And who knows what else they've added?"

"You had no knowledge of this?"

"None. I wasn't consulted, and this was never even mentioned as a possibility."

"How can they do that?"

"Oh, they can do it. I was working for AquaCorp when I designed it. They put up the big bucks." Hannah cursed. "AquaCorp's point man, Ebersole, alluded to this the other night. They must need me for something, and they knew I'd be furious when I found out what they had done."

"What do they need you for?"

"I don't know. Ebersole has been trying to reach me since we left. He left this message on my e-mail. I guess he figured the only way he could get a response from me was to show me this."

Eugenia pointed to the laptop. "I hope you didn't access e-mail from here."

"No, I had Kirov stop at a hot spot so that I could retrieve it all without giving away our position." Hannah pulled out her disposable phone. "And now I need to call Ebersole. But if someone is monitoring his phone lines, looking for me, I'd rather be hitting a different cell tower. I'll call from someplace else."

Eugenia grabbed her jacket. "I'll go with you."

She frowned. "I don't need a bodyguard."

"That's not why I'm going." Eugenia picked up Hannah's jacket and tossed it to her. "Dublin is a great city. We need to see more of it."

They caught a cab to the Temple Bar area, a popular neighborhood jam-packed with bars and restaurants. It took only a few minutes to find a pub that did not seem to be overrun with tourists. Eugenia went inside to get a table while Hannah found a quiet area outside to make her telephone call.

Ebersole's assistant put her through immediately.

"A less secure man might think you were avoiding his calls," Ebersole said calmly.

"What in the hell were you thinking?"

"Ah, I see you got the photo."

"Please tell me that was something your art department guys mocked up."

"Nope. It's the real deal. That picture was taken at our machine shop in Norfolk. Where are you, Hannah? Let's discuss this in person."

"Not possible. I can't believe you would modify my design without consulting me."

"It wasn't our call."

"Whose call was it?"

"Who do you think? You saw the photo. Who do you think paid for the modifications?"

Hannah knew. She had known since she had spotted small missile tubes in the place where she had specified a gentle curve of the hull. "The U.S. Navy."

"They wanted their own design team to do the modifications. They said it was a security matter."

"That's ridiculous. I do a lot of work on military projects."

"I know. But they had some specific ideas about what they wanted, and I think they didn't want a fight from you."

"The only reason I would fight them is if I saw they were screwing it up."

"That's what I wanted to talk to you about."

"What a shock."

"The Navy-modified vessels aren't performing up to snuff. They have nowhere near the mobility of the subs you used in Marinth."

"Funny," she said sarcastically. "Isn't mobility usually a requirement for military applications?"

"The Navy doesn't think this is such a laughing matter. We're sitting on a fleet of attack minisubs that—"

Her hand tightened on the phone. "What do you mean 'a fleet'?"

"Seven have been completed. Six more are still under construction, but we've ceased work on them until we can figure out what
needs to be done."

"Seven?" Hannah's voice was shaking with anger. "You screwed
up my design and repeated your mistakes seven times? Are you serious?"

"Hannah, please. Calm down."

"How can I? I can't believe you blundered into this."

"The Navy was in a hurry to get these vessels up and running."

"Why didn't AquaCorp stand up to them? There's a magic word
I use when someone tries to talk me into something I know is not a
good idea. You know what it is? I'll tell you. The word is no."

"It's not that simple."

"Yes, it is. I say it all the time."

"It was a multimillion-dollar contract. We have a responsibility
to our stockholders."

"And I have a responsibility to the bank that holds the mortgage
on my condo. And I have a responsibility to my niece and nephew to
make sure they can go to college. But I still know when to say no."

"It's a mess, Hannah. I'll be the first to admit that. But we need
your help to fix it."

"Unbelievable. Between the Navy's stupidity and AquaCorp's
greed, I don't know who to be more furious with . . ."

"Hannah, please. We need your help."

Hannah took a few deep breaths before continuing. "I'll say this
for your people, they sure earned their security clearances. Not one
of them said a word about this to me."

"They probably didn't want to be anywhere near you when you
found out. I know I didn't."

"So the subs are a complete disaster?"

"Actually, no. They handle fairly well, even with the increased weight from the weapons systems. They're just a bit sluggish on certain types of turns. The Navy engineers have tried to lick it, but they're having problems. We just got approval to bring you into the project."

"Approval from the Navy, not from me."

"Come on, Hannah . . ."

"If the Navy didn't have enough faith to include me from the beginning, I don't see why I should have to clean up their mistakes."

"Do it for AquaCorp, Hannah. We bankrolled the Marinth expedition for you."

"Only because you knew the military project wasn't working out, and you thought you might need me."

"That was a consideration, yes."

"But it's the Navy that's out all those millions on this stupid project, and I'm perfectly happy to let them twist in the wind."

"Wherever you are, Hannah, let me send a private jet for you. We've brought the subs to Las Palmas in the Canary Islands, so they'll be convenient for you. Since the *Copernicus* is still there, I assume you're going to return there. Come and take a look at the subs in action."

"That's just not possible right now."

"When will it be possible?"

"Maybe never."

"Please, Hannah. We'll work with you. Anything you want."

"Even if I wanted to help, which I don't, I'm tied up right now. I'm not available."

"What if I sent you a packet with all the information on the subs and where we're at so far?"

"Go ahead. I can't guarantee I'll look at it."

"I'll have a courier bring it to you."

"No. E-mail it to me."

"It's a fairly extensive packet. Blueprints, reports, videos of the subs in action . . . It will be easier to just send someone out with it."

"Nothing's easier than an e-mail. Scan it all, compress it, and send it to me."

"It's not the most secure method of transit. This is classified, re-member?"

"Then encrypt it. Use the same key we used before the Marinth expedition."

"Hannah, why be difficult about such a simple thing?"

"It's the only chance you have of my even *possibly* helping you. I'd take it if I were you."

Ebersole was cursing under his breath. "If I do this, when will I hear back from you?"

"I can't promise you ever will. But it's your only shot, Ebersole." Hannah cut the connection.

Damn him, damn AquaCorp, damn the U.S. Navy. She shouldn't have called. She knew it would only annoy her, but Ebersole had reeled her in with that photo of her mangled creation.

Eugenia poked her head out of the bar. She studied Hannah's upset expression and slowly nodded. "Hannah, get in here. You have to start drinking. Immediately!"

A HALF HOUR LATER, HANNAH WAS still nursing her first beer while she watched Eugenia down her third beer-and-whiskey-shot combo. A folk trio was performing in the wood-paneled bar, almost completely drowned out by the boisterous local crowd.

"You seriously need to catch up." Eugenia wiped the foam off her upper lip.

"It wouldn't matter," Hannah said. "Alcohol doesn't work on me when I'm angry. I'm lucky that way. Or unlucky, depending how you look at it."

"Definitely unlucky. So what are you going to do about those subs?"

Hannah leaned back in her chair. "Ignore it for now. It's the Navy's problem, not mine. We have to stay focused on what's happening here."

"You're going to help them, Hannah. You know it, and I know it."

"Why do you say that? They betrayed me. They hung me out to dry."

"Ah, but those vessels are still your children. Bastard children, perhaps, but they're still mostly yours. I don't believe you'll turn your back on them."

She scowled as she took another drink. "Well, maybe not. But I'll still make the Navy and AquaCorp sweat a little."

"Good. I approve." She leaned back in the booth. "The decision is made. Now relax and enjoy yourself for a little while before we go back to the house." She studied Hannah. "This episode has given me a new viewpoint on you. I've thought of you as an explorer and inventor. I always knew you were a powerhouse, but it never occurred to me that you could be very important to the military."

"I try not to be. I've worked for them before. Hell, they're an important factor in my profession. But I try to avoid it whenever possible." Her lips tightened. "Because of stupid mistakes like this."

"No idealistic attitude about military use?"

"It's my country. The military protect my country. If they start going down a path I think is wrong, then I'll have to think again." She shook her head. "Though the military have their own bureaucracy that's positively maddening. But it's not as bad as the government red tape."

"Still, you put up with it. You could go anywhere in the world and write your own ticket. I do believe you may be a patriot."

She shrugged. "We make mistakes, but we have a fine, basic structure to correct them. That gives us a better chance than any other country in the world." She paused. "And that's worth fighting for. Yes, I'm a patriot." She glanced at Eugenia. "You live and work in the U.S. You must think we're okay."

Eugenia nodded. "I've always liked your country. It's dynamic. I envy you. Kirov and I really no longer have a country. I wasn't wanted in the country after I left the KGB. He was on the run for so long that when he could return to Russia, there was nothing left there for him."

"Kirov can take care of himself." She smiled at Eugenia. "And I refuse to feel sorry for you. No one is more successful or has a better time than you."

"Oh, yes." She took another sip of beer. "I like my life very much indeed. I'm . . . settled. Kirov, on the other hand, is still searching. Who knows where he will end up?"

"Who knows? I can't imagine anyone more capable of carving out a place for himself wherever he decides to land," Hannah said. "Good luck to him."

"That sounds final."

"I have my own problems. Kirov wants to deal with things in his own way and could step out of the picture at any time. If I can't depend on him being there, I won't let myself become involved. It would be stupid. I don't need him."

"Ah, but do you want him?"

She looked down into the foam on her drink. Did she want him? Charisma, magnetism, the heat she felt when she looked at him.

Oh, yes, there was no question that she wanted Kirov sexually. That didn't mean she would toss wisdom to the winds and take him.

She finished her drink. "Drink your beer, Eugenia. It's time we got back to the house."

AT TEN THE NEXT MORNING, Kirov entered the apartment and was surprised to see Driscoll and Charlie, each wearing a brown uniform, standing in front of a full-length mirror.

Kirov smiled. "You're working for UPS now?"

Driscoll adjusted his right pant leg. "Actually, these are the uniforms worn by the people who service Gadaire's refrigeration unit. A ninety-year-old woman in Dundrum made them for us. She's a wizard at this sort of thing. I showed her a photograph, gave her our sizes, and she turned these around in less than sixteen hours."

"Sounds like Hong Kong service. Another handy person to know," Kirov said.

Driscoll shrugged. "You don't survive in my business without having a large network of talented people in your circle." He flexed his arms. "It's a good fit, and she found just the right material. We could walk through the service center's front doors, and no one would look at us twice."

Charlie struck a variety of poses in front of the mirror. "I have to say, I look damned good. Not all men could pull this off, but I most certainly do." He lifted the collar of his uniform shirt and spoke in a seductive growl. "At your service, Miss Anna. And is there anything else I can help you with?"

"That settles it. I do all the talking," Driscoll said. "You sound like a bad porn film actor."

Charlie laughed. "Aren't they all bad?"

"Not as bad as you just sounded. But you definitely look the part." He motioned toward a set of schematics pinned to the wall. "Now get back to work studying the refrigeration unit."

Charlie made a face. "But we're only *pretending* to be repairmen."

"We'll have to fix the compressor while we're there, remember? We'll practice on one very similar to it."

Charlie shook his head. "More homework . . ."

"That's ninety percent of any job, my boy. Particularly my job. Now get to it."

While Charlie studied the schematic, Driscoll and Kirov stepped out onto the balcony and looked at the Aviva Stadium. It sparkled in the morning sun, reflecting intense rays of light onto several neighboring buildings.

Driscoll reached into his back pocket and produced an envelope. "This came this morning. Thank you."

"What's that?"

"It's my offer letter from Dennison Security. A very generous salary, plus the responsibility for hiring a five-person staff."

"Congratulations."

"You're the one who made it happen, Kirov. I'm grateful."

"It wasn't difficult. The owner and I were in the Russian Navy together."

"Ah. Your connections at work."

"That didn't really matter. He was already aware of you and your reputation. He's thrilled to have you on his staff, keeping his clients from getting robbed by people like—"

"People like me." Driscoll smiled.

"Exactly."

"However it happened, I'm grateful. I can bring my son along and put him on a good path. That's something I couldn't have done in my younger days." Driscoll looked at Charlie through the closed glass door. "His mother was right to keep him from me all these years. I would have just screwed him up."

"I'm sure that's not true."

"It is. I was pretty screwed up myself, so it couldn't have gone any other way." Driscoll looked down. "You know, as you get older, and you see the people near and dear to you pass on, the world can become a much sadder and more unfriendly place. That's why it's been such a joy to suddenly have Charlie in my life. It's not the same as raising him from birth; but in our case, it's probably better."

Kirov smiled. "Then you're both very lucky."

"Do you have children?"

"No."

"Ever think about it?"

Kirov nodded. "I was married once, and my wife and I wanted to have a big family. She had it in her head that she wanted five kids. Not four, not six, but five. She had even started naming them. She wrote prospective names on pieces of paper and put them on the refrigerator. If she got tired of looking at the name after a week or so, it was stricken from the list."

"Interesting system."

Kirov smiled. "Yes, it was a special time." He abruptly turned away. "Well, you have work to do. I'll leave you to it. Congratulations again, Driscoll."

AGENT ELIJAH BAKER ADJUSTED his telephone earpiece and braced himself for another barrage of excuses. The two agents he had brought with him to Ireland had botched the operation at every turn.

"I tested those tracking pellets myself," Agent Bradley said. "They should have worked anywhere in the city."

"So what happened?"

"I don't know. Hawlings and I put them in every pair of shoes that Bryson had with her, and in her coat pockets. They disappeared off our monitors within an hour."

"Yes," Baker said bitterly. "That's when you offered me your 'local interference' theory. You thought it would pass. In the meantime, Hannah Bryson vanished."

"Well, I'm calling to tell you that the tracking pellets reappeared on our monitors just a little while ago."

"All of them?"

"Yes. Every one."

Baker's face brightened. Maybe Bradley and Hawlings weren't such total screwups after all. "Did you reestablish visual contact with Bryson?"

"Not exactly."

Uh-oh. "What does that mean?"

"We followed the signal. It led us to the General Post Office. Specifically, a trash receptacle in front of the building."

"Hannah Bryson's shoes were in the trash?"

"Uh, no. The pellets themselves had been removed and placed into a small gift box. The box was wrapped in decorative paper and labeled to you."

"To me?"

"Yes, sir. 'To Elijah Baker, with love.' We took the liberty of opening it. Inside, the pellets were arranged in the shape of a heart."

Very funny, Kirov. "Any activity on her mobile phone?"

"No, sir. Not since yesterday morning."

"Okay. Stand by, Bradley." Baker cut the connection and cursed under his breath. He should have had Hannah Bryson tailed rather than relying on those damned GPS tracking devices. Shit.

"Tough day at the office?"

"Yes." He turned toward the bed at her question. "We're no closer to finding Kirov than we were yesterday. We're now a bit farther, actually."

Anna Devareau sat up in bed and pulled the covers around her, leaving her shoulders bare. "I told you that you should have let me handle it."

"And how would you have handled it? Kidnap Hannah Bryson and torture her until she tells you what we want to know?"

Anna shrugged. "Much more effective than your approach."

"I think this requires more finesse."

"Your finesse isn't getting you very far right now." She leaned back in bed and smiled sweetly. "Sometimes, my darling, a blunter instrument is required."

CHAPTER
11

HANNAH OPENED THE DOOR OF her rented house to see Kirov standing on the front porch.

"I'm moving things up," he said curtly.

He pushed past her before she could open the door wider for him to enter. "By all means, please come in."

He ignored her sarcasm. "My sources tell me that Gadaire will be back in the country within forty-eight hours. We'll need to execute our plans tomorrow."

Hannah took in a deep breath. "Nothing like a little pressure. Is Driscoll ready?"

"He needs to make sure his contact at the telephone company is prepared, but otherwise he's all set. The man's a pro."

"That's more than I can say for the two of us."

Kirov put a reassuring hand on her arm. "We'll do fine."

Hannah looked up at him, surprised. His voice was gruff, but his smile was almost comforting. It wasn't a side she had often seen in Kirov. "If you say so."

"I do. You look tired. Have you been getting enough sleep?"

"I tossed and turned most of the night, thinking of ways to torture AquaCorp."

He chuckled. "The entire corporation or someone in particular?"

"All of 'em."

"What did they do to deserve the wrath of Hannah?"

She waved her hand. "Long story."

"I see," he said absently. He changed the subject. "Before we finalize our plans, I'm going to need your help."

"That's what I'm here for. What do you need?"

"I need to tap into that amazing memory of yours. We were interrupted before I could take photos in the lab yesterday. I'd like to take another look around . . . through you."

"I thought this might be coming down the pike," Hannah said. Ever since she was a small child, she had possessed a photographic memory that enabled her to recall the tiniest details with only a brief glance. As a second-grader, she convinced her teacher of her powers of X-ray vision by describing the previously glimpsed contents of a purse and desk drawer. As much fun as she'd had with her unique ability as a child, she chose to keep it hidden from the majority of her adult friends and associates. It was too easy for people to ignore her genuine achievements while they were being dazzled by circus stunts. As she had told Melis, she preferred not to deal in mental hijinks. "So you want to see my dog and pony show again."

"It would be a great help."

Hannah sat on the living-room sofa as she motioned for Kirov to join her. "I'll do the best I can."

"I have faith in you," he said quietly. "I've seen you do it before under much more difficult circumstances."

"I remember." The last time she'd had to dredge up memories

had been to recall the details of that horrible night Conner had been murdered. It had been a nightmare. This would be much easier.

Anything would have been much easier.

Don't think about it. Concentrate on the present. "As you know, I can't just pull it up right away. I need to take a minute and put myself back in the time and place."

"We have all the time in the world."

"You just told me that's not true." She leaned back on the sofa and took a deep breath.

Think back. See the sights, smell the smells . . .

They had slipped through the open lab door, leaving behind the voices and shuffling feet in the corridor.

The heavy wooden door squeaked as it swung closed behind them . . .

Pungent odors in the lab. Chemical smells . . . Sulfur?

Their footsteps had echoed on the white-tiled floor. Her shoes had even squeaked a couple of times. And there was a slight buzzing from the fluorescent lights above.

Those lights . . . one of them flickered. It was all the way to the left, third from the front.

And with that one detail, the entire room suddenly came into razor-sharp focus.

She opened her eyes. "Okay. I'm there. What do you need?"

"Heating and air-conditioning vents?" he said quickly.

She smiled. "No rush, it's locked in now. It's not like it will suddenly evaporate." She glanced around at the lab in her mind's eye. "It's funny, but I don't see any. Wait. There they are. Surface-mounted slot diffusers. Long narrow strips low on each of the side walls." Hannah imagined herself turning from the front of the room to the back. "They run the entire length of the room."

Kirov shook his head. "Amazing."

"What else?"

"Do the refrigeration cases have temperature readouts?"

Hannah strained to see the upper right-hand corner of the cases. "Yes. LCD readouts, not illuminated."

"Can you see the temperatures?"

With difficulty, she read the small panels. "Forty-four degrees, forty-four degrees, fifty-one degrees. And that's all I can make out. I can't see the ones on the other side of the room from where we were standing."

"Okay, what about motion sensors? I didn't see any, but we should be sure."

"None that I can see in the front . . ." Hannah imagined herself turning, her eyes skimming past the lab's smooth walls. "And none in the back, either. And no visible alarm panels."

"Good. And each of the desks has a gas spigot for burners, is that correct?"

"Yes. With an L-shaped handle to control it."

"And I assume there's some kind of master switch at the front of the room that enables them all."

Hannah felt her eyes narrowing to see the front of the room. "There's a box mounted on the instructor's table. There's a slot for a small key. That's probably it."

"Excellent."

"Anything else?"

Kirov shook his head. "No, that's all I needed. It's an incredible gift you have, Hannah."

She left the lab and focused her attention back on Kirov. "Not really. It's a trick. It's nothing compared to true intelligence, imagination, and creativity."

"Things you are also blessed with."

She shrugged. "I have to work harder at those things, but the satisfactions are much greater."

"I could see that."

Hannah stood and gestured toward the kitchen. "Would you like some coffee? I think Eugenia bought some terribly strong French roast, and there might be some—"

"I don't want any coffee."

There was a note in his voice that made her stiffen warily. Her gaze flew to his face.

"Ask me what I do want," he said softly.

She didn't need to ask. It was there in his expression, the tension of his body. She hadn't been expecting this. The sexuality had come out of left field. Her chest felt suddenly tight. She could feel the heat scorching her cheeks.

"Ask me," he repeated.

"It's fairly clear. But all I'm offering is coffee."

"Hannah . . ." Kirov took her hand, his thumb gently, sensuously rubbing the palm.

She felt a flash of heat travel from her palm to the sensitive flesh of her wrist. "Don't *do* that."

"No?" He stood up and stepped close to her. "It's time. We both want it."

"I don't do everything I want. I have a mind and will."

"A beautiful mind," he murmured. He moved slowly closer, his hand sliding around to the back of her neck. He kissed her. "A magnificent will." He kissed her again. "It was the first thing about you that I noticed and admired." His thumb was rubbing the nape of her neck, and she felt a jolt of sensation with every movement. "But since then, I've come to appreciate many other things." His tongue licked gently at her lower lip. "You have wonderful shoulders. Your breasts are incredible." His hands slid down to cup her hips. "It's a turn-on just watching you walk . . . Free, bold, no compromise . . ."

She was on fire. She couldn't breathe. "You're trying to seduce me."

"Now that was an obvious statement not worthy of you. Yes. I most certainly am." His big hands were opening and closing on her buttocks. "I pray I'm succeeding. Am I?"

This wasn't smart. Why couldn't she move away from him?

Then she did move, but it was toward him. Her lower body arching into him.

He inhaled sharply, and his fingers dug into her hips, jerking her closer, rotating them against him. "What a wonderful answer. Do you like this?"

She bit her lower lip to smother a cry. "Dammit, of course I like it." She was almost panting. "It's sex. That doesn't mean I—"

"Shh." He kissed her again. "Do you recall I said something to you once. *Pomni, ya vsegda ryadom.*"

"'Remember, I'll always be with you'?" she said shakily. "Funny thing to say to a woman just before bailing on her."

"The irony has not been lost on me. Of course, I thought I was going to die at the time. I was speaking in terms of emotions and memory."

"Thanks for coming back to clarify." Dear God, her entire body was readying.

"Allow me to be more literal this time." He kissed her again. "I mean it, Hannah."

"So I should jump into bed with you?"

"It would be my most earnest desire." His hand moved to caress her breasts. "I'll make it your most earnest desire too. I promise, Hannah."

Her breasts were swelling beneath his touch, the muscles of her stomach clenching. Her cheeks were burning with heat. She could feel her resistance eroding. Why was she even trying? This was what she wanted. *He* was what she wanted.

"Eugenia told me she won't be back until this afternoon," Kirov whispered. "Where's your bedroom?"

"Why did Eugenia—" She stiffened as a thought stabbed through the hot haze Kirov had wrapped around her. "But I know why she'd tell you." She stepped back and pushed him away. "Eugenia is your buddy. She wants you to have everything you want in life. She told me when I asked her to help find you that you were the important one in the equation. So when you decide you want a roll in the sack with me, naturally she'd find a way to help make it happen."

"You're not being reasonable. No one was plotting. Perhaps she did want to give me the opportunity. It wouldn't surprise me." He frowned impatiently. "But what difference does it make what Eugenia wants? It's what we want."

"It matters because I don't want to be manipulated by her or you. You're both masters of the game, but not with me, Kirov. I'm not having it."

"Then you'll cheat both of us. Why aren't you having it? You wanted it, dammit."

"Yes, I did." God help her, she still did. She was shaking just looking at him. "But you were seducing me, Kirov. You admitted it. And I was letting you do it. Everything that's still hurting and unresolved between us, and you made it go away." She jerkily shook her head. "When I go to bed with a man, it will be my will, my decision, and not because I'm 'seduced' against my better judgment. I'm not that weak." Yet she had been within a hair of tossing that damn judgment out the window. "You come in here mumbling romantic Russian phrases and telling me that I mean something to you. Well, I'm not listening."

"That's quite clear," Kirov said. "And since that's the case, I'd better take my leave. I'm not . . . myself at the moment." He turned and strode toward the door. "Which means I'm tempted to drag you down to the floor and make you listen in the most basic way possible. But I'm a civilized man." He whirled to face her as he reached the door. His face was flushed and his eyes blazing. He didn't look civilized. He was radiating pure male lust. She had never seen him like that before. "And as a civilized man, I'll let you have your space and go my way. It's still going to happen, but you've chosen to put both of us through hell until it does. If you want me, call me. I promise I won't try to seduce you. I'll let you seduce me. I've no qualms about sexual persuasion. I'd enjoy it." He opened the door. "I'll see you tomorrow, Hannah."

She stared at the door as it closed behind him. Was she an idiot? Lord, she had wanted to go to bed with him. Her body was still swollen, aching. She wanted to run after him and tell him that . . .

Pride and self-will were all very well, but neither was going to keep her from being in a fever whenever she looked at him from now on.

She was not an idiot. Whatever relationship she might have with Kirov, it couldn't begin without absolute honesty and knowing exactly where she intended to go. She had to be true to herself.

Dammit.

Bergerac, France

GADAIRE DROVE DOWN THE GRAVEL road that would take him to the long-abandoned vineyard that had belonged to his grandfather. By all accounts, the wine produced there had always been

mediocre at best, but his grandfather had been savvy enough to
"incentivize"—bribe—the local tour guides to steer their groups of
palate-challenged tourists to the main house for tastings. There the
gregarious and bosomy servingwomen would seal the deal by taking
orders for scores of cases each day. After his grandfather's death,
however, no one had picked up the torch, and the vineyard had become an overgrown eyesore.

But now, after all these years, it was serving some purpose again.

Gadaire followed the road around to the rear of the main house.
He parked next to the small trailer that housed a roaring power generator. He climbed out of his car and entered the building through
a cracked and peeling door.

Dr. Timothy Hollis called out from across the large concrete-
floored storage room. "Mr. Gadaire, good to meet you."

Hollis was a thin man with shoulder-length black hair. With
loosened tie, rolled-up sleeves, and sweat-stained shirt, he had obviously been working inside for quite a while. Gadaire wondered what
his associates at the Louvre would think if they saw their respected
curator now.

Gadaire shook his hand. "Sorry I'm not Anna. I know you're
disappointed. She was tied up with business out of the country. And
I trust that the rather spartan work environment hasn't been too
much of an impediment."

"It's been very peaceful. And believe me, I can understand the
need for privacy. I'm honored to be given the opportunity to work
with such a valuable find."

"Even one you can never talk about?"

Hollis quickly ran his hands through his perspiration-soaked hair.
"My findings from this trellis have given us many answers we've been
looking for. With those answers in mind, I can go out and find other

evidence that supports them. I won't need the trellis once I've done that."

Gadaire nodded. "It could put you years ahead of Melis Nemid or any other researcher."

"Which means more grants and more resources to continue my work. Trust me, it's very difficult to get Marinth research funding if your name isn't Melis Nemid. This project may be a secret, but it's still an amazing opportunity for me."

"Good. I'm anxious to see your findings."

"You won't be disappointed." Hollis motioned for Gadaire to follow him to the other side of the large room. "Let me show you what I've been doing here."

They walked toward the other end of what was once the winery's main tasting area. Gadaire looked at several shallow trays, each filled with a different-colored liquid. Next to each were small molded pieces in the same hue.

"What's this?"

"The trellis is missing dozens of pieces of jewels, quartz, and colored glass. It was quite a job to reconstruct it. In some instances, there are enough remaining fragments for me to know exactly what color to replace the missing pieces with. In other cases, I had to look for interactions in the surrounding stone framework."

"Are the colors really that important?"

"Yes. Some figures in the Marinthian language can have a drastically different meaning depending on the color they are written in, so color is crucial."

Gadaire glanced at the trays on the floor. "So you used these to fabricate replacement pieces?"

"Yes, out of polyurethane. I've come up with an extremely accurate re-creation."

"So where is it?"

Hollis smiled. "It was made to be viewed outdoors, with the sun shining through it. I thought you should see the full effect."

Hollis motioned toward the crumbling double doors that led toward an enclosed patio where tasters had once enjoyed their wine outside. As Gadaire followed him, he saw that the trellis was now suspended between a pair of six-foot platforms. The multicolored panels were now brightly illuminated by the afternoon sun, taking on a breathtaking glow.

"Incredible, isn't it?" Hollis looked at Gadaire, then the trellis. "This is exactly how it looked during the final days of Marinth."

"Stunning," Gadaire said. He looked down at the white-tiled patio and caught his breath. "But nothing like that. Oh, my God."

Gadaire was staring at the colorful mosaic that the sun and trellis had projected onto the patio. The razor-sharp image and vibrant colors literally left him speechless. He shook his head in amazement.

Hollis pointed to the projected image. "These were all over Marinth, but this one was special. It was the work of an educator, a scientist, who discovered too late what caused Marinth's downfall."

"But were there specifics?"

Hollis smiled and knelt beside the projected image. "Right here." He ran his hands over a small, narrow, green and yellow symbol in one corner of the image. "This is one of my reconstructed pieces which turned out to be the most important part."

"What does it mean?"

Hollis handed Gadaire a sheaf of papers. "My final report. It's all there. I've included high-resolution photographs of the projected image, along with my symbol-by-symbol translation of the message. Melis Nemid herself couldn't have done a better job for you."

Gadaire quickly shuffled through the papers, paying particular attention to the last two pages. He looked up with a start. "You're absolutely positive about this?"

"No doubt. It's exactly what you were looking for, isn't it?"

Gadaire let his hands fall to his sides. "This is better than I even dared to dream."

"I thought you would be pleased."

Gadaire smiled. "You thought correctly. You deserve a handsome bonus, Dr. Hollis."

"I wouldn't refuse one if offered." He grinned. "Though I would enjoy it much more if it was delivered by the lovely Anna."

"She is lovely, isn't she? And so interested in you. You wouldn't believe how much in depth we discussed your successful completion of the project."

Hollis's face lit. "Really? What did she say?"

"I've no time to tell you everything." Gadaire reached into his jacket. "But believe me, she would have loved to deliver this herself."

He pulled out a semiautomatic handgun and fired four times into Hollis's chest.

Aviva Stadium

Dublin, Ireland

DRISCOLL AND CHARLIE SAT inside their van two blocks from the stadium. A game was under way, and the cloudy night sky was ablaze with the arena lights.

Driscoll chuckled as Charlie unfolded the refrigeration unit schematic. "If you don't have it down cold by now, we're in trouble."

"Cold? Is that a pun? I have it, don't you worry. Just a refresher. I just hope your friend was able to upload that virus to the stadium power system."

"He said it was taken care of last night, and I believe him. He's never let me down before."

"There's always a first time."

"You're right about that, son. But if you surround yourself with good people, you increase your odds. I'm more worried about my telephone guy. All automated maintenance alert calls to the service center are supposed to be intercepted and routed to me here. If it doesn't work, we could find ourselves bumping into the *real* service team. That could be awkward."

"I have a question." Charlie glanced up from the schematics. "Why on earth did you make this your career? I figure most thieves do it because they're lazy. But this is harder than any work I've done in my life."

Driscoll smiled. "I didn't do it because it was easy. You're right, it's hard work. And if you don't do it right, you'll spend years of your life in prison."

"Then why do it?"

Driscoll looked out the windshield for a long moment. "When you grow up in Bray like I did, people have a habit of looking down their nose at you. Shop owners, bankers, pretty much everyone. I think in the beginning, it made me feel smarter than them. However much they tried, they couldn't stop me from taking whatever I wanted. Makes you feel kind of powerful, you know?"

Charlie nodded. "Yeah."

"But you're not. It's fun, and you get a bit of a thrill. But in the end, you're just a parasite, leaching off someone else's accomplishments. Once you realize that, it's a hell of a lot less fun."

"But you did it for a long time."

Driscoll shrugged. "I was good at it. Doesn't mean I always liked it." He patted Charlie's arm. "This security job we have lined up, though, that's my idea of fun. Good money, and we'll be helping to catch the parasites."

"You won't feel like a rat turning on your own kind?"

"My own kind? Most of 'em are dirtbags, and don't you forget it. It's all part of the game, my boy. The smarter we are, the smarter they'll have to be. And I have a secret for you, most of 'em aren't very smart."

Driscoll's mobile phone rang, and he checked the caller ID tag. "This is it. Gadaire's refrigeration system is reporting a malfunction." He smiled at Charlie. "We're on."

Driscoll started the van and drove around to the stadium's security entrance. He pulled up to the guard booth and spoke to the uniformed guard. "Safe It Systems. We're here for an emergency repair on a refrigeration unit in one of the owners' suites. Security knows we're coming."

The young man in the booth picked up a phone and talked to someone for a few seconds. He started filling out a drive-on pass even before he hung up the phone.

He reached in and placed the pass on the dashboard in front of Driscoll. "Okay, go up the ramp, turn right, and drive until you see the signs for service and catering parking. Go to level three, suite four. Security will be waiting there to let you into the suite."

"Thanks."

They followed his directions, parked, and unloaded the van. They each carried large toolboxes, and Charlie pulled a small trunk on wheels behind him.

"So far, so good," Charlie whispered, as they walked up the main concourse.

"We're not done yet." Driscoll glanced around as the crowd cheered a goal. "Keep your wits about you."

They approached the entrance to Gadaire's suite just as a blue-blazered security officer arrived. "We would appreciate it if you could make this fast," the officer said. "Mr. Gadaire doesn't like anyone to have access to his suite when he's not here."

"Won't be a problem," Driscoll said. "His refrigeration unit sent us a diagnostic report, so we know exactly what needs to be done."

They entered the dark suite, and the guard flipped the light switch. No lights. "I heard we had a power surge here," the guard said. "I hope that won't mess things up for you."

Driscoll shook his head. "It shouldn't. The unit has a twenty-four-hour battery backup." He gestured toward Gadaire's office. "I believe it's back there. We'll get started."

"I'll need to stay with you."

"Of course. Care to lead the way?"

Driscoll glanced over and saw that his son was sweating buckets. Not unusual for a rookie, but it wasn't good for the casual image they had to project. Driscoll tugged at the large blue bandanna protruding from Charlie's pocket and pointed to his forehead. As they walked with the guard to Gadaire's office, Charlie pulled out the bandanna and tied it around his head.

"Ah, a customized model," Driscoll said upon seeing the unit. "Beautiful woodwork. The factory only makes these with stainless or glass doors." Driscoll looked at the keypad below the door handle. The moment of truth.

"Do you have the combination?" the guard asked.

"When there's a malfunction, my service code will open it."

Charlie shot him a nervous glance.

Cool it, lad. Remember your poker face.

Driscoll punched the six-digit service code he had seen at the holistic medicine practice.

The keypad didn't respond.

He held his breath. Cripes. His worst fear come true. How in the hell were they going to—

The lock clicked, and the small display read OPEN.

Success!

They were in.

ANNA DEVAREAU DOWNSHIFTED her orange Lamborghini Gallardo Spyder, letting the slack-jawed businessman in the next lane get a good long look. Her car always made the guys look, but she knew that *she* was the reason why they couldn't look away.

She flashed him a smile. Could she make this horn-dog crash into the tanker truck ahead of him? It was a game she had often played in her teens and early twenties, but perhaps now it was time to see if she still had the magic.

Her phone beeped, and she turned from the salivating businessman. Oh, well. Of course she still had the magic.

She touched her earpiece. "Anna Devareau."

"Miss Devareau, this is Charles Ames, Security."

"Of course, Charles, I recognize your voice." Keep it soft and intimate. Ames had done her many favors. "Is everything all right?"

"Yes, nothing to worry about. We were told to inform you of any unusual occurrences since Mr. Gadaire is out of the country. We just got a call from the Aviva Stadium security chief. The refrigerated cabinet in Mr. Gadaire's office went on the fritz, and he wanted to let us know that the service technicians are already there working on it."

Merde. "How did it happen?"

"Some kind of power surge. It's no big deal. The situation is under control."

She shook her head. The idiot probably thought Vincent was just using it to chill his wines collection. Of course he thought it was no big deal.

"Get your ass over there now," she said harshly, forgetting all about soft and intimate. "Take a couple of your men with you."

"Excuse me?"

"Make sure the contents of that cabinet are protected."

"Stadium security is taking care of it. But if you'd like, I can—"

"Stop wasting time. Get over there now." Anna cut the connection. Dammit.

Calm down, she told herself. It was probably just like he said, no big deal. But still . . .

She gunned the engine and sped toward the Aviva Stadium.

Trinity College
Dublin, Ireland
8:40 P.M.

KIROV AND HANNAH STOOD in the shadows of a tall elm tree, watching as an occasional student walked across the dark campus. Hannah patted the pockets of her bulky jacket.

"That's the fourth time you've checked your pockets," Kirov said. "You're not nervous, are you?"

"I sure as hell am. I don't like walking around with this stuff on me."

"Just another couple minutes. As soon as we get Driscoll's text message."

Hannah watched Kirov as he angled his watch into the illumination of a streetlight. He was as cool as usual, and his attitude toward her was almost impersonal. She had not known how he would respond to her after that turbulent meeting. But Kirov was the same man she had come to know; confident, authoritative, in command of the situation. She wasn't quite as cool as he appeared to be and tried to mask it. It wasn't like her. Yet she kept remembering his face, the sexuality . . . Yes, the seduction of the senses.

Forget it. Clear your mind of everything but the job at hand as Kirov was doing.

Kirov's phone buzzed. He glanced at the small screen and smiled. "Driscoll's in."

Hannah breathed a sigh of relief. "Hallelujah. Let's move."

"Good luck."

"You too."

Kirov sprinted away, and Hannah moved quickly toward the botany building. Adrenaline surged through her, and the sensation was so strong and intense it felt almost alien, as if she had momentarily inhabited someone else's body.

Get a grip. Focus.

She stepped off the sidewalk and ran around to the back of the botany building, toward an entrance that opened into a corridor of faculty offices. The entrance was locked at night, but Kirov had earlier slipped a piece of metallic tape over the doorframe's strike plate.

Here's hoping it was still there.

She pulled the door, and, to her relief, it swung open easily. She slid inside and bolted up the stairwell. Three flights later, she pushed open the door and stepped out onto the roof, where the large HVAC units roared.

She unfastened her jacket, pulled out two heavy plastic bags of liquid, and gently rested them on the roof. She tugged at her jacket's lining, where she had taped a disposable aluminum cake pan. She pulled out the flattened pan and unfolded it to its original rectangular shape.

She unscrewed the caps on the plastic bags and poured their contents into the pan. Before she had even finished emptying the bags, smoke rose from the mixture.

Hannah smiled. If only Dad was around to see this. It was a home-brewed version of the liquid smoke that model-train hobbyists used in their locomotive engines. The familiar odor brought back a rush of memories of her father, his massive train collection, and the hundreds of feet of track that snaked throughout her childhood home.

The real fun would come when her concoction hit the building's heated vents.

Hannah lifted the pan and emptied the liquid into the building's air-intake unit.

Aviva Stadium

Dublin, Ireland

THE STADIUM SECURITY officer grabbed Charlie's arm. "What are you doing?"

Charlie held up the white lab trays he had pulled from Gadaire's refrigeration unit. "I need to move everything to this portable air-cooled locker."

"Is that really necessary?"

"The owner of this unit would probably say so," Driscoll said. "He must have had a reason for keeping this stuff cool, whatever it is. We need to keep the door open to make our repairs. But I can leave it out if you'd like to take responsibility."

The guard shook his head. "No, it's okay. Put it in."

Charlie placed the sample trays in their rolling locker, then cleared the refrigeration unit of several bottles of medicine and two champagne bottles. He closed the rolling case's lid.

Driscoll opened his toolbox and smiled at the guard. "This won't take long."

CHAPTER
12

KIROV CHECKED HIS WATCH AND glanced up the sidewalk. Dr. Lampman would be walking past at any moment, fresh from his evening lecture course. But if Hannah hadn't completed her mission, he would continue right past the botany building and make his way to the faculty parking lot.

Exactly what they did not want to happen.

Kirov squinted at the building. Was that . . . ?

Smoke.

A little bit at first, then much more, clearly visible in the rooms with lights on. It spilled out of several open windows on the second and third floors.

The building's fire alarm sounded, and flashing red lights whirled inside, playing against the ever-thickening smoke.

Good girl, Hannah.

Kirov glanced back toward the sidewalk. Several students had stopped, and behind them, he recognized the awkward gait of Dr. Simon Lampman. Right on schedule.

The professor stared in horror at the building. He cursed aloud and ran toward the downstairs lab entrance.

Kirov was just a few yards behind.

Lampman fumbled with his keys, unlocked the door, and threw it open. Kirov caught it before it closed and watched as the man ran down the smoky, dimly lit corridor. Lampman charged into his lab. Kirov moved forward to see him open a cabinet, pull out a large leather case, and dump hundreds of papers on the floor. Lampman then unlocked two refrigeration units and carefully pulled out several trays, which he then stacked in the case.

The smoke grew thicker, and the alarms seemed even more piercing than before. Lampman was coughing, and Kirov felt his own eyes water. As nostalgic as Hannah had been for the odor of her liquid-smoke concoction, it only reminded Kirov of the putrid odor given off by the diesel backup generator of his old submarine.

He crouched into an alcove as Lampman carried the leather case toward another set of refrigerated lockers at the end of the corridor. On his way he stopped to open a drawer near the lockers and stuff two DVDs and a folder in the case. He unlocked the refrigerated lockers and transferred a series of translucent round containers into the case. With the case still open, Lampman paused. He glanced between the lab and the refrigerated locker in front of him, almost as if making a mental checklist. He nodded to himself, closed the case, and ran back toward the entrance.

Kirov stood up to intercept him, but he felt a sharp jab in the middle of his back.

"Careful, now."

Kirov turned. It was the long-haired kid with the book bag. He looked older close-up, and certainly more menacing. Especially with the semiautomatic in his hand.

Lampman froze. "What's happening?"

The kid did not take his eyes from Kirov. "Nothing to worry about, Doctor. Mr. Gadaire sent me to protect you."

"Protect me?"

"From people like this."

The kid glanced at the leather case. "Do you have what you need?"

Lampman nodded.

"Good. We're leaving. All three of us."

Aviva Stadium

Dublin, Ireland

DRISCOLL SHOWED THE GUARD his digital thermometer. "Forty-two degrees. Perfect as perfect can be."

"Good." The guard motioned toward the wheeled case. "Now get everything loaded back in. I need to lock this place up."

Charlie opened the lid of their rolling case and quickly pulled out the items he had placed inside. He and Driscoll moved the objects back inside the refrigeration unit.

"That's everything?" The guard looked into the empty case. He then nodded toward the refrigeration unit. "Okay. Seal it up."

Driscoll closed the door and once again keyed in the service code to lock the unit. He picked up the toolboxes while Charlie grabbed the handle of their wheeled case.

"That does it." Driscoll gave the guard a minisalute. "Thanks for your time."

He and Charlie walked out of the suite and made their way down the concourse. Charlie moved quickly, several paces ahead.

"Slow down," Driscoll said. When Charlie drew closer, he whispered, "Not too quickly. Don't want to look like we're in a hurry."

They took the elevator down to the parking garage, loaded up the van, and climbed inside the back. Driscoll opened the rolling case, then pushed the diagonal corners of the bottom panel until it sprang open. He removed the false bottom and examined the samples. "Well done. I didn't even see you drop this down."

Charlie smiled. "That was the idea, wasn't it?"

They climbed up front, started the van, and pulled away.

KIROV FELT THE GUN BARREL pressed firmly against the base of his spine as he continued down the smoky corridor. He glanced back at the kid. "How do you think you're going to pull this off? The fire department will be here any second, and I'm sure campus police are outside."

"You're right," the kid said. "I should just kill you."

Lampman looked as if he was having a panic attack. "I can't be mixed up in this."

"Too late," Kirov said. "Do have any idea how many men have already died for those samples you're holding?"

"You're about to be one of them," the kid said.

Move.

Kirov ducked and whirled around. Before the kid could reposition the gun, Kirov pounded the kid's hand against the wall and pierced his wrist with a small needle. Seconds later the kid dropped the gun and fell to his knees. Two seconds after that, he was out cold.

Lampman backed away. "What in the holy hell . . . ?"

Kirov raised the needle. "This was meant for you. I'll take that case now."

Lampman clutched it close to his chest.

Kirov picked up the gun and put it in his waistband. "Now, please. I don't want to have to use this gun, but I will."

While Lampman thought about it, Kirov reached out and wrenched the case away from him.

Lampman made a sound of protest. "You can't—"

"Tell the police whatever you like. But the truth won't look good for you, and Gadaire's not going to like police involvement. And if it's your reputation you're worried about, give that some thought too."

Kirov ran down the hallway and disappeared in a plume of smoke. He extended his hands in front of him. Where in the hell was that back door?

Wait. That sound. The familiar purring of an engine outside. Ahead and slightly to the right.

Using the engine sound as his guide, Kirov moved down the smoky corridor.

How much farther could it be?

Then, finally, he saw an intense light from outside, shining through the glass doors and cutting through the smoke.

Kirov pushed the doors open and stood in the illumination of a motorcycle's headlight beam. The motorcycle's rider roared toward him and skidded to a stop.

Hannah flipped up her helmet's windscreen. "What are you waiting for? Climb on!"

Kirov jumped on the back of the motorcycle. As fire-engine sirens wailed in the distance, Hannah gunned the motorcycle's engine and roared away from the campus and onto Pearse Street.

Aviva Stadium
Dublin, Ireland

ANNA STOOD IN GADAIRE'S OFFICE, her hands clenched as she stared into the refrigeration unit. "They're gone!" She struck the adjacent cabinetry with the heel of her hand. She turned toward Carl Dyson, the arena's director of security. "We're missing some valuable items here. Where are those repairmen?"

"They just left," another security officer said as he entered the room. "But I was with them the entire time. They didn't take anything."

"Idiot!" she said through her teeth. "How long have they been gone?"

He shrugged. "Minutes."

She darted toward the exit. "Get back to your control room and pull up your surveillance video. I want a make, model, and license-plate number of the vehicle they were driving right now."

Dyson stammered, "That isn't possible. It will take time."

"It's possible if you want to keep your job. I want it before I get to my car." She stopped in the doorway and turned around. "And before I leave the parking lot, you'll also tell me what direction they were heading."

"WEST ON LANDSDOWNE ROAD," the stadium security chief said in Anna's earpiece as she roared out of the parking garage. "And we're positive it was a Mitsubishi Delica L400 van, navy blue or black."

"Still no license plate?"

"No, we just looked at the guard gate camera feed, and there was mud spattered on it. We have a partial . . . It begins with the letters K and L."

"Got it."

"And we called the service company for that refrigeration unit, and they had no idea that it was in need of repair. They say it wasn't their guys. We're about to call the police."

"No police."

Silence. "Did I just hear you correctly?"

"I said no police. Mr. Gadaire would not want the attention."

"A crime was committed on stadium property. I don't have any choice but to—"

"The crime was committed against Mr. Gadaire and Mr. Gadaire alone. I'm telling you, no police. We'll take care of it."

"I'll have to discuss this with the general manager."

"Discuss all you want, but Mr. Gadaire will be extremely unhappy if his wishes aren't followed. Call back when you have more information."

She waited for the security chief to hang up before speaking to the other party on the conference call. "Did you get that, Ames?"

The security chief cleared his throat. "Yes. But we really might want to consider bringing the police into this."

"I'm not going through this with you, too. No police. That's what we pay you for. Where are you now?"

"Haddington Road, close to the stadium."

"Okay, you stay on that road and go to the ferry terminal. They may be heading to Liverpool."

"What about you?"

"I'll go to the Beach Road and drive south. They'll want to get as far away from here as quickly as they can."

"It might help us to know what they took, Ms. Devareau. What are we trying to recover?"

"White sample trays, probably in some kind of cooler."

"What are we dealing with here? Is it safe for us to handle?"

Considering the dangerous materials that were Gadaire's stock-in-trade, it was a legitimate question.

"Yes, Ames. Just get it back. Stay in touch."

Anna ended the call and peered through the windshield.

Although the thieves had several minutes' head start, she could make up the time.

Traffic lights optional.

Anna punched the accelerator.

Beach Road
Dublin, Ireland

DRISCOLL DROVE DOWN THE DARK road and checked the rearview mirror. All clear. So far, so good.

He glanced over at his son, whose face was bathed in the pale blue dashboard lights. "We did it. We deliver the goods, and we're on our way to the good life. Are you sad about leaving here?"

"No. I need a new start."

"That's exactly what we'll get. My offer letter says we'll be based in Sydney for eighteen months, and after that we'll have a choice. You can even come back to Ireland if you want."

"My mum's here, and my friends are here. But I don't know. I've never even been anywhere else other than here, England, and Scotland. I've always wanted to see a bit of the world, and I figure this is my chance."

"That it is. And nothing will make me happier than to show it to you. But you know, as many wonderful things as I've seen all over the world, something always drew me back to Ireland. Even when it was very risky for me to be here."

"Home?"

He nodded. "I've tried my best to develop a sophisticated façade, but I'm just a sentimental Irishman at heart. You may feel the same way about returning here as I do."

"I might." He looked at his father. "And there's a girl."

Driscoll chuckled. "There usually is. Why didn't you tell me about her?"

"She left me. She didn't think I had enough ambition. That was about the time I decided to look you up. Damn, I was glad to see you."

"Despite all the awful things your mother probably said about me."

"They weren't all awful." Charlie smiled. "But I'd like to come back here a big success. Maybe she'll think of me differently then."

"You never know, son. In any case, maybe you'll think differently of you. That's more important." Driscoll glanced at the rearview mirror. "Someone's tearing up the road behind us."

Charlie turned to look. "Police?"

"Nah, too low to the ground. A sporty Italian number. We'll let 'em pass."

The car sped up and roared alongside them for a moment.

Even in the darkness Driscoll could see the electric orange paint job and sleek, distinctive lines of a Lamborghini sports car.

"Wouldn't mind coming back here driving one of those," Charlie murmured.

Driscoll's brow furrowed. "I don't like this."

The Lamborghini roared ahead of them, then behind, like a panther positioning itself over its prey.

Driscoll cut the wheel hard right and turned off on a side road. Before they had even completed the maneuver, however, the Lamborghini spun around in a perfect 180 and charged after them.

Driscoll's hands tightened on the steering wheel. "She has speed on her side, but we have bulk."

"She?"

"I caught a glimpse back there. I think it's Gadaire's woman." His lip curled. "Your beloved Anna."

The Lamborghini whipped right and left, as if looking for

another opening to move alongside. Driscoll matched the sports car move for move, keeping it behind him.

For the moment.

Charlie reached under his seat and fumbled for something.

"What are you doing?" Driscoll asked.

"I brought some insurance." Charlie pulled out a rolled-up towel and unfolded it to reveal his revolver. "No one's gonna stop us."

"Put that thing away. I don't use guns."

The Lamborghini roared past them.

"Shit!" Driscoll pounded the steering wheel in frustration.

"Don't let her block our way. We need to get back to the Rock Road."

Driscoll glanced over at him. "Put the gun away. Right now I need you to—"

He gasped. With a squeal of tires, the Lamborghini had spun around in another perfectly executed 180 and faced them with blinding headlights. The car peeled out and hurtled straight toward them.

"She's crazy," Charlie said.

"Or she knows she has better airbags than we do."

Charlie lowered his window and took aim at the advancing sports car. He fired once, twice, then repeatedly, but none of the bullets appeared to find their mark.

Driscoll gripped the wheel harder. "Either you're a rotten shot, or she's got some wicked bulletproof glass."

Charlie was cursing as he jabbed his arm out the window and fired again. Still the Lamborghini raced toward them.

At the last minute, Driscoll cut the wheel to the left.

"That boulder!" Charlie shouted.

The van clipped the boulder and rolled down a steep embankment before coming to rest on its side in a ravine.

Charlie tried to pull himself up. "Dad . . . Dad!"

Driscoll felt the cold wetness in his nose and mouth. Blood.

"Charlie . . . Get away from here."

"I'm not leaving you."

Driscoll tried to shift in his seat. "I can't move."

"Then I'll carry you."

"Don't be stupid."

The Lamborghini's headlights appeared over the embankment above them.

"Get away from here. Now."

"The samples!" Charlie turned back toward the rear compartment, but the wheeled refrigeration case was upside down behind Driscoll.

"No time, son. Get to Kirov, tell him what happened. Do you still have your gun?"

"No, I—" Charlie looked up at the road above. "I lost it when we went over the embankment."

"It's okay. Run, Charlie. It will be doubly hard if you make me worry about you, too. Go!"

"No."

"Then go find the gun. We can't do anything without a weapon."

"I should have held on to it." Charlie climbed out of his still-open window and turned back, his face twisted in agony. "Dad . . ."

"It's going to be all right. She's a woman. They have no use for violence. I'll tell her a pack of lies, and she'll go away. I've never asked much of you, but I want you to obey me now." He said softly, "I'm proud of you, Charlie. Now go."

Charlie backed away and bolted into the brush.

Driscoll looked up at the Lamborghini's headlights, twin spears cutting through a light mist. As he watched, Anna Devareau stepped in front of them and made her way gracefully down the embankment.

She crouched next to the upside-down van. "Who are you working for?"

"Only myself."

"You're lying." She walked around to Driscoll's side and shattered the already-splintered window with one fierce kick. Fragments of glass stuck to his already-bleeding face. She knelt next to him, a smile on her beautiful face. "Who hired you?"

"No one."

She reached inside and pressed her thumbs to his throat. "I'm crushing your larynx, old man. But I'll give you one more chance. When I let you go, you'll give me a name. Then I'll take my property and go away. Do you understand me?"

He couldn't breathe; more blood ran from his nostrils.

Anna released her thumbs. "The name."

Driscoll spat in her face.

Anna smiled, making no attempt to wipe away the bloody saliva dribbling down her cheek. "Oh, you're going to pay for that, old man." Then a frown crossed her face as she looked up to see more headlights as cars stopped on the road above them. "Too bad. We could have had fun."

Anna hooked her left arm under his chin and braced her foot against the door.

She hurled herself backwards, cleanly breaking his neck.

Wicklow, Ireland

12:10 A.M.

KIROV, HANNAH, AND EUGENIA sat in silence in the small rental cottage overlooking the Irish Sea. The property was obviously geared to vacationing golfers with its kitschy golf-themed aesthetic and close proximity to the world-class European Club.

"Where is he?" Hannah said. "It's been too long. He should—"

"I hear something," Eugenia jumped to her feet.

Kirov was ahead of her, peering out the front window. "It's Charlie." He strode toward the door and threw it open.

Charlie stood there, dazed. "He's dead."

"We know." Hannah ushered him into the room. "We've been listening to the police bands to find out if Gadaire's people have reported the robbery." She put her hand gently on his arm. "I'm so sorry, Charlie. Are you okay? You look terrible."

"No, I'm not okay. My dad is dead. I think I'm going to be sick."

"The police are talking about it as if it were an accident," Eugenia said. "But they've only been talking about your father. We were afraid Gadaire's people might have gotten to you."

Charlie dropped down on a leather hassock. "I saw him die." He shook his head. "I saw him die, and I didn't do a damn thing."

"I'm sure there was nothing you could have done," Hannah said.

"There was. I should have helped him. I was watching from behind some bushes near the top of the embankment. Dad told me to go back and find the gun I lost when we wrecked. I was halfway up, but then I saw her coming, and I stopped. She looked so slim and fragile. I should have stayed. My father told me to go away, that she was a woman and wouldn't hurt him."

"She?" Kirov asked.

"Anna. She snapped his neck." He shook his head in wonder. "It looked so easy for her. I wanted to come back and tear her apart, but then she was gone. I ran back to the van, but he was dead. He was dead. I didn't know what to do. Other people were stopping, coming down. And he'd told me to meet you."

"The samples?" Hannah asked.

Charlie shook his head. "No. Everything went off fine, but when that bitch caused us to wreck, I had to leave the sample case in the van. I'm sorry."

"So am I," Kirov said. "You did the right thing, but it's damn bad luck. I hate to leave Gadaire in possession of those samples. Between the samples and the artifact he hijacked, he may have everything he needs." He turned to Hannah. "What do you want to do about it?"

She looked at Charlie, who was obviously on the verge of breaking down. "We should stick with Eugenia's plan. We're going to take the boat to England. Then we can hire a small plane, and we'll take the samples to Melis at the lab in Athens."

"But you don't have all of the samples. I screwed up. That bitch took them," Charlie said. "Kirov said it was important that we steal every one of them."

"We'll take the samples we have. Maybe there will be something in Lampman's research papers we took with the samples that will help us keep ahead of Gadaire."

"I don't give a damn about those samples anymore. I'm not going," Charlie said flatly.

"Yes, you will," Kirov said. "It's not safe for you here."

"I don't care. I'm going to stay and make sure Gadaire and his bitch pay for what they've done."

"They will." Kirov clasped his shoulder. "I promise you."

"When?"

"Soon."

"I want to do it myself. Tonight."

Hannah moved closer to him. "I know how you feel. We all do. But you have to be smart about this. If you blunder after them, they'll kill you. And as soon as the police identify your father, it won't take a lot of legwork for Gadaire's people to figure out that you may have been the one that helped him. They'll come after you, Charlie."

"Good. Bring 'em on."

"No," Kirov said. "Maybe we can use that aggression, but it will have to be later. On our terms. Charlie, trust me."

Charlie rubbed his forehead. "I don't even know where I would go."

"After this is over, you'll go to Australia just like you were going to do with your father."

"That security company wanted him, not me. I was just going in on his coattails."

"I'll speak to them. You'll have a place there. You'll have every opportunity that you would have had before. It's a good opportunity, Charlie. Take it."

Charlie shook his head. "I can't just run away. She *killed* him."

"Let us handle this for now," Kirov said. "I promise you that Gadaire and Anna will pay, but they have money, power, and a small army backing them up. We need to be careful. Your father wanted you to be safe. That's why he sent you away. If you really want to strike back at them, wait for the right moment. It's what your dad would have done."

Charlie thought about it. "Yeah, maybe, he was always telling me to be patient." He added fiercely, "But I can't be patient. Not for long. They killed him. They killed my dad."

"One day at a time, Charlie." Eugenia moved toward the door. "Our boat is waiting for us. We should go."

"Come with us, Charlie," Kirov said quietly. "We'll need your help."

Charlie hesitated, looking between them. He finally nodded. "Okay. I don't know what else to do. But I can't promise anything." He started for the door. "Everything has changed now."

* * *

"HE'S RIGHT, KIROV," HANNAH said as she gazed at Charlie, who was standing leaning against the deck rail several yards away. He hadn't spoken a word since they'd left Ireland two hours ago. "Everything has changed for him. At first, I was having problems with him. He's definitely a diamond in the rough. But he was trying so hard, and you could see how much he loved his father."

"Yes," Kirov said. "And his father loved him. After all the years apart, they'd found something good. They wanted to have a chance at a decent future that would keep them together." His lips twisted. "That made it easy for me."

Hannah glanced at Kirov. His expression was as somber as his tone. "I believe I detect a hint of Russian melancholy. Made what easy?"

"Manipulating Driscoll to do what I needed." His lips tightened. "I liked Driscoll, Hannah. I liked his humor and his cleverness and the way he—Shit. It didn't have to be this way. I thought Driscoll's plan had a good chance of succeeding, but I should have dug deeper, maybe found a backup that would have—"

"Stop right there," Hannah said. "Your men might have treated you like a god when you commanded that sub, but you are *not* Superman. Driscoll's plan was brilliant and should have been as safe as any plan could be. There was nothing that you could have done to make it safer unless you'd hired an army battalion to run interference for him."

He didn't answer. His eyes were still fixed on Charlie.

She wasn't getting through to him.

She grabbed his arm and whirled him to face her. "Listen, I know what a hang-up you have about responsibility, but it's time you got over it. You weren't responsible for the death of your wife or your crew all those years ago. You were a victim. You're intelligent. You know that's true. Unless you live in a vacuum and don't make any move at all, there's always going to be a reaction to any action you take. You offered Driscoll exactly what he wanted, and you had already delivered. He was a professional, and he wanted this chance. He was excited about it. He was proud of his talent and was liking showing it off to Charlie." She paused. "It all went wrong. I'm sorry and angry too. But, dammit, stop being angry with yourself and focus on the people who killed him."

He didn't answer for a moment, then turned to look at her. "Are you finished?"

"For the moment."

He smiled faintly. "Good. I don't know how much more I could take. No sympathy, no soppy assurances of understanding. Just a sharp slap to bring me back to my senses. There's no one like you, Hannah."

"A circumstance for which many people are very grateful."

"Only if they're fools." He reached out and took her hand. "I'm not a fool, Hannah."

His grasp was strong and warm. No sexuality. Comfort, camaraderie, a rock to cling to in the darkness. She wanted to keep on holding it.

"You're not backing away from me," Kirov said.

"Because you're not a fool," she said. "And you're not trying to seduce me."

He chuckled. "Wrong time. Wrong place. Besides, I told you it was in your court. I'll just make myself available for any erotic game you want to play." As he felt her sudden tension, his hand tightened on hers. "It's okay, it's fine. We can wait," he said quietly. "We'll take this. It's good too. Right?"

Yes, it was okay, Hannah thought. The tentative bond that

they'd formed during the weeks since they'd met had been stretched taut, but was still in place. They were learning more about each other every day, and that was causing tremors in the relationship. But then nothing stayed the same. As she'd told him, unless you lived in a vacuum, there was always action and reaction. She didn't want to live in a vacuum.

And she didn't want to let go of his hand.

She looked away. "Yes, we'll take this, Kirov."

CHAPTER
13

IT WAS COLD ON THIS DAMN boat, Eugenia thought as she looked out at the moon-dappled water. She had never liked boats. They were too slow for her, and she'd never liked the idea of the only escape being that icy sea. She didn't know how Kirov had stood it on his sub all those years. But then she and Kirov were different in as many ways as they were alike.

Her glance shifted to Kirov and Hannah across the deck. Kirov wasn't as grim as he'd been when he'd first boarded the boat.

Hannah's doing?

Probably. Kirov could be moody, and Hannah wouldn't put up with it. Good for her. Eugenia believed that the only way to keep from plummeting was to soar and look to the sky. If you kept busy and positive, no one could take you down.

Her glance moved to Charlie, standing alone at the rail. He was hurting and couldn't see anything but his own pain. If left alone, he'd either spiral into nothingness or get himself killed. Pity. He had potential.

Oh, what the hell. She needed a project.

She jumped to her feet and strode over to where Charlie stood. "We'll be arriving in another hour." She leaned her elbows on the rail. "I'll be glad to get off this junk heap. Seven hours is too long."

Charlie didn't answer.

"How about you?"

"I don't care," Charlie said dully. "I haven't paid much attention."

"That's right. You're too busy hulking here feeling sorry for yourself."

He stiffened with shock. "Go to hell."

"Ah, a response. Maybe you're alive after all. I wasn't sure. You're acting more like a zombie."

"I want to be alone."

"You've been alone. That's over now. It's time to come back and join the war."

He scowled. "I'll join the war as soon as you show me Anna Devareau and Gadaire."

"That's right, you only act if the situation is set up for you. That's what your father did, didn't he? He called the shots and made everything neat and tidy for you. Then you ambled in and helped out."

"Shut up."

"And that's what you still want to do. You'll lean on Kirov and the rest of us, then try to step in and get your revenge."

Charlie's hands fell on her shoulders. "Shut up."

"Do you think that's what your father would want you to do? Maybe so. He was very protective of his little boy." She paused. "But do you think that he'd be proud of you? I don't think so."

"He was proud of me. He told me so."

"He was proud of the fact that you'd kept out of jail. He was proud of the fact that you'd turned into a good-looking kid with a fair amount of intelligence and wasn't completely obnoxious. Other than that, what have you done to make him proud?"

Charlie's hand tightened on her shoulders with bruising force. "Why are you saying this?" he asked hoarsely.

"I liked your father. He had style and wit. He was a complete person." She paused. "You, on the other hand, are a confused collection of bits and pieces. It's a wonder he bothered with you." She moved her shoulders. "It's a wonder I'm bothering with you. You're hurting me. If you don't let me go in three seconds, I'm going to break at least two bones in your rib cage. Then I'll start on mutilating your penis. You know I can do it."

"Yes." His gaze was suddenly searching her face. "But why would you want to? If I'm such a piece of crap, why would you bother?"

"Do we have a breakthrough?" She shrugged off his hold and took a step backwards. "Are you thinking about something besides yourself?"

He slowly shook his head. "Hell, no, I'm thinking about my dick. That's damn important to me."

She smiled. "Speaks the universal man."

"Why are you being such a bitch to me?"

"I told you, I liked your father." She made a face. "And I have to admit, I may be close to liking you, Charlie."

"So that's a reason to take a knife to me?"

"It's my way. Cut, clean, and cauterize." She looked up at him. "And then start over with a clean slate. Are you ready to listen to me?"

"Do I have a choice and still keep my dick?" he asked ruefully.

"You'll have to discover that for yourself." Her smile faded. "I think you're torn with guilt about your father's death. For playing the obedient son when you know you should have taken matters into your own hands and stayed to help him. Is that true?"

Charlie's eyes closed with pain. "God, yes."

"Then you made a mistake, and it's one you can't take back. The only thing you can do is try to make the best of it. You're not going to do that by wringing your hands and brooding. But you could make Driscoll's death mean something."

When his eyes opened, they were glittering with moisture. "It did mean something. He had more guts than I'll ever have."

"You haven't been tested. Not really. But life isn't about dying well, it's about living well. Your father was experienced enough to know that. What kind of man do you want to be, Charlie? Would you like to be like your father?"

Charlie hesitated. "I don't know. He was smart and funny and a real good guy. I loved him. Could I be like him? I don't think so. I get too mad. I want to swing out. He was smooth as glass, and I'm just a rough kid from the streets."

"There's such a thing as change and growth." She let the idea sink in. "Anything's possible if you want it bad enough. Driscoll loved you, and the best gift you could give him would be to not go back to being what you were when the two of you came together. I think your dad would have wanted you to be all you could be. But it doesn't matter a damn what anyone wants unless it's what you want."

He was silent a moment. "How would I do it?"

"I can start you out. I've led a far rougher life than you have, Charlie. I've had to pull myself up out of the mire, but I know how to negotiate that mire. First, since I know you're not going to be able to concentrate on anything until you make Gadaire pay for your father's death, I can teach you how to do that with lethal efficiency. You're good for an amateur, but a professional could put you down in a heartbeat." She paused. "If you hadn't lost your gun when you went over that embankment, we wouldn't be having this conversation. Everything hinged on that. A principal rule is always to protect your weapons."

He slowly nodded. "I can see that."

"If you survive Gadaire, and I find you teachable, I may take you back to New York with me, and we'll see if we can file off some of those other rough edges. I often deal with Fortune 500 companies and countries who want their business. I know that jungle too."

"I don't care about that right now," he said impatiently. "Gadaire. I want to learn how to kill him and the bitch."

"Understandable." She turned away. "But I'll continue teaching you only as long as you do everything I say. The minute you explode or go off on your own, it's over. Your time for being immature ended when Driscoll died. I won't put up with juvenile displays." She met his gaze. "Think about it."

"I don't have to think about it," he said quietly. "I'll do whatever I have to do. When do we start?"

She shrugged. "We're on a job. I'll have to find the time."

"What do you mean?" He frowned. "I want to—" He stopped. "Whatever you say."

"Yes, it is." She smiled faintly as she turned away. "And that particular lesson will take you far."

Weston Executive Airport

Dublin, Ireland

7:30 A.M.

GADAIRE STEPPED OFF HIS private jet and glared at the man waiting in the hangar. It was Charles Ames, his director of security. The bastard had ushered him safely through some of the most dangerous countries on earth, yet he hadn't even been able to protect an office surrounded by a large security force.

"You know I don't tolerate failure, Ames," he said as the flight crew unloaded his luggage.

"Neither do I."

"Then how in the hell did this happen?"

Ames didn't speak for a moment, then said reluctantly, "They found the one weak link in our defenses. The service company needs immediate access in case the refrigeration unit fails. By posing as employees of that company, they bypassed all the safeguards we have in place. When your unit failed, it basically told us to roll out the red carpet for them."

"It's only because of Anna that we retrieved my merchandise. You should be feeling pretty damn stupid about that."

He shrugged. "We screwed up. It won't happen again."

Not if I kick your sorry ass to the curb, Gadaire thought. Instead, he merely nodded. "I'm more concerned about what happened at the college. Not only did Dr. Lampman lose all of the working samples I gave him, he lost many of his notes. I thought you said things were under control there."

"Our man on campus was injected with a quick-acting sedative. He gave us a good physical description of the thief, but we don't have much to go on yet."

"Unbelievable." Gadaire turned toward him. "I need two things from you. I need my property back, and I need to know who did this to me. It has to be the same people who arranged to hit me at both sites. Do we have any leads?"

"Yes, sir. We have a description of the man who stole the TK44 from Dr. Lampman. It was the same man who supposedly blundered into Lampman's workroom a few days ago. He was with a woman that time. Lampman's tail didn't get a photo, but we sent a sketch artist to work with him when the actual theft happened." He pulled out two charcoal sketches from his briefcase. "We're not sure about the identity of the man yet, but we think he's Nicholas Kirov, Russian submarine commander, and the same man who interfered with our dealings with Samuel Debney in Venice. We convinced Debney to tell us his name, but that's all he knew about him. Kirov's been very hard to trace. This time the only break we had was that he was recently linked with the woman in question." He handed him the other sketch. "Positive ID on her. Hannah Bryson. You may have heard of her."

"Oh, yes. I recently took something very precious away from her. Now she's trying to punish me?" He gazed down at the sketch. "It seems the bitch didn't like being stung. I wonder how she'll like what I'll do to her when I catch up with her." He handed the sketch back to Ames. "I want a complete report on both of them on my desk by the time I get home. Friends, family, business associates. Get me a telephone number for both of them."

"Bryson won't be hard, but Kirov . . . I believe he worked with the CIA at one time, and he covers his tracks."

"Work on it. This is the second time that bastard has gotten in my way. I don't want there to be a third. In the meantime, I'll deal with the woman." Though he wasn't going to fool himself that she would be easier than Kirov. He knew just how deadly a woman could be. "I'll make her wish she'd never been born. I want her to hurt. I want to see her cut to pieces." Anna might enjoy doing that, he thought. Though she preferred working on men. No, he wanted to reserve that pleasure for himself. Bryson and Kirov had made him look like a fool. He needed to set an example. "Find them."

"I'll get right to work on those numbers." Ames turned away. "I'll see you back at your suite, sir."

Ames might be there before he arrived, he thought, annoyed. His limo wasn't here yet, dammit. No, there it was, pulling in at the far gates. He had time to make that call to Devlin that he'd meant to do before he left France.

Devlin answered the call on the first ring.

"Devlin, I had good news in France. The project is a go. Proceed as planned."

"Immediately?"

"As soon as possible. Two days max."

"It may take a while to—"

"No longer than two days, and I want a name."

"You'll have it." Devlin hung up.

Devlin wouldn't fail him, Gadaire thought. Not like those damn security men who had let him be stripped of his dwindling supply of TK44.

The limo pulled into the hangar, and the driver jumped out to help the flight crew load Gadaire's luggage into the trunk.

Gadaire climbed into the limo, but called back to Ames at the last moment. "Meet me in my office at six. You can give me your progress report then."

The driver closed the door behind him.

"Welcome back, my love." Anna sat in the car with her long legs stretched out and crossed in front of her. She held up a champagne flute.

"This is a nice surprise." Gadaire kissed her. "A bit early for a drink, don't you think?" Anna seldom drank. He always thought it was because she never wanted to lose control.

"Apple juice. The tumblers are being cleaned."

"I see. Not that I couldn't use a drink right now. Or four."

She nodded. "I know. I'm sorry you had to cut your trip short."

"Ames has found out that the bastards behind it are Hannah Bryson and Nicholas Kirov. We need to know how to find them. Call in every marker and work your charms. This is important."

She took a sip from her glass. "Too bad I didn't find out more from the old man before he passed on to a better place."

"Dammit, you couldn't have brought him in? We have people on the payroll who could have made him talk."

"None better than I am, darling. There were too many witnesses. Two minutes later there were half a dozen people there. And I still needed to retrieve your precious cargo."

"What do we know about the dead man?"

"His name was Martin Driscoll. In his day, he was a pretty good thief. He was only convicted once, and that was several years ago."

"Has he worked for any of our competitors?"

"Not as far as I could find out. We're still looking into that."

"Any luck tracking down his partner?"

"Not yet. The other man was quite a bit younger, in his twenties. Driscoll usually worked alone, and he had no known associates. I have people on it."

"Good."

She took another sip from her glass. "Judging from your phone call, it sounds like France was a success."

Gadaire smiled. "A rousing success. I didn't want to discuss it on the phone, but I have the best possible news."

She gave him a questioning look.

"Anna, we hit the jackpot."

"You don't mean—"

"It's the missing piece of the puzzle. The artifact was everything we hoped it would be."

Anna laughed. "I can't believe it!"

"It's true. I've informed our friends in Pakistan that we may only be days away. I'm expecting a call from them this afternoon."

She kissed him. "You never stopped believing."

"No, but you can see why I was so upset about what happened here last night. We can't let anything derail us now. There's too much at stake." He nodded at the small cooler on the floor. "Are those the TK44 samples you recovered?"

"Yes, I wasn't sure what you wanted me to do with them."

He picked up the cooler and opened it. "We'll take them back to my office in the stadium. I'll have Ames put a couple guys there around the clock, at least until after—" Gadaire's voice trailed off as he stared into the cooler.

"What is it?"

"I think there's a tray missing." He started moving the samples. "Dammit, where is it?"

She frowned. "Are you sure?"

He felt the tension and anger tightening his chest as he searched frantically. "I don't see it." He glared at her. "Where is it, Anna?"

She stared him in the eye. Her voice was icy. "Just what are you accusing me of, Vincent? I suggest you keep on looking. Count them."

He did as she suggested. They were all there. One had slipped beneath the tray above it.

"You're right." He closed the cooler. "I just thought there might have been a screwup."

"And you were the one who made it," she said coldly.

Gadaire leaned back in his seat. He had gone too far. If he couldn't trust Anna, who in the hell could he trust? If she hadn't performed so brilliantly last night, he could have lost everything and had to start the project over. "You're right, as usual. I was out of line. Forgive me."

Anna relaxed a little, but her demeanor was still chilly. "I can understand that it's been an upsetting night for you. But you really should think before you speak."

And she wasn't going to let it go without him paying for that mistake. It might not be at this moment, but it would come. "You're absolutely right," Gadaire said. "Let's forget about it."

"Of course. But Vincent . . ." She leaned close to him. "Don't ever question my loyalty again. I killed a man for you tonight. And we both know it probably won't be the last time."

"Not if you have your way." He chuckled. "I'm sorry, Anna. To make it up to you, let me tell you how I dispensed with your admirer, Hollis. It will amuse you."

Stodwell Airport

London, England

"GADAIRE KNOWS THAT WE stole the TK44." Kirov hung up his phone. "Walsh said that Gadaire's men are questioning everyone on the street about us. Very intense. Sometimes brutal."

"Is Walsh angry?"

"Yes, but not with us. Or he wouldn't have warned us." He added, "It was bound to happen, Hannah. It was just a matter of time."

"I know." But it still made her uneasy to know that Gadaire was using all his considerable resources in Dublin to track them down. "What do we do now?"

"Proceed as we planned. We're being careful. That's all we can do." He paused. "Unless you want to stop."

She shook her head. "We can't do that. Driscoll died. How many other—" She drew a deep breath. "I'm ready. Make the call."

"I could do it."

"No, I told you, I want to do it. Gadaire's not real enough to me. He's a shadow figure who destroys everything around him. I don't want to think of him as bigger than life."

"Then let's cut him down to size." He dialed the number. "Three minutes."

She took the phone.

Gadaire answered on the fifth ring.

"You bastard," Hannah said angrily. "You killed him. You're not going to get away with it."

Gadaire didn't speak for a moment. "Who is this?" He answered himself. "Why, I believe it must be Hannah Bryson."

"Yes."

"How delightful. Is Kirov with you?"

"Not at the moment. He keeps telling me to calm down. I can't calm down. She murdered Driscoll in cold blood."

"Anna never acts in cold blood. Her blood always runs hot."

"Driscoll was a good man. He didn't deserve to die."

Another pause. "Then he shouldn't have gotten in my way. He was lucky his death was comparatively easy."

"Easy. She broke his neck." She added shakily, "It's not going to do you any good. We're not going to give up. We'll find that trellis. We'll take every bit of that TK44 away from you."

"Not a chance."

"And I hear you're looking for us. You won't find us. Do you think we're stupid?"

Another pause. "No, I think you're a *bitch*." His smooth voice was suddenly vicious. "Yes, I've been looking for you. And I will find you. And, when I do, would you like to know what I'm going to do to you?"

Kirov checked his watch and held up one finger.

"I'm going to hurt you more than you can dream." Gadaire's voice was laden with malice. "I'm going to cut off your breasts and then start on every limb of your body. How dare you waltz into my territory and steal my property."

"It's not your property. Neither the trellis, nor the TK44."

"It's mine because I say it's mine. Possession is everything. I won't have you getting in my way. I'll find you and Kirov, and I'll make you wish you'd never been born."

"Empty threats."

"I'll show how empty they are. You're nothing. I'll do whatever I have to do to—"

"Cut it," Kirov said.

She hung up.

She drew a deep breath and tried to keep from shaking. "Was I on it long enough?"

He nodded. "He had time to trace. And it was clear he was doing it. There were a lot of pauses while he tried to stretch the call."

She shuddered. "Ugliness. I've known what a monster he was. He's always been hovering in the background, but it's different actually hearing his voice. All that malice . . ."

"Yes, it must have been very satisfying for him." He added, "He got very personal with you. It made me angry. I knew it was going to happen but I didn't realize it was going to cause me to react quite that strongly. It appears I've become somewhat barbaric in my attitude toward you. I believe I may have to go back and pay Gadaire a visit."

"No, don't be stupid. Promise me you'll stay out of Dublin."

He didn't answer.

"Dammit, promise me."

He shrugged. "Very well. We'll just have to try to draw him into a trap on our own ground."

"It was worth it?"

"Red herrings are always worth the effort. It will buy us time and security."

"I take it the trace won't lead him here."

He shook his head. "The call will be traced directly to the University of Edinburgh."

"How is that going to happen?"

"It's an old spy trick. Tape two telephone handsets together, mouthpiece to earpiece, earpiece to mouthpiece. It's a hard relay. If they try to trace the call, it will only lead to the office where you have two phones fastened to one another. These days, the poor audio quality is a dead giveaway, so it's important to temporarily hardwire the earpieces and mouthpieces together. I have a contact in London who does very good work."

"Of course you do," Hannah said. "And I guess he owed you a favor?"

"No, actually I now owe him one. Especially since he'll want to be reimbursed for his time and travel expenses." He smiled. "And those of two look-alikes who resemble us who will make sure they're seen and noted in those hallowed halls of learning. They should keep Gadaire's men busy tracking them."

"So now we're free and clear."

"For the time being. I've contacted some friends in Athens, and they assured me there was no sign of a Gadaire presence there, but I always believe in safety measures." He turned away. "Come on. It's time we got on the plane. Eugenia and Charlie are waiting for us."

She nodded and moved toward the small jet waiting by the hangar. It had been worth it, she told herself. All that ugliness had purpose.

Kirov glanced back at her. "You did well," he said quietly.

Just a few words, but they made some of the ugliness go away. "Sure I did. Now let's get on that plane to Athens and forget that bastard."

"YOU GOT IT?" GADAIRE ASKED. "Dammit, I held her on the line long enough."

"Yes, I think we got the trace." Ames had a phone pressed to his ear. "Though it was close. You shouldn't have threatened her and made her—"

"Are you telling me it's my fault if you screwed up?"

"No, sir. I wouldn't do that."

No, Ames knew better.

Gadaire's hand slowly clenched on the desk. He hadn't played it as well as he should have done. He had just been so angry when he'd heard Hannah Bryson's voice. He was so close to making the biggest score of his life, and Kirov and that woman were standing in his way.

Okay, calm down. Go on with what needed to be done.

It was only a matter of time until he had both of them in his sights.

"We've got it," Ames said. "Edinburgh University. Edinburgh, Scotland."

And the university that had one of the finest botany departments in the world. He'd initially been considering sending the TK44 to Professor McDaniel instead of Lampman to research.

Now it appeared McDaniel was going to get his chance at it after all.

But not for long.

"Go," he told Ames. "Get a team up to Edinburgh right away. I want those samples and Bryson and Kirov brought back here."

"You want them alive?"

"That's what I said, didn't I?"

Oh, no, don't kill them. I have plans for you, Hannah Bryson.

CHAPTER
14

Marinth Science and History Museum
Glyfada, Greece

"THAT'S IT, ISN'T IT?" KIROV pointed to a large white building built atop an oceanside bluff. "The Marinth Museum?"

He drove the rental car along the coastal highway with Hannah sitting beside him and Eugenia and Charlie in the backseat.

"That's it," Hannah said. "I've never actually been there, but I've seen enough pictures to know what it looks like. There's nothing else quite like it."

"It's not open to the public yet, is it?" Eugenia asked.

"No, the official opening is still a few weeks off. But the research labs have been in operation for over two years. Melis and her team are anxious to get a look at the TK44 alga samples we're bringing."

"Does she know where we got them?" Kirov asked.

"No, and it should probably remain that way. Plausible deniability, you know."

"Right," Kirov said as he drove the winding road that took them to the museum's back entrance. After passing through the security gates, they were met on the driveway by a tall young man obviously of Middle Eastern descent. He shook Hannah's hand as she climbed out of the car. "Good to see you again, Ms. Bryson. I'm Dr. Aziz Natali."

"I remember you from the expedition." She smiled. "You're the one who never sleeps."

"Not when I'm on a project I love. But when I finish here, I'll probably sleep fourteen hours a day."

"Sounds like a plan." Hannah introduced him to Kirov, Eugenia, and Charlie. "So where is Melis?"

"She has a visitor and said she'd be late. She entertained him on the boat last night." He motioned down to the coastline almost a mile below, where *Fair Winds* was docked next to a tram that connected the waterfront area to the museum.

"The fund-raising never ends," Hannah said.

Aziz smiled. "In any case, she should be here soon."

Hannah was still taking in the spectacular vista before her, with the miles of the Greek coastline giving way to the breathtaking blue waters of the Aegean. "Not a bad place to come to work every day."

"I'd rather be out on the ocean, but this will do." Aziz shrugged. "Melis tells me you have some special TK44 samples that should go straight to the lab."

Hannah lifted the portable cooler. "Right here. Just lead the way."

Aziz motioned for them all to follow him through the automatic sliding glass doors of the museum laboratories. "We've only been back a couple of days, but we've been working nonstop to try to crack this."

"Any success so far?" Hannah asked.

"A little. We know that exposing these particular alga to high concentrations of nitrogen causes them to grow at an incredibly accelerated rate. They spread like nothing we've seen. But as far as we can tell, they wouldn't represent a danger to local populations. There has to be something we're missing."

Kirov pointed to the cooler. "The answer may be in there. Professor Lampman produced these in his lab. If you can analyze what he did, it might yield a solution. Some of his notes are also in there."

Aziz' eyes lit with eagerness. "We'll get right on it. Melis has made it our top priority." He swiped his badge on a wall-mounted scanner, and the doors opened to reveal a large lab that literally gleamed with brushed aluminum and polished glass on almost every surface.

Hannah looked around in amazement. "I can see why Melis is always fund-raising. This is incredible."

"It's a dream," Aziz said. "We just don't feel like we're studying history here. We feel like we're making history. Melis Nemid has ruined me for every other job I'll ever have."

"That's not necessarily true," Hannah said. "But you might have to go out and make your own amazing jobs."

"I guess you're right. It worked well enough for you, didn't it?"

Hannah nodded. "And Melis."

Aziz took the portable cooler from Hannah and handed it to a lab assistant. "Prep these for the bioscanner, please."

"May we take a look around the museum itself?" Eugenia asked.

Aziz nodded. "Of course. The tech people are still working on the interactive exhibits, but almost everything else is in place. I'll take you down there."

Five minutes later, they entered the museum's grand atrium, framed by half a dozen massive pillars that had been brought up from the ocean floor. Between the pillars were striking multicolored mosaics that Hannah remembered seeing in *National Geographic* after Melis's first Marinth expedition.

Eugenia spun completely around, trying to take in everything. "This is incredible. It makes me wish I'd lived in Marinth." She looked at Hannah. "I had no idea they'd created things of such beauty."

"Most people don't. It's one thing to see a relic in a book or magazine, but another actually to stand in front of it. The Marinthi-ans were technologically savvy, but they also took pains to make things aesthetically pleasing. They felt it would stimulate their cre-ativity."

Charlie stood in front of a series of mosaics depicting a massive fishing party on the open sea. He shook his head in awe. "My father would have loved these. We went fishing together once. It was kind of nice."

Kirov stepped toward the mosaics. "Your father would have al-ready planned how to walk out of here with them."

Charlie managed a smile. "That he would've."

"I'm sorry I'm late." Melis was hurrying toward them. "It took me longer than I thought it would to get through breakfast and get up here."

"Forgiven." Hannah gave her a hug. "Aziz told us you were wheel-ing and dealing with a guest."

"Wheeling and dealing? Yes, you might call it that." Her gaze had zeroed in on Kirov. "You must be Kirov. I've heard about you. I'm Melis Nemid."

He stepped forward and took her hand. "And I've heard about you. You must be extraordinary for Hannah to feel such loyalty for you." He introduced her to Charlie and Eugenia. "And your mu-seum is magnificent. We dropped the TK44 samples in the lab but couldn't resist a look around."

"Good. I want everyone to appreciate Marinth as much as I do."

"Not possible," Hannah said. "But we can come close."

"Go ahead and look around. I have something to do, then I'll meet you back at the lab."

Kirov nodded and started down the corridor with Eugenia and Charlie following behind. Hannah was about to go after them when Melis's hand grasped her arm.

"Wait. I have to speak to you alone."

Hannah looked at her in surprise. "Alone? There's nothing about the samples that Kirov and Eugenia shouldn't hear."

"It's not about the samples. It's personal."

Melis's expression was grave. Hannah gazed at her in concern. "Is it Pete and Susie? Are the dolphins okay?"

"I suppose they are. They didn't come with me when I left Marinth."

"I'm sorry, Melis. I know that worries you."

"It does, but that's not the problem." She was moving down the corridor. "I got a phone call yesterday afternoon."

"Your Jed?"

"Jed is fine. Will you stop making guesses and let me talk?" she added ruefully. "Though it might be easier if we made it questions and answers. It's not about me, Hannah." She opened a paneled door. "It's about you. Someone is here to see you."

Hannah gazed at her in bewilderment. "What is this—"

"I had to come, Aunt Hannah." Ronnie stood up from the chair where he had been sitting. "Please don't be angry."

She stared at him in shock. "Ronnie?" She couldn't take it in. "What . . ."

"I had to do it." His dark eyes were desperately earnest in his thin face. "You need me. Please don't be angry."

"Of course I'll be angry." She crossed the room and hugged him close with all her strength. "Later. Are you okay?"

"I'm fine." He clung to her; his voice was muffled against her. "I tried to stay, but I couldn't. I had to know you were all right. I have to help you."

"The telephone, Ronnie." She tried to steady her voice. "All you have to do is call me, and I'll be there."

"You're too far away. I have to be close, so I can take care of you."

She drew a shaky breath. "We've got to talk about this." She pushed him away. "After you tell me how you got here. Did your mother bring you?"

He shook his head.

"Then how—" She was trying to get it straight, and what she was suspecting was not good. "Your mother does know that you're here?"

He nodded. "I wouldn't worry Mom like that. She thought I was spending the weekend with my buddy Mark. I called her last night after I got here and told her where I was and that I was safe."

"And she didn't know before? Ronnie, how could you just take off and leave your mom and Donna?"

"They have each other. You don't have anyone."

"I don't need—" She ran her hand through her hair. "And how did you get here? You're twelve years old and an unaccompanied minor. How did you get from Boston to Athens by yourself? Surely they wouldn't let you on a plane without all kinds of signatures and an adult to give permission."

"It's not that hard," he said casually. "I checked it out on the Internet. I had a passport from that time Dad brought me to London to visit you at that *Titanic* site. I had money in my savings account from working at soccer camp last summer."

"But how did you get on the airplane by yourself?"

"I wouldn't have been able to do it on a U.S. carrier. But European airlines are cooler about it. Unaccompanied kids travel all the time with no red tape at all. I just walked up to the ticket counter as if I knew what I was doing and got on the plane."

"Unbelievable," she murmured.

"That's what I said," Melis added from behind her. "You automatically think children are going to have volumes of rules and strictures to keep them safe."

Hannah had forgotten Melis was standing there. "And how did you get involved? How did you find him?"

"He found me." She smiled at Ronnie. "Though I was second choice. He came to the museum asking for you. When the receptionist told him that you weren't here, he asked for me. He said that you told him that you were coming here."

She had mentioned it casually in that conversation with Ronnie, but she'd had no idea he'd pick up on it and run.

Not run, fly, she corrected herself dryly.

"Melis has been really nice to me," Ronnie said. "She took me to have dinner on her boat last night."

"Melis, I'm sorry that you—"

"Stop right there," Melis said. "Ronnie has been no bother. I enjoyed having him. I was a little lonely last night."

"Lonely? Don't mention that word," Hannah said. "It seems to trigger something in Ronnie. You might have a permanent houseguest."

"That wouldn't be so bad." Melis and Ronnie exchanged glances. "He's really eager to meet Pete and Susie. I think they'd get along just fine." She looked back at Hannah. "I was there when Ronnie called his mother. I talked to her myself and told her that I'd take care of him until you arrived. She wants you to call her."

"Thank heaven. I'd hate to have Cathy worrying about him. I'll call her right after I have a talk with Ronnie."

"Why don't you go for a walk on the balcony?" Melis suggested. "The weather is wonderful this morning." She grinned. "Sunlight can be very soothing."

"Good idea. I can use a little soothing." She nodded at Ronnie. "Let's go. We have some tall discussing to do."

"Hannah."

She looked back at Melis. "You're looking all worried and protective. I should have expected it. Conner could charm the birds from the trees, and Ronnie is just like him. It will be all right. I'm not going to be too rough on him."

"I think he can take care of himself," Melis said quietly. "I just want you to know that everything I said to him I meant." She made a shooing motion. "Now, out into the sun with you."

What could she say to him, Hannah wondered, as they walked along the long terrace balcony. It had to be right. Sensitive and yet firm.

"You're trying to decide how to tell me to go home," Ronnie said. "Dad used to say that he could almost hear your mind clicking when you had a problem." He smiled. "He said that it was like the gears in one of the machines that you invented."

"Well, the gears are stuck right now." She gazed out at the sea. "I'm going to have to wing it. You know I love you. You know I'd like nothing better than to have you with me. It's just not the right time. I'm having a few problems."

"Then that's why I should be with you."

She'd said the wrong thing. Naturally, as protective as Ronnie was, that would be a red flag. She tried another direction. "You're missing school and soccer season. It's not the right time for you either."

"I can do makeup in my classes. I don't care about soccer. It doesn't seem important right now."

After facing the murder of his father, she could see how anything else would dwindle in importance. "Your mother and Donna. You said you had to take care of them."

"They can do without me for a while. They have each other and Grandma. You're alone."

Lord, he was stubborn. Stubborn and solemn and endearing.

"Ronnie, I'm not alone. I have my crew."

He shook his head. "They're not close to you. Not like Dad used to be. They might not be there when you needed them."

She was searching wildly for an answer. "I'm working with a man named Kirov. He used to be a submarine captain, and he's very responsible." That was certainly the truth. "He'd never let anything happen to me."

"A submarine captain." He was frowning. "They're pretty cool, but I don't know . . ."

"Ronnie, he's brilliant and tough and—"

He was shaking his head. "I can't go home. I don't know him. I have to be sure."

She gazed at him in exasperation. "Why are you being this way?"

He was silent a moment. "I told you about my dream about Dad. I couldn't stop thinking about it. It seemed okay if I came to you on my own. I think he'd want me to be here." He looked up at her. "So I have to stay, Aunt Hannah. Until I'm sure everything is safe for you."

What was she supposed to say now? "I can't keep you with me. I've got business that's going to keep me on the move."

"That's what Melis said. Is this Captain Kirov going to be with you?"

"Yes, I'll be very safe. So you see, there will be no place for you to stay. You should go home."

He shook his head. "Boston is too far away. I have to be close." He smiled. "And I have a place to stay. Melis said I could stay with her on her boat. That way if you need me, I won't have to cross the ocean to get to you. I won't be that far away."

"Melis is very kind, but I don't think—"

"I won't be in her way. She said I could help with the dolphins and maybe even have her crew teach me about boats and sailing. Dad showed me a little on the lake at home, but he didn't have much time."

Because Conner was always with Hannah traveling to the far ends of the oceans. She had cheated Ronnie of those experiences with his father.

"It's all right, Aunt Hannah." Ronnie's gaze was on her face. "When he was home, it was great. It was the way he wanted it. I didn't understand when I was younger, but he explained."

She reached out and hugged him fiercely. "You sound like a little old man. I want you to be young again. I want you to jump and run and play."

His face suddenly lit with a smile. "Then let me stay on Melis's boat and play with the dolphins."

"Clever." She made a face. Then she cradled his face in her two hands and stared down into his eyes. "If I sent you home, you'd come back, wouldn't you? You'd find a way to hop on another airplane."

"Dad wants me here."

She sighed resignedly. "If I let you stay, it would only be for a little while. And I can't promise until I talk to your mother. You'd have to promise to stay with Melis on her boat and not chase after me."

"Okay." He had a second thought. "As long as this Kirov guy is what you say he is. I'll have to see him and make sure that Dad would have trusted him. Where is he?"

And now he wanted to vet Kirov to see if he measured up? It would have been amusing if it hadn't been ridiculous. How would Kirov react to a twelve-year-old critically assessing his character and abilities?

Oh, what the hell difference did it make? It *was* amusing. Let Kirov deal with it.

"Kirov is still in the lab." She strode toward the balcony door a few yards away. "Come on. I'm sure he'll be delighted to meet you."

Kirov looked up from the Lampman papers spread on the lab counter. "I was wondering where Melis whisked you off to." His gaze went to Ronnie. "And you are?"

"Ronnie Bryson," Hannah said. "He's my brother Conner's son. He decided to hop on a plane and come to see me."

"Interesting." He smiled. "I'm a friend of your Aunt Hannah's. I'm very happy to meet you, Ronnie."

"She says that you were a submarine captain."

"That's true, among many other professions. I've moved around a lot."

"Where?"

"Name a place. I've probably been there."

"But you're not going to go anywhere now. You're going to stay with Aunt Hannah?"

Kirov's brows lifted at the boy's intensity. "As far as I know, that's the plan."

"No, you've got to promise."

Kirov's gazed shifted to Hannah. "I don't believe he's speaking for you. Am I missing something?"

"He just wants the assurance that I'll be safe. He's worried about me." She met Kirov's gaze. "And like you, he believes I need protection. I can't convince him otherwise."

"Really?" He nodded and smiled. "I'm very good at reassurance." He turned back to Ronnie. "And I'm extremely good at taking care of people around me. Would you like to hear my qualifications?"

"Yes."

He chuckled. "Then by all means we need to talk. Would you

like to accompany me to the balcony?" He started for the door. "Stay here, Hannah. We really don't need you for this."

"And I've no desire to listen in on your conversation. It would probably annoy me."

"Oh, I'm sure it would." He opened the door and let Ronnie precede him onto the balcony. "Though we both have the utmost respect for you, Hannah."

She stood watching them through the glass French doors. They were both leaning with their arms on the railing. The two looked strange yet oddly companionable together. The tall, powerful man and the thin, gangly boy with the tousled brown hair. Ronnie's expression was intent, serious, as he listened to Kirov. Kirov's expression was equally grave, but lit with an occasional small smile.

"Is everything all right?" Melis had come back into the lab and was strolling toward her. "Is he staying?"

"Yes, I didn't have much choice. He's like Conner, easygoing, but rock stubborn if it was something that meant something to him."

"He's a great kid. I like him a lot," Melis said. "I'm going to enjoy having him on the *Fair Winds*."

"Thank you for having him. At least with you he'll be safe. I was afraid he'd insist on being with me. I couldn't let that happen."

Melis's smile faded. "Because you're afraid he'd be in danger."

"I don't know what's going to happen. I don't have the right to put him in a position that might be . . . volatile." She shook her head ruefully. "I was able to convince him that I didn't need him to protect me, but I had to throw Kirov in to add weight. He didn't trust my judgment, so I had to let him do his own appraisal."

Melis's gaze followed Hannah's to the man and boy standing on the balcony. "And how is Kirov taking it?"

"It's a challenge. He's enjoying it."

Melis's eyes narrowed. "But you hoped that he might feel a little uncomfortable dealing with a boy."

"Maybe. It was too much to expect. Kirov never loses his cool, and I've never found anyone he couldn't handle."

"Including you? I thought I detected a little tension. You haven't resolved your differences?"

"It doesn't matter. We can work together." She looked back at Kirov and Ronnie. Ronnie's stance and attitude had changed; relaxed, even eager. "I think he's won him over. You'll definitely have Ronnie as your guest."

"He'll work his way. He'll enjoy it more." Her gaze was on Kirov. "I can see how Ronnie would be swayed. Kirov's very impressive. Not in the usual style, but there's enough power and magnetism to stop you in your tracks." She paused. "And I admit, when I met him, I felt a sense of . . . I don't know. He made me feel as if there wasn't any mountain he couldn't climb."

And he'd clearly won Melis over. "Yes, he is impressive." She changed the subject. "What did Ronnie's mother say when you talked to her yesterday?"

"Cathy is a very smart woman. She knows her son. She knows you. She said Ronnie is having a very bad time, and she knew that you'd do what was best for him."

"I'm trying. I still have to talk to Cathy. I hope this is best for him."

"I think it will be." She paused. "I've never told you, but I had a terrible childhood. I was scarred. And then I found the dolphins. They healed me. I don't know how. It could be that just the fascination and working with them completely absorbed me. It could be that I loved them, and that was enough. Love itself is a great healer. Pete and Susie will be good for Ronnie."

Melis was a very private person, and it hadn't been easy for her to reveal that intensely personal part of her life. It moved Hannah that she would do it to put Hannah at ease with her decision. "Yes, I think they might," Hannah said quietly. "And you'll be good for him, too. I don't know anyone with whom I'd rather leave him."

Kirov was clapping Ronnie on the shoulder, and they were both turning to come back into the lab.

"It's okay, Aunt Hannah," Ronnie said. "As long as you stay with Captain Kirov. He'll make sure everything's all right."

"Call me Kirov, Ronnie. Captain is too formal, and that's all in the past. I hope we're friends now."

"Yes, sir." Ronnie smiled eagerly. He turned to Hannah. "He's going to tell me all about how they lived on a nuclear sub."

It was clear Ronnie had been completely won over. "How nice. And I'm glad you approve of him," she said dryly. "If you think he's so competent, perhaps you'd consider going home?"

His smile faded. "No, I have to be here. Cap—Kirov promised he'd tell me if there was any trouble. I might have to help. He's only one man."

"Really?" she murmured. "And I thought you believed he was an army."

"Navy," Kirov corrected. "I'm much better on the sea than ground tactics." He turned to Ronnie and held out his hand. "But you have my word that nothing will happen to Hannah when you're not with us."

Ronnie shook his hand. "She's very smart. I know she'll pay attention to you."

Kirov's eyes were twinkling with mischief, but his tone was solemn. "I'll make every effort to assure that she does."

Hannah drew a deep breath, struggling to keep her frustration under control. "I could hardly help it. You manage to—"

"So Ronnie will stay with me on the *Fair Winds*," Melis interrupted quickly. "That's wonderful. Will you be able to spend the night with us, Hannah?"

"I'm not sure." She turned to Aziz, who was working at a table across the lab. "What kind of progress are you making?"

"Good." His eyes were shimmering with excitement. "Those notes of Lampman's are leading me in an entirely new direction. He was very far along. If I can combine my research with his, I may have a breakthrough."

"How soon?"

He shrugged. "It will come when it comes. But I'm close. I'll let Melis know as soon as I do."

"I'll stay here with him," Kirov said. "You go with Melis and your nephew. Show him a little of the city. Athens is an experience no one should miss. I'll call you if there's anything to report."

"Okay. You're right. While he's here, he should see a few sights." She looked around the lab. "Where are Eugenia and Charlie? Still in the museum?"

"No, Eugenia said they were going for a trip in the countryside to do a little target shooting. It seems she's taken Charlie under her wing."

A very lethal wing, Hannah thought as she turned away with Ronnie. "Heaven help him."

"Not necessary," Kirov said as he went back to the notes he'd been studying previously. "Eugenia will take good care of him."

"DO YOU THINK YOU CAN DO IT?" Eugenia asked. "It's a hundred yards."

Charlie squinted against the glare of the strong sun and zeroed in on the small tin can on the lower branch of the olive tree. "I can do it." He carefully aimed, lining up the shot.

The tin can was blown off the tree limb.

"You're a good shot," Eugenia said.

"Damn straight."

"But not good enough. When you can do that running at full speed and dodging in and out of those bushes and boulders, you might be able to stay alive under any kind of conditions Gadaire could throw at you."

"It's a waste of time. There's no reason why I can't just go after him in Dublin or—"

"You'd better hope that you don't have to face him on his turf in Dublin. There's a hell of a lot more cover in terrain like this. Now try again. My way."

He shook his head. "No one could make that shot running at full speed."

"The hell they can't." She checked her automatic. "Put three tin cans on that branch and get out of my way."

He shrugged and did as she asked.

Eugenia gazed at the target for a moment.

"Not easy, is it?" Charlie asked sarcastically.

She could feel the adrenaline start to surge. "Piece of cake." She took off running. She hit one can before she reached the boulders. She hit the next as she reached the trees. She fell to her knees and took the third shot at close range. It blew off the branch.

She got to her feet and turned to face him. "Point taken?"

He was staring at her dumbfounded. "Damn you're good."

"Yes, not the best. I don't get enough practice anymore. When I was eighteen and working with the KGB, I was awesome." She reloaded her gun. "But I'm good enough for most situations I might run into." She looked at him. "*You* are not. Are you ready to try again?"

"I'm going to make an ass of myself. There's no way I can—"

She chuckled. "I believe I intimidated you. Perhaps you need a little motivation." She walked over to the ground where they'd tossed their belongings and pulled out her computer. "And there's a lot to learn besides just how to shoot the bad guys. You can lose the game before you even get to that point. If you can be one step ahead of the enemy, then your bullet will be there waiting for him when he takes that step."

"Put yourself in his shoes?"

She nodded. "In most cases you can do it with no problem. Defense. Self-defense. It's common tactics. It's only when you run into someone who's out of the ordinary that you have problems." She had been keying in the computer. "You might study Gadaire and Anna Devareau's dossier and see if there's anything about them with which you can identify." She turned the computer around for him to see the photos and dossiers. "Gadaire will be easier."

"You're saying women are tougher to decipher?"

"Not always. But never underestimate an antagonist because she's a woman."

He glanced at the last tin can she'd shot from the branch. "I'm not likely to do that."

"But you might decide that she has skill but not intent. I've dealt with women who were as tough as nails and had no compunction about pulling the trigger."

"Anna Devareau killed my father. I watched her do it. I know what she is."

"No, you don't." She looked down at the picture on the screen. "You don't really know anything about her. I doubt if even Gadaire does. She reveals only what she wants to reveal, what she thinks is necessary at the moment. I doubt if she has ever revealed a potential weakness."

"She's so beautiful," he whispered. "Even when she was coming down that embankment, I couldn't believe anything that beautiful could be a threat. Even my father wasn't worried about her."

"No?"

"At least he told me he wasn't." He shook his head. "But he's smarter than me. He had to have known what she is."

"Read the dossiers, then we'll get back to practice."

He shook his head. "I'll read them later. I'm going to get back to work." He started to pick up the tin cans and set them in place. "You wanted motivation; I've got motivation." He gave her a cool glance. "And I'll do that run better than you did. Not the first time. Maybe not even the tenth. But I'll do it."

She nodded slowly. "I think you will. Get to it."

Orissa, India

IT WAS A SCENIC LITTLE COVE, Devlin thought, and more prosperous than most of the villages he'd visited.

Half-dressed children were running and playing on the shore. Fishermen were on their boats taking off their catches for the day.

A small hotel was perched on the hill, and he could see the tourists in the restaurant on the veranda that gave them a fine view of the pretty village below.

Devlin had never liked India, too hot, too muggy, too poor. But even he could see that this place was . . . pleasant.

And it was the right place.

He reached for his phone.

He had a name to give to Gadaire.

Orissa.

GADAIRE SAT IN HIS CAR NEAR the Trinity College campus and waited for his phone to ring. He flipped the switch on the bug-jamming device in the console next to him. He wasn't even sure if he could trust it. The damn thing had been installed by the same security expert who had recently failed him so badly. He would just have to trust Ames and his device's ability to counteract any kind of attempt to listen to his conversation. Too bad he—

The phone rang.

Gadaire answered it. "Right on time. Funny, you're quite punctual when I have something you want."

Nibal Doka ignored his sarcasm. "My associates are intrigued by your proposal. They're interested in exploring this further."

That's what happens when politicians allow foreign ambassadors to be chosen by bribes, Gadaire thought sourly. They wind up with imbeciles like Doka. " 'Interested' and 'exploring' are code words for 'a waste of my time,' " Gadaire said. "Do we have a deal or not?"

"You're promising something that has never been done before, and you expect my associates to wire you a quarter of a billion dollars in advance. Surely you can understand their hesitancy."

"If I were a merchant they had never done business with, then yes. But I have a reputation and experience. I've been in this business for over ten years, and I've had dealings with each and every one of your associates. I've always delivered for them and all my clients. My reputation depends on it. Why would I endanger that?"

"They want a demonstration."

"No free samples."

"Who said anything about free?"

That's what he had been waiting for. "I'm listening."

"Give us an example of what your TK44 can do on a limited basis, and we pledge to move forward and give you free rein to initiate the other plan you mentioned." He paused. "The destruction would have to be significant."

Gadaire sat in silence for a moment. Considering the money

involved, he had suspected they would put him to some kind of test. Not an unreasonable demand, and he'd already made preparations to meet it. "For the right price. I could get started right away."

"And what is that price?"

"Five million dollars. That will buy them a very dramatic demonstration that India will remember for centuries. And when I succeed, we immediately move forward with my original proposal. Two hundred and fifty million for India's entire coastline."

"You have a deal, Mr. Gadaire. Five million dollars will be wired into your account within the next hour."

Damn.

He was taken aback by the quick acceptance of his terms. That meant Doka was authorized to pay more than just five million. No matter. Small potatoes compared with the bigger prize that awaited him down the road.

"A pleasure doing business with you," Gadaire said. "Please give my regards to your associates and tell them not to make any vacation plans that involve India. It may be in some turmoil for the foreseeable future."

He hung up and sat there, trying to control his excitement. Everything was falling into place. Thanks to Devlin, he had a choice test site that he could hand over to Doka on a silver platter. And Lampman had promised that he'd have the TK44 process finished in a few days.

No, not in a few days. He had to have it now.

He quickly dialed Lampman. He couldn't remember if Lampman was teaching a class that day, but he didn't give a damn one way or the other. He could tell his students to go to hell.

Lampman answered. "Good morning, Gadaire."

"Tell me I didn't just promise something that we can't deliver."

"It depends entirely on what you promised."

Lampman sounded strange, Gadaire thought. Confident, cocky, even. A far cry from the contrite little man who had been so terrified after losing those samples. As a student of human nature, he knew this could be a sign of excellent news.

"You told me you wanted some clues from the historical record," Gadaire said. "I gave it to you. I trust it was helpful."

"You could say that. As encouraged as I was by my initial experiments, I'm even more encouraged now, Mr. Gadaire. There's something you really should see."

"Are you in your lab?"

"Actually, I'm outside the city. Can you come right away?"

"You're summoning me?"

"Consider it less of a summons and more of an invitation. I can take pictures, but I think you'd rather see this for yourself."

The nerdy little bastard was positively giddy. That alone might make the trip worthwhile. "Where are you?"

"I just sent you an IM with my GPS location. It's kind of in the middle of nowhere, but the phone should give you good directions."

Before Gadaire could reply he heard the instant-message-notification tone. "Okay, I'm on my way. Don't be alarmed if a few friends get there before I do."

CHAPTER 15

Dunslaughlin, Ireland
3:14 P.M.

GADAIRE'S CAR ROLLED TO A stop on the country road eighteen miles northwest of Dublin. Two of his bodyguards stood at the roadside with Lampman, and two more rode in a car behind Gadaire.

He glanced at the area on either side of the desolate country road; it had been a good five minutes since he had last seen a sign of civilization.

"You weren't kidding about your friends arriving first," Lampman said. "You didn't tell me I'd have to put up with the most invasive pat-down I've ever had in my life. I thought I was going to have to endure a cavity search."

"You actually might have enjoyed it. My men are exceptionally good in that area. Excuse the precautions. A man in my business is frequently a target, so I rarely accept invitations that put me in isolated areas."

"Then you should consider looking for another line of work."

"Retire? It's a thought. It might depend on what you're going to show me today."

"Then you may be on your way." Lampman smiled. "You were aware that I was less than enthused when you gave me the information from that trellis. I was skeptical. I had a tough time believing that something so simple could have triggered this effect. And even if I had accepted that premise, I seriously doubted that a scientist of the time could have figured it out."

"But he did?" Gadaire said.

Lampman motioned for Gadaire to follow him down the dusty road. "We've seen Oxygen Minimum Zones, or Shadow Zones, in our oceans before. What usually happens is that nitrogen-rich pollutants cause huge populations of plankton to grow on the water's surface. Those plankters decay and fall to the ocean floor, where they are decomposed by billions of microbes. It's a feeding frenzy. The trouble is that those microbes also consume oxygen. Lots of it. They consume so much oxygen that there's none left for anything else in the area."

"That's what happened in Marinth?"

"I don't think so. Not exactly. We saw this happening with phosphate runoff from laundry detergents. Once sewage-treatment plants were improved, and phosphate levels subsided, these pockets healed relatively quickly. In Marinth, things were much more serious. The coastal regions didn't heal for many years, perhaps even centuries. Once this Marinth TK44 alga was activated, it apparently spread like nothing we've ever seen. It just continued to spread and breed microorganisms that leached all the oxygen from the waters."

"This part I know."

"Then you also know what activated this destructive property. You found a hint in that trellis."

Gadaire smiled. "Corn?"

"Sounds ridiculous, I know. But it's true. Corn is something that can exist only with human helping hands. It doesn't grow in the wild. It was developed just in the past few thousand years from a wild grass called teosinte."

"I thought it came from Mexico."

"It did, and it spread through the Americas. Europeans weren't even introduced to it until a few hundred years ago. But after Marinth was discovered, we found out that they also cultivated teosinte to develop a type of corn of their own. A close cousin, if you will. We knew it happened late in the history of their civilization, but it now appears that it helped end their civilization." He shook his head. "Such a humble thing to cause the fall of the most glorious culture known to man."

"How could that have happened?"

"The Marinthians had begun burning the stalks and cobs in their ovens. It's possible that the resulting air pollution settled on the coastal waters and activated this alga. Or perhaps they tossed the stalks and cobs into the river as waste. Either way, this Marinthian educator was right. That was the beginning of the end."

"Are you sure about all this?"

"As a scientist, I want to know why this effect happens. I still don't know, and I won't until I can get more of the TK44 alga to study. But for your purposes, I can tell you it works. And it works quickly."

"You seem very positive."

Lampman smiled and gestured toward the small pond that had just appeared in Gadaire's line of sight. "Why don't you take a look?"

"You're joking, right?"

Lampman shook his head.

Gadaire felt a jolt of excitement as he walked quickly to the water's edge. The pond's water was dark green. Hundreds of dead fish, frogs, and insects floated in the muck.

Gadaire looked at Lampman. "You're telling me that you did all of this?"

"That's exactly what I'm telling you." Lampman held up a small stack of eight-by-ten photographs. "Here it is, just forty-eight hours ago."

Gadaire took the photos. He hardly recognized the clear water and beautiful, tranquil image. He glanced up. "Forty-eight hours?"

"It should have taken weeks to reach this stage. I told you, it's like nothing we've ever seen."

Gadaire knelt at the water's edge. "You mixed the alga samples with actual cornhusks?"

"I did that in the lab, and after I observed a strong reaction, I synthesized a chemical solution with some of the elements that could have caused it. As soon as I can narrow down the element—or elements—that are activating the alga, I can be more efficient."

"This is fantastic," Gadaire whispered.

"I told you it was worth the trip."

"Absolutely." He looked down at the dead water, sucked of every gasp of life. "I was afraid I might have to pull back if you didn't come up with something. But now I can go forward."

"Well . . . not quite. Not yet. You'll need massive quantities for the kind of operation I think you have in mind."

Gadaire waved his arm over the pond. "What about all this?"

"It's a start, and you'll eventually be able to grow and harvest all you need. I can help you with that . . . for a substantial increase in my fee and certain other considerations."

Gadaire's eyes narrowed. "What considerations?"

Lampman smiled. "I don't want to be an employee. I want to be a partner."

It was what Gadaire had been expecting for some time. Lampman was hungry and wanted to feed. "I pay you well."

"But my duties have expanded. You have me not only doing

vital research but analyzing coastal waters for potential breeding grounds for the alga. Naturally, it made me curious as to what you're doing in India. I'm not a fool."

"I've never thought you were." Throw the bastard a bone. He wasn't going to live long enough to enjoy it. "Perhaps I might let you have a small percentage of the profits if you agree to get your hands dirty and help me with information on how to produce and safely harvest this alga. You can do that?"

Lampman was beaming. "I told you that I could."

"How quickly?"

"We can create a TK44 algae farm here and perhaps in nine months or a year we . . ."

"That's not soon enough. I can't wait that long."

He frowned. "You have no choice."

"I always have a choice. Tell me my options."

"There's only one place on earth where you can get the amount you need. Marinth."

"Then you've just made my choice for me. Prepare to work your ass off . . . partner. I'm going to need all the information I can get about how to grab the alga safely and get out quick." Gadaire turned and strode back toward his car. "I'm going to Marinth."

"YES!"

Elijah Baker hung up his phone and strode back into the living room of his suite. "Hannah Bryson has been spotted in Athens," he said to Anna, who was curled up on the couch. "She was seen down at the docks where Melis Nemid's ship is moored. I've sent Mendoza to follow up."

"Then we'll have her." Anna swung her feet to the floor, her face lit with eagerness. "And Kirov?"

"We don't know yet. He hasn't surfaced."

"The lab at the museum?"

"Off-limits. Once Mendoza gets there, he'll find a way to explore that possibility. My agent on the ground couldn't get in to check."

"Then he's a fool. I'd find a way."

"I don't doubt it," Baker said. "But then he doesn't have your . . . talents."

"You're talking about sex?" She smiled as she slipped on the heels she'd kicked off earlier. "Sex is helpful. But it's brains that carry the day. I think you'll agree I have both. Gadaire is so sure that they're somewhere in Scotland, but I had a hunch she'd stay near Melis Nemid. That's why I suggested you send a man to stake out the Athens museum. And it paid off, didn't it?"

"In spades."

"You should listen to me more often, and I'd have my darling Vincent delivered to you tied in lovely pink ribbons."

"I have my own plans." And he still didn't know how much he could trust Anna. He'd been trying to get the goods on Gadaire for years, and it had been a nightmare of frustration. Gadaire had been virtually untouchable because of his connections with high-ranking government officials who used him for their covert operations, providing guns and ammo to U.S.-supported rebels in third-world countries and similar tasks. Every time Baker tried to arrest him, he'd been released within hours. But when Baker had gotten wind of the Marinth case, he'd seen his chance. Ecoterrorism on a grand scale. He would get his conviction. No one would be willing to help Gadaire on this one and risk their own careers. It was time for the big push.

Anna smiled. "Yes, and I'm sure your plans are brilliant. If you'd share them with me, I could find ways to make them better. Why else did you come to me?"

Why? He'd approached Anna to appeal to her supreme ambition. He hadn't been disappointed. In exchange for her help, he'd told her she'd be exonerated of all charges against her and Gadaire. The weapons business would be dismantled, but she'd retain control of the other business that she owned jointly with Gadaire, a business worth close to a hundred million dollars. She'd get her independence and wealth. Baker would get his conviction. Gadaire would be destroyed. Perfect.

More than perfect. He hadn't realized that he would also get Anna in his bed. He should have suspected that she always had to be in control of the situation, and sex was the logical weapon. He would have been a fool to refuse that particular manipulation when performed by one of the most skilled courtesans in the world. As long as he didn't lose his head and kept focused, it was an unbelievably satisfying arrangement.

"Gadaire hasn't indicated that he suspects you're dealing with me?"

She chuckled. "Gadaire suspects everyone. But I've made sure he needs me in such a multiplicity of ways so that he's reluctant to think me anything but loyal."

"I wouldn't want anything to happen to you."

"I'm touched." She smiled. "It's always good to have a man like you taking care of me."

She needed taking care of about as much as a cobra ready to strike. But there was something vaguely erotic about risking that bite. He touched her cheek with his forefinger. "You're valuable to me too. And I don't have to worry about your loyalty. Everything you do for me, you do for yourself."

"I wish you'd let me do more." She took his finger and brought it to her lips. "Digging out information is so boring. I'm a woman who likes action. What did you tell Mendoza to do about Hannah Bryson?"

"Just to keep a close watch. When Kirov surfaces, we'll gather them both in and put them away until they won't be a threat to the operation."

"Is that safe? As I told you, Gadaire knows that Kirov is the one who staged the heist of those samples. You wouldn't want him to reach Kirov before you do. It would complicate your plans if there was a conflict. This project is enormously important to Gadaire, but he could back off if he believes Kirov could cause it to blow up in his face."

"That's not going to happen. Mendoza is a trusted member of my team. He's been in my confidence from the beginning. He knows how important it is to move carefully."

"I hope you're right." She gave him a quick kiss. "But you'll find a way to fix the situation if it does." She headed for the door. "I'll call you as soon as I hear more about the results of Lampman's experiments. That could be the goad that puts everything in motion. Gadaire was supposed to meet with him this morning."

"I'll be waiting to hear from you."

BAKER MIGHT HEAR FROM HER or he might not, Anna thought with annoyance as she got into her Lamborghini. He was being too casual about Hannah Bryson, trusting her to Mendoza's surveillance. He'd lost her once before at that hotel when he should have closed in immediately and forced her to tell him where Kirov was. He was a fool who had too many rules and scruples with which to contend.

She had no such worries. She was not yet sure which way she was going to jump, but she had to protect the option that Baker had opened to her. It might be the best way to gain her independence and still be rich as Midas. But Gadaire had the potential for being much richer, and that was alluring. Why be queen of the world when you could be queen of the universe? It might be wise to stay with him and shave off more from his bank accounts than she had already. She was walking a delicate line until she made her decision.

At any rate, Hannah Bryson and Kirov had to be removed from her path.

She reached for her phone and dialed Charles Ames, Gadaire's security chief. Ames was smart, had contacts, and could be manipulated. "Charles, Hannah Bryson and Kirov have surfaced in Athens. I need you to arrange for them to disappear."

He hesitated. "Mr. Gadaire's orders?"

"Not this time." She'd had Ames do private kills for her before in past years. She'd paid him well and found him to be very discreet. "I prefer not to bother him. We both know that he'd approve."

"Then why not tell him?"

"Well, you see, there's a question of just how I knew where Bryson and Kirov were to be found. I have to protect my sources. You understand. You have sources to protect too. I just want Bryson and Kirov to be discreetly put down and not bother Gadaire again. No trouble for you. No trouble for me. No trouble for Gadaire."

"Discretion is expensive." He paused. "So is confidentiality."

"Double your usual amount. I wouldn't think of trying to cheat you."

He was silent a moment. "The other jobs I did for you had nothing to do with Gadaire. This could be more dangerous."

"But the money is wonderful. And I'd be very grateful."

Another silence. "Where are they?"

"Hannah Bryson is staying on Melis Nemid's boat near the Marinth Museum. I'm not sure about Kirov. I'd bet he'll be near Bryson."

"I'll have to hire men in Athens. I won't risk my men here talking to Gadaire. That will be more money."

He was going to do it. "Whatever it takes."

"Right away?"

"As soon as possible. Tell me when it's done."

"Oh, I will." He paused. "I like doing favors for you, Anna. It makes me feel close to you."

He had never called her Anna before. That could mean a sexual advance he might feel confident she couldn't refuse. Or it might mean that she must be wary of a lack of respect that could lead to possible blackmail. She could deal with either, but not until he was finished with the job she'd given him. "I know you'll do a good job, Charles." She hung up the phone and started her car. It hadn't gone as smoothly as she'd hoped, but she would get what she wanted. Bryson and Kirov would die, and she would be one step closer to where she wanted to be.

That was all that was important.

Athens, Greece
Plaka District

"WHAT IS THIS THING I'M EATING?" Ronnie asked as he took another bite of his lunch. "It tastes fishy, but good."

"I have no idea," Hannah said as she took a sip of her coffee and glanced up at the ruin of the Parthenon on the hill above them. "But I'm glad you're enjoying it. It's probably not as healthy as your mom would like, but there's always an exception."

"It's *gavros.* Baked anchovies." Melis looked around the outdoor café where they were sitting. Red-and-white umbrellas shaded the white tables, which were occupied almost exclusively by tourists. "I thought you'd enjoy a taste of Greece."

"Mom took me to a Taste of Boston festival once." He chuckled. "It wasn't anything like this."

"Well, Boston doesn't have ancient ruins as a backdrop," Hannah said. "We're still a young country."

"Yeah." Ronnie took out his iPhone and took several pictures of the café on the Plaka, an area packed with restaurants and small gift shops. "This place is awesome."

"It's a tourist trap," Melis said. "But it's fun. You'd better stop taking pictures and finish your lunch. You've been snapping shots all morning. You must have enough to fill an album."

"I thought I'd e-mail them to Mom and Donna. But some of them are pretty lame." He started to view the photos. "I'd better go through them and blow some of them away."

"Technology." Melis shook her head. "Kids these days are amazing. They just accept the miracles. That phone camera would have never been possible when I was growing up. I had an old Brownie. Is that iPhone one of your gifts to him, Hannah?"

She shook her head. "Cathy and Conner gave it to him. I usually opted for sports equipment." She smiled as she watched Ronnie's intent face as he flipped through the photos. He had enjoyed himself this morning. For this brief time, he seemed to have returned to the boy she had known before Conner's death. "Where to this afternoon, Ronnie? Another museum or back to the *Fair Winds?*"

He didn't answer immediately and when he looked up his expression was absorbed. "I don't know. Why don't we ask Kirov what he wants to do."

"Kirov?" Hannah asked.

"Yeah, I called and asked him to come and meet us here when we were at that last museum. We were having so much fun, I thought he'd like it too. He said he'd come as soon as he finished going through some test results with Aziz."

"You didn't tell me," Hannah said.

"A surprise." He glanced back down at his photo gallery in the phone. "I knew you'd be happy to see him. You like—" He frowned. "Here's another one."

"Another what?"

"Wait a minute." He made some adjustments to the photo display. "Isn't this weird? Practically everywhere we went this morning, this guy was there too."

Hannah stiffened. "Really?" She said casually, "Probably a tourist hitting the same sights. Let me take a look."

He pushed his phone across the table to her. "Some of the pictures are of him inside the museums, but a couple of them are shots outside on the streets."

She looked down at the gallery and enlarged the photos. A, burly man in his forties with sandy hair and a weathered, freckled face. He was dressed casually, wearing khakis and a navy Windbreaker. Nothing threatening about him. He looked like the tourist she'd told Ronnie he probably was.

Probably. The museum shots appeared very innocent. He was never looking directly at them, but at a vase, a painting, a sculpture.

The two street shots were more suspicious. He looked . . . intent.

"Well, he evidently is on the same tour circuit we are."

Ronnie nodded. "And he likes the same restaurants."

"What?"

"Look at the last photo."

A sandy-haired man sitting at a table beneath a red-and-white umbrella.

Her gaze flew to Ronnie's face. "Where is he?"

"Two tables behind you. By the bar."

She forced herself not to turn around, but she felt a prickling on the back of her neck.

"He's having the same kind of food I'm having," Ronnie said. "That *gavros* thing."

"Then he has good taste." She handed Ronnie his phone back. "But I think we should make a decision about what we're going to be doing." She got to her feet. "Finish your lunch. I think I'll go out on the street and see if I can see Kirov. If he's not in sight, I'll give him a call and get his estimated time of arrival."

"That might not be a bad idea." Melis was looking at Ronnie's phone. "Ronnie and I will be with you as soon as we finish." She smiled. "You know, Ronnie, you didn't get a chance to see the Marinth Museum yet. It's my pride and joy. Why don't we go back to the boat, then go up to the museum later?"

"We'll ask Kirov." He was sipping his lemonade. "He may want to go somewhere else."

"By all means, we wouldn't want to do something Kirov wouldn't like," Hannah said dryly. "We'll certainly check." She made her way through the tables toward the low wrought-iron gate that bordered the street. She carefully didn't glance at the table beside the bar.

Not yet. Not until she was at an angle that wouldn't be obvious to the man at the table.

By the time she had reached the street, she'd reached the correct angle.

Navy Windbreaker, sandy hair. But he'd stopped eating and was watching her.

Not good.

She went out beyond the wrought-iron barrier and casually looked up and down the street. She shook her head and waved at Ronnie and Melis. Then she pulled out her phone.

Kirov answered immediately. "Hannah?"

"I'm at an outdoor restaurant in the Plaka. It's on Adrianou Street. Don't come anywhere near here. Something's happening."

Kirov muttered a curse. "I'm already on my way. I'll be there in a few minutes."

"No, we're being followed. Heavyset man, khaki pants, and navy Windbreaker. Looks like a tourist. He hasn't made a move toward us, but he may be waiting for you. Baker's man?"

"Maybe. Maybe not. Are there lots of people around?"

"Yes, the café is packed."

"Then all of you stay there until I get there."

"No way." She smiled and waved again at Ronnie. "I'm not running any risk to Ronnie and Melis. They're out of here. I'm putting them in a cab and sending them back to the *Fair Winds*. I'll try to distract our tail until they're away from the café."

"Dammit, stay where you are."

She hailed a cab. "I don't want to chance anyone following their cab. I want all his attention on me. I'll try to lose him in the streets. I'll meet you at Melis's boat." She hung up and motioned for the cab to wait. She walked quickly back to the table. "Kirov said that he'll meet us at the *Fair Winds*. Come on, the cab's waiting."

"Right." Melis got to her feet. "Finished, Ronnie?"

He nodded and jumped to his feet. "But he said he was coming here."

"Change of plan." Hannah herded them to the cab. "He definitely wants to show you the Marinth Museum. He said he'd become an expert while he was waiting for Aziz."

"I believe I know a little more about it than he does," Melis said as she got into the cab. "And I think I can fill in the gaps."

Ronnie nodded. "You know everything. Is there anything about the dolphins at—"

Hannah glanced over her shoulder.

The sandy-haired man had gotten to his feet and was moving toward them.

She slammed the cab door. "Oh, darn it, I forgot those souvenirs I was going to buy for you, Ronnie. I'll go pick some up at that booth across the street and take the next cab." She motioned to the driver to go. "See you at the ship!"

"Hannah!" Melis said, as the cab left the curb. Then she quickly recovered. "Fine, get a souvenir mug for me."

Hannah turned quickly away with a lightning glance behind her.

He was still in the café, but talking or pretending to talk on his mobile phone. The cab was turning the corner and was out of sight.

Move!

She turned and hurried down a narrow passageway between restaurants. She cut through to the back alley and turned left, resisting the urge to look behind.

Garbage cans lined the deserted alley, and window-mounted air-conditioning units roared and dripped water onto the cobblestones. Tubs filled with animal fat lined the back of several of the restaurants; fish scales were scattered on the ground behind others. She started to have doubts. What if the guy didn't follow her? What if he had circled around and was waiting for her ahead in any one of the many narrow passageways between buildings?

A sound behind her. Metallic clattering, then the sound of scuffling. She spun around.

Kirov and the man in the navy Windbreaker had knocked against a pair of garbage cans as they fought over Kirov's gun.

Kirov struck him in the throat with the handgun's butt, and the man doubled over, struggling to breathe. Kirov reached inside the man's jacket and pulled out a semiautomatic. Kirov lightly kicked the man's calves. "Any more down there?"

The man shook his head, then suddenly barreled into Kirov with his shoulder. Kirov spun the man around and rammed his face against the brick wall.

"You're annoying me," he said.

The man's mouth was still pressed against the brick wall, and his answer was unintelligible.

Kirov reached into his pocket and drew out his wallet and flipped it open. "Paul Mendoza, carpet salesman."

"That's right," the man managed to say.

"I don't think so. Somehow you don't look like a salesman to me. First, I hear you've been stalking my friends all over Athens, now you're creeping after a defenseless woman in a deserted alley. I'd be well within my rights to pulverize you."

Mendoza angled his mouth away from the wall. "Then call the cops."

"That would be okay with you?"

"Yes, I haven't done anything wrong."

"That shoulder roll is something they've been teaching at Langley for a few years. I never thought it was very effective. You might want to pass that on to the higher-ups."

"I don't know what you're talking about."

Kirov turned to Hannah as she approached them. "I'd bet he's one of Baker's U.S. government agents."

She made a face. "That's scary, considering the fact that his cover was blown by a twelve-year-old."

"Let me go or have me arrested," Mendoza said. "Your choice."

"There's a third option we haven't explored. Tell me who you are and why you're following her."

Mendoza didn't answer.

"Let me assist you. You're looking for me, and you work for Agent Elijah Baker."

"He just wants to talk to you."

"I don't have a problem with talking. It's the 'detained indefinitely' part that bothers me."

"Baker is only trying to do his job. I was only supposed to watch and report."

"As a first step. Once he zeroed in on both of us, you might have been given other orders."

"We're not hit men. He might have told us to keep you confined, but that would be the extent of—"

A Humvee turned into the alley from the end of the block.

"I think we're about to run out of breathing room here," Kirov said. "If you promise to behave, we can find someplace to discuss this like—"

A gunshot! A chunk of plaster exploded next to Hannah's head.

"Get down!" Kirov shouted.

A hail of bullets sprayed the building wall as they ducked into an alcove.

"Friends of yours?" Hannah asked.

"No." Mendoza stared at her with glassy eyes.

"Are you okay?"

With shaking hands, he pulled open his jacket. A bloodstain spread across the front of his shirt.

"Kirov!" Hannah gasped.

Kirov folded the man's jacket over the stain. "Keep pressure on it." He turned back toward the Humvee as it drew closer. Kirov raised the gun he'd taken from Mendoza, but another hail of bullets pushed him down before he could fire. "Trapped," he murmured. He glanced around, trying to find an out. He suddenly noticed a tub of animal fat beside them. He felt the outside of the tub. "Warm."

"So what?" Hannah said.

"Stand back." Kirov pulled a lighter from his pocket and lit it. He jerked off the tub's lid and tossed the lighter inside. The fat ignited and flames shot high from the container's rim. He turned back to Hannah and Agent Mendoza. "Get ready to run."

Kirov kicked the tub over. The grease fire roared over the alley, the flames shooting higher as they hit patches of water around the Humvee's front tires.

Shielded by the flames, Kirov, Hannah, and Mendoza bolted from the alcove to a passageway between the buildings that would take them back to the street. Kirov crouched and aimed his gun back toward the alley. "Keep going!"

Mendoza collapsed in the narrow passageway.

Hannah leaned over him, trying to pull him up. "Come on. Just a little farther."

He shook his head. "I can't. Go . . ."

"Like hell. Come on!"

As Kirov knelt with the gun extended before him, the Humvee peeled out and sped away. The grease fire burned and crackled as tenants from the other buildings started to appear in the alley.

Kirov put the gun away and leaned over the agent. "We'll get you help."

Mendoza's breathing grew shallow. "You have to stop," he whispered. "You're helping Gadaire."

Kirov's eyes narrowed. "What?"

"We're trying to get him . . . but . . . you're screwing it up."

"He shouldn't be talking," Hannah said.

Kirov crouched beside the man. "What do you mean?"

Mendoza tried to speak, but no words came. He tried again. "Gadaire . . . the scientist . . . Trinity. India. Stay out of . . . it. We'll get . . . him. It'll be okay . . ."

"Just relax," Hannah said. She looked at Kirov. "I'm going to get him help. Stay here with him, and I'll run to one of the—"

"He's dead."

Hannah's gaze flew back to Mendoza. The agent's eyes were still open, his face frozen in that last tense, urgent expression. Shit. This was no way for a person to leave the world.

Kirov stood up and took her forearm. "Let's go."

"Shouldn't we stay and—"

"No. Quickly."

Before Hannah could process what had happened, she was on her feet and moving through the passageway. They emerged on the sidewalk and passed the dozens of excited pedestrians who had heard the noise and seen the smoke rising from behind the row of shops and restaurants.

Kirov nodded toward the crosswalk. "This way."

Hannah and Kirov walked to the next block, rounded the corner, and made their way to his rental car. They climbed in and drove off as the sirens wailed in the distance.

Kirov checked the rearview mirror. "I think we're okay now."

Hanna drew a deep breath as she leaned back in the seat. "Who just tried to kill us? Gadaire?"

"I'm guessing it was his people. They must have figured out that we're here in Greece."

"Then what was the agent saying about your helping Gadaire?"

"Maybe just that I'm interfering with his and Baker's investigation. I'm not sure. I was more interested by what he was saying about Gadaire's working with the Trinity College scientist."

"Lampman? But we knew he was doing research for Gadaire."

"But it sounded like he wasn't working *for* but *with* Gadaire. A subtle change in status. And what was Mendoza trying to say about India?"

Hannah shook his head. "We can try to figure that out later. What disturbs me most is that apparently everybody in the world seems to know we're here."

"Yes. Evidently our red herring has played out. We've got to leave Athens right away."

"That opens up a hell of a can of worms," Hannah said. "We can't just walk away. It must be fairly obvious to Gadaire what we're doing here. Melis's people in the lab are still working on those samples, and we have to guarantee their safety." She bit her lip. "Ronnie. That's what scares me the most. I want to send him home on the next flight, but if Gadaire's people have been watching us, that might be the worst thing to do. By now they know who he is and what he means to me."

"Then what do you propose we do?" Kirov asked.

Hannah thought for a long moment. Every solution had dangers. Just try to pick the one that had the least number of threats.

"We leave right away. All of us."

"All of us?"

"Yes, we take the lab with us."

"How do you think we'll do that?"

"We take Melis's boat. Melis and the lab guys can take whatever they need from here and move it to the lab on *Fair Winds*. It's one of the most advanced laboratories anywhere. We move fast and hope that those men who attacked us in the alley will be slowed down by having to wait for orders. With luck, we can be hundreds of miles away before nightfall."

"Where do we go?"

"Nowhere. The middle of the ocean. The one place we can go and not be found."

Kirov shook his head. "Technology is too good for you to say that. You know that."

"I know it's not a perfect solution. But we can move if we see a threat. Planes can search areas for days without spotting boats in distress on the ocean. And would Gadaire really waste time to go after us if it proved that difficult? He appears to have other more urgent plans in mind."

"It could be the safest bet for the time being," Kirov said slowly.

"If you can think of any way that would be safer, tell me. I'll listen. But we can't keep looking over our shoulders, and that's what will happen if we stay here."

"India . . ."

"You want to go to India? You don't even know what Mendoza meant."

"No, but Lampman might know. Lampman might know a lot."

"You idiot. Dammit, you promised me. That's right, go back to Dublin. They'll be waiting to cut your throat."

"Probably." He thought about it. "No, I'll go with you on the *Fair Winds*. I can always helicopter out later. I want to make sure that Gadaire's people aren't trailing you. But I have another idea about Ireland . . ."

"I'm sure you do." She was just grateful he was going to stay out of danger for the time being. Hannah reached for her phone. "I've got to have Melis call the lab and get them moving down to the ship. I want to be out of the harbor within the hour."

Kirov nodded. "Good plan. I have a few calls to make myself . . ."

CHAPTER
16

THE DECK OF THE *FAIR WINDS* was already teeming with activity when Kirov and Hannah pulled up to the dock. The crew was preparing to weigh anchor, and Aziz was speaking animatedly to Melis. He turned to Hannah as she boarded the boat. "There you are. You appear and I lose my beautiful civilized lab and I'm thrown back into the primitive."

"Primitive, my foot," Hannah said. "I've seen the facilities on board, and they're awesome. You'll do just fine, Aziz."

He grinned. "I know I will. I'm far enough along so that I don't require all the sophisticated testing equipment. I can bring along what I need."

"How fast can you move?"

"I have my assistant packing up right now. I told him that if he didn't have everything on board in an hour, I'd get a new assistant." His eyes were twinkling. "That's a fate worse than death for an eager young scientist. I know just how he'd feel. This project is the job of a lifetime." He turned back to Melis. "It will work out. I'm so close. Give me another day or two, and I'll have your answer."

"You'll have the time. As long as those days are on the briny deep." She turned and walked toward the captain, who was motioning to her.

"You're that near to an answer?" Hannah asked Aziz.

He nodded. "I wouldn't con Melis. I'll hand it to her on a silver platter." He turned and strode down the gangplank. "But now I've got to go back to the lab and help pack up."

She turned back to Kirov and found him talking to Eugenia and Charlie, who had just come on board.

Eugenia smiled as Hannah came toward them. "It seems I missed some excitement. How disappointing. But to make up for it, Kirov has promised me that I won't have to go on another boring boat ride. I do hate boats."

"So you told me," Charlie said. "You were stinging me with that tongue so much that I hardly noticed the journey."

"Just a little to wake you up a bit."

Kirov glanced at Hannah. "Eugenia and I are going to do a little reconnoitering. We'll be back before it's time to leave."

"Reconnoitering?"

"The boat is probably being watched. We need to find Gadaire's man and take him out before he can report any activity."

"I'm going with you," Charlie said.

"No." Eugenia's voice was firm. "This isn't a learning exercise. Kirov and I are experienced and know what we're doing. You're an amateur. We can't risk mistakes."

Charlie's face flushed. "I won't make—"

"No." Eugenia said again. "Stay here and keep an eye on Hannah." She smiled. "You'll get enough action in Dublin." She turned and walked down the gangplank with Kirov. "I think I spotted a possible near the office of the marina," she told him. "I'll go there, and you head for the museum. It would be logical that they keep an eye on the lab."

Two of a kind.

Hannah watched them walk down the dock and felt the same frustration that Charlie must be experiencing. Dammit, she wanted to run after them and try to help.

No, her place was here. She had to make sure that Melis and Ronnie were safe.

"You're going back to Ireland?" she asked him.

"According to Kirov." Charlie's hands clenched on the rail. "I'm surprised Eugenia is letting me trail along. After all, I'm just an 'amateur.'"

And Hannah was surprised that Charlie was obeying Eugenia's orders when he obviously wanted desperately to join them. Charlie was changing, she realized. He was more mature, a little less egocentric. "We could use help setting up Aziz' lab. Unless you'd prefer to stand here and glower at Eugenia as she goes about her business."

He grimaced and turned away. "You sound just like Eugenia."

"That's not bad. I respect her."

"So do I. Where is this lab I'm supposed to set up?"

"Go see Melis. She's in charge." She gave one last glance at the direction in which Kirov and Eugenia had disappeared and turned away. She had her own work to do.

But first she had to find Ronnie. She hadn't seen him since she'd come on board, and it wasn't like him not to be in the middle of things. She went to look for him.

She found him alone at the rail on the starboard side of the ship. "Ronnie?"

He didn't look at her. "You lied to me."

She had half expected that reaction. He was too smart not to have realized what was going on after she had called Melis. "Yes, I did. I'm sorry. I just wanted to get you out of there so I could find out what was going on."

"You should have told me. How can I protect you if you don't let me know what's happening?"

How to explain in a way that he would accept? "It's instinct, Ronnie. Caring for people is a two-way street. You want to protect me. I want to protect you. Think about it. If you had to lie to me to keep me safe, would you do it?"

He thought about it. "Maybe. But it's wrong."

"Yes, it is." She paused. "I should have trusted you. I was in a hurry, and I didn't want to make explanations. After I saw those photos you took, I just wanted to get both of you away from there." She smiled faintly. "By the way, that was very clever of you to be so observant. I was impressed."

"No big deal. I was a little scared about him." He scowled at her. "But you seemed not to be worried. So I thought it was okay."

And damaged his trust and pride. She had to get that trust back. "Will you forgive me if I promise never to lie to you again? Not even if I'm scared and want to keep you safe?"

"You treated me like a kid. Oh, I know I am a kid, but you should have—"

"You're right. I'm wrong." She covered his hand on the rail with her own. "I'll never lie to you again."

He was silent a moment. "And you'll let me help if something like that happens again?"

"That's a hard one." She sighed. "Yes, I promise."

He turned and buried his head against her. "Good. I hated to be mad at you, Aunt Hannah. But I couldn't let it happen again."

Her brows rose. "By any chance, did you just manipulate me to get what you want?"

"Maybe. But I didn't lie." He lifted his head and smiled. "I wouldn't do that."

She gave him a quick hug and pushed him away. "Make yourself useful. Go to Melis and have her give you something to do. We need all hands to get this ship under way."

"Aye, aye." He started down the deck. "And I think it's smart to go out to sea. Much less chance of anyone finding you."

"Harder anyway. I'm glad you approve."

"Oh, I do. Was it Kirov's idea?"

"No, it was *not*."

She watched him as he headed down the deck toward Melis. Had there been a hint of mischief in that last question? Possibly. Ronnie was growing up and fully capable of subtle humor . . . and manipulation. But hopefully the agreement that they'd struck wouldn't be uncomfortable for either of them.

Her smile faded as she started after Ronnie. Time to get busy. Like Charlie, she wanted to stand waiting and watching for Kirov and Eugenia to return. But the time would pass quicker if she kept busy.

Kirov returned alone almost an hour later. He was . . . charged. Every muscle of his body seemed wired. She had seen him like that a few times and knew what it meant. She dropped what she was doing and walked toward him. "Mission accomplished?"

"We got rid of two. I don't think there were any more."

"Dead?"

He shook his head. "We weren't sure if either of them were Baker's men. Didn't want to throw out the baby with the bathwater. So we put them to sleep for a good long time. They'll wake up with ferocious headaches when we're far out to sea." He turned to Charlie, who had strolled up to him. "Eugenia is waiting for you at the museum. Take off."

Charlie nodded and headed for the gangplank.

"And we should take off too," Kirov said. "When do we sail?"

She turned away. "We're ready to go. You were keeping us waiting."

THE SUN WAS GOING DOWN IN a purple-scarlet explosion on the horizon, turning the sea into a glory of shimmering color.

"That's nice," Ronnie said as he leaned on the rail. "I left my camera in my bunk, or I'd take a picture of it. We've been sailing for hours, Aunt Hannah. Are we safe now?"

"I think so." Don't lie just to make him feel safe. Damn, that was difficult. Every instinct with children was to keep them secure and happy. "No sign of pursuit, and Kirov made sure that no one reported our departure. Yes, there's an excellent chance we're safe."

"So we just sail around out here? Why don't we go to Marinth?"

"Because Marinth isn't safe right now. We'll go later."

Ronnie was silent a moment, his gaze on Melis's silhouette a few yards away framed against the scarlet sky. "She'd like to go there, I think. She's sad, isn't she?"

"Yes, she misses her dolphins."

"I know, she told me. It's hard to have a dolphin for a pet. It's not like they'll come whenever you whistle."

"She does have a whistle, but she seldom uses it. They're not her pets. She regards them as friends. They've saved her life more than once. Not many people understand dolphins. They're a very strange species. Pete and Susie like humans, they even interact with them; but they still have a strong family herd instinct with their own kind. Particularly the dolphins of Marinth. It's as if they call Pete and Susie back to them."

"She looks lonely. I think I'll go to her and see if—"

A high, shrill sound broke the silence. Another followed.

Then the shrillness broke until it sounded like laughter.

Melis straightened at the rail. "Pete?" She was peering down at the sea below her. "Pete!"

Ronnie and Hannah hurried to stand beside her.

"They're here?" Hannah asked.

Melis nodded. The soft rose flush on her face was from the setting sun, but the luminous glow was pure happiness. "Pete and Susie. We're so far from Marinth, I didn't expect to—but here they are."

"They came looking for you," Hannah said softly.

"Yes." She fell to her knees, her gaze on the dolphins, who had both come close to the ship and were chattering up at her. "It's about time you wandered out here. I've missed you."

Ronnie dropped to his knees beside her. He was staring in fascination at the two sets of huge dark eyes gazing up at them. "They're . . . beautiful."

"Don't flatter them," Melis said. "They're already too vain. Particularly Susie."

"Which one is Susie? They look the same."

"Susie is on the left. She has a dorsal fin with a V in the center. Pete is larger and has darker gray markings on his snout. It won't take you long to get to know them at a glance." She laughed. "Susie is going to make sure that you do. She's flirting with you." Susie had swum over to Ronnie and was chortling up at him. Then Pete swam close, nudging her aside to get to Ronnie. "I believe you've made a hit, Ronnie."

"Look at their eyes. They're glowing like cat's eyes."

"They're brighter than cats'. They have to function in depths and withstand light levels that would hurt human eyes."

"I . . . want to touch them. Would that be okay?"

"I think they'd like that. Dolphins can't smell, and they swallow everything whole, so they don't taste it. But touch is important to them. They spend about thirty percent of their time in physical contact with other dolphins." Melis sat back on her heels. "Would you like to swim with them?"

Ronnie's eyes lit up. "May I?"

Melis nodded. "Go get your swimsuit on. Hurry."

He jumped to his feet and ran toward the stairs.

"Is it safe?" Hannah asked.

"Yes, I'll be in the water with him, and the dolphins won't let anything happen. I've seen them cradle a swimmer between them to keep him from drowning." She pulled off her swim dress. "And it's an experience he won't forget." She kicked off her thongs. "They like him and took to him right away. I don't know quite what's happening, but I think they want him to come to play with them. Maybe they sense . . . I don't know. They have wonderful instincts."

And Ronnie was ecstatic, Hannah thought. Why not let him forget the threat hanging over them and enjoy all the beauty and wonder of this moment?

"I'm ready!" Ronnie was running toward them. "Do I just jump in?"

"Be my guest." Melis dove into the sea.

Ronnie was laughing with excitement as he followed.

Hannah came closer to the rail, watching the dolphins jumping, circling around them, even butting Ronnie playfully with their snouts.

He reached out and gently touched Pete's snout. "It's warm . . . I thought he'd be cold from the water."

Pete went still beneath his hand, staring into the boy's eyes for a long time.

What was going on between them? Hannah wondered.

Magic.

Mystery.

Understanding.

And something else.

Healing.

Trinity College

Dublin, Ireland

1:40 P.M.

RAIN POUNDED THE SIDEWALKS and formed massive puddles as Eugenia and Charlie, dressed in hooded slickers, made their way to the west side of campus. Some students, apparently caught without umbrellas, dashed back and forth between buildings.

Eugenia pulled her hood lower over her forehead. "I don't understand how you Irish can be so cheerful when it's gloomy and rainy so much of the time."

Charlie smiled. "Aye, but there's always a sadness there, just under the skin. We drink to keep it mashed deep down."

"Ah, that explains a lot." She gestured to a vine-covered building ahead of them. "That's the botany department's greenhouse. Dr. Lampman always goes there to check on growths and cultures at about 1:45 every weekday except Thursday."

"How do you know?"

"Research. It's the first rule of dealing with any unknown quantity, especially someone who may be an enemy. Remember that."

"I will. I'll put it on my list." His lips twisted. "A list that's getting longer and longer."

"A list that will get longer still, especially if you want to take on Anna Devareau. If you try before you're ready, she'll squash you like a bug."

"I understand, Master Yoda."

She gave him a perplexed look. "What's a Yoda?"

"You're kidding, right? *Star Wars,* little green guy, teaches the heroes how to kick ass . . ."

"I don't like science fiction."

"You're missing out."

"I doubt it. Anyway, it's always important to do your research. It's not exciting, but it's vital. I know your father believed in it."

He nodded. "He drove me crazy with that stuff."

"In this case, it's already been done for us. Kirov logged Lampman's schedule when he was planning how to take the alga samples. Lampman evidently follows a strict routine. That's good for us."

They entered the arboretum and followed the signs that pointed them toward the adjoining greenhouse. In a matter of minutes, they moved into the white-tiled structure. The rain was still pounding outside, rattling the upper panes and running down the sides, distorting their views of the outside world like thousands of fun-house mirrors.

"What time is it?" Charlie whispered.

"Always wear a watch. Put that on your list right now. Lampman should be here any—" She stopped and looked ahead. "There he is."

Lampman was standing on the other side of the greenhouse, hunched over a table of plants. He held a clipboard in front of him, jotting down observations. He either had not heard them, or he did not care that there were suddenly others in his vicinity.

"Hello, Dr. Lampman." Eugenia smiled as she and Charlie approached him. "How are you today?"

He glanced up from the clipboard and responded absently, "Fine."

"Sorry to interrupt your work, but I wondered what you might think of this." She unzipped her rain slicker and pulled out a stack of photos. "Some of these got a little wet, sorry about that." She showed him the first picture, a shot of two badly decomposed corpses in the driver and passenger seats of a car parked in a wooded area. "These were David and Patricia Hermann, though in the picture it's difficult to tell who is who. The driver's skull is a bit bigger if you overlook the smashed-in forehead. That's probably David, don't you think?"

Lampman stepped back and held the clipboard close to his chest. "Who are you?"

"Not important right now. These two people were software engineers whom Vincent Gadaire hired to hack into the encrypted files of Senate Appropriations Committee members. He wanted a peek at a new antimissile system. Gadaire got his peek, but the U.S. government started to figure out what the Hermanns had done. Gadaire didn't want the trail to lead back to him, so he made sure they would never give him up to the authorities. Their bodies sat in their car at the bottom of this ravine for months before they were found. There was a crude attempt to make it look like an accident, but multiple contusions in an automobile interior looks quite a bit different than thirty-five blows from a baseball bat."

Lampman moistened his lips. "Why are you here? Why are you showing this to me?"

She held up another photo of a corpse with no head or hands. "They eventually identified this one as a defense contractor who was providing classified countertactical weapons to Gadaire. Again, it looked like he was about to cut a deal that included giving up Gadaire." She held up yet another photo, this one of a bald man missing half his face. "Antonio Venti, who helped Gadaire broker a deal with Al Qaeda. Also killed as he was about to give evidence . . ." She held up a clipping from a French newspaper. "This is Dr. Timothy Hollis, a curator at the Louvre in Paris. He's recently vanished without a trace." She paused. "He's one of the world's foremost experts on Marinth."

Lampman stiffened in shock.

Eugenia smiled. "Yes, Marinth. Do you think Gadaire hired him, too?"

Beads of sweat collected on Lampman's forehead. "I don't know what you're talking about."

"Gadaire is a dangerous man to work for, especially if he thinks you may incriminate him. He has a history of eliminating any threat."

"Assuming that I would ever do any work for this man, why would I ever endanger my life by doing such a foolish thing?"

Eugenia smiled. "But you've already done it. About five minutes ago."

"What are you talking about?"

"You know that Gadaire has been having you watched. Remember the night the samples were taken from you?"

Lampman opened his lips to speak, then closed them again.

Eugenia reached into her pocket. "Then it shouldn't surprise you to learn that he—or his security team—are monitoring your phone calls. How else would he be able to keep such close tabs on people who hold such sensitive information about him?"

Lampman was sweating profusely now. "You haven't answered my question. What exactly did I do five minutes ago?"

"You used your mobile phone to make a call to the authorities. Ireland's Special Branch C-3 Section, to be specific."

"But I didn't." Lampman patted his chest. "And my phone's right here."

Eugenia lifted her own phone. "And here. I spoofed your number and user account information. And it turns out that my friend here is an exceptional mimic."

Charlie nodded while Eugenia pulled up a recording application on her phone and played back a portion of a conversation that sounded very much like Lampman speaking to a female special branch agent.

". . . I had no idea what Gadaire had in mind. If I had known, I would never have gotten involved."

"You did the right thing by coming to us, Dr. Lampman. I know it wasn't easy to do."

"I have a few samples of the alga he wanted me to work with. I can bring it when I come in. But I need to know I'll be protected."

"Of course."

Lampman's nervousness was being replaced by pure horror.

Eugenia stopped the recording. "I played the part of the agent, by the way. I can't stand hearing my own voice, but I think Gadaire will be convinced. Don't you?"

"You bitch," Lampman said.

Charlie shrugged. "You're an easy man to imitate. It helps that some of your classroom lectures are on the Internet. I really think I captured your essence."

"Who *are* you?"

"Eugenia, your savior, or the woman who's going to take you down. Your choice."

"This is insane," Lampman said. "I'll have you both arrested."

"Not likely," Eugenia said. "Unless you would really like to call Special Branch C-3 Section, and I wouldn't recommend that. Gadaire will be pissed enough that you called them once."

"He'll believe the truth. I know he will."

"Do you really?" Charlie asked skeptically.

Lampman didn't answer.

He was on the edge of breaking, Eugenia judged. Time to tighten the final screws in the coffin.

She walked to a row of greenhouse windows that were almost completely fogged from condensation. "Here's what I think has been happening in the past five minutes. It starts with the phone call. A low-level member of Gadaire's security staff hears it, then plays it for his boss. He, in turn, plays it for Gadaire. If Gadaire is not available, he plays it for Anna Devareau. Before the recording is even finished playing, the security chief is ordered to kill you. There may be a discussion about how to do it, and whether or not it should appear to be an accident or natural causes. Then they come to a decision." Eugenia wiped away some of the condensation and peered outside. "Look, they're discussing it with your faithful shadow right now."

Lampman walked slowly to the window and stared down at a young man standing in the rain. He was talking on his mobile phone. "Him?"

Eugenia nodded. "I suppose he has the day shift. There are a few different ways they could go. They could inject a syringe of poison into your iced tea. You could be struck by a hit-and-run driver as you walk to your car. Or, if they really wanted to be crass, a bullet would do the trick. Any of those methods would keep you from talking to the authorities about Gadaire's latest hobby." She nodded toward the young man on the phone. "They're probably discussing it with him right now."

Lampman looked at the person outside. Like the other young man who had been tailing him, this one also carried a backpack and appeared to be a student. As the rain came down harder, he pulled his jacket tighter around him, revealing the awkward bulge of a shoulder holster.

Eugenia turned from the window. "You can also be sure that Gadaire is having your e-mail monitored. We've spoofed your address and crafted quite an e-mail from you to the authorities, including lab photos of those samples. It may be overkill, if you'll pardon the expression. I seriously doubt you'd still be around by the time Gadaire would read it."

Lampman asked hoarsely, "What do you want from me?"

"Information. That's all."

"That's all? You've just ruined my life. Why would I help you?"

"To save your life."

"How can you do that?" he asked bitterly. "You've just finished telling me that you totally destroyed every—" Lampman froze as he stared out the window.

The young man had pocketed his phone and was suddenly walking with purpose toward the greenhouse.

"Our recording must have gone up the chain of command," Eugenia murmured.

Charlie turned toward Lampman. "And this guy's orders have come down. What now, Professor?"

Lampman glanced frantically from Eugenia to Charlie. "I don't want to be on the run for the rest of my life."

"You won't be," Eugenia said. "You'll just lie low for a few days. I promise. After that, Gadaire won't be a problem."

"He's coming. He's going to kill me."

"We'll take care of it." Eugenia motioned to Charlie, and they pulled out their semiautomatic handguns. "We came prepared." She gestured toward the greenhouse floor. "Have a seat. Keep low."

Eugenia and Lampman crouched behind a plant rack as Charlie sprinted to the other side of the greenhouse. She turned to Lampman. "But there's a price. Tell us what Gadaire is planning in India."

"I have no idea."

Eugenia gave him a disgusted look. "You're not cooperating. I believe we'll have to leave."

A heavy door opened, then swung shut in the connected building. Firm footsteps echoed in the long corridor.

"We have less than a minute," Eugenia whispered. "Such a short time to decide whether you want to live or die."

The footsteps grew closer.

"India," she said.

The pace quickened.

Lampman desperately glanced around, then whispered, "Orissa, India. Chilika Lake. It's just a test run for the whole country."

"And Gadaire is there?"

"I'll tell you later. Please."

"Now."

"He's not there yet. He's leading a team to Marinth to harvest the TK44 alga he needs. Please, that's all I know. You have to help me."

The footsteps stopped. "Dr. Lampman?" The young, male voice spoke again. "Sir?"

Looking at the reflection in the greenhouse glass panes, Eugenia watched the young man as he moved down the center of the room. Meaning, of course, he would be able to see them.

"I'm Paul Reilly, sir. Mr. Gadaire sent me," the young man said, glancing from side to side. "He gave me a message for you. He said that he'll need your help to—"

The kid froze when he was just yards away.

Reilly had spotted her and Lampman in the glass, Eugenia thought.

He reached into his jacket.

Now!

She jumped to her feet and whirled around with her gun extended before her. Before she had even completed the move, Charlie had appeared out of nowhere and coldcocked him from behind.

Paul Reilly turned, dazed, and Charlie finished him off with an undercut to the jaw. Reilly's gun slid across the floor as he fell unconscious.

Eugenia picked up the gun and smiled at Charlie. "Well done."

"Improvised, like all the best jazz," Charlie said.

She turned to Lampman. "Stand up. We need to get you out of here. Gadaire's people may already have more on the way."

Charlie pointed to the man crumpled on the floor. "I'll find something to tie him up with and dump him in the gardening shed in the back."

"Good. I'll meet you at the boat," she said. She took Lampman's arm and walked with him out the building's side door. The rain had eased up to a gentle sprinkle.

"Where do I go?" he said dazedly.

She handed him a set of keys. "It's a furnished apartment we were using. Sixteen-oh-two Kinney, Unit D. Rent's paid until the end of next month."

"Next month."

"You won't need it anywhere that long. Don't go home, don't go to work, don't go anyplace you normally go. Don't check e-mail. Get as much cash as you can right now and don't use your credit cards. And give me your phone."

"Why?"

"Give it to me."

He pulled out a mobile phone from his breast pocket and handed it to her. She gave him another one in return. "This one is a disposable. Use it until this is over. I'm going to call you on it before we leave Dublin and get more details on Gadaire's plans."

"Whatever you want." He shook his head as they left the building. "I can't believe any of this."

"I'll be in touch."

"Yeah. Wonderful."

Eugenia watched him walk down the sidewalk to the street that would take him off campus. He was getting off easy, but it would be worth it if they could get the goods on Gadaire. Once she was sure he was permanently out of sight, she walked around the rear of the arboretum, where Charlie and the young man, Paul Reilly, were smoking cigarettes outside the back doors.

"He's gone," Eugenia said. "It worked like a solid-gold charm."

Charlie and Reilly laughed and bumped fists. "I told you Paul would come through for us," Charlie said. "We've known each other since we were six, and he's always had the theater in his blood."

Paul cocked an eyebrow at him and spoke in his working-class Irish brogue. "Is that your way of calling me a poof? If so, I've got plenty of stories about you I can tell."

Eugenia smiled. "You were very menacing, Paul. Your masculinity is intact."

"That's a relief. But I didn't appreciate Charlie whacking me so hard. He seemed to be enjoying himself far too much."

Charlie shrugged. "What can I say? I got inspired." He glanced at Eugenia. "What did you find out from Lampman?"

"Enough. We'll talk later. Right now we'd better get out of here before Gadaire's real security guy arrives on the scene."

"How did you know he wouldn't burst in during our theatrical extravaganza in there?" Paul asked.

"It was a calculated risk, but Kirov's notes said he typically gets a sandwich and makes calls while Lampman does his work in the greenhouse." She checked her watch. "Let's go. I don't want to be around when he returns and finds that Lampman is long gone." She turned to Paul. "Can we reimburse you for your stellar performance?"

"Nah, I had a great time." He smiled. "And now Charlie owes me. Don't worry, I'll collect in kind."

"But now I owe you, too," Eugenia said. "I'll have to see what I can do . . ."

* * *

"I HATE THIS," HANNAH SAID with bared teeth. "I feel like a prisoner."

Kirov chuckled as he leaned lazily back against the deck rail. "You're in the middle of the ocean, the sun is shining, the breeze is blowing, and you can go anywhere in the world by only telling Melis to up anchor and take off. You're not being reasonable."

"I don't have to be reasonable. And we can't just take off with Gadaire hovering like a vulture. It's not safe for Ronnie and Melis."

"True."

"Why haven't we heard from Eugenia? Aren't you worried?"

"Not yet. It's only been two days. She's probably setting up for the kill."

She turned to look at him. "Are you speaking literally?"

"No, she wouldn't kill Lampman except in self-defense. But if he's working with Gadaire with full knowledge, then he'd probably deserve it as much as the doctors who worked in the concentration camps for Hitler."

"Do you think he does have full knowledge?"

"Mendoza seemed to think so." He smiled. "Stop fretting, Hannah. She'll get back to us."

"I don't fret." Her gaze ran over him. He was sitting on the deck, barefoot, wearing khakis and a white T-shirt, and looked like a beachcomber. A very virile and tough beachcomber. He had been perfectly at ease during the last two days. When he hadn't been helping Aziz in the lab, he had been with Ronnie and the dolphins, or just lazily sunning as he had been this afternoon. He was showing her a completely different side of him. "I just want something to happen."

"No, you want to cause something to happen." He tilted his head. "And you don't have enough to do. Why don't you go play with Melis and Ronnie? They seem to be having a good time with the dolphins."

"Don't you be patronizing to me," she said softly.

"Sorry."

No, she should be the one who was sorry. She was behaving ir-rationally.

"Melis and Ronnie are doing quite well on their own. Ronnie is almost as enthralled with the dolphins as Melis. And she's a good teacher. I'd be in the way."

"And you want to do something with purpose."

"Yes." It wasn't only the lack of anything purposeful to do, it was being at close quarters with Kirov. It didn't seem to bother him. He was the picture of lazy . . . sensuality.

Where had that word come from? Sensuality.

She knew very well that it was one of the underlying elements beneath her discontent.

"I could find a way to keep you busy," Kirov said softly as he met her eyes. "But I can't break my promise. It has to come from you."

She couldn't look away. She could feel the heat moving through her. "A jump in the sack to while away the boredom?"

"Whatever you want. I'm easy." His smile faded. "No, I'm lying. I can't promise it will be easy. I want it too bad. Sometimes I wake at night and I lie there thinking of all the ways I want us to come together. And they're all hard and wild and not at all easy." He shook his head. "Maybe later. Maybe after we've had that first taste. But you'll have to set the rules. I've discovered that I'm not nearly as civilized as I believed."

His eyes were intent, his lips full and slightly parted. She could see the whiteness of his teeth against the tan of his skin.

That first taste.

That phrase was resonating within her as she remembered how she had tasted him, touched him, brought him to her.

The sun was hot on her face and throat, and her body was remembering too much. Lord, it was tempting. Why not give in just one time and take what she wanted? But she knew herself, and that wouldn't be enough. She forced herself to pull her gaze away and turned back to look at the sea. "I don't think so. I believe I can find—"

"Where's Melis?" Aziz had burst out of the door leading below-decks to the lab. His face was flushed, his eyes blazing. "I've got to see Melis."

Kirov sat up straight. "She's over there with the dolphins. Is it what I'm thinking?"

"Hell, yes, I'm a genius." He was hurrying toward Melis. "I've found it. I can destroy it," he said over his shoulder. "She's going to be over the moon that she didn't take a sneezing cat instead of me."

"Sneezing cat?" Hannah followed him. "What does that have to do with—"

"Private joke." He was focused on Melis. "I've got it! We're golden, Melis!"

Melis whirled to face him, her face luminous. "You're sure?"

"I destroyed three samples in a four-hour period. The alga bit the dust."

"Those samples were tiny. How long will it take to produce enough to kill off a sizable amount?"

"That's not so easy. I'm in the early stages."

"How long?"

He shrugged. "Six months to a year."

"Damn," Kirov murmured. "In six months, there's no telling what damage could be done to the coastlines."

"It's the best I can do. I may be a genius, but I'm not a miracle worker. Just stop it from happening until I can—"

"Just stop it from happening. Easy to say," Hannah said. "We don't even know how close Gadaire is from being able to launch an attack on the coasts."

"Eugenia will be able to tell us," Kirov said.

"When she calls," Hannah said. Back to square one. Everything depended on what Eugenia could find out from Lampman.

Dammit, Eugenia, call us.

CHAPTER
17

THEY DIDN'T GET A CALL FROM Eugenia until nearly seven the next morning.

Hannah tensed as Kirov's phone rang.

He nodded as he checked the ID. "Eugenia." He put the call on speakerphone. "It's about time. We've been waiting very impatiently. Hannah is tired of basking in sun and sea."

"Better than here. It's been raining buckets for three days."

"Are you safe?"

"Yes, we're fine and so is Lampman. Though he's a little shaken at his brush with the real world of Vincent Gadaire." She paused. "So shaken that he can't stop talking. He was dazzled by the thought of all the money and power that Gadaire dangled in front of him, and I was forced to point out that he would probably be dead within the next few months. I would have called you yesterday, but I had to phone Lampman once he was settled and get every detail." Her tone became brusque. "It's dirty. Very dirty. Gadaire has got a deal to seed the coast of India with TK44 alga. Environmental Armageddon."

"Dear God," Hannah said.

"But his clients want a demonstration. He's chosen a small village on the east coast. There's a large lake at the mouth of the Daya River. Chilika Lake. It's a very popular tourist destination, and it sustains over a hundred and fifty thousand fisherman from villages all over the region. He'd planning on dumping a large batch of the TK44 alga there and destroying that area to show his clients it can be done."

"When?"

"Right away. He's greedy and wants to score the bigger deal." She paused. "But science takes time when you're dealing with alga. He's not willing to wait for Lampman to grow his own stock. He's going after Marinth."

"No!" Hannah tried to regain control. "How could he? There's no way that he could access that alga bed."

"Nedloe Rentals out of Grand Cayman. Minisubs that Iran sold to Nedloe when they brought out their new models. Nedloe promptly sold them to Sodkar Rentals in Somalia. At great profit since they have the pirate contingent operating out of there. Sodkar rents out the subs and trained pilots as a package. The subs aren't nearly as sophisticated as yours, Hannah, but adequate for farming the alga beds." She paused. "And for defense. The Iranian Navy didn't sell them the weaponry that went with them, but I'm sure that Sodkar added their own brand."

"Shit."

"Gadaire doesn't intend to be stopped. He hired enough subs and crews to make an all-out effort. Lampman said he's going in fast and combing those beds, then getting out. He'll go direct to India and drop off his trove."

At that pretty little village that would be dead within days of Gadaire's visit. "When is he planning on hitting Marinth?"

"Lampman thought he was there now."

Hannah was stunned. It was sickening to think of Gadaire already raping the waters with which she had become so familiar.

"We can't let him do that."

"Then work it out. We've stashed Lampman in a safe place, and Charlie and I are on our way to you." She hung up.

Kirov gazed at Hannah as he pressed the DISCONNECT.

"There's your answer."

"It will kill Melis. Those bastards in her Marinth."

"Then the answer is to get them out," Kirov said. "And that means heading for Marinth. How far away are we?"

"About seventy miles."

"Do we have a base? Is the *Copernicus* still in Marinth waters?"

She nodded. "And we have *Conner Two*. *Conner One* is still under repair." Her hands clenched. "But even if we had both of them, they have no weapons. They could be blown out of the water if they try to intercept those subs."

"Then we'll have to find a way to lure them to the surface." Kirov raised his phone again. "I'll arrange for a helicopter to pick us up." He started to dial. "Damn, that will take time to get here from Las Palmas."

"Yes." Lure them to the surface? Difficult if not impossible. There had to be a better way. Think, dammit. She was in such a panic that was almost impossible too. *Conner Two?* Any way to use—

She stiffened as it came to her.

"Hang up." She reached for her own phone. "I'll get a helicopter. I'll get a whole damn armada." She was dialing quickly. "I hope."

Ebersole answered on the third ring. "Is this good news, Hannah?"

"Maybe. Are those minisubs you want me to modify still in the Canary Islands?"

"Yes, they're still at Las Palmas. I persuaded AquaCorp to be patient. I knew that you wouldn't want anyone else to do the changes. It was only a question of your getting over that first irritation."

"How clever. You're right. I'll do the modifications. I'll even supervise a trial run before I start them." Dear God, and what a trial run it will be. "But on my terms. I don't have much time. I want those subs on their way to the *Copernicus* right away. I'll meet them there. Who's in charge?"

"Lieutenant Dalgo."

"Tell him I'm the sole authority once he reaches the ship."

"No problem."

"And I want an AquaCorp helicopter to pick me up on the *Fair Winds* within the hour. I'll text you my GPS coordinates as soon as we hang up."

"I'll send my own helicopter." He paused. "You can see we're ready to cooperate in any way. I'm glad that you decided to help us out, Hannah. You're going to make me look good at the head office."

"That's not my main goal in life, but in this case I may not mind your taking credit. Get moving, Ebersole." She hung up.

Kirov was laughing. "I'll be damned. We may just have a chance."

"No chance about it. We'll do it." She had to believe that. "And after we do, Ebersole will probably have me thrown in jail and toss away the key."

"Trust me. I'll break you out."

And he would, too. "That's comforting." Comforting and warm and making this lonely decision easier. "Now we've got to decide how to do this. That AquaCorp helicopter will be here before we know it."

"I'm already working on it." He looked at Ronnie, still playing with the dolphins. "I think you have some prep work to do before we take off. Melis . . . and Ronnie."

"Right." She was already heading toward Melis. "Neither of them is going to be easy. They'll both want to go with us . . ."

THIRTY MINUTES LATER, SHE watched Ronnie climb on board. She had been right; persuading Melis to stay here and away from the trouble zone had been almost impossible. Only the fact that someone had to keep Ronnie safe had made her finally acquiesce.

"Did you see me? Pete and Susie are awesome. Did you know dolphins can hear from a distance of—" Ronnie's eager smile faded as he saw Hannah's expression. "Something's wrong."

"Yes, and no." She had promised to be honest, and she wouldn't lie. "We've got a problem with men who are trying to steal something in Marinth. But we can go after them in one of my subs and stop them."

"I'm going with you."

"No, you know how small those subs are. You have to have technological knowledge to operate them. You don't have that knowledge yet." She added quickly, "You will soon. That's one of the first things I'll teach you when you come back this summer. But you can see that it's not possible now."

He slowly nodded. "Then I'll be surface support like Dad was sometimes."

"I'm not going to need that support. This is going to be a very fast operation." She paused. "And I need you here to protect Melis and the dolphins. Just because you can't go out and slay the dragons this time doesn't mean that there isn't work keeping the home fires burning."

"Is Kirov going with you?"

"Yes."

"Then you'll be safe." He looked back at the dolphins arcing out of the water. "Are you sure you want me to stay and take care of Melis and the dolphins?"

"It would be a great favor," she said quietly. "Melis has a great crew, but she likes you with her. She feels comfortable with you."

"I like her. Will she trust me to take care of her?"

He was so solemn, so adult, in his child's body.

"Yes, I think Melis will trust you."

"Good." He gave her a faint smile. "It's going to be pretty boring. You come back soon and listen to Kirov."

She gave him a quick hug. "You won't be bored. Pete and Susie will keep you entertained. We'll be back before you know it." She got to her feet. "Now you go back to the dolphins. I'll go tell Melis that you're going to stay with her. Then I have to throw some things together. That helicopter should be here anytime to pick us up." She paused. "Thank you for understanding, Ronnie."

"You didn't lie to me." He looked up as the sound of a rotor pierced the silence. "There it is. You'd better hurry, Aunt Hannah."

Melis was watching the helicopter descend as Hannah approached. She turned. "I still don't like this, Hannah. I'd rather be with you." She held up her hand. "I know. Ronnie. Don't worry, I'll keep *Fair Winds* far away from Marinth. We'll stay right here on the Atlantic-Tenerife sea-lane and I'll be able to zip over to Las Palmas at the first hint of trouble."

"Good." She squeezed her hand. "Kirov and I won't let this happen, Melis. We'll find a way."

"I know." She turned as Kirov joined them. "Take care of her, Kirov." She smiled. "Or you'll have to answer to Ronnie."

He watched the helicopter descend. "Heaven forbid. The mere prospect terrifies me."

HANNAH COULD SEE THE CREW gathered on the deck of the *Copernicus* as the AquaCorp helicopter carefully descended. It was good to see those familiar faces. Captain Danbury, Matthew, and Kyle were front and center of the welcoming party.

"No minisubs yet," Kirov observed, scanning the waters surrounding *Copernicus.*

"They'll be here. It takes longer to dispatch a fleet of subs than it does one helicopter."

The crew was stepping back as the helicopter stirred a tornado of wind that blew their hair and clothing into wild disarray.

"It's about time you got back here," Matthew said as he opened the helicopter door for her. "Just skip off and leave us with all the work."

"I've always been a slacker." She jumped out. "This is Kirov. Introduce him to the team, will you?" She turned back to the helicopter pilot. "Thank you. You were very prompt. I may need you again so stay available. I'll call you."

"My pleasure, ma'am. I have orders to be at your disposal."

She turned back to Kirov as he took off. "I'd rather have had him stand by on the ship, but we can't risk him hearing things he shouldn't and reporting back to Ebersole." She looked out at the tranquil blue waters off the bow. "It's so still. It seems impossible that Gadaire's subs are somewhere down there. Maybe they haven't arrived yet."

"Verify." He turned to Captain Danbury. "Send a man out in a small craft. There has to be a central supply-and-control ship in the immediate area. Tell him to take all care and report as soon as he spots it."

"Yes, sir." Danbury turned crisply, then stopped short. He looked at Hannah. "Is it okay?"

She smiled with amusement. She had never seen Danbury react that quickly and politely to anyone. It had to be the invisible air of command that surrounded Kirov. "Do as he says."

"I'm feeling very second mate," Kirov said. "It's most unsettling."

"You'll get used to it."

"Not likely." He moved over to the rail. "How many of your men will be capable of operating the minisubs?"

"Out here? Only Matthew, Josh, and me." She frowned and called to Matthew. "I don't see Josh, Matthew."

"You know Josh. He always goes off on a toot after a spell at sea. He didn't know you'd be wanting him. He's in Las Palmas. I'll give him a call, and he'll be speeding back here."

"Don't bother. He'll be too late. We're moving fast." She turned back to Kirov. "It appears to be just Matthew and me. Kyle can take second position in Matthew's sub."

"And I'll take second position in yours."

"You've not been trained."

"Not on your subs, but I can wing it. You'll remember I have a certain eclectic background in submarines." His brow knitted in a thoughtful frown. "That may still not be enough. I wish we knew how many subs Gadaire was able to put down there. I suppose we could draft the Navy pilots who are delivering the subs."

"I won't draft them. They're military, and they have no stake in this."

"When India and their neighbors go to war over India's de-stroyed coastal waters, they might have a big stake."

She shook her head. "I won't trick them as I did AquaCorp. The only thing I can do is explain and hope for volunteers. But first I have to get my own guys with the program." She gazed out at the water. "Gadaire will be on that supply ship, won't he?"

"I can't imagine him letting anyone else head the operation. It's too important to him."

"So close. Maybe we could strike at him and avoid having to go after those harvesters."

He shook his head. "Not unless we could take him unaware. And then we'd have to get rid of those subs anyway because Gadaire could order them to surface and turn them loose on us." He shrugged. "I have a few ideas on how to take Gadaire out. But now we have to concentrate on stopping them from harvesting that TK44 alga. We don't know how much he's siphoning off and immediately shipping out to hit that village in India."

She nodded. "I guess I knew that. I was just hoping." She turned toward Matthew. "What about it, Matthew? I told you on the phone what the stakes were in this. Are you and Kyle going to be on board with it?"

"What about these new weapons systems that have been installed?" Kyle asked. "None of us have used them before."

"In a way, you have. They're based on the motion-control gloves that we use for the other functions. I had Matthew jury-rig a weapons simulator setup downstairs with the gloves and personal computers. Is it done, Matthew?"

He nodded. "But very crude, Hannah. I had to work fast."

"I'll look it over. While we wait for the subs to get here, we can get in as much practice as we can." She gazed soberly at Matthew and Kyle. "No pressure. AquaCorp is going to be ready to toss all of us into the brig when they find out about this. If you want to opt out, I'll understand."

"I'm in," Matthew said immediately. He smiled. "Sounds like fun."

"I'll do it," Kyle said slowly. "If I can make heads or tails of the weapons system."

"Thank you." Hannah checked her watch. It was only noon, but it seemed much later. "I don't know how much time we'll have. Get on those simulators." She gazed soberly after them as Matthew moved away. "I'm scared," she told Kirov. "I love those guys. What the hell am I getting them into?"

"You're saving the planet. Feeling responsible? Welcome to the club." He headed for the door. "Come on, you don't have time to worry and bite your nails. Show me that mock-up of the weapons simulator."

THE MINISUBS HAD STILL not arrived an hour later.

"Where *are* they?" Hannah said, in frustration. "Maybe I should call Ebersole."

"I wouldn't," Kirov said.

"What do you mean? Gadaire is *out* there. Captain Danbury got a report from the man he sent out to do a search that he'd sighted an unidentified vessel clear on the far side of the Marinth site. He couldn't get close, but it definitely wasn't a minisub. He said what he might have seen was the top deck of a regular submarine. One minute it was there, the next it was gone." She shook her head. "We have to get him while we can, dammit."

"We will. Just don't be in such a big hurry. We may need the extra time."

Her gaze flew to his face. What she saw there caused her eyes to narrow. "You've been very quiet for the last hour. What are you up to?"

"I've been thinking about the prospect of your being thrown into jail, and I decided that I believe we should do something to keep that from happening. It would be a major inconvenience for me to have to break you out. Bribes, weapons, getaway cars . . . No, let's work around that."

"I can hardly wait for you to tell me how."

"We can't get AquaCorp to authorize the possible damage to their subs, but we can cushion the resulting aftereffects . . . if it's a government-sanctioned attack on Gadaire and his Somalian crews."

"There's no way we can get that sanction. It would take weeks to batter through all the red tape."

He took out his phone. "Then we deal from the inside out."

"What are you doing?"

"Baker's been trying to find me. I'm going to let him do it."

"You can't let—"

"We've run out of options," he said quietly. "And you've been so busy getting ready to fight Gadaire and snatch away that TK44 alga that you haven't stopped to think what would happen if it doesn't work. What if he manages to stave us off and sends that bundle of TK44 to India?"

"That won't happen."

"I hope not. But I believe in preparing for the worst-case scenario." He added, "Because I've had experience that they do happen."

Yes, Kirov had experienced the ultimate worst-case scenario. His whole crew dying of bacteria exposure on the *Silent Thunder*. His wife murdered.

"I know you have."

"Then we have to send word to Chilika Lake, India, that something is going to happen. If they know the alga is going to be dispersed in the waters, maybe they can stop it."

"It's not likely. There's no time."

Kirov nodded. "I agree, but we've got to give them a chance to try."

Hannah nodded. "I know. I wasn't thinking. I don't like believing in a worst-case scenario." She drew a deep breath. "Okay, how do we do it?"

"Baker. Let him save Chilika." He smiled. "And maybe our asses along with it." He started to dial. "Let's see how fast he can do it."

"DAMN YOU, KIROV." BAKER'S tone was harsh. "I'm supposed to believe anything you tell me? You were responsible for my agent being butchered in that alley. Mendoza was a good man."

"We all seem to be confused about the concept of responsibility. You're the one who sent Mendoza into Gadaire's path. You knew what could happen."

"I didn't know that Gadaire knew where you were."

"Really? Then your intelligence is very faulty."

"Apparently, it is." He paused. "You're sure about Chilika Lake?"

"I'm sure. It's in Orissa, India. Issue a warning."

"I'll have to think about it," he said absently. "I don't want to start a panic."

"If you think about it, it's going to be too late. We don't know whether Gadaire is going to send an immediate supply of the TK44 alga to the area for seeding. It could be on its way now."

"I won't be pushed into doing something that could cause damage to those villagers."

"Issue a warning," Kirov repeated. "And contact the U.S. naval presence in the area and tell them that you're going to need assistance to stop a terrorist threat at Marinth. I'll need their cooperation."

"Strange." Baker's voice was sour. "You haven't been interested in cooperation before this."

"Circumstances change."

"I have my own plans for capturing Gadaire."

"Alter your plans. Think about it this way: what would happen if you had information that Al Qaeda was trying to retrieve plutonium from a location on the ocean floor? Would you ignore it? Of course not. Because if you did, they might use it to build an atomic bomb. Gadaire is on the brink of creating a weapon just as devastating, and you know that he'll sell it to anyone and everyone who will meet his price."

Baker was silent for a moment. "What kind of naval support are you looking for?"

"Actually, it's on its way." Kirov told him about the Navy minisubs en route to the location. "And Hannah Bryson herself is here to supervise the operation. It's the best equipment for the job, and she's the best person to carry it out. But we also need the cooperation of those Navy minisub operators. Call the Navy Command and tell them that Lieutenant Dalgo is to be under our orders when the minisubs arrive at the *Copernicus*."

"This is a lot to ask, Kirov. None of this jibes with our own intelligence."

"If I'm wrong, and I hope I am, they'll find that nothing is going on down there. And the Navy will have the services of Hannah Bryson to refine their newest fleet of minisubs, which is something she's reluctant to do. But if I'm right, this is our best chance of stopping Gadaire." Kirov paused. "Look, Baker, you can take full credit for any success and blame us if it goes wrong. You can't lose."

So it would appear, but I don't like the idea of having so little control, Baker thought. And why hadn't Anna told him about Gadaire's plan? Either Gadaire didn't trust her any more than Baker did and hadn't told her, or she had been playing him for a fool and had jumped back in Gadaire's camp. Either was possible.

"I've got to verify. I'll call you back in five minutes." He hung up the phone and thought for a minute. Then he called to Graham, his assistant, in the other room. "I'm going to make a call. I want you to verify where that cell phone is picking up at."

"Right."

Baker waited another minute and called Anna's number.

She answered immediately. "I was just thinking about you, darling."

"Were you? I haven't seen you in two days."

"Gadaire is being very suspicious. I have to be careful."

"Have you found out anything more?"

"No, but I should know something soon. You know I'll call you as soon as I do." She laughed. "No, I'll come to you. That's always more entertaining for both of us. Isn't it?"

"No one can deny that you have entertainment value. I can hardly wait."

"Neither can I. Good-bye, darling." She hung up.

Baker did not hang up in case Graham needed the line open.

She had sounded just as casual and seductive as she always did. Every word meant to convince and entice.

"I've got it," Graham came out of the other room.

"Don't tell me," Baker said. "She's not in Dublin. The Canary Islands?"

Graham shook his head. "Orissa, India."

"Shit!"

He punched in Kirov's number. "You'll have your naval support. Stop Gadaire from harvesting that alga. Pronto."

"I take it we've been verified. Have you called Naval Command?"

"Not yet."

"Do it." Kirov hung up.

Chilika Lake

Orissa, India

ANNA GAZED THOUGHTFULLY at the twinkling pinpoints of light along the shoreline. It was an exceptionally warm evening, but much more tolerable than the day's blistering heat. She turned and watched the men take the last of the barrels of corn-teosinte chemical extract off the boat and pour it into the water. She should have probably contacted Baker before this, but once her decision had been made she was busy.

It was still okay. She had smoothed it over. By the time Baker realized what was happening, the final delivery would be made here.

She called Gadaire. "Fifty more barrels to be dumped, then I'm out of here. How close are you?"

"I've got another two hours of harvesting before I'll even have enough in the nets to send to Orissa. I'll send Ames to do the dump in Chilika Lake. But we'll have to work for hours longer to completely strip the beds."

"No trouble?"

"Not a sign of it. We spotted Hannah Bryson's ship when we first arrived here. But they're no longer sending down exploratory subs since AquaCorp pulled the plug, and we made sure we were far enough away so that they couldn't see us. It just means having the subs operate at longer range."

"Smart, darling. I'll see you soon. If there are any problems, let me know." She hung up.

But there weren't going to be any problems.

Not for her. Never for her.

It was just a matter of eliminating the potential before they developed.

HANNAH STOOD ON THE DECK OF the *Copernicus* next to Kirov and Lieutenant Dalgo, looking over the seven modified Conner-class subs being serviced in the water. Four of their pilots were now on board at the stern and waiting for their subs to be turned back over to them. Two others had been sent back to Las Palmas at Hannah's request. When the subs had arrived only fifteen minutes before, Hannah had been impressed by their pilots' skill as they executed maneuvers around the ship.

"It must be an amazing feeling to know that you created these." Dalgo smiled, and Hannah instinctively smiled back. Dalgo was in his late thirties, but his boyish good looks and faint Southern accent gave him a disarming charm.

"I didn't," Hannah said. "They're mostly mine, but there are design elements I never would have chosen. So it's a strange feeling. Like waking up and discovering that all your children have been replaced by imposters who look almost, but not quite, like your sons and daughters."

"Imposters trained to kill," Kirov said.

Lieutenant Dalgo watched as two more minisubs were readied on deck near the crane. "I know the manufacturer and Navy brass think there are performance issues with these babies, but that's only because they've seen how well your original versions handled. My guys love them exactly as they are. Anything you do to improve them is just icing on the cake."

"They may like my subs, but I don't get the impression that they're

happy about me and Matthew joining them in this operation."
Hannah glanced at Dalgo. "Are they?"

"They're Navy guys, what do you expect? They know they're the
best underwater pilots in the world, and your guys are just as sure
they are. And now my guys are going into what could be a combat
situation with civilians calling the shots. You even insisted that two
of my pilots stand down and permit you and your pilot, Matthew
Jefferson, to use their subs."

"Only two subs. Actually, I'd prefer having more of my people if
I had them available. I was trying to be reasonable and compromise."

"Tell that to the two pilots on their way back to Las Palmas." He
made a face. "Let's just say that my officers are uneasy."

"Aren't we all?"

Dalgo motioned toward Kirov. "And they're probably not crazy
about a former Russian submarine commander being down there
with them. You may think the Cold War is over, but it doesn't feel
that way to guys who are out there playing hide-and-seek with Russian subs every day."

"That's ridiculous. Kirov has probably done more to keep the
U.S. safe than any of them have done."

"Don't be defensive, Hannah," Kirov said. "Their attitude is
perfectly reasonable."

"I don't care. It's stupid. We have to work together." She turned
to Matthew, who was working a few yards away. "Come on, Matthew, let's go meet these guys. Introduce us, Lieutenant." She glanced
at Kirov, who had not moved. "Coming?"

He shook his head and leaned lazily back against the rail. "I'd
prefer to stay back and observe. It's not often I get the chance of seeing you in attack mode."

"I'm not attacking. I just have to make them see sense."

Kirov smiled. "Sometimes it ends up being the same. Protect your team, Dalgo."

Dalgo gave him an annoyed look as he escorted Hannah and Matthew over to the four pilots at the stern. "I'm sure most of you recognize Hannah Bryson. And this is Matthew Jefferson, one of her test operators for the civilian version of the Piranha subs."

As many times as Hannah had recently read and heard that name—the Piranha Project—she could not get used to it. But "Conner" now did not seem right, either. Not for these missile-equipped little brutes.

"Nice to meet you."

There was only a noncommittal murmur from the four pilots.

"I'm not a pilot, but I designed these submersibles. I know what they can do and what they can't do. Matthew does, too. We're going into what might be a dangerous situation, and I need you to trust us as your wingmen down there."

No acknowledgment. Keep pushing. "And Nicholas Kirov has more experience in submarine warfare than all of us put together. We're lucky to have him."

The temperature went down a few more degrees.

Great, Hannah thought. "How about some quick introductions? Pretty soon we're all going to be just reduced to voices on a radio, so it would help for me to hear what you each sound like."

The one female pilot, an African-American woman whose hair was pulled back in a ponytail, extended her hand. "Lieutenant Theresa Reynolds. We'll watch your back down there, Ms. Bryson."

Matthew smiled. "We'll watch yours."

Hannah shot him an exasperated look. Knock off the bravado, she wanted to tell him. We're going to need these people.

A tall, strapping young man nodded toward Hannah. "Lieutenant Derek McCallister." Probably a high-school football star, Hannah thought. Fullback. How on earth could he fit into some of those Navy minisubs?

"Lieutenant Commander Steve Sandford," another of the pilots said. He was thin, not athletic, like the others. Computer geek, she guessed.

The last of the pilots looked somewhere over her head as he spoke. "Lieutenant Gary Helms." Then he said tightly, "Are you going to tell us why we're doing this?"

Dalgo said quickly, "We're on a need-to-know basis here, Helms. We should concern ourselves with objectives and strategy."

"Wait a minute," Hannah said. "You haven't told them the reason they're going to risk their necks down there?"

"Ms. Bryson, perhaps if you and I can speak privately for a moment."

"No, I don't give a damn about 'need-to-know.' I figure if you're going to put your life on the line, you should know why." She turned toward the pilots. "I'll make this quick. We've recently discovered that the Marinthian civilization was destroyed by an interaction between their polluted waste and an algal growth unique to this area. We believe that someone may be trying to harvest large quantities of this growth to use as a weapon. We need to stop them."

Helms turned to Dalgo. "That's not exactly what we were told."

"Need to know," Dalgo repeated. "We just obey orders."

Hannah turned toward Dalgo, who was obviously annoyed that she had given away mission details that the military had wanted to keep confidential.

Too bad.

She turned and strode back toward Kirov.

"Enjoy yourself?" Kirov asked. "Yes, I can see that your adrenaline is surging."

She knew what he meant. She did feel as if at last she was doing something. She shrugged. "I don't know if I did any good."

He smiled. "I believe you made a dent. I was impressed."

Dalgo joined them a moment later. "I wasn't expecting quite that action on your part, ma'am."

"Expect it from now on. I won't be anything but honest with the people I work with." She paused. "There was some definite coolness frosting the air back there. Not that I blame them. You should have told them. Blind obedience sucks."

"I gathered you felt that way. So did they," Dalgo said. "Orders are orders. But I think that you managed to defrost them a little."

"But there's still resentment that civilians are going to take a major part."

"And one of them is a rascally Russian," Kirov said.

"They'll get over it," Dalgo said. "I'm just asking you to look at it from their point of view. This has all happened so quickly that they're still trying to get their heads around things. They've been essentially vacationing in the Canary Islands for the past week, waiting to do a few low-stress runs for you. But it's suddenly turned into something very different."

"I'm sensing a lot of negatives." She stared him in the eye. "Are your men up for this assignment, Lieutenant?"

He looked away from her and out at the minisubs in the water. He suddenly grinned. "Yes, ma'am. It's my duty to look at all the negatives. But, to tell you the truth, my guys were bored out of their minds doing those low-stress runs in the Canary Islands. They'd mutiny if I didn't let them take a shot at a duty like this."

She motioned toward the subs on deck. "Then let's go to Marinth."

CHAPTER
18

GADAIRE STOOD IN THE CONTROL room, as it were, of the handmade diesel submarine that he had sold to a tribe of Somali pirates two years before. Although he had brokered the purchase and sale of the vessel, he had never actually seen it and was surprised by the poor quality of the workmanship. Constructed in a mountaintop workshop outside of Bogotá, it was one of dozens of subs built by the Revolutionary Armed Forces of Colombia for the purpose of smuggling cocaine to Central America and Mexico. This particular model, forty-five feet long and capable of depths of over three hundred feet, was constructed to hold eleven tons of cocaine. More than enough to store his alga harvest from the Marinth ocean floor.

"Do you think they're finished down there?" The sub's "captain," Jorge Silva, was less a naval officer than a heavy equipment operator. Silva had been part of the team that built the sub in Colombia and had gone with it to Somalia to train its new owners. Two years later, however, he had still made no effort to move back home.

"No, it's going to take more time," Gadaire said. He pointed to an experimental low-frequency radio he had brought to keep in touch with his minisubs on the ocean floor. "This system doesn't work worth a damn, but stand by in case they can make contact."

"Will do."

Gadaire restlessly paced the length of the control room, which was manned by all six of the sub's other personnel. The room, like the rest of the sub interior, was quite crude in appearance, with chipped black-rubber flooring and exposed hydraulics tubes running along the bulkhead. Welding scars randomly crisscrossed the superstructure, almost as if laid on the fly to plug leaks. It was a shit hole, Gadaire thought, but it would get the job done. Such subs evaded air and sea patrols along the South American coast every day, and this one would do the same here. It would be a simple matter to move his precious cargo to the Fuertenventura Airport, where he had a plane waiting. From there, he was off to Orissa, India. By the time he arrived there, Anna would have completed stage one of the plan that would change their lives—and the lives of millions—forever.

It was finally happening, he thought exultantly, and no one was going to take it away from him. Not Elijah Baker, not Nicholas Kirov, and certainly not Hannah Bryson.

BACK INTO THE VOID, HANNAH thought. She was descending into the dark depths, piloting a vessel she hadn't even known existed just a few days before.

"How does it handle?" Kirov asked.

"Not bad, but we've been in free fall for the last twenty minutes. Ask me again when we get to Marinth. How are you doing with the weapons controller?"

He raised his hands, showing off the black-and-silver controller gloves. "Good. It's very clever of them to include this onboard simulation routine in the software. It's helping me to learn, but even experienced users can use it to warm up and quicken their response times."

Hannah leaned back and gazed at the dazzling 3-D graphics on the monitor in front of Kirov. "Nice. They should release it for the PlayStation in time for the holiday season. They'd make a fortune."

Hannah checked her far-more-utilitarian sonar screen to see seven blips representing her and the other subs descending to Marinth. She would occasionally catch sight of one of their running lights through the viewing ports, but they were far enough apart that they usually existed as mere blips on the screen in front of her.

"What if we're too late?" Hannah said. "We had to waste a lot of time on deck. What if Gadaire has already taken what he needs from here?"

Kirov shook his head. "He couldn't have. He hasn't had enough time."

"If Gadaire succeeds, I could never forgive myself," she whispered. "And India could just be the beginning."

"You *will* forgive yourself because we'll do everything possible. And that's all anyone can ask of themselves."

"He has to be stopped right here, right now."

Kirov gently rubbed her arm. "If he's here, he will be."

Hannah smiled as she looked down at the controller glove on her arm.

"Watch it with that thing. You might have just launched our missiles."

AFTER ANOTHER TWENTY MINUTES, Hannah established the audio link between her and the other Piranha subs. "We're approaching downtown Marinth, everybody. I'm not seeing any activity on my sonar yet. Anybody else?"

The other pilots radioed their negative responses.

"Okay, slow to a holding pattern. I'm turning on the lights."

Hannah transmitted the signal, and in a few seconds the large light towers bathed Marinth in their bluish white glow.

The common radio-communications frequency was filled with the pilots' awestruck gasps and exclamations at the sight before them.

Dalgo cut in. "We're not tourists here, people. We have a job to do. Eyes peeled."

Hannah spoke into the radio. "Continue south-southwest. The only area of mapped TK44 is beyond the ruins. We'll set up our perimeter there."

Although Hannah had studied all the additional equipment installed in her subs, she was most impressed to see one piece of technology in action—a tiny laser projector that tracked all of the other vessels in their group, superimposing the pilot's name over where she saw each of them in the viewport. They moved low over the city, keeping a tight formation as their running lights cast blue and green highlights over the structures.

"Incredible," Kirov said. "I can see why Melis made this her life's work. I'm sure there has to be a fascinating story in each and every one of those buildings."

"That's true," Hannah said, but moved her shoulders uneasily. "But something's not right here."

"What do you mean?"

"I can't put my finger on it. The feeling is totally different today." Hannah glanced out the viewports. Then it hit her. "The dolphins."

"What dolphins?"

"That's just it. There aren't any. Not one. Sometimes I'll see hundreds on the way down. Sometimes less, but there are always dolphins in some quantity."

"Where do you think they are?"

"I don't know." Hannah glanced outside. "I don't like this."

Dalgo's voice came over the radio. "Hannah, is everything okay?"

She had forgotten that everyone could hear her. "For some reason, the dolphin population has deserted Marinth. It could be that our sonar or radio waves are unfamiliar to them, or . . . I don't know. This is unusual."

An alert sounded from her instrument panel, and through the radio Hannah could hear that the other pilots were also getting it.

"Incoming," Dalgo shouted. "Brace yourselves."

Hannah saw a white streak ahead of her. It moved from right to left, and as she watched, it turned and headed straight for her and Kirov.

"Hold on!" Kirov flipped a switch and raised his glove to eject a mass of highly reflective particles from the upper compartment of their vessel. The missile roared overhead and exploded fifty yards behind them, shaking the tiny craft.

"Where did that come from?" Hannah shouted. "Any visual?"

"Dead ahead," Theresa said. "I saw the ignition flash. And here's another one!"

More shrill alarms emanated from the instrument panel. Another streak of light raced toward their formation.

"It's not heading for us," Kirov said. "It's heading toward—"

"Dalgo!" Hannah shouted in horror.

A heartbeat later, Dalgo's vessel exploded!

Hannah's front port was filled with a retina-searing light. Her sub rocked, and the alarms sounded even more persistently. Escaping oxygen from Dalgo's sub ignited a fireball that shot high above the rest of the formation.

"Oh, my God." Hannah stared in disbelief at the place where his sub had been. Her front-port readout with Dalgo's name faded out. Two people dead.

"Grieve later," Kirov said roughly, picking up on her stunned expression. "Stay in the here and now, Hannah."

Hannah nodded. Kirov was right. He knew about staying alive in combat situations.

Stay in the here and now.

Lieutenant Sandford shouted to the team, "Maximum depth, everyone. I repeat, maximum depth. Hug the seafloor. We're giving them a shooting gallery here." He spoke with such authority that Hannah had a tough time reconciling his voice with the slight, geeky man she had met on the surface.

"Check your diagnostics," she said to the team. "Those blasts could have caused some damage. Matthew, you were closest to Dalgo. Make sure your left rear flap still has full extension."

The team dropped into the city until they hovered mere feet over the seafloor.

"I got a fix on them," Theresa said. "Both missiles were fired from due south-southwest."

"They're covering the TK44 seabed," Hannah said. "We need to get over there."

"Okay," Sandford said. "We'll spin up, take positions on the perimeter of the city, and continue in an elliptical pattern. We'll coordinate and converge on the seabed. Reynolds, you take McCallister east, I'll take Helms and move from the west."

"What about me and Matthew?" Hannah asked.

"Hold your position."

"And do what?"

"Await orders."

"Like hell."

"I don't have time to argue."

"Neither do I. Matthew, you go with Reynolds and McCallister. I'll go with Sandford and Helms."

Sandford cursed. "I can't babysit you, Bryson. They're firing missiles at us."

"Then let's stop talking and move."

Hannah heard more cursing from Sandford, but this time he had obviously tried to muffle the outburst by placing his hand over the microphone. "Just don't get in our way," Sandford said. Then he spoke to the team. "Okay, let's go. And keep your eyes open for missile flashes."

Still hovering low over the ocean floor, the team split up and moved to opposite ends of the site. Once there, they each began the long sweep toward the TK44 seabed.

Hannah turned toward Kirov. "Anything you would do differently?"

"If I were Sandford?" Kirov paused. "I might have tried harder to make you stay back there."

"You couldn't have talked me into it either."

"I know that, but Sandford doesn't." Kirov flipped down a pair of goggles that gave him an infrared view of their surroundings. "And Sandford isn't thinking like the enemy. If you're going to fight a battle, you need to take your opponent's point of view. What's their objective here?"

Hannah thought for a moment. "The alga in that seabed."

"Exactly. If we want to stop them, perhaps we don't waste time with hidden targets. They've taken their positions, and they're just waiting to pick us off as we approach. Maybe the best way of stopping them is to remove the reason for their mission."

Hannah's eyes widened. "Destroy the TK44?"

"All of it. It only grows in that one area, correct?"

"Yes."

"That's what we should be attacking. With that objective re-moved, Gadaire's minisubs would have no reason to engage us. I'm sure they're fairly short-range vessels. What would be left for them to do?"

Hannah thought about it. "They'll need to rendezvous with the mother ship."

"Yes, if we could follow them . . ."

Hannah's eyes met his. "Gadaire."

"They might lead us right to him." He smiled slightly and re-peated, "The first rule of warfare: think like your enemy."

Hannah turned on her microphone. "Sandford, do you read me?"

"Copy, Bryson."

"I propose we hang back and hold positions. Send an all-frequency warning to the trespassers. Tell them that we're about to open fire on the TK44 seabed."

"To try and draw them out?"

"That's what they may think. But it's really to give them a chance to get clear before we blow them to hell."

"Negative, Bryson. We have strict orders not to harm the ar-chaeological site or the surrounding area."

"The alga field is outside of Marinth. The archaeological site won't be touched," she said.

"We already have a plan, Bryson. And they're no longer just tres-passers, they're murderers."

And the victim was Dalgo, one of their own. Hannah couldn't blame them for that bitterness.

"This is purely a commercial job for them. If they can remove that TK44, then they continue to get paid. They'll kill again to pro-tect their mission. Let's end it for them right now."

"Negative, Bryson."

"Listen to me. I'm angry about what happened to Dalgo, too. But this is a better way of beating them."

"Please keep all chatter on this channel to a minimum, Bryson."

Hannah switched off her microphone. "That idiot."

"He's not," Kirov said slowly. "And that's what disturbs me. I'm afraid he knows exactly what he's doing."

Hannah felt a chill. "You think he has orders to—"

Another high-pitched alarm sounded from the instrument panel, and Matthew's tense voice came over the radio. "We're under attack on Marinth's west slope. Two attack minisubs, maybe Iranian Guardian class. Missiles fired, and we're returning the favor."

Hannah looked out her viewport and saw the intense flashes of light near Marinth's western spire. "I'm going over there."

"Negative," Sandford said. "Stay on our present course."

Static from the radio.

More alarms.

Anguished screams.

"I have to get over there," Hannah said. She gripped the navigation stick. "Hang on."

"No," Kirov said. "Don't do it."

"I *have* to do it."

"No. He ordered you not to go. Do not abandon your commander."

"He's not my—"

Another flash of light from the west.

"McCallister's been hit," Theresa said. "But I just destroyed one of the enemy minisubs. The other one is retreating. Matthew is in pursuit."

Hannah adjusted her microphone. "Stay sharp, Matthew. Don't let him lead you back to the alga field. There may be others waiting there."

"That's exactly what he's doing, Hannah. I'm easing back. I'll see you on the down-low."

Hannah cut her microphone and turned to Kirov. "That's strange."

"What?"

" 'See you on the down-low.' That's what Matthew and I say when we want to communicate with just each other without company execs or anybody else listening in. That's our code to switch to a low-frequency subchannel."

Hannah made the change and switched on her microphone. "Are you here, Matthew?"

"Yeah, I wanted to talk to you about this alone. It's about this sub I'm chasing . . . You're going to think I'm crazy, but I'm positive it's Josh."

She couldn't speak, or even breathe, for a long moment. "You're right. I think you're crazy."

"It's him, Hannah. Art experts can tell an artist's work by the brushstrokes. I can pick out a minisub pilot's work a mile away. Especially Josh's. We've been working together for years. The way he banks a turn, how he eases off the power to ride over his undercurrent . . . It's him, Hannah."

"Shit."

"Do you think I want it to be him?" Matthew asked. "He's my friend."

"Gadaire's spy on your Marinth expedition?" Kirov said.

She had already thought of that. Dammit.

"Matthew, flash him the 'down-low' signal with your lights."

"I'm on it."

Hannah looked at the laser projector readout on her viewport for some indication where Matthew was even though she couldn't actually see him from the other side of Marinth. She turned to Kirov. "If we're close enough, we flash running lights at each other when we want to go to our private channel. Uppers-lowers-uppers."

"Do you think Josh will respond?"

"I don't know." She shook her head. "I'm still having a tough time believing it's true."

She heard a brief burst of static and a slight low-frequency hum on their audio channel. "It is him," Hannah whispered. "He just switched over." She spoke into the microphone. "Josh, it's Hannah. And that's Matthew behind you."

Silence.

She adjusted her headset. "We know it's you, Josh. No one pilots a sub like you. Do you want to tell us what's going on?"

Matthew cut in. "Talk to us, buddy."

Still not a word.

Hannah spoke softly. "Two men are dead, Josh. They were good men. You would have liked them. I can't believe you would have had anything to do with—"

"I didn't," Josh blurted out. "I wouldn't do that."

"Then why are you working for Gadaire?"

Josh paused a moment before answering. "He makes weapons, Hannah. Just like you've done on occasion."

"It's not the same."

"It's all just a matter of degree, isn't it?"

Hannah looked ahead and realized that her formation would soon move beyond the well-lit city center and toward the darker valleys that lay beyond. "There's a line, Josh. You spied for him, and now you're willing to kill for him?"

"No one was supposed to get hurt. I'm just here to protect the mission."

"Are you really that naïve? Gadaire puts you behind the controls of a submersible with missile launchers, and you think no one is supposed to get hurt?"

"It's just a job. An extremely well-paying job. Just like I work for you and your weapons."

He was rationalizing. She could argue with him all day or just appeal to the Josh she had known for years. "Help us. Please. How many more of you are down here?"

"Why would I tell you that?"

"Josh, don't do this. If Gadaire succeeds, millions of people could be killed."

"I don't want you to become one of them, Hannah."

Matthew's voice cut in. "Josh, you need to get to the surface now."

Josh laughed incredulously. "Is that an order?"

"Your hull is damaged. I think your partner's already dead back there, and you will be, too, if you don't get topside in a hurry."

"You're a bad bluffer, Matthew."

"I can *see* the damage. You climbed into a ten-year-old retrofitted piece of shit and took on Hannah Bryson's latest subs. How did you think it was going to end? You're putting even more stress on it right now. Slow down!"

"I don't believe you."

"You're wobbling. Everything in there probably feels like it's about to shake loose. Doesn't that tell you something?"

"Oh God, yes." Josh didn't say anything else for a moment. "Stay back, Matthew. There are three more Guardian subs in the alga field. I'd bet you're already in their sights."

"Josh!" Matthew's voice was agonized.

Hannah heard a sickening roar, a rush of static.

Then nothing.

The only sound was the whisper-quiet engine of her sub. "Matthew?"

"Yeah." Matthew spoke hoarsely. "He's gone, Hannah. His hull ruptured, and he . . ." The words caught in his throat. "Josh is gone."

Hannah closed her eyes.

"Hannah," Kirov said gently.

"I know." Her eyes opened, and she said huskily, "Stay in the moment." She drew a deep breath. "Okay, Matthew. Let's rejoin the party and finish this." She switched back to the team's radio frequency. "Are you there, Sandford?"

"Nice of you to drop back in, Bryson."

"There are three Guardian minisubs in the alga field. One or all three may be harvesting, but they're all weapons-equipped."

"Just how do you know this?"

"Trust me. We're almost there. Watch your hyperspectral scanner readings. Their targeting systems will heat up as they lock in on Matthew. He's over there now." She shared a worried glance with Kirov. "Don't wait for your onboard system to identify the spectral signature. When they heat up, lock on and fire. Matthew's life depends on it."

"They'll have a head start in locking in on their target," Helms said.

"I'm sure our systems are faster," Hannah said. "Are you comfortable with that, Matthew?"

"Comfortable isn't really the word. But since I'm here, may as well use me to draw them out."

Hannah searched for their other subs in her viewport. "Where's Reynolds?"

"Trying to tow McCallister to the surface," Sandford said. "He has fairly substantial damage, so it's just the four of us."

Kirov was staring intensely at his console. "I have two targets lighting up."

"Wait for my order to fire," Sandford said.

Hannah was incredulous. "Have you been listening to me?"

"Guys . . . ?" Matthew sounded panicked.

"Easy, Matthew. Firing at two targets," Kirov said. "Missiles engaged."

Hannah felt the sub's engines automatically revving to counteract the thrust of the twin missiles firing from each wing.

"Dammit, Kirov!" Sandford shouted. "Everyone stand down."

Hannah saw two more missile flashes, and she realized that Matthew had also fired. She watched the four trails as they rocketed over the ocean floor. The trails converged, and Hannah lost sight of them. Seconds passed. A bright, almost blinding, light filled her viewport, and a low rumble shook her submersible.

She shouted into her microphone. "Matthew, are you okay? Matthew?"

No reply.

She checked her viewport indicator. Matthew's name still appeared on its surface, so at least his transponder was operational. But that was no guarantee that he—

"I'm here." Matthew's voice. "Still in one piece."

"Good," she said. "I can breathe again."

"I can confirm two minisubs destroyed. I got a visual."

"What about the third?" Sandford asked. "If there is a third."

"There is. I saw it. It was trying to tow a large sled. Probably the TK44 they harvested."

"What do you mean *trying* to tow?" Hannah asked.

"The sub may have been damaged in the explosion. They cut and ran. The sled is still here on the ocean floor."

"You have a visual on that?" Sandford asked.

"Yes, I'm coming up on it now."

"Good," Sandford said. "We'll be right there."

Within a minute, Hannah, Sandford, and Helms cruised over

the massive crater created by the missile strike. The water was still thick with blast sediment.

"Amazing," Hannah said. "The entire alga field is gone." She looked ahead and saw Matthew hovering over the large underwater sled, an enclosed contraption similar to the type she had used to collect artifacts from the ocean floor. Hannah studied her sonar screen. "We can track that last minisub. There's a good chance it will lead us straight to Gadaire."

"Negative," Sandford said. "We'll secure the sled and prep it to bring to the surface."

"What?" Hannah said. "Hell, no. They're getting away."

"That's not our priority."

"Why not? This may be our only chance to positively link this operation to Gadaire. For God's sake, he murdered your commanding officer down here."

"Our orders are to secure the TK44. With that field gone, this may be the last of it left on earth."

"Good. Let's destroy it and go after that sub."

"Those aren't our orders."

Out of the corner of her eye, Hannah saw Kirov nodding. This was what Kirov had feared, she realized.

"You want the weapon," Hannah said. "That's what this is all about, isn't it? That's why you didn't want to fire into the alga field, even though Matthew's life was on the line. You just want the damned weapon."

"I have my orders, Bryson. And now you have yours."

"It won't do you any good. Melis Nemid's scientists are already developing a chemical to counteract it."

"Good," Sandford said. "We don't want a superweapon that we can't control. Control is everything."

Hannah turned to Kirov. "It's exactly what you thought."

"I would have been happy to be wrong." He met her gaze meaningfully. "But Sandford is right. Being in control is very important."

She slowly nodded as she understood what he was trying to tell her. She spoke into the microphone. "Do what you want, Sandford. I'm going after that sub."

"If you do, I'll have your security clearance revoked. You'll never work on another military project as long as you live."

"Really?" Hannah checked her sonar screen and eased the mini-sub backwards. "I guess it will come down to who has more powerful friends, Sandford."

"Don't do this . . ."

Matthew entered the conversation. "I'm coming with you, Hannah."

"Sorry, Matthew. I think your weapons system may have a little glitch. I want you to get to the surface."

He hesitated. "Are you sure?"

"Yes, it's for the best. Good luck."

Hannah accelerated upward and turned off her radio so that she wouldn't have to hear Sandford shouting at her. In another two minutes, the group's running lights were tiny dots in her rearview monitor. She turned toward Kirov. "We should be able to catch up with that sub, especially if it's damaged."

He nodded. "I'm surprised Matthew gave up so easily. He wanted to come with us."

"He'd never argue with me when the safety of his vessel is at stake. And besides, I talked to him before we left the *Copernicus*. He knows he's needed back there."

MATTHEW SPUN HIS SUB AROUND and rose above Sandford and Helms, gazing down at the sea sled they had hooked between them. They were towing it in tandem, slowly bringing it to the surface.

"Just be glad you didn't take off with her," Sandford said. "It was a career-wrecking move. You're too smart for that."

"If you say so."

"I do. Have you considered a career in the Navy? We could use you on our team."

"I've already been in the Navy. I liked it. I just like my life better now." Because I don't have to deal with pricks like you, Matthew thought.

He felt a low rumble in the water. What the hell . . .

It was as if an oil tanker was approaching.

Matthew stared at his instruments, not quite believing what they told him. "Guys, look at your sonar. The entire right side of the monitor is covered by . . . something. I've never seen anything like it." Matthew leaned forward and looked out his viewport. He gasped. There, hard starboard, was a massive shadow that might have been left by a dozen oil tankers.

"What the hell is that?" Helms whispered.

"We need to get out of here," Matthew said. "Drop that damn sled."

"No way," Sandford said. "Don't even think about letting go, Helms."

As the shadow drew closer, Matthew realized that he had seen it before, on that terrifying last afternoon in Marinth. "My God, dolphins. Thousands and thousands of dolphins. And I think they're pissed."

The first wave hit Sandford, Helms, and the sled like a wall of stone. Matthew, now over a hundred feet above them, was spared the brunt of the attack, but he was still capsized by their brute force. He watched as the other two vessels tumbled through the water, struck repeatedly, and swept away from the sheer force of the on-slaught.

Helms released his vessel's claw-grip on the sled, leaving Sand-ford alone to wrestle it with the mechanical arms. "I've got to use the missiles!"

"They're too close and almost a solid mass," Sandford said. "We'll blow ourselves up unless we can get some distance from them."

Before Helms could regain control, another wave of dolphins struck them, flipped the sled upward, and slammed it against Sand-ford's viewport.

"It's the sled, dammit," Matthew yelled. "Let go of it!"

The dolphins' crushing force was now directed almost entirely at Sandford. They spun around him, slowly at first, then faster and faster. Their speed and sheer mass made navigation impossible, and his sub spun with their current until the accumulated force flung him from the whirlpool and wrenched the sled from his grip.

The dolphins, moving as one, swam toward the lights of Marinth and circled back in a long arc.

The water still churned as Matthew raced toward the sled.

"Good man," Sandford said. "Grab it."

Instead, Matthew moved his sub fifty feet over the sled, then froze in place. "Keep away, guys. Dammit, I've just had a weapons malfunction. Hannah warned me . . ."

Sandford managed to right his vessel, though he still apparently had difficulty with the propulsion system. "What kind of malfunc-tion?"

"Two mines discharged. Get back!"

The softball-sized explosive charges dropped through the water and fell directly onto the sled's top surface.

They exploded, incinerating the sled and its contents.

After the last of the shock waves had subsided, Matthew called out on the radio. "Oops. Are you guys all right?"

"This is treason," Sandford hissed.

The dolphins had completed their long arc around the city and had almost finished their return trip. "Hold tight," Matthew said. "Our friends are back."

Matthew braced himself for another pounding, but this time the dolphins passed overhead and circled for a full two minutes. Then they rushed toward the surface in a corkscrew pattern.

"What the hell was that about?" Helms said.

Matthew took a moment to catch his breath. "They obviously weren't happy with you. We went through the same thing when we brought up the trellis. Maybe they somehow knew we shouldn't have those things."

"Don't give me that new-age crap. I'm bringing you up on charges," Sandford said. "Hannah Bryson may never work again, but you're going to jail for that stunt you pulled with the mines."

"Weapons malfunction," Matthew repeated. "They released on their own."

"Bullshit."

"Must be something your military people did to the control system. You really shouldn't have monkeyed around with Hannah's design without consulting her . . ."

CHAPTER
19

"WHAT THE HELL HAPPENED DOWN there?" Gadaire shouted into the radio of his Colombian-made submarine. "Five of my mini-subs went down, and only one is coming up?"

That one survivor, Lane Garvin, had managed to raise him on the underwater wireless system. His voice was thin and laced with static. "They were ready for us. Some kind of attack minisub I hadn't seen before. Sort of . . . winged."

It had to be Bryson's minisubs. None other came close to that description. Gadaire cursed. He had already sold those minisubs she had destroyed, and this was going to cost him dearly. "How much of the TK44 did you get?"

Garvin hesitated. "None of it."

"Tell me I didn't hear that correctly." His voice was low and vibrating with anger. "Tell me I didn't contract a bunch of fools to carry out the most important project of my career. Can you tell me that?"

"All hell broke loose. I was lucky to get away with my life. My ship is damaged. I have to get out of this thing before it takes me down to the bottom."

"Where are you now?"

"Maybe a couple miles out. I'm heading straight for you. Prepare to take me aboard."

"Has it occurred to you that you may be leading them to me?"

"I don't think so."

"You don't think so? Break off, Garvin. Do you think you're the only one in trouble? I'm having to go on the run myself. I don't dare go to Fuertenventura as I planned. They could be waiting for me. I'll have to change course for Las Palmas. I'll radio you with new rendezvous coordinates later."

"I have you on my sonar. I need to keep pace with you. I'm not sure how much longer my vessel can last."

"I said break off."

"And I said I can't."

Gadaire nodded to Asad, a bald Somali with light brown skin. Since the submarine was not equipped with an integrated weapons system, the Colombians had devised an effective solution to combat the military and police patrols that might discover and pursue them. Asad, in his capacity as weapons officer, had adopted the technique for use in Somali waters. He climbed the steel ladder that would take him to the outside top deck.

"Okay. I can see you're in a bad situation." Try to sound sympathetic toward Garvin. As sympathetic as a cat toward a mouse. He turned back to the control board and changed course to intercept the Atlantic-Tenerife sea-lane that would lead him to Las Palmas. Then he upped the speed.

Damn Bryson and Kirov. All his escape plans were centered on that airport at Fuertenventura. He'd be lucky to get to a safe haven before anyone caught up with him. He turned back and spoke again on the radio to Garvin. "All right. We'll wait ten minutes."

"That's all I need."

That's all *I'll* need, Gadaire thought. He climbed the ladder and joined Asad on the top deck.

BOOM.

"What the hell was that?" Hannah asked. The explosion came from up ahead, in the direction of the minisub they had been pursuing. "Are they firing at us?"

"Too far away," Kirov said. "But it's possible that with the damage sustained, they—" He looked at his instruments. "Wait. It's gone."

"Did we lose track of it again?"

"I don't think so. I'm picking up some diffuse matter in the water ahead . . . Debris."

"The minisub?"

Kirov nodded. "Either its damage was worse than we thought, or—"

"Gadaire," Hannah said. "That fits with his M.O., doesn't it? Eliminate anyone who might incriminate him?"

"We need to be careful," Kirov said. "Remember Captain Danbury's report on Gadaire came back that he was probably in a submarine himself."

Hannah slowed her rate of speed. "But we aren't sure."

"I'll broaden the sweep, but it doesn't look like he has a ship in the area. It would be much easier for him to travel undetected in a sub."

Hannah studied the sonar. "So far I'm not detecting anything. There's only one ship in the area, and it—" Hannah felt a chill run through her. She had been so intent on tracking the minisub that she hadn't made the connection, hadn't realized how far and in what direction they'd been traveling.

They had just reached the Atlantic-Tenerife sea-lane.

"Oh, my God."

COULD HE BE SO LUCKY?

Gadaire stared at the schooner in the distance.

He was in the control room reworking his route to Las Palmas when he'd spotted the distinctive masts of *Fair Winds*. He hadn't even been aware that the schooner was still in these waters after the most recent Marinth expedition concluded.

True, it was Melis Nemid's ship, but could Hannah Bryson actually be on board?

Doubtful.

But Melis Nemid would almost certainly be there. He felt a surge of excitement mixed with the sheer rage he was feeling. Hannah Bryson and Kirov had orchestrated this nightmare. They had put him on the run as he hadn't been since he had first started in the arms business. He felt . . . diminished.

He couldn't let them get away with it. He would search them out and butcher them if it took the rest of his life.

But he would take what satisfaction he could until he could find them. Although this mission had been a miserable failure, he could still take away some victory if he could hurt Bryson in some way.

And what better way to hurt her than to blast her friend Melis Nemid to kingdom come?

*　*　*

"MELIS, YOU NEED TO GET EVERYONE on board into flotation vests," Hannah said tersely into the radio. "Give the order to uncover and prepare the lifeboats. Immediately."

Before even questioning Hannah, Melis ordered her captain to prepare *Fair Winds* for an emergency evacuation. She came back on the radio. "Okay, Hannah. Why did I just do that?"

"Gadaire's in the area. We believe he might be in a sub. We just ruined his plan, and he might decide to take a parting shot at you before he goes on the run."

"What kind of weapons?"

"We don't know. He may have just destroyed one of his own minisubs, so there could be a heat-seeking component."

"Dammit." Melis's voice dropped to a tense whisper. "We're defenseless against something like that."

"I know. We're going to find him, Melis. But get your crew ready in case the worst happens."

"I will. And I'll take care of Ronnie. Don't worry."

Don't worry? She was scared to death. "Thanks, Melis."

"Good luck."

Hannah turned toward Kirov. "Anything yet?"

"No. Next time you're looking for a way to make another breakthrough on these tiny subs, come up with a sonar system with a broader sweep."

"I'll work on it. Any ideas for right now?"

"Push closer to *Fair Winds*. If we still don't get a reading, we should break the surface and take a look around. If he's using a sub, I doubt if it's sophisticated enough for underwater launch tubes. He'll have to surface to make a strike."

*   *   *

"HURRY." GADAIRE STOOD ON THE top deck of the submarine, watching Asad quickly position and lock down the heavy iron tripod and gyroscopic stabilization unit for his deck-mounted rocket launcher.

Asad gave him a noncommittal glance but said nothing. They both knew Gadaire's urging was unnecessary. Asad was moving with utmost efficiency. Whatever Asad was getting from the Somalis, Gadaire was sure the man could make much more from some of his other clients. Another conversation for another time.

On the tripod's underside, Asad connected a thin piece of string attached to a marble sphere. It hung from the contraption like a pendulum, though it remained rock steady as an indicator that the gyroscope was doing its job even on the choppy seas.

Asad hunched over his eyepiece to line up *Fair Winds* in his sights.

HANNAH PUSHED THE ENGINES HARD and broke through to the surface, leaping over the waves. The electronic periscope immediately scanned the surrounding area and highlighted visual points of interest. *Fair Winds* was displayed on the monitor immediately, but after another few seconds it also showcased something that they couldn't quite make out.

"What is it?" Kirov asked.

"I think it may be pay dirt. I'm crossing my fingers." Hannah magnified the image and showed what appeared to be two men walking on water.

"Can you get a closer view?"

Hannah magnified the image, and it was immediately apparent that the men were standing on the deck of a small submarine. Hannah tapped her finger on the device between them. "Damn, is that—"

"It's a rocket launcher," Kirov said. "No time to waste. What's the range on our surface-to-air missile?"

"Far enough, in a perfect world." Hannah put on her left controller glove.

"What are you doing?"

"There isn't time to move closer," Hannah said. "You line up our show with the stick. I'll watch the targeting monitor and fire."

"Do you know what you're doing?"

"I've read the manual. Whoever designed this weapons system has a sense of humor." Hannah held up her hand wearing the controller glove and balled it into a fist. "Hurry. Line up the shot."

Kirov swung the targeting scope around.

"That's Gadaire himself," Hannah said as she looked at the scope's enhanced image. "And they're ready to fire!"

"TELL ME WHEN," ASAD SAID without expression. "All is in place."

Gadaire could feel the exhilaration soaring through him as he gazed at *Fair Winds*. There was some activity on the ship. Had one of the crew spotted them and sounded the alert? Too late. One word, and he would send death hurtling toward Melis and her crew. He could taste and savor the triumph and godlike power.

I wish you could see me, Hannah Bryson. This is what I am. This is only the start. I can take anything and anyone away from you.

And I will, bitch.

He turned to give Asad the order.

"GET READY," KIROV SAID. He struggled to focus the electronic scope's crosshairs in the deck beneath the men.

"What's wrong?"

"We're rocking too much . . . I can't get it."

Hannah looked at the monitor as she held up her gloved hand. "Come on . . ."

"Now!"

Hannah flipped up her middle finger, and the missile launched from the tube over their heads.

GADAIRE LIFTED HIS BINOCULARS and stared at the minisub that had appeared a few hundred yards off his port side. Although the vessel protruded only a few feet over the waterline, he recognized those fanciful curves immediately from the television commercials and magazine articles. It was clearly one of Hannah Bryson's Marinth minisubs.

Fine. He had a rocket for that one, too.

His gaze narrowed at it. This vessel looked different somehow. "Was that—"

There was a white flash over the viewport.

"Shit!"

Asad had seen it too. He swung his rocket launcher around.

"Too late!" Gadaire yelled. He leaped from the deck as the missile exploded against his submarine.

His eardrums burst. The blast hurled him thirty feet over the water.

Ringing in his ears. Numbness all over.

Another explosion rocked the sub from within. It split open, and a fireball roared through what was left of the craft's superstructure. No one could survive that hell.

Except him, he realized. He had survived, as he always did. He always found a way to survive.

He watched, motionless in the water, as another explosion tore the sub apart, leaving only twisted wreckage and debris in its wake.

Gadaire smiled. They had failed. He would live to take revenge on Kirov and Hannah Bryson.

The burning mass slowly went under and sent a small wave toward him. He tried to turn and swim away.

He couldn't. He couldn't move.

What the hell? He couldn't move at all, he realized.

He was paralyzed.

No!

This couldn't be happening. Surely he was just stunned from the blast. Just concentrate. Focus.

Water lapped at his nose and mouth.

He still couldn't move.

No! No! No!

A burning wave rolled toward him, on fire from the oil in the water.

Must get out of the way . . .

He couldn't.

No!

The blazing oil consumed him, frying his face and hair, and still all he could do was expel a hoarse whisper where there should have been a scream.

His lungs filled with the burning oil.

Oh God, no . . .

HANNAH STARED AT THE BURNING oil and debris where Gadaire's submarine had been. Had it not been for the black smoke still rising into the sky, she might have thought it was all just a nightmare.

It didn't seem possible. Only a minute before she had been hideously afraid of the malice that was Gadaire. Now he was gone, no threat to Melis and Ronnie. No threat to anyone else in the world from the bastard.

She leaned back in her seat and tried desperately to catch her breath.

Kirov leaned close to her, straining against his seat harness. "Hannah," he said gently.

"Yes?"

"You can put your finger back down now."

"YOU DO LIKE TO MAKE A grand entrance," Melis said, as Hannah and Kirov got out of the minisub they'd docked alongside the *Fair Winds*. "I'm only glad you weren't the center of that huge explosion. Ronnie and I were worried."

"I was a little worried myself." Hannah hugged Ronnie. "How are you doing?"

"Okay." His gaze was on the water where Gadaire's sub had disappeared. "What happened out there?"

What could she say? She had promised him the truth. "We had to get rid of Gadaire."

Ronnie turned to Kirov. "The bad guy?"

Kirov nodded. "The very bad guy. He was trying to hurt many people. Including you and Melis."

Ronnie shook his head. "We would have been okay. We can take care of ourselves." He grinned at Melis. "Isn't that right?"

She nodded. "We're a good team. But he was concerned about you, Hannah." She paused. "And Pete and Susie. They disappeared right after you left the *Fair Winds* early this morning."

"Early this morning," Hannah repeated in wonder. The sun was going down now in a blaze of scarlet, and it seemed impossible that everything that had transpired had happened in the course of one single day.

Kirov met her gaze and smiled. "But it was one hell of a day."

She nodded. "So it was." She turned back to Melis. "I don't think that you should be fretting about Pete and Susie. I believe they got a call and had somewhere else to go. I'm sure they'll be back soon."

"A call?"

"You told me that the dolphins communicate. I had a radio message from Matthew on the way to the ship that indicated a call had definitely gone out." She gave a relieved sigh. "And that Matthew was safe, thank heavens."

"A call," Melis murmured. "It's what I've been afraid of all these years. That they'll answer that call and never come back. You're sure that they're safe? I can take it if they leave me as long as they're all right."

Hannah hesitated. How could she assure Melis that the dolphins were safe? There had been deadly missiles flying down there in the depths. Explosions and shrapnel and all kinds of weapons that could kill a dolphin venturing too close. Pete and Susie were friendlier than the other dolphins and that could have been lethal for them.

Melis read that hesitation and her expression became haunted. "You're not sure."

Hannah couldn't lie to her. "Things were . . . happening. We've got to hope for the best."

"Oh yes, hope. And pray." Melis turned and headed for the steps leading to the lower decks. "Let's go down to the galley and get a cup of coffee, and you can tell us all about it."

Hannah nodded. "That would be good." She reached for her phone. "As soon as I call Eugenia and tell her about Gadaire."

Melis paused before going down the steps. "Was Anna Devareau on board that sub?"

"We don't know for certain," Kirov said. "But I can't see her crammed in that antiquated monstrosity. She would definitely want an escape route. I'll bet Eugenia and Charlie are going to be checking under every rock to see what they can come up with."

"More than likely." Hannah wearily rubbed her temple. "I know Charlie won't give up until he knows for certain."

"You're tired." Kirov leaned forward and kissed her forehead. "Go down to the galley and get your coffee."

"You're not coming?"

He shook his head. "I'm going to take the sub back to the *Copernicus* before Sandford can charge us with piracy." He headed for the sub. "And then I have a few other things to tie up. Things aren't quite as they should be."

She stiffened. "Dammit, you're going away again. I know it."

"Yes, I am. But I'm coming back soon." He called to Melis, who had started down the steps. "I'll be back in time for your grand gala opening at the museum." He ducked inside the sub. "I promise."

"And I'm supposed to believe you?" Hannah asked.

But he'd closed the metal door and couldn't hear her.

She went to the rail and watched in helpless frustration as he backed away. No, this couldn't be happening. They had been so close, every move as if they were connected by invisible bonds. Stifle the panic and the shock. Anger. Be angry with him. She wanted him here so that she could scream at him, pound at him, tell him that it wasn't fair that he was leaving her again.

She wanted him here . . .

"It's okay, Aunt Hannah." Ronnie was beside her. "He said he'd be back."

Which was a promise Kirov hadn't given her the last time, she thought bitterly. "It doesn't matter. We don't need him." Ignore the hurt, the sudden loneliness. It wasn't as if she couldn't survive without him. Their relationship was tentative at best, and this move on his part showed just what an enigma he really was. She would have to decide whether that enigma was worth all the pain and bewilderment he was putting her through to solve it. Dammit, he was evidently giving her plenty of time to make that decision. She put her arm around Ronnie's shoulder. "Come on. Let's go down to the galley and I'll tell you a rip-roaring tale that will shiver your timbers, my lad."

He chuckled. "Dad always used that corny phrase. What does it mean?"

"I don't know. We'll have to look it up. It probably has some—"

"The dolphins," Ronnie interrupted. His smile had disappeared and his gaze was on her face. "I'm scared, Aunt Hannah. You think something could have happened to them. Melis could see it too."

"I don't know anything. Let's not borrow trouble."

"I . . . love them." His hands clenched at his sides. "They're my friends." He gazed at her helplessly. "When I'm with them I feel . . ."

Healing.

Dear God, as terrible as it would be for Melis to lose Pete and Susie, it might be even worse for Ronnie. Another loss with which he'd have to cope.

"Ronnie, even if they don't come back it doesn't mean that they're not alive and happy with their own kind," she said gently. "Sometimes we just have to let go and trust. They'll always be with us even though we may not see them."

Ronnie gazed out at the sea. "Except in our dreams . . ."

She hadn't expected that connection with his dreams of his father and it nearly broke her heart. "Yes." She squeezed his shoulder. "Now come with me and don't let Melis see how upset you are. You don't want to worry her."

"I know. I promised I'd take care of her for you." He swallowed hard as he started down the deck. "She loves them too. She taught me—" He stopped short. His head lifted, listening. "What is . . . ?"

A chortle. A squeal.

Hannah's gaze flew to the water.

"There they are!" Ronnie ran back to the rail and was waving in sheer ecstasy as if the dolphins could understand him. "They're here! Pete and Susie!"

Jumping and arcing in the water, joyously diving and surfacing in a giddy dance of life. There was no question that Pete and Susie had come back to them.

"Thank God," Hannah whispered.

"They came. I knew they would. I knew it!" Ronnie's face was luminous as he whirled and ran for the door to the galley. "I've got to go tell Melis."

Hannah turned back to gaze at the dolphins. So much joy. So much life.

"Proud of yourselves, aren't you?" Hannah said softly as she finally turned away. "Maybe we're a little proud of you too. Go ahead, you have a good time. Now that we know you're safe I've got to go tell Melis what you've been up to."

EPILOGUE

Two Weeks Later
Marinth Museum
Athens, Greece

"YOU LOOK BEAUTIFUL, AUNT Hannah." Ronnie suddenly grinned. "But I like you better in jeans and your faded blue shirt. All that sequin and stuff looks like it belongs to someone else."

"It does." She straightened the chocolate brown silk skirt of her gown and stood up from the vanity in Melis's private suite in the museum. "Melis borrowed it from a designer friend in Rome. A big favor since all his models are size zero and it had to have massive alterations." She ruffled his hair. "And my shirts are honorably faded by sun, sea, and hard work. So I agree that they suit me much better. Are your mom and sister here yet?"

He nodded. "They're talking to Melis. She's showing them the trellis that just arrived from France. Melis's husband, Jed, flew them here on his private jet. Donna is excited out of her mind that she got to come for the official opening of the museum. Mom bought her a pink dress with lots of ruffles."

"Then you should be with them."

He shook his head. "No, they don't need me." He gravely offered his arm to her. "I came to escort you down to the party, Aunt Hannah."

She was touched. "Thank you." She took his arm. "It's very kind of you, Ronnie." She moved toward the door. "And I've been thinking that since we're going to be working together next summer, maybe you should drop the aunt and just call me Hannah. It's more professional. And it might keep you from taking any flack from the team."

"Hannah," he repeated the name tentatively. "Just like Dad."

"Exactly what Conner called me." She smiled. "It would have been weird for him to call me anything else. He was my brother, for goodness sake. But suit yourself. I'll answer to anything."

"Hannah," he said again. He gave her a brilliant smile. "I think I'll like that. I think Dad would like it too."

She dropped a kiss on the top of his head. "Maybe he would." They had reached the top of the staircase leading down to the main hall of the museum.

Chatter.

Glittering crystal chandeliers.

Men in tuxedos, women in colorful silk gowns.

Music.

Crowds.

"Oh, Lord," Hannah said. "Not my cup of tea."

"I'll stay with you," Ronnie said quickly. "But there are lots of people you know. Matthew, Kyle, the whole team. Eugenia, Charlie . . ."

Bless him. He thought she was nervous. "I know." She started down the stairs. "It's okay. I have to go to these things occasionally. I just get a little claustrophobic. Give me a fancy party, and I start yearning for sand and sea."

"Then go out on the balcony. You can see the sea. I saw Kirov out there."

"Kirov?" Her gaze flew to the French doors. "He's back?" Kirov had been gone the entire two weeks since that last day at Marinth. She had not heard a word from him, dammit.

Ronnie released her as they reached the bottom of the stairs. "Go out and talk to him. I'll go get Mom and Donna . . . Hannah." He disappeared into the crowd.

She stood there a moment, then started for the French doors.

"Hannah."

She turned to see Eugenia making her way through the gala crowd toward her, with Charlie in tow. She was dressed in a strapless gown of pleated scarlet silk, but it was no more vivid or full of vitality than the woman who was wearing it.

Eugenia gave her a hug. "You look superb. I can almost believe you belong in this high-class fish tank. Melis gave a wonderful party, but she had to invite all her rich benefactors. It causes a certain lack of spontaneity." She gestured to Charlie. "Does he not look splendid?"

Charlie did look splendid in a tuxedo that was as finely tailored as those of the Greek shipowners across the room. Splendid, darkly handsome, and even . . . sophisticated. He made a face. "She made me do it."

"You look great, Charlie." She looked back at Eugenia. "Anna?"

Eugenia shook her head. "She's still out there somewhere. She must have been tipped off about what happened to Gadaire. Baker said he thinks she flew the coop with close to a hundred million dollars converted to gold and other liquid securities."

"Damn."

"I'll find her," Charlie said quietly. "It will take time, but I'll kill that bitch."

Hannah believed him. Charlie was beginning to become a formidable force. "Be careful. She reminds me of Medusa with her head of writhing snakes. There are too many ways for her to strike at you."

"But he's learning all the best ways to cut off Medusa's head." Eugenia beamed. "Charlie's making great progress. In the meantime, he's going to New York with me to apprentice at slightly less violent endeavors."

"When do you leave?"

"After the gala." She glanced at the balcony. "Kirov was looking for you. He told me he brought you a present."

"What?"

She shrugged. "I don't know. But being Kirov, I'm certain it will be unusual." She kissed her cheek. "I will see you later. Come on, Charlie. I hear there is going to be some kind of glorious ring of fire exhibit on the veranda shortly. The Marinthians were supposed to have used it at their ceremonial functions."

"Interesting," Hannah said absently. She started for the French doors.

"I can see that you're positively fascinated by the prospect," Eugenia said. "Tell Kirov that he must bring you. Melis will be disappointed if you don't show."

"I'll be there." She opened the French doors. Kirov was standing twenty yards away bathed in the golden glow of the Aegean twilight. Powerful, dark, vital, in stark contrast to the softness of the light all around him.

Her heart was pounding. Keep cool, dammit. She mustn't be so vulnerable.

He turned to face her. "I came back." He smiled. "I kept my promise. See how I've improved?"

"Sort of." She came toward him. "No explanations. Just 'see you' and 'don't worry, I'll be back.'"

"I explained. I told you I had a few things to do."

"One of them wouldn't have been getting Baker to call off Lieutenant Sandford and AquaCorp from trying to do a hatchet job on me? They've been amazingly low-key. Not a looming jail sentence in sight."

"We had a few discussions. It's interesting what physical threats and a little blackmail can do to improve a situation."

"Blackmail?"

"I pulled out all the stops, from a juicy little tidbit I learned about Baker's investigational techniques to threats of a media blitz about the Navy sacrificing the glory of Marinth on the altar of modern warfare."

"And would it have hurt you to have told me what you were going to do?"

"I'm making good progress. You mustn't expect too much of me."

"Why not?" She stopped before him and gazed into his eyes. "I want to be able to expect everything from you. I'm tired of being cautious and understanding and—"

"Understanding?"

"Well, maybe not. I don't have that much patience. But I'd like to work on it."

He tilted his head. "I believe I'm seeing a change in attitude. Is that true?"

"It's possible."

"*Ya blagadaryu boga,*" he said softly.

"Now don't go spouting Russian to me. You did that before and then took off into the wild blue yonder."

"I was just thanking God for his miracles." He reached out and touched her cheek. "This particular miracle."

"Don't touch me. Not yet. I have to know where all of this is going. I'm not going to try to tie you down, but I have to know that I'm not just a—I have to mean something to you."

"Where is this going?" Kirov repeated. "Somewhere solid, somewhere warm, somewhere magical. I've wanted to make love to you. I've wanted to kill for you. I've wanted to protect you. I want to stay with you and listen to you and have your nephew tell you how wonderful I am." He nodded. "I'd think that would indicate that you mean something to me. Oh yes, I believe I may be much farther along than you on this journey, Hannah."

Somewhere solid, somewhere warm, somewhere magical.

"Not necessarily," she said unevenly. "You're so good at all those pretty phrases. But I'm much more grounded than you are. And I've had time to think. Heaven knows you were gone long enough. I was a little insecure when you took off this time, but I got over it. I thought about how we'd been together and I decided you'd be an idiot not to give us a try. I believe you may genuinely care for me. I know I care for you."

He smiled. "Are you afraid of the word love, Hannah?"

"I'm wary of it. I want you to be wary of it. Before I say it, I want time to explore every single facet of it. Are you good with that?"

"Oh yes, I'm all for exploration." He bent, and his lips touched hers. "Every single part of you."

"That sounds purely sexual."

"Yes. We can address the cerebral and spiritual later." He kissed her again. "I want to encourage you in the proper direction. Because I believe I'm about to be seduced. Is that a possibility?"

"Yes."

"Then should I step back and let you do it?"

"No, it's not easy for me. I think we'd better just let it happen." She put her hand on his throat. "Your heart's beating so hard," she whispered. "I love to feel it . . ."

"It's about to jump out of my chest." He took her hand away

from him and kissed the palm. "And unless you want to do something socially unacceptable on this balcony, we'd better get out of here."

She couldn't breathe. She was so dizzy it was hard to think. "Melis. We have to go see her ring of fire."

"The hell we do." He drew a deep breath. "Yes, as a matter of fact, we do." He took her wrist and started to pull her toward the veranda. "I received permission from Melis to use her giant ring to give you your present."

"What?"

They had reached the veranda, and in the center was a huge upright ring lit with orange-red flames. Guests were just beginning to trickle in from the museum, and they had no trouble reaching the area before the ring.

"What are we doing here?" Hannah asked.

Kirov took out a large brown envelope from his inner jacket pocket and handed it to her. "The last samples of TK44. I got them from Gadaire's safe and Lampman's lab. Baker's men were all over both places, and it took a while for me to manage to get them. But I knew you'd want them."

She nodded. "And so will Melis. She destroyed all of the TK44 she had at the labs. It's dangerous having them out there. Aziz' remedy is a breakthrough, and we know it works because he tried it out on Lampman's polluted pond in Ireland and it completely eradicated the alga. But we have to be as certain as we can be that it's all been totally destroyed."

He half bowed. "Then would you like to do the honors?"

She took the envelope. "By all means." She stepped closer to the flames. "Do you know, this is somehow right. TK44 alga destroyed Marinth. Now it's being destroyed by one of Marinth's symbols."

Slowly, one by one, she dropped the samples into the fire. She tossed the envelope in after them and stood there watching the flames devour the alga. "Death of Marinth. Death of TK44."

"Oh, Hannah, you're so wrong," Kirov said softly. "Marinth's still alive. She's only sleeping." He took her hand and began leading her from the veranda and down the steps. "Ask the dolphins . . ."